SISTER
NORTH

Also by Jim Kokoris

The Rich Part of Life

SISTER
NORTH

JIM KOKORIS

ST. MARTIN'S GRIFFIN
NEW YORK

www.stmartins.com

www.jimkokoris.com

Library of Congress Cataloging-in-Publication Data

Kokoris, Jim.
    Sister North : a novel / Jim Kokoris.
       p. cm.
    ISBN 0-312-27540-4 (hc)
    ISBN 0-312-33507-5 (pbk)
    EAN 978-0312-33507-6
    1. Women television personalities—Fiction. 2. Loss (Psychology)—
Fiction. 3. Missing persons—Fiction. 4. Spiritual life—Fiction.
5. Waitresses—Fiction. 6. Wisconsin—Fiction. 7. Nuns—Fiction. I. Title.

PS3611.O58S57 2003
813'.6—dc21   2003047149

First St. Martin's Griffin Edition: October 2004

10 9 8 7 6 5 4 3 2 1

To my mother and father

ACKNOWLEDGMENTS

Special thanks are due to the following people who helped make this book possible:

Pat and George Brixie, my in-laws, for watching the kids and helping me find the time to write; Alicia Brooks, my editor, for her insight and her determination, which made this a better book; Lynn Franklin, my agent, for her usual and needed counsel and support; Gordon Mennenga, my teacher, who pushed me to get it right; Jonni Hegenderfer, my business partner, for putting up with me; Ursula at the La Grange Park Library for giving me a room in which to write; and my three sons and wife, Anne, for their ongoing love and support.

SISTER
NORTH

One

Nine months after his divorce, Sam stopped wearing underwear. It was a practical decision rather than any type of statement. After Carol left him, he remained committed to underwear, thinking it a fundamental part of his life. He worked in a very proper, very conservative Chicago law firm that had a dress code, and while the dress code did not specifically mention underwear, it was definitely implied.

After he was fired, he began to reassess the need. Maintaining a clean fleet of boxer shorts took time, effort, and money. He had made one, halfhearted visit to a Laundromat but found the experience so depressing—so many homeless people were there hovering about like ghosts—that he never went back. He then entered a very decadent phase of wearing boxer shorts twice and throwing them out. Finally, after his dry cleaners began charging him three dollars a pair, he made the decision to liberate himself and gave up on underwear altogether, throwing away every last pair. He was very drunk when he did this.

Not wearing underwear was just one of a series of small changes Sam had made since Carol and his job had left him. Other interesting additions to his ever-evolving lifestyle included using regular gas in his car, drinking instant coffee, living in the Get Down Motel, and listening to other people have sex.

It was the loss of underwear that galled him the most. While lying naked on his bed in Room 12 of the Get Down and balancing a can of beer on his stomach, he reconsidered his decision. His body was cold, and he felt exposed and vulnerable in a childlike way. Suddenly he was ashamed of his nakedness, ashamed of everything. Not wearing underwear was crass, even uncivilized. He felt tears forming in the corners of his eyes. I am civilized, he thought. He finished his beer. I'm drunk, he thought.

The motel was strangely quiet for midafternoon. This was prime affair time at the Get Down, and the rooms were usually occupied, with the walls rattling and the beds in high squeak-and-shake mode. Sam sat up, pressed his ear against the wall, and thought he detected a muffled moan, but soon realized it was his stomach growling. He lay down again.

He was in the midst of deciding whether or not to go to the mall and buy some boxer shorts when the phone rang. It was Maureen from his office. She was only nineteen and had a childlike voice and a sweet, simple mind, both prone to hysterics.

"Mr. Gamett?"

"Hello, Maureen."

"Thank God I found you. Thank *God*. Are you coming back to the office today?"

"What time is it?"

"It's three o'clock."

"No, I'm not."

"Mr. Hurley is here," she whispered.

"Who?"

"Mr. Hurley, the man who wants to divorce his wife secretly."

Sam crossed his feet at the ankles and noticed he still had his socks on. He felt hope stir. At least he still had socks.

"Mr. Gamett? What should I do about Mr. Hurley?"

"Mr. Hurley," Sam repeated.

"He's been waiting for two hours. You said you were going to see him after you got back from lunch."

"I had to go to court."

"What should I tell him? He looks mad. He's swearing a lot under his breath. He's in the bathroom now. He might be swearing in there, I can't tell though."

"Tell him I was called to court, then reschedule for tomorrow. Can you do that for me, Maureen?"

"I don't think so."

"I know you can."

"I don't think so. He has a glass eye."

"Glass eyes can't hurt you."

"I know, but a lot of people coming in here are weird. It's scary sometimes. Like that man who didn't have a nose, the one who had it cut off by his wife."

"Ex-wife." Sam cleared his throat. That man *was* scary. "Be brave, Maureen. Remember our talk about being brave? We're doing important work. We're helping people. We're helping people who don't have noses."

Maureen took a deep breath. "Okay. I think I can do this. Should I do it now?"

"No, wait until he comes out of the bathroom." Sam had to be very literal with Maureen.

Maureen whispered again. "What happens if he starts swearing at me?"

"If he does that, tell him I'll sue him."

"That might make him madder."

"Maureen, just do this."

"What happens if he has a gun?"

"He doesn't have a gun."

"The man without the nose had a gun. He showed it to me."

"Well, he was just trying to impress you. He was overcompensating."

"Overcompensating? You mean because he didn't have a nose?"

"That's right, Maureen. Because he didn't have a nose."

Maureen took another deep breath. "All right, Mr. Gamett. I'll do it. I'll do it if you say so. Can I put you on hold though while I tell him? He's coming out now. I just heard the toilet flush."

"All right."

Sam propped himself up on an elbow and searched for the TV remote while he waited.

"Mr. Gamett? Are you still there? Guess what? He swore at me." Maureen was breathing fast and talking in a rush, as if she were reporting live from the scene of an accident.

"He did?"

"He did. He said he wasn't someone to trifle with."

"He said 'trifle'?"

"He said he was a veteran, and taxpayer, and he ain't no pussy."

"He said all that? How fast does this guy talk?"

"Then he said the 'f' word."

"Where is he now?"

"He went back to the bathroom."

Sam punched a pillow. "Maureen, I'm not coming in to see this guy. Tell him something else. I have to go. The guy is nuts anyway."

"Mr. Gamett, please. What do I tell him? I'm scared." Then she whispered again. "That glass eye is *so weird*."

"Give him some excuse."

"What excuse?"

"I don't know. Figure something out." Sam hung up the phone. "Just figure it out."

Later, he watched the History Channel again. He had gotten hooked on it a few months ago when one of his regular clients had wanted him to sue the channel because its frequent running of Holocaust documentaries caused him great emotional distress. Sam had dropped the case but become addicted to the channel. It was one of the main reasons he stayed at the Get Down. The other reason was that it was free. He had handled the divorce of Nezlo, the owner, and taken free lodging as payment for getting his Internet-ordered bride deported back to Russia after she gave him a venereal disease.

Patton had just relieved Bastogne. Sam watched with admiration as Patton, hands on hips, ivory revolver in holster, jaw resolute, reviewed his exhausted but victorious troops. An amazing feat, the narrator said. Sam repeated this out loud, then looked around the room and wished someone were with him to share the breaking news. Patton, you old son of a bitch. Sam opened another beer. Patton, you old *dog*.

Sam stared at the television set until the *Battle of Bastogne* was replaced by *The Building of the Hoover Dam*. He watched as American men, in construction helmets and carrying blueprints, squinted in the hot sun as they conferred in shirtsleeves, their faces optimistic, no problem too large. These were men with purpose, men with plans, building something that would stand the test of time. Years later, these very same men probably drove by the dam with their grand-children in their Chryslers, pointed out the window with pride, and said, "I built that; your goddamn grandfather built that."

Sam drank some more beer and swished it around the sides of his mouth before swallowing. He had nothing to show for his life. No wife. No kids. No hydroelectric dams. Never even wore a construc-tion helmet. He wouldn't know how to read a blueprint. In fourth grade, at his mother's urging, his father had tried to build a go-cart with him for the Soap Box Derby. His father was terrible with tools, though, and eventually they had both gotten frustrated. After three hours, it had still looked like a milk crate. His father had said forget it, and took him to a movie—*Iced*. It was about an old man who killed people by hanging them on meat hooks in an ice locker. On the way home, his father said, "Let's tell Mom we went to the park."

The Building of the Hoover Dam was followed by an in-depth history of coin-operated vending machines and their impact on culture. Sam watched this last show for only a few minutes before flipping through the other channels. He paused momentarily on ESPN, then settled on the Weather Channel. An unusual cold front was developing over the Rockies. Sam stirred on the bed and was considering going to the bathroom when the phone rang. He stared at it and counted fifteen rings before answering.

"Hello, Maureen."

"Mr. Gamett? He's gone. He finally left."

"What did you tell him?"

"I said you suffered a serious head injury."

Sam paused. "Maureen," he said, "why did you say that?"

"I figured he might feel sorry for you."

"What did he say?"

"He swore."

"Did you reschedule our meeting?"

"No."

Sam propped up some pillows and lay back on them. He was actually glad Maureen had called. He was in the mood to talk.

"Did anything else happen? Did Microsoft call, looking for help on any of their antitrust suits?"

"Mr. Gamett? I have to go. Good-bye."

"What? Where are you going?"

"Home. I have a date, and I'm late. Bye!"

Home. Sam glanced around the room, slowly hung up the phone, got up, and walked to the bathroom, where he removed three beer cans from the sink. He splashed his face with cold water and looked in the mirror. It surprised him how much he hadn't changed. He appeared the same, despite everything. Hair wasn't even gray at forty-five. Never got fat, reasons unexplained. The thought that he wasn't aging normally momentarily scared him. His heart and mind weren't telling his body things; his hair, waistline, skin, were still blissfully in the dark. He splashed more water, then tried to make a muscle with his arm. He couldn't make a muscle, he had no muscles. He opened his mouth and checked his gums in the mirror. He had no idea what he was looking for. Some sign of deterioration or decay. But his gums appeared fine. He looked at his face, studied the well-proportioned chin and the strong nose, the slight scar on his left jaw, a white mark just below the ear. He fell off a bike when he was nine, crashed into a door. He ran his hand over the scar, touched it with his fingertips, and remembered the pain, the tears. Then he stared into his eyes. He stared until the room behind him disappeared, until his body melted away, until it was just his eyes in the mirror, empty and dark.

Two

The next day, when Joe Lux, a fifty-five-year-old construction firm owner with a history of public indecency, walked into his office, Sam took a mind-clearing breath and tried to rally a can-do attitude.

"So, Mr. Lux," he said, "masturbating in public again."

Lux cringed. "Bizarre," he said, sitting down. "I don't understand that one at all. That one is way out there. Left field."

Sam read the file. "According to the police report, you were caught inside the home of the Garcia family. You were masturbating in their shower." Sam emphasized the word *masturbating*. Most of his flashers hated that word, preferring the harmless, almost whimsical, "playing with myself," by way of explanation.

Lux shook his head. "I don't know how that happened. It's all a big misunderstanding, really."

"I don't know how it can be a misunderstanding, Mr. Lux. There's not a lot of ways to misinterpret what you were doing."

Lux cringed again, his shoulders jerking. "Just for the record, it wasn't really in public. I was taking a shower. I thought I was at home. In my own house." He raised his hands incredulously. "Next thing I know, this broad is hitting me with a broom. So I run out to the garage. That's where the cops found me. I should be suing her. She should have been arrested for assault. I made an honest mistake."

Sam tried not to sigh but felt a long, sad breath seep out of him. Ten years ago, he had argued before the Illinois Supreme Court. Now it appeared that he was specializing in masturbatory law.

"Where do you live again?" he asked.

"In the city. Logan Square. But I'm moving. To the suburbs."

Sam glanced up from the file.

"A gated community," Lux said.

Sam went back to the file. "According to the report, the Garcias live in Berwyn. That's quite a ways from Logan Square."

Lux stared at him.

"So, not only were you in the wrong house, masturbating, you were in the wrong town, masturbating."

Lux hunched forward in his chair and folded his hands on his lap. He was a thick man with a full head of gray hair worn slicked back like Elvis. "Yeah," he said. "So they say. But that's just their story. I got a different version."

"What's your version?"

"Trust me, it's different." Lux shook his head. "Personally, I don't know what the big deal is. Just say for the sake of argument that I did what she said; it's not like I was hurting anyone. Who was I hurting? I was alone. What was I hurting? What? The environment?"

"You need help, Mr. Lux. You have a history of doing this."

Lux leaned back in his chair, shook his head, and laughed. "What do you mean by that, a history? What am I, George Washington?"

"You've been arrested six times for this."

"Oh, so now that's"—Lux stopped and made quote marks in the air with his fingers—"a history. I'm fifty-five years old. Six times. That means I do this, allegedly do this, once every, what, eight-nine years?" He patted his knee in disbelief. "So now that's a history. Jesus Christ."

Sam ignored Lux and rooted through the file again. He was relieved that Lux at least didn't try to blame his affliction on aliens. A growing number of his clients had begun hinting at alien influence in their crimes. Near the back of the file, he found one of the priors, vaguely remembered it.

"Last year, you were arrested for a DUI. They arrested you at a tollbooth."

Lux shook his head again in a can-you-believe-this way. "Oh, *that*. That was strange, too."

Sam looked up, saw alien craft hovering just over Lux's head, ray guns poised. "What do you mean, strange?"

"Peculiar."

Sam waited.

"I went to a party, came home, went to bed. Next thing I know, I'm at a tollbooth, and they're cuffing me."

"You didn't have any clothes on," Sam read. "You were naked. You were in your car, naked. And you were, let's see . . . masturbating."

Lux shifted in his seat and focused on the floor again. "That's what they told me. I don't remember that part though."

"You have no memory of it? Leaving your house naked? Driving your car naked?"

Lux shook his head. "Nope. I can honestly say I don't have any recollection of that event. Nothing at all. *Nada*." He paused and turned serious and thoughtful. "It was like my memory was erased."

"Erased," Sam repeated.

Lux ran his tongue over his top lip. "Like I was *planted* there. Like I was . . . set up."

Sam waited.

"Hey, listen. I've got a lot of enemies. It's a tough business. We shouldn't rule that out."

"Rule what out?"

"That I'm being set up."

Sam closed the file, then shut his eyes and rubbed his forehead. He had drunk at least a six-pack the night before, and his head was producing a persistent, dull ache he had begun to associate exclusively with cheap beer. "So what you're saying, Mr. Lux, what you're saying is that your competitors may have had something to do with your ongoing problem?"

"It's possible. Yes. Conceivable."

"That they may have taken you to your car, naked, made you drive, then somehow tricked you into masturbating."

"I'm just saying that's a possibility." Lux leaned close to the desk. "You don't know what I've seen in my business. People will do anything to make you look bad."

Sam folded his hands in front of him and stared Lux in the eye. He was actually beginning to admire his tenacity, to say nothing of his imagination. He could learn from this man. "I'm just curious, Mr. Lux, how would your enemies go about making you do these things? Say, masturbate in another person's home?"

Lux gave Sam a long, meaningful look. Sam thought he might be offended, might tell him go to hell, but instead he said, "Hypnosis."

Sam exhaled. He was disappointed. Next to aliens, hypnosis was his clients' second most popular defense. He should have seen this coming.

"I hypnotize very easily. I mean *very* easily." Lux snapped his fingers. "Like that. You could hypnotize me right now."

"I don't want to hypnotize you. And I don't think that's your problem."

"I just think the whole thing is suspicious, that's all I'm saying. They always seem to crop up when a big job opens for bid."

"So, you think you're being set up . . . being planted somewhere?"

"Yeah, I do. I definitely do." Lux uncrossed his legs and pulled his chair closer to Sam's desk. He glanced once over his shoulder. "Has that ever happened to you? You feel like you've been planted somewhere, you just wake up and you're at some weird place doing some weird thing? You got no idea how it happened? Don't know how you got there? You're just *there*."

Sam took a deep breath and closed his eyes. When he reopened them Lux was staring at him. "That ever happen to you?" he asked again. "Ever? That feeling? You got no control. You just wake up, and you're *there*?"

Sam didn't say anything. He just looked into Lux's dark, empty eyes, recognized something, and suddenly felt afraid.

For lunch, Maureen brought Sam a large tomato stuffed with tuna salad and presented it with a flourish, taking it out of the bag and holding it up near her smiling face as if it were a prize on a game show.

"Stuffed tomato," she said in her breathless voice. She placed it on his desk on top of a napkin. "It's really good for you. Especially the tuna salad."

Sam gazed blankly at the tomato. It looked like an exploded human brain. "I didn't know it was lunchtime," he said.

"It is." Maureen sat in the chair across from Sam, then opened another bag and pulled out a plastic cup of soup. Sam watched her blow on a spoonful and thought again about how young and pretty she was. She had huge blue eyes that always seemed surprised, and brownish blond hair that she wore in pigtails that day. Whenever he looked at her he was reminded of every girl he had ever had a crush on in high school. He assumed she had a crush on him. He always assumed women had crushes on him and was frequently surprised when he discovered they did not.

"I've got something else for you, Mr. Gamett," Maureen said.

"You got me something else," Sam said. He picked up his plastic fork and tried to make sense of the tomato.

"I got it at a garage sale."

Ever since he had hired Maureen to work in his storefront office, she was constantly buying him little knickknacks. Everything she gave him had some sort of inspirational bent to it: self-help books, posters of kittens trying to climb trees, pictures of golf courses at dusk, a little boy looking dejected after he struck out. (*Try, try again!*) Last week she had given him a framed photo of a nun riding a bike on a country road. The nun was smiling broadly, her legs spread wide, her shoes extended outward. (*Go Sister!*) Maureen had insisted on hanging the picture in Sam's office, next to the clock. He had no idea why she had bought it and even less idea why he had let her hang it up.

"Can I give it to you now?"

Sam rubbed his head again. "Sure," he said.

She reached down, pulled out a framed picture from a bag, and held it up. *Take Time for Six Things*, the title read.

"I think this is so neat," she said. Then, just as Sam feared, she began to read off the six things to take time for, in her soft, singsong voice.

"Take time to work—it is the price of success," she started. She peeked over at Sam and nodded after she read this. He stared down at the tomato.

"Take time to help, it is the source of happiness. Take time for beauty for it is God's gift. Take time to play, for it will keep you young."

He looked up from the tomato. Maureen smiled at him expectantly, waiting for an appropriate comment.

"What number was that?" he asked.

"That was four." Maureen cleared her throat. "Take time to laugh—it is the singing that helps life's loads. And finally, take time to live, for our time is brief."

Maureen smiled so brightly when she finished that Sam couldn't help but smile back.

"Isn't that neat?" she asked.

"Very."

Sam smiled again. He was going to have to fire her, he knew it. As much as he liked her, he needed a different type of secretary, someone with a few miles on her. Someone who walked around with her bra strap showing, a raspy voice, a cigarette dangling from her mouth. Maybe an ex-prostitute, or even a current one. She could bring in business. Maureen was entirely too nice and too sweet for the job.

"Like it?" Maureen asked. She held it out for him.

"Yes," Sam said. "I do." He refused to take the thing from her, so she put it down on the desk.

"Where are you going to hang it?"

"Somewhere." Sam scanned his cramped, messy office. "Definitely . . . somewhere."

"That's nice." Maureen sipped some soup, then made a face. "So hot," she said. She blew on a spoonful again.

"Are you still living in that hotel?" she asked.

"Yes. It's temporary though."

"I drove by there yesterday. It's right on my way home. It looks pretty small."

"It's bigger than it looks." Then, since he didn't want her to feel sorry for him any more than she already did, Sam added, "It has a pool. It's nice in the summer."

"I know. But when I drove by there yesterday I saw a car in the pool."

"There was? Oh, yeah, that's right. It was an accident." The woman in Room 16 had driven her station wagon into the pool two days ago. She was trying to run over her boyfriend. Sam had managed to give the woman his card before the cops came.

Maureen gave him a sad smile. "Things will get better for you, Mr. Gamett. I know they will. Deandra told me."

"Deandra."

"My astrologer."

"You asked your astrologer about me?"

"Yes. She said you were going to go on to big things."

"Why don't you ask her about yourself?"

She shrugged. "I already have. I know all about my future. I'm going to have lots of kids and live by the water and marry a man who plays the piano."

"The piano."

"Not professionally. For recreation."

Sam nodded. He had no idea how he was going to fire her. He might leave her an inspirational note. (*Try, try again—you're fired!*) He imagined her coming in to work and reading the note, imagined her crying and taking back all the knickknacks, the nun picture, the framed six things, the stuffed tomato. He sighed and pushed the tomato away. He could never fire her. He might just have to quit himself.

"Well, time to get back to work," he said.

Maureen examined her watch. "Really?"

"Yes. I have a lot to do."

Maureen looked surprised. "You do?"

Sam held up an empty file. "Yes," he said quietly. "I do."

After Maureen left, Sam wrapped the tomato in the wax paper it had come in, placed it in the bottom of the wastebasket, and stepped to the front of his desk to lie down on the floor. A year ago, he would have been downtown, maybe in a staff meeting, pretending to listen to Charlie, his ex-father-in-law, review cases and thinking about lunch. He had held memberships in three clubs and frequently met clients there, discussing nothing of importance over chilled Manhattans and warm salmon salads. Afterward, he would stroll La Salle Street, taking his time getting back to the office, wondering where he was going to have dinner and hoping that Carol would have to work late so he didn't have to see her. If only Carol hadn't awakened one day and decided to leave him, he could have kept that life. Maybe he should have hypnotized her, made her think he was wonderful, made her forget things: his indifference toward her, his lack of ambition, his constant flirtations with his harem of miniskirt-wearing, gum-snapping secretaries that he insisted on hiring at the firm.

He adjusted himself on the floor, placing a thick but soft file under his head, and began his after-lunch ritual of tracing his downfall. He chose not to analyze the obvious, that being a terrible husband had cost him his marriage and being a lazy lawyer had cost him his job. Those were merely symptoms. He had to dig deeper. He suspected the seeds of his current situation were actually sown years ago. In eighth grade, at St. Francis, he was given the role of Jesus in *My Boss Is a Jewish Carpenter*, the school play Father Pocius wrote and directed. Sam had no desire to be in the play, but Father Pocius had insisted, saying he had a "Jesus air" about him. "It's because you're so handsome," his mother explained. "They want a handsome Jesus." Despite his initial reluctance, Sam quickly warmed to the part. When he smashed up the temple, he did it with zeal, throwing things over his head and stomping on them with both feet. And when he was crucified, he wailed so convincingly that his mother told him later that she feared he was really hurt. After the final performance, he received a standing ovation.

He now blamed that early success for his ego problems, his self-centeredness, his belief that he was special and different, that rules did not necessarily apply to him. For months after the play, he had thought people were looking at him during Mass, secretly *worshiping* him. Maybe if he hadn't wailed so convincingly, or if he had been cast in a different role—instead of Jesus, maybe Judas—he might have developed a different perspective on life, been more eager to please and be liked.

He must have dozed off because the next thing he remembered

was hearing a small commotion outside his office. Maureen was speaking loudly, and her voice had an unaccustomed edge to it. He glanced at his watch. He wasn't expecting anyone for another two hours at least.

He sat up just as the door to his office opened. A short, young man, with blinding white hair and a brown leather jacket zipped all the way up to his chin, poked his head in.

"Are you Mr. Gamett?" he asked. "Sam Gamett?" His voice was quiet and dull and had a slight Southern trace to it.

Sam quickly stood up and walked toward the door. "I'm Sam Gamett. Who are you?"

The man hesitated before entering the room, trying to shut the door. Maureen was right behind him, pushing the door back open.

"I'm sorry, Mr. Gamett, but he wouldn't wait. He said he knew you."

"It's all right," Sam said. He reached behind the man and shut the door.

"I need to see you," the man said softly.

"What's your problem?" Sam walked back to his desk and ran his hands through his hair. The man had a flat, disconnected look about him. He was skinny and pale and couldn't have been more than twenty years old.

"It's my daughter," the man said. He sat down. Sam remained standing, his arms folded across his chest.

"You said I knew you?" Sam asked.

"Do you work with Bobby Noelke?" The man was looking past Sam, at the wall behind him.

"Oh. Bobby." Sam finally seated himself. Bobby was another lawyer he sometimes did business with. He worked downtown and did quite well. He had bounced several DUI cases Sam's way because of his overload. Bobby meant money. Sam reached for a pad and pencil. "What's your name?"

"Roger."

"What's your last name?"

"You do a lot of work for Bobby Noelke?"

"Yes," Sam said. "We work on some projects."

Roger leaned back in his chair and rolled his head around a bit. There was something off about him. He's probably high, Sam thought. Many of his clients were drug users. "What's your problem, Roger? Why are you here? You mentioned something about your daughter."

"I lost my baby girl. My daughter."

Sam picked up his pencil again. "I'm sorry to hear that. What do you mean lost?"

"Lost her to my wife. She divorced me. I can't see my baby girl no more."

"That can be very difficult. When did this happen?"

Roger rolled his head one more time, then looked evenly at Sam. "Yesterday. Wendy left me, and now they took my girl."

"That's too bad. Maybe we can do something about it. Did Bobby give you the case file? If not, he can fax it to me so we don't waste time. I'll call him. I'm surprised he didn't call."

"Bobby was my wife's lawyer," Roger said. "Wendy's lawyer. You worked for her, too."

Sam paused, thinking. "Wendy Stets? Yeah, that's right, I helped Bobby a little on that. Last month, I think." As soon as he spoke, he felt something in the room change, felt Roger's eyes shift to him, saw them flicker.

Roger unzipped his jacket and squeezed his eyes so tight that his forehead scrunched up.

Sam cleared his throat and glanced at the closed door. "What's this about?" he asked.

"Mr. Gamett, do you believe that Jesus Christ died for our sins?"

Sam slowly stood up. "You know, Roger, I'm pretty busy right now. So, if you don't mind, you're going to have to leave."

Roger leaned toward the desk. It was only then that Sam saw the reddish brown stain on the front of his white T-shirt.

"Is that blood?" he blurted. "Your shirt. It's all over your shirt."

Roger opened his eyes and looked past Sam. "It's Bobby's blood."

Sam stepped back from the desk, almost knocking over his chair. "What do you mean, Bobby's blood? What are you talking about?"

"He started bleeding after I shot him."

"You shot him," Sam said. For some reason, he started to laugh.

Roger continued to stare past Sam while his knees bounced up and down. "He's dead," he said.

Sam stopped laughing and saw the cold, flat nothingness of Roger's eyes. He teetered backward and reached out for the edge of his desk. *I can talk myself out of this.* But when he saw Roger reach under his jacket and pull out a black gun with a short, thick barrel, Sam knew he was going to die.

"Listen, Roger, I had nothing to do with your case. I just looked at some papers."

"You worked with him," Roger said. "You talked with Wendy, too."

"Please," Sam said. Roger was shrinking, disappearing into the blackness that was closing in on them. Sam looked around the office, saw its clutter, papers and files. I'm going to die here, he thought. His knees buckled. I'm dying right now.

Roger got to his feet. He was crying. "I'm sorry," he said. He raised the gun and aimed it at Sam. His hand was shaking.

"Please," Sam said. "Please. Don't, Roger. I can help you. Put the gun down. Please put it down."

"I'm sorry," Roger said. He was holding the gun with two hands, while wobbling back and forth on his feet.

Sam stood frozen, tears falling down his face, clutching the desk, saying the word "please," over and over.

"Please," Sam said one last time. That's when Roger fired.

Sam felt a flicker of heat flash past his ear and heard Maureen scream. He opened his eyes and saw her standing behind Roger, holding flowers.

"Run, Maureen!" Sam yelled. "Run!" Roger whirled and fired again. Maureen's head jerked back and she flew out into the hallway, one shoe popping up in the air behind her. Roger kept shooting in her direction.

"Stop!" Sam yelled. "Jesus, stop!"

Roger turned to face him. "I only have one bullet left," he said. "I was going to kill myself after I killed you. But I only have one bullet left now." He was crying, long tears streaking his face. "One bullet, one bullet. I don't know where to get more bullets around here. Do you? Do you know where I can get more bullets?"

Sam closed his eyes.

Roger stamped his foot. "What should I do?" he screamed. "What should I do?" He backed away from Sam and bumped into the wall, causing the picture of the nun on the bike to fall to the floor in a crash. Roger picked it up and looked at it, cocking his head like an inquisitive bird. Then he dropped it to the floor and pointed the gun at Sam.

"Do you believe in Jesus Christ?" he said calmly.

Sam covered his face with his hands, not sure of what to answer. "No," he said.

"I'm sorry, Mr. Gamett, what did you say?"

"Yes," Sam yelled. "Yes. I do."

Roger considered this answer. "Do you?" he asked. "Do you really? Most people say they do, but they don't. Most people lie." His voice was a whisper. He held the gun with both hands. "It's important that you tell me the truth. I need to know. Do you believe in Jesus Christ?"

"I don't know," Sam said through tears. "Yes. Yes I do. I do." He knelt down and pressed his face on the floor and closed his eyes. "I believe in Jesus Christ."

Roger was quiet. Sam heard him breathing, sharp, short rasps. "Good. Because if you do, none of this matters."

Then he pressed the trigger.

CHAPTER

Three

Afterward, Sam just watched TV: talk shows in the morning, soap operas in the afternoon, the History Channel in the evening, the Weather Channel late at night. The programs all blended together, a collage of faces, voices, and blue light. Occasionally, something would catch and hold his interest, offer brief traction against his downward slide, but most of it was a slippery slope.

When he did manage to sleep, he caught glimpses of Maureen as the young mother she would never be. Sometimes she was walking in a large green field by a lake, sometimes she was in a park by a pond filled with brown reeds that swayed in a breeze he could not feel. Small children would be trailing her, dancing in muted sunlight, their backs glowing halos. When Maureen saw him, she would offer an unbearable smile and walk away.

Carol had called several times, as had his father-in-law, Charlie. A cousin from Washington, DC had also called once, leaving a message. Sam talked to no one. He was past words.

He spent most of his time in bed. Occasionally, he would muster enough energy to go across the street to the convenience store, but lately even that was proving to be too much.

Tonight he had strayed from his usual pattern of shows and watched a VH-1 *Behind the Music* on the Go-Go's, an A&E biography on Sonny Bono, a few minutes of the movie, *Cool Hand Luke*, and an Andy Griffith rerun on Nick at Nite. *The Andy Griffith Show* actually held his interest for a while. Barney and Andy were hunting a criminal in an abandoned barn. When Barney drew his gun, Sam switched channels.

It was close to midnight and time for the Weather Channel anyway. He found the maps and reviews about high-pressure zones and lake temperatures sufficiently sleep-inducing and tried to end his day with them. He propped himself up on some pillows. If he slept at all, it was usually sitting. He opened a new beer and slowly began to press the remote on his way to Channel 34.

He had talked about the weather with Maureen's mother at the wake. He had shown up near the end of it, drunk and with nothing to say. He had apologized for being late, blaming the thunderstorm that had flooded underpasses on the Dan Ryan Expressway. It was on the radio, he said. The rain was going to last all week. Maureen's mother had taken his hand and said one of Maureen's uncles had called from his car and said the same thing. She gazed at him for a while with desolate eyes, then faded into the crowd. He stayed only a few minutes and never approached the casket. When he returned to the motel, he had pounded the wall of his room with his black, wing-tipped shoes until the night manager knocked on his door and threatened to call the police.

As he continued to make his way to the Weather Channel, Sam noticed that the stations were suddenly changing at a slower pace, then not at all. He stared down at the remote, then back up at the screen. Nothing. He pressed down hard, fighting panic. He relied on this remote, needed it. He looked at the TV. A woman in a nun's costume was talking. He pressed the button. Nothing. Still the same woman in the nun's costume. He pressed again, then again, and again. This could not be happening.

He removed the batteries and turned them over carefully in his hands. Accomplishing nothing, he put them back, got out of bed, and approached the TV, holding the remote in front of him with both hands like a divining rod. He kept pressing and walking until he was just inches from the screen. Nothing changed. Just the nun and Sam.

He threw the remote against the wall and watched as it broke into flying pieces. He ripped the covers off his bed and threw them, too, against the wall. Finally, he took hold of the sides of the TV and shook it with his hands, shook it like he was trying to strangle the breath out of it.

"Goddammit!" he yelled. "Goddammit."

It was while he was choking the TV that he recognized the nun. Then he felt his jaw drop.

"You have the power to change," the nun said.

Sam stared at a piece of the broken remote on the floor, then back up at the television.

"When bad things happen to you, people, well-meaning people, say it's God's will. But that's not God's will. Our God does not test people, our God does not bring forth tragedy and pain. Our God loves and forgives. Our God offers hope. Don't turn on God, don't give up on Him. He won't give up on you."

It turned out the nun was a real nun, Sister Maria North, the nun from the picture Maureen had given him, the nun riding the bike. *Go Sister!* Maureen must have watched this show. Sitting cross-legged on the floor, he, too, watched Sister North, broadcasting live from Lake Eagleton, in northwest Wisconsin. She was taking calls from viewers.

"I'm sorry," a man's voice said. Sam inched closer to the TV and listened as a truck driver told Sister North how he had crashed into a minivan on a mountain road, killing two teenagers.

"I should have seen them," the man said, his words chokes and sighs. "But it was late, and I was tired. I was half-asleep and shouldn't have been driving." He briefly broke down, his voice dissolving into a whisper. "It was my fault. I should have seen them. I should have been paying better attention."

Sister North gently readjusted her thick, black glasses, her eyes wide and sad. "I understand," she said.

Sam leaned closer and raised the volume with suddenly trembling fingers.

"I can never forgive myself," the man said. "Two boys dead. I can never forgive myself."

Sister North shook her head. "You didn't plan for it to happen. You didn't want it to happen." She held out her hands, palms up. "It just happened."

"I can't forgive myself," the man said. "I never will."

"You must," Sister North said. "Forgiveness is God's grace. It is His gift. Accept it."

Sam sat frozen, his hand still on the volume button. He sat there mesmerized as Sister North took other calls, offering comfort and advice to all.

When she told one caller, we all have pain, Sam nodded.

When she told another, we all have sinned, Sam said yes out loud.

When she said she was taking one more call, Sam grabbed the phone.

He was immediately put on hold. After a minute of waiting, listening to absolutely nothing, a hopeless, depthless silence, a woman with a soft voice came on the line and asked what he wanted to talk to Sister North about. He was stunned by the question and felt his lips move, felt his own breath against the receiver. He closed his eyes and swallowed. When he opened them he could already taste the tears at the corners of his mouth.

"I want to know why I'm still alive," he said in a raw, empty voice he did not recognize. Then he hung up.

• • •

Sam spent the week at the end of things, the final strings of his tied-together life unraveling. In the afternoons, he braced himself and got up and ran across the street to the convenience store for beer. The clerk, a tired old man with dirty hair and tattoos on his thin wrists, looked at Sam's unshaven face and bloodshot eyes with a mixture of fear and sympathy.

At nights, he waited patiently for Sister Maria North, her voice and words, first a curiosity, then a salve, soothing and cool. Her voice was plain and her words direct. She was a sturdy life raft that Sam clung to.

He tried to write down what she was saying, using a small, red spiral notebook he found in a pocket of his briefcase. He took the best notes he could, recording her message:

"God is hope."

"God is people."

One of her shows was dedicated to the mystery of faith, another to the healing power of prayer. Near the end of the week, Sister North focused on self-examination. Life is an accumulative experience, she said. Things add up.

Sam listened to what she told him, taking most of her pronouncements at face value, open now to all possibilities. Despite the fact that his father had been a minister, he was not a religious person. He didn't believe in God, but he found himself believing in Sister North. Her logic and sincerity made him feel better, made him see hope as a tangible, necessary thing. After her show, his spirits were temporarily raised; for a few minutes, he felt he was not alone, felt he might have a friend, someone who understood and forgave, someone who offered fresh starts and clean slates.

During the days, he lay in bed and imagined conversations with her, confessing all. At night, near the end of the show, he called her 800 number and listened to the busy signal keep time with his heart.

On Friday, he finally got through.

"Yes?" It was the same woman's voice as before, soft and calm.

Sam stared at the receiver. "I want to talk to the nun. To Sister North," he said.

"There's a long wait."

"I'll hold."

The woman put him on hold, and Sam waited, rocking back and forth in the bed, listening again to the silence, everything, the world, his life, suspended. After ten minutes, the woman came back on.

"Are you still holding for Sister North?"

"Yes."

"It will be a while."

"I'll hold."

"You may want to try back tomorrow."

"I'll hold."

Sam propped himself up on the bed and turned up the volume of the TV. A woman had just announced she was going to kill herself, but Sister North seemed unfazed.

"Now, why would you want to do that?" she said.

"Because there's no reason to go on," the woman said.

Sister North smiled and peered over her glasses. "There are always reasons to go on. There are hundreds of reasons to go on. Thousands. And you know that; otherwise, you wouldn't be calling me. Listen, dear, you're in a bad way. That doesn't mean you'll always be in a bad way. Tomorrow might be better. Next week might be better. And wouldn't it be a shame if you weren't around to enjoy it?"

The woman started to cry.

Sister North folded her hands in front of her and stared into the camera. "Never give up hope, my dear. Hope is the light that never goes out."

The next caller, a man with a loud, breathless voice, said Sister North had cured his wife's cancer.

"After we saw you, it went away," he said. "We came up to the lake and you touched her and now she's cured."

"I didn't cure her."

"You prayed for her. Right in front of her. I was there. Do you remember? It was last month, and we came up to see you at your house."

"I remember. But we all prayed, if I recall." Sister North smiled. "We all prayed. I'm so glad your wife is better."

"God bless you, Sister North."

Sister North smiled again, but shook her head.

A minute later, the woman came back on the phone line with Sam.

"Are you still waiting?" she asked.

"Yes," Sam said.

"It's going to be a while."

"I'll wait." More than ever, Sam wanted to talk to this magical woman.

"We're running out of time," she said.

"It's okay. I'll wait."

The woman sighed. "If that's what you want."

A few minutes later, the show ended, though, and he was disconnected. He stared at the dead receiver and gently hung it up.

That night he dreamed he was finally talking to Sister North, her voice clear and clean.

"Never lose hope my son," she said. "God loves you."

"He doesn't love me," Sam said.

"God loves you. The signs are everywhere. Open your eyes, Sam. Open your eyes."

Signs. Sam opened his eyes and clutched a pillow in front of him, cradled it like the Christ child, and waited for bushes to burn.

Four

He had a vague sense of where Lake Eagleton, Wisconsin, was. North and west. Or north and east. He wanted to believe that a divine force was guiding him and that he would somehow find himself in the town that broadcast Sister North's show. Eventually, he knew, he would have to get a map.

He drove in the right-hand lane of the tollway with the radio off, the silence a welcome relief after weeks of television. After he passed the Wisconsin border, though, he found himself thinking, something he tried to avoid doing. He turned the radio on, first to a classical station, which made him think even more, then to an all-sports talk show, then to an oldies rock station. "Just My Imagination," by the Stones, was on. He turned the volume up, the song pushing his thoughts underwater, gasping and kicking.

He gripped the steering wheel with both hands and tried to focus on the road. After spending so much time in bed, he felt disoriented in motion. Continuing in the right-hand lane, he hugged the shoulder, driving slower and slower. Several cars honked, many of the drivers making faces or obscene gestures, as they passed. One young girl, drinking a can of Coke in the passenger seat, casually gave him the finger without looking at him.

Finally, when he realized he was going only thirty-five miles an hour, he pulled over at a gas station just south of Milwaukee. He filled up with regular, leaning against the car and breathing in the cold spring air in gulps. When he was finished, he went to the men's room and washed his face over and over again with lukewarm water.

In the checkout line at the gas station food mart, holding a bottle of water and package of Twinkies, things finally crashed over him, a terrible wave of sadness, despair. Maureen. Roger. His wife. His life. He saw everything at once spread out before him like a map, one thing leading to another, and thought, And I'm on my way to see a television nun.

A cold tightness gripped his chest, icy fingers, and he tasted something bitter rising in the back of his throat. He dropped the Twinkies and the water on the floor and ran out to his car.

He was sitting there taking deep breaths when he heard a pounding on the passenger side. A short, Hispanic man, with thick black hair was knocking on his window.

"You Burt?" the man yelled. "Burt Hoff?"

Sam simply stared back at him.

The man opened the door, threw a green duffel bag in the back, then got in the front seat next to Sam.

"You're late," the man said. "Let's go."

They had driven for close to five minutes before a somewhat dazed Sam finally got around to telling the man he wasn't Burt Hoff.

"Didn't think so. Burt Hoff didn't sound like he had a car like this. Beemer?"

Sam looked around the car for confirmation, nodded.

"Burt Hoff ran a classified looking for someone to split gas with him to Minneapolis. Supposed to meet him here."

Sam stared straight ahead and noticed that it was almost dark.

The red taillights of the cars in front of him burned like warning signs.

Finally, he said, "I'm not going to Minneapolis."

"Where you going?"

"Lake Eagleton, Wisconsin."

The man was silent. He nodded for a while. "Where's that again?"

"North," Sam said. "Northwest."

The man took this in too, thinking. "Yeah, that's the direction I'm going."

"I think that's farther than Minneapolis," Sam said.

"That's okay. I'll get a ride from there. Been at that store for six hours."

"I think it's a lot farther."

"That's okay."

Sam shrugged. He didn't really care. "If that's what you want," he said.

He kept driving, the highway a treadmill. He had no idea what he was doing, but recognized where all this was leading: a desolate road, a knife, a brief struggle.

"Can I ask you a question?" the man asked.

"What?"

"Ask you a question?"

Sam waited.

"You drunk?"

Sam looked over at the man. "No," he finally thought to say.

"You driving so slow. Just wondering. I always drive slow when I'm drunk. You know, just thought you were being careful because maybe you were fucked up. Taking precautions."

"I'm not drunk."

"Yeah, well don't make a difference to me. Long as you got air bags."

They drove a little longer. A station wagon with a missing taillight passed them. Sam glanced over and saw a small child strapped into a car seat. He waited for the child to give him the finger, but the station wagon pulled away.

"Hey," the man said, "all right if I ask you another question?"

Sam took a deep breath. "Sure."

"You ever been buried alive?"

Maybe the one question Sam did not expect. "No." He counted to three, then carefully asked, "Have you?"

The guy sniffled and shrugged. "No. The last guy I got a ride with, though, he tells me he was buried alive three times. Two times by accident. That's bullshit. Maybe once, but no one gets buried alive three times. And I told him that. He got all pissed off and everything, said he's got a condition that makes him seem dead. Everything dies on him, but he ain't dead. He secretly alive. I listened to him, went along with him, because I didn't want to get him too excited in case maybe he does got that condition and it kicks in and he's driving, you know? Thing was, he kept talking about it. After a while, he made it seem like I was the crazy nut because I never was buried alive. So I started thinking maybe it was more popular, getting buried alive. Maybe it happens more. A common thing. That's why I asked. Curious."

Sam switched into the left-hand lane and passed a minivan that was actually driving slower than he. "Well," he said, "that seems like a strange condition. Too bad for that guy, huh?"

"Too bad for me. Stuck listening to him. Nut, man. Wouldn't shut up."

They drove in silence, the traffic sparse and moving fast. Sam wondered again how far Lake Eagleton was, then wondered again what he was doing.

"Guess what I do," the man asked after a while.

Kill people, Sam thought. "I don't know," he said. He turned on the radio. Another Stones song. "Tumbling Dice." His favorite when he was fourteen. He played it constantly, jumping around his room, pretending to be Mick and Keith, the grinning devils. After "Tumbling Dice," yet another Stones song, yet another one of his favorites, "Rocks Off." The music lifted him for a moment until he realized it was probably a sign, realized that his life was probably flashing before him on the radio. The abandoned road, the knife, imminent.

"I'm a magician. Do tricks."

"What?"

"For kids' parties, mostly. Minneapolis is a good birthday town. More money, lots of kids. I can get $125 an hour in Minneapolis. You want to see a trick?"

The knife, now. "Okay," Sam said.

"You got a knife?"

The car swerved.

"Hey! Watch it!"

"Sorry."

The man sat straight up in his seat and put his hand on the dashboard. "You sure you ain't drunk?"

"I'm not drunk. I'm sorry."

"I got kids depending on me." He sat back and crouched down low in the seat. "Anyway, as part of my act, I'm learning this new thing, with a knife and some string. Complicated though. You cut the string into pieces, then it kind of comes out whole in like one piece."

"I don't have a knife."

"Yeah, I don't got no string."

The man coughed and squirmed in his seat. "Everything's an illusion, you know? Sleight of hand. Magic is mysterious, you know? But it's hard, too. I'm lucky. I got quick hands, that helps. Can juggle, do shit like that. You gotta work at it, though, make people believe. People want to believe in magic."

Sam drove for a while before saying, "Interesting."

"You ever do magic?" the man asked. "Any tricks? When you were a kid?"

"No. I watched TV when I was a kid."

"TV," the man said as if he vaguely remembered it. "Yeah, I watched some TV."

More silence, another Stones song. "Brown Sugar." *English blood runs hot.* Sam was part-English. When his mother told him that, he spent an entire week talking with a cockney accent until a bully at school punched him in the stomach and called him a fag.

"This the Stones?"

"Yeah."

"You like the Stones?"

"Yeah."

"This a CD?"

"Radio."

"Someone from the Stones die?"

Sam was concerned. The prospect of a dead Stone cut him. Keith, Mick, Charlie were like family. "I don't think so. Why, did someone die? Did you hear that?"

"I don't know, they keep playing Stones songs. They do that when people die. They played Jim Croce for a month when he died. I remember that. Same thing with Lennon."

"I can see Lennon," Sam said. "But not Jim Croce."

The man laughed. "Yeah, who is Jim Croce right? He only had one song. That LeRoy thing."

" 'Bad, Bad LeRoy Brown.' "

The man snapped his fingers. "Yeah, I hated that song. They kept playing it over and over."

Sam nodded, then relaxed for some reason. "I remember that. I was in high school. They played Jim Croce for an entire day."

The man laughed again. "Hey, before I forget, my name's Willie. Willie Martinez."

Sam nodded.

"You got a name?"

"I'm Sam," Sam said.

"Sam, I know you're probably in a hurry, but you hungry? I ain't eaten in a while."

Sam realized he hadn't really eaten in days. "Yeah," he said. "I guess I could eat."

They stopped at a place called the Brat Stop, where Sam ate french fries and drank several beers while watching Willie wolf down three cheeseburgers. Throughout the meal, Willie kept up a steady banter about the weather, women's bodies, and why he should have been born taller.

"I got the arms and legs of a tall person," he said, swallowing. He stretched his arms out to his sides to emphasize the point. "But got the torso of a short guy. Parts don't match up."

Sam sipped his beer and watched Willie eat. His face certainly didn't match up. It was a patchwork of mismatched features: low-slung ears that stuck out wide, a nose pushed slightly to one side, and eyes set so deep that Sam had a hard time even seeing them. His hair, too, was out of proportion. Black, and wavy, it jutted out to one side, ending abruptly like a cliff.

"What you staring at?" Willie asked.

Sam glanced away, down at his beer.

"Looking at my hair, aren't you?"

Sam didn't say anything.

"Got a bad haircut. Gave it to myself. Thought it would be easy to do. Just look in the mirror and cut, but it's hard. Harder than it looks."

"Yeah, well, it'll grow back," Sam said, and signaled for another beer.

"Yeah, that's what I'm thinking."

By the time they left the restaurant, it was very late. Since Sam was pretty lit up, he asked Willie to drive to a motel. He made him go to four different places until they found one that had full cable TV.

"You must really like cable," Willie said, as they pulled off the highway and into the parking lot of a place that looked remarkably like the Get Down.

Sam was sure that Willie would drop him off and steal the car, but Willie walked with him into the small motel office and waited patiently by the counter while Sam got a room.

"Hey, you okay?" Willie asked.

"Yeah, I'm good," Sam said, as they walked outside. The rain was coming down in sheets, and the parking lot was turning into one large puddle. They both walked through it without comment or concern. When Sam finally got to his room, Willie asked if he could sleep in the car.

Sam turned around to face him, no longer sure exactly how they knew each other. He had had a lot of beers.

"It's late. Won't get no ride now," Willie said. Water was streaming down the sides of his dark face.

"Here," Sam said. He started fumbling for keys.

"Looking for these?" Willie asked. He held out Sam's car keys.

"Keep them. I don't care. Sleep in the car. Listen to the radio if you want, keep the heat on. I don't care."

Willie pointed the keys at Sam and headed to the car, almost sauntering. "Thanks, man. Sleep tight."

Once inside the room, Sam immediately turned on the television. It was well past midnight, and he was late. He frantically flipped through the stations, squeezing the life out of the remote. They had stayed too long at the Brat Stop. Now he was afraid he had missed the show.

He found her on Channel 49. She was talking to a caller about forgiveness.

"Forgiveness is God's grace," she said.

"But I can't forgive him. He killed my son."

"It was an accident, my dear. You said so yourself."

"My son," the woman said. She started to cry.

Sister North took off her glasses and rubbed the bridge of her nose with a short, thick hand.

"When I was a girl, my brother was killed in a hunting accident," she said matter-of-factly. She put her glasses back on. "He was my older brother, and naturally I was upset and angry. I knew the boy who killed him, I knew him well. They had been drinking and gotten careless."

"That's terrible," the woman said. She stopped crying and sniffled.

"I forgave him, though it took time, and it was very difficult," Sister North said. She folded her hands in front of her and looked tired and old. "But I forgave him. For his sake, my brother's sake, and my sake. Forgiveness releases you."

Sam stared at Sister North's image, her eyes swimming in thick glasses, a large owlish face sitting on a short, thick neck, and felt the familiar sense of comfort she brought him. He picked up the phone and dialed her now memorized number. He was shocked when someone answered after only three rings.

"Hello?"

"Hello." It was the same woman's voice, softer than usual.

"I'd like to speak to Sister North. The nun," he said.

"There's a long wait," the woman said.

"I'll wait."

Sam was put on hold. He raised the volume on the TV. Sister North was telling another woman to gather herself together and calm down. The woman was crying, saying she had dreamed of Satan the night before, and he had looked just like Regis Philbin.

"Hello?" The calm voice again. "What do you want to talk to Sister North about?"

Sam hesitated. He didn't want to sound crazy or come on too strong. "I want to know how I can be a better person."

"Do you need Sister North to tell you that?" the woman asked.

He turned away from the TV and stared at the phone, confused. "What?"

"It will be a while," the woman said.

"I'll wait."

"If that's what you want."

He was put on hold again. He didn't think Sister North's staff was particularly courteous and thought he might offer this piece of constructive insight to her once they finally spoke. He readjusted himself on the bed, propping up a pillow behind him.

A few minutes later, the woman was back on the line. "You're still holding." She said this, rather than asked.

"Yes."

"What do you want to talk to her about again?" the woman asked.

"It's personal," Sam said. He had decided not to like this woman.

"You're going to be on TV you know."

"I know."

"Well, it can't be that personal."

"It is."

"Call back later, then."

"I'll wait."

"If that's what you want."

Sam felt his face flash hot. "You know," he started to say something, then caught himself. Instead, he slammed down the phone.

He turned the volume up higher. Sister North was talking about the importance and need for self-examination and reflection.

"Reflect on who you are, and where you're going. Know your faults," she said. "Assess things. Assess who you are. Examine both the good and the bad."

She concluded her show by reading a Psalm.

"'Praise the Lord who heals the brokenhearted. God heals the brokenhearted and binds up all their wounds. God fixes the number of the stars and calls each one by name.'" She peered into the camera, her eyes wide. "Good-bye," she said. Then Sam thought he saw her wink.

· · ·

When the show ended, Sam searched his pockets for his little red notebook while walking over to the desk. He thought this was the perfect opportunity to assess himself, particularly now that he was safely drunk.

He wrote:

1. *Self-centered*
2. *Selfish*

He stopped and stared at the two words. He thought those two redundant. Can you be self-centered but not selfish? He tried to imagine a self-centered but generous person. Regardless, he was both, always putting his interests ahead of others.

He next added *vain* to the list. He thought he was good-looking, knew it in fact. He had put himself through college and law school working as a model, appearing in newspaper ads for local department stores wearing suits, pajamas, and, once, tight-fitting underwear. He was "discovered," as his mother used to say, when he was seventeen by a neighbor, Mrs. Mardiks, who was a photographer. "You look like a mannequin," she said as she took his picture in front of her apartment. A month later, he appeared in the *Chicago Sun-Times* for Marshall Field's wearing a three-piece suit. His mother referred to the clothes he modeled as "outfits." She would say, "You look nice in that outfit," or "that outfit is smart-looking." He had posed for ads off and on for years in a variety of outfits, always smiling, his head tilted in one direction or another, his hands in his pockets or on his hips. His friends had teased him, but he didn't mind; the money was good, and he needed every cent of it to escape his parents. The work eventually tailed off as he got older, but by that time he had just enough to pay for law school.

Next he listed, *underachieving*. He should have made more of himself. He had suspected this for some time. He got very high test scores in school but very average grades. His teachers were constantly telling his mother that he was a classic underachiever. When his mother first told him this, he thought she said *classy* underachiever, which Sam took as a reflection on his stylish clothes. His mother fretted over the label, claiming his father was a classic underachiever as well. "Push yourself," she would say time and time again. "You can't get by on your looks forever." Once they were going through revolving doors at Marshall Field's, and his mother, who was ahead of him, suddenly stopped pushing. Since Sam wasn't pushing at all, the door came to a complete stop. Sam remembered his mother whirling around and pointing a finger, remembered her mouthing the words through the glass, *"Push yourself."* His mother was always trying something, anything, to keep him from ending up like his father.

Then, *unloving*. From the start, his marriage had been a commercial for divorce. He had married Carol because she was rich: Her father was the managing partner in the city's largest law firm and owned a Bentley, something that impressed Sam very much at the time. She had married him because she was fat.

They had met in law school and while friendly, never dated. Sam regularly slept with a number of women, and Carol, a good forty pounds on the heavy side, was someone he never considered. After graduating, their paths frequently crossed. Sam worked in the District Attorney's Office, a job he was ill suited for—it required effort and dedication—and Carol worked for her father's firm in criminal defense. Occasionally, they would have lunch to discuss deals and cases. It was during one of those lunches that she asked him to accompany her to the firm's Christmas party, which was held at her parents' house in Hinsdale. Sam said yes and, after seeing the house, the swimming pool, the tennis courts, and the photos of the family jet, immediately started to revise his position on heavy women.

She had four sisters, all of them attorneys. Sam, always terrible with names, could never keep them straight. When they weren't around, he referred to them as the Smart One, the Big One, the Pretty One, and the Really Big One. They all hated Sam, thinking him not worthy of being in their family, which traced its lineage back to the first Archbishop of Canterbury. The Really Big One in particular had it in for Sam, glaring at him whenever they would meet.

They dated for years, Sam always discreetly seeing other women on the side: waitresses, models, law students. He preferred thin, facile women who asked little if anything of him other than sex. He seldom paid for dinner. He was relatively content with his life and saw no reason to change his situation until the small, personal injury law firm he had joined started making demands, asking him to work full eight-hour days and show up at the office before ten in the morning. It was only then that Carol became a serious option.

The first few years of marriage had been peaceful, if not somnolent. They both worked at her father's firm and tended quietly to go their separate ways on weekends, Carol to her parents' home and Sam to their 1.2-million-dollar town house on the Gold Coast, where he spent his time sipping single-malt scotches and watching satellite TV, when he wasn't on a golf course or in the tanning booth. He was comfortable with the relationship: Carol was very quiet, had a considerable trust fund, and, in certain, dark clothing, the ability to appear thinner than she was. Sam was handsome, looked good in a tux, and agreeably escorted her to the numerous firm and family functions they were required to attend.

Things started to change when Carol began dieting, however. It started innocently enough, with her eating grapefruit for breakfast instead of pound cake. This soon led to aerobics, jogging, and, finally, a personal trainer from Bosnia named Rigo. At first, Sam watched the weight loss with curiosity, then with amazement, and finally with fear. He suspected the diet was part of a bigger plan, a plan that would ultimately involve him. In the end, his fears were confirmed. Once she was down to 110 pounds, she decided to shed Sam.

She told him she wanted a divorce when they were at the bottom of a toboggan chute. It was at the firm's holiday outing that she announced this. They had gone down the chute together and fallen sideways into the snow, landing with the toboggan on top of them. Sam was the first to stand up. As he was brushing snow off his ski pants, Carol said, "I think I want to go it alone." She was still lying on her side in the fetal position when she spoke, her head half-buried in snow. Sam had thought she meant go it alone on the toboggan, so he said fine and turned and headed up the hill. When she didn't come home that night, or the night after, he began to read more into her statement. A week later she called him in the middle of the night, and simply said, "You are incapable of loving anyone but yourself," in an odd, faraway voice that Sam sometimes still heard.

Sam next printed *too quiet*. Like Carol, he wasn't much of a talker. His habit of silence unsettled people, his coworkers, his friends, his bosses. It used to particularly annoy his mother. "Speak up," she used to say, "speak your mind." Throughout his life, Sam made an effort but found words clumsy. At parties or bars, he preferred to stand in corners and wait for women to gravitate toward him, and in meetings he would stroke his chin thoughtfully and agree with the consensus. Secretly, he admired people who had the gift of gab and was envious of the give-and-take others fell into, the easy chitchat about the weather, sports, or politics. He tried but could never quite achieve the outgoing personality everyone seemed to expect from him.

He added *inept* to the list, thought about it, and then changed it to *not handy*. He had no practical, real-world skills. He was terrible with technology, could barely change a lightbulb, couldn't cook, and knew next to nothing about cars. Anytime he tried to take on a project, whether it was paying the bills, painting a wall, preparing a brief, or washing a car, someone—his mother, his wife, a female coworker—would invariably step in and redo it, start to finish.

He studied the word, then decided to change *not handy* to *lazy*. After a few more minutes, he added *inept* next to it in parentheses. He wanted to be honest for once and use this as a blueprint for the rest of his life.

He turned to a new page in the notebook and decided to focus on his good traits for a moment, end the day on an upbeat note. He searched inward, quickly scanned his life, the blank page in front of him a sobering mirror. He tried to think of something positive to say about himself, but couldn't. Finally, in desperation, he wrote, *always rewinds videotapes before returning them*, then immediately erased that and wrote: *down deep, a nice guy.*

He almost always gave change to homeless people near the train station. When he was young, he had sometimes chosen the worst athletes to be on his team because he felt sorry for them. In high school, he had once purposely run a little slower in a track meet so his friend Pat Bogi, who was extremely short, could win his first race. And when he was a boy, he used to say his prayers every night.

Feeling a little better about himself, he added *relatively honest, nonviolent*, and finally, *good golfer*. Sam closed the book and looked in the mirror above the desk. The lamp was throwing shadows, obscuring one side of his face. He moved his head slowly back and forth, in and out of the darkness. Light and dark, dark and light. He was still pretty drunk.

While he was staring into the mirror, it occurred to him that he hadn't done anything good in a long time. He had been self-absorbed and selfish for years. Yet, despite his history, he thought he might have small, gurgling pools of goodness in him waiting to be tapped. He remembered something that had happened to him a few months earlier. He was driving back from court and had gotten stuck in a traffic jam at a tollbooth. When he tried to change to a lane that was moving, no one would let him cut in. Finally, after ten minutes, a man in a beat-up Buick waved him over and let him slide his car in front of his. When Sam got to the tollbooth, he considered paying the man's fifty cents as a way of thanking him. He didn't, of course. He paid his own toll and roared off in his BMW. The intent was there, but he had failed to follow through.

He examined himself in the mirror, his face still in half shadows, and vowed to change. From now on, he would act on his impulses, step over the line that separated the indifferent from the good. He would change.

He stood up, walked over to the window, and pulled back the drapes. It was raining heavier than ever. It was freezing out, too. Willie, he thought, must be cold.

He immediately turned and pulled a blanket and a pillow from the bed, then walked outside. When he got to his car, he knocked on the passenger window, waited, and knocked again. The windows were fogged up, and he couldn't see inside. He knocked again, and again, then finally just yanked on the door handle. It was unlocked. Willie was stretched out, sound asleep, with his mouth open, his feet propped up on his duffel bag.

Sam stood in the rain, trying to figure out the best way to approach this situation. He finally threw the soaking-wet blanket on top of Willie and tossed the pillow onto his lap. He was about to leave when he decided to adjust the blanket a bit, tuck Willie in, so to speak. That's when he woke up.

"The fuck you doing?" He lurched forward and tried to grab at Sam's arm. Sam jumped back and fell in a puddle, water splashing.

"I was giving you a blanket." Sam had to yell this over the rain.

"You some kind of fag?" Willie yelled. "Touching me!" He threw the blanket off himself.

Sam stood up. "I thought you might be cold."

"Fuck you!" Willie said, then slammed the door.

"No," Sam said. He pointed at the car. "Fuck *you*!" He staggered a moment, turned, and stomped off.

That probably didn't go as well as it could have, he thought once he was back in his room. He stripped off his clothes and crawled into bed.

No dreams that night. But as he slept, he sensed things in motion. Everything was in front of him, but he had no way of knowing that for sure.

Five

In the morning, with sun streaming past the open drapes, his mouth dry, and his head cracking, Sam saw things more clearly. From virtually every perspective, giving Willie the car keys had not been smart. He needed a car to go north, or just to go. He wasn't even sure where he was.

He lay in bed and stared at the ceiling, then stood up and walked over to the window. No Willie. No car. No surprise. He deserved it. As punishment, he would spend the rest of his life here, wherever "here" was. He imagined himself living in the motel forever, decorating his room for the holidays and eventually taking a job here, first as janitor, then as the night clerk. He would ask for Saturday off, settle for every other Sunday.

He went to the bathroom, turned the faucet on, and washed his face. Then he took a long, hot shower and tried to decide next steps. Maybe there were no next steps, he thought.

He was drying off and imagining the police report, "man willingly gave hitchhiker his car," when he heard a single knock at the door.

He wrapped a towel around his waist. Through the peephole, he saw Willie holding two paper cups, the steam rising.

"I found a place down the road, a coffee place," he said, when Sam opened the door. "I didn't know if you wanted cream though."

Sam stared at Willie, not quite comprehending. Willie was supposed to be gone and far away.

"You want cream?"

"No. This is good," Sam said, taking a cup from Willie's outstretched hand. "This is fine."

They drove for a while in silence, Sam's head full of tremors and aftershocks. Willie was slouched in his seat, staring out the window at the rolling countryside that had replaced the truck stops and billboards. Sam squinted into the morning sun and wished for sunglasses. The light hurt.

"Hey, sorry about last night," Willie said. "Kind of lost it."

"I probably scared you."

"Scared me a lot. Was sound asleep. Felt you touching me."

"I wasn't touching you," Sam said. "But I'm sorry. It was stupid. I'm sorry. I won't do that again."

"Yeah, well I don't like being touched. Especially by some guy."

"I wasn't touching you," Sam said again.

Sam switched into the left lane. He wanted to drive fast while he still had coffee in him.

"Where you going again?" Willie asked.

"Lake Eagleton," Sam said, almost sheepishly.

"Yeah, that's what you said. How come you heading there?"

Sam hesitated. "A little vacation. I need a rest."

"You ever been up that way before?"

"No. I heard about it though."

"How you hear about it?"

A TV nun told me. "A friend. It's supposed to be nice."

"Yeah, vacation. Get away from it all. I hear you. Sometimes you gotta do that. Go someplace and cool down. I went on a vacation couple years ago. Had to get away. Things were crazy, job bad, woman bad, everything falling apart. Needed to go someplace quiet, you know, no commotion, just go somewhere and be alone in peace and quiet, tranquil-like, and get my head together."

Sam was momentarily interested. "Where did you end up going?"

Willie shrugged. "Vegas." He picked at his teeth with a fingernail. "Had a free ticket."

Sam slowed down and glided back to the right lane. Driving fast still made him nervous.

Willie yawned and shuffled his feet on the floor a little. "Heard another flight attendant got sucked out of an airplane," he said. "Heard it on the radio this morning."

Sam didn't say anything. His head was pounding worse than ever. He was in no mood for further conversation.

"Yeah," Willie said. "Saw it on TV, too. At the coffee place. They had kind of a reenactment on *The Today Show*. They had a woman in a wind tunnel, blowing around. I think it was Katie Couric, but I couldn't tell because she had a space suit on. That's the third flight attendant to get sucked out this year. They're just flying along and a door gets opened and, bam, they get sucked out. Out into space. Weird, man."

Sam fought the urge to look up at the sky. While he no longer feared Willie was going to stab him, he feared he might not stop talking.

Willie continued. "Flying dangerous. If I was a flight attendant, I'd wear like a rope or something around me, you know, tie it around me and connect it to a pole or something. A leash, maybe, but not around my neck. Door opens, and I'd be like 'whoa!' you know, I'd be surprised, but at least I'd be okay, because I'd be leashed."

Sam changed lanes and drove faster even though he was already going eighty.

"If it was like a strong leash, I mean."

Sam sped up to ninety.

"Maybe a chain."

"Can you not talk right now?" Sam blurted out. "I have a headache."

Willie, hurt, put his hands up in front of him. "No problem, man. Hey, we don't got to talk. I don't give a shit about no flight attendant falling out of the sky. Ain't no friends of mine." He slouched even lower in his seat, and mumbled, "We don't gotta talk."

They were quiet, Sam gradually calming down. After a while, he began to feel guilty about snapping at Willie. He wasn't a *bad* guy. He had brought him coffee. And he hadn't tried to kill him yet.

He slowed down. "We can talk now," he said.

Willie didn't say anything.

They drove under a viaduct, the car momentarily awash in darkness. "The leash idea is a pretty good one," Sam offered. "Each passenger would have to get one though."

Willie ignored the obvious gambit, stuck out his chin, and stuffed his hands in his pockets.

"In case they wanted to walk around the plane, and a door opened," Sam said.

Willie closed his eyes.

Sam sped up again. This was ridiculous. He wanted to get to Lake Eagleton as soon as possible. He wanted to get rid of Willie and sort things out. In the light of day, without the benefit of beer and a TV, his whole plan of heading north seemed, at best, ambiguous. If he drove fast, he could probably be there by late afternoon. After that, things got vague. He imagined meeting Sister North. But then what? Salvation? Redemption? Forgiveness? A chance to be cohost? He wasn't sure he was ready for this. He wasn't sure about anything.

He switched into the right-hand lane and exited the tollway.

"Where we going?" Willie asked.

"I want to get some coffee," Sam said.

Willie pointed toward the cup holder between them. "You still got some there," he said.

"I need more," Sam said.

The minimart was large and airy, with a surprisingly large fruit display in the front and a pastry counter in the back. Sam sat at the counter and ordered coffee from an overweight woman with a face like a fish. Out of the corner of his eye, he watched as Willie slowly walked around the minimart, hands in his baggy pants pockets. He apparently was out of his funk and seemed to be thoroughly enjoying his shopping experience, a calm, curious look on his face. He stopped in front of the fruit display and began to examine a bunch of bananas, holding them up to his eyes as he turned them, searching for some rare flaw that could render them worthless. He glanced over at Sam.

"Bananas," he said, smiling. He put the bananas down and picked up two apples, extending them in Sam's direction.

"You want some apples?"

Sam shook his head. Willie flipped one of the apples up in the air and caught it, then did the same with the other, this time turning around and catching it with one hand behind his back. He winked at Sam after he caught it. Sam turned back toward the counter.

When his coffee came, Sam held his cup with both hands and blew on it, while his mind slipped backward. When he was about sixteen, he and his family had driven this way to his grandparents' cottage. It was during that trip that his father had made the great change and decided to become a minister. Up until that point he had been a security guard at a power plant, a job he hated and always seemed on the verge of being fired from because of his long hair and inability to get to work on time.

His father announced his decision while they were fishing in Sam's grandfather's old fifteen-horsepower boat. It was a sunny morning, and they were near the shore, casting in silence, their lines floating and bobbing in the water. It was very early—his father firmly believed that you couldn't catch fish after 8 A.M. Sam did not want to be there. He was apprehensive about fishing with his father. The last time they had tried, they had almost capsized when his father, high out of his mind, claimed he saw a flying fish and started yelling and jumping around in the boat. His father always fished while high. He said it broadened his awareness and allowed him to sense where the fish were. According to his mother, his father had "inner demons," and smoking marijuana was his only way of dealing with them. She hated that he smoked it, though, and complained about it incessantly.

"I've made some decisions, Sammy," his father had said as he changed their lures, tying and pulling on the knots. Sam ignored his father and threw his line into the water.

"About things."

Sam said nothing. His father usually made strange pronouncements that had little meaning or impact on Sam's life.

"Let me ask you a question, Sammy. Do you think much about the Lord?"

"You mean God?" Sam asked.

"The Lord."

"You mean God?"

"Yes, Sammy. They're the same person."

"No. I don't think about *the Lord*." Sam rolled his eyes.

"Well, I have been thinking about Him lately. I've been thinking about Him a lot. I've been talking to Him a lot, too."

"Yeah? Do you guys get high together?" Sam asked. "You and . . . *the Lord?*" Like his mother, he hated the fact that his father smoked pot. He wanted to smoke it, too, because most of his friends did. He couldn't, though, because he didn't want to do anything his father did and end up guarding power lines and meters with a flashlight strapped to his belt.

His father threw his line into the water. "I'm not going to do that anymore," he said. "That's over now. I'm going to make a change. I'm going to live a life of grace and purpose." Sam looked at his father. He could tell he wasn't high, and was surprised.

"Grace and purpose," his father said again. He squinted in the sun, his face wrinkling up. "You don't believe me, do you, Dude? You're disappointed in me. Think I'm a big zero."

Sam watched his line bob and remained silent. He did think his father was a big zero. He was constantly working or volunteering for some charity, or community organization, giving away what little money they had. Despite the fact that the family car was a beat-up Pinto and that they lived in Uptown, a run-down area of Chicago, his father insisted on donating his time and money to various causes. The week before he had given fifty dollars to a school that taught English to Cambodian refugees, money Sam wanted for tickets to a Fleetwood Mac concert.

His father shook his head. "I know you think I'm too extreme, that I don't take care of you and your mom. I try to do what's right, but I realize that I'm not approaching it the right way," he said. He was quiet for a moment before saying, "But all that's going to change now. I've accepted Jesus."

With that, he put down his rod, stood up, and extended his arms to keep his balance. "I'll be back in a few days," he said. "Tell your mom not to worry." Then he jumped overboard.

He disappeared under the water and reemerged, his thick black hair slick and shiny like a sea otter's coat. He floated on his back to shore, turned, and waved once to Sam, then walked into the woods, water dripping from his jeans. He was gone for almost two days, and Sam's mother was frantic. She had been planning a surprise birthday party for him, and baked a chocolate cake through tears and worry. When he finally returned, he ate the entire cake and drank a half gallon of milk. "From this day on," he said, "everything is going to be different."

Surprisingly, it was. His father attended a seminary for a few months in Iowa, then came home and worked at a not-for-profit organization that helped children get their cleft palates fixed for free. He helped so many children with their palates that the local paper ran a story on him, calling him "Mr. Palate."

His father gradually drifted away from cleft palates and started his own church, the Church of Light. It was a mixture of several religions, and most of its members were people like his father. Disenfranchised souls, his mother said. His mother had initially been mortified when his father made the conversion from Catholicism, covering her ears with her hand whenever his father would try to explain how he had gotten the calling. Eventually, though, she accepted it. His father had stopped smoking pot, dressed better, and started wearing small, round reading glasses that made him look thoughtful and introspective. A number of his sermons were reprinted in the newspaper, and Sam's mother cut them out and sent them to Sam's grandmother, who never liked Sam's father. ("See, you and Daddy were *wrong, wrong, wrong!*" she wrote on top of one of the columns.)

Despite his father's urgings, Sam only went to the Church of Light a handful of times. When he did go, however, he was secretly impressed with his father's sermons about finding one's way in a material world poised for nuclear war. His father was a good speaker and radiated confidence and strength when he spoke in his new, low, and clear voice, which Sam didn't recognize or altogether trust. Gradually, the Church of Light began to attract more and more people, families and elderly couples, all wanting to hear and see his father.

The more popular his father became, and the more causes he was involved with, however, the more Sam withdrew from him. Despite his new standing in the community and his mother's apparent acceptance of his chosen calling, he was still embarrassed by his father's ponytail and battered Pinto with Jesus bumper stickers and the fact that they still never seemed to have any money. Once, the day before Father's Day, after Sam had graduated from high school, his father pleaded with Sam to come to church. He was going to give a sermon about the special bond between fathers and sons and thought Sam would enjoy it. A number of children who had had their palates fixed would be there as well. Sam reluctantly said he'd come and was embarrassed how excited and happy his father was when he told him. The next day, though, he got up early and went to the new shopping mall and stayed there most of the day, purposely avoiding church. His father never mentioned his not going, though his mother said he was very disappointed and had delayed the sermon for twenty minutes with the hope that Sam would eventually show up. Sam made a point of avoiding his father as much as possible after that and left for college a few months later.

Sitting at the coffee counter, he pulled out his little red assessment notebook from his front pocket, and wrote, *Bad son*, then flipped it shut.

"You want a refill?" the woman behind the counter asked.

"No, I'm good," he said. He turned and looked for Willie. He found him standing by the fruit display, juggling three apples and smiling, the fruit flying in small, silent arcs. He watched as the apples flew faster and faster, watched as Willie's hands blended into each other, faultlessly moving with a grace and purpose that Sam suddenly wanted to believe in.

CHAPTER

Six

They approached Lake Eagleton from the top of a large hill. They saw the lake first. It was strangely round, a large circle of water shimmering in the early-May light. The town bordered the east side of the circle, a small, solitary line of low buildings and frame houses painted pink by the setting sun. Behind them, an ocean of pine trees rose and dipped, flowing toward the horizon. The town, pressed hard between the woods and water, looked to be fighting for space, clinging to life.

"There it is," Sam said. He lowered the window and felt the warm air full in his face.

Willie, who had offered to drive the last hour, was clutching the steering wheel hard and squinting, his face just inches above the dashboard. Off the tollway and on the back roads, he seemed to have shrunk into a scared, scrunched-up ball, overwhelmed by the lake and the land. Driving down the hill, he read a sign welcoming them.

"Lake Eagleton, population ninety-six." He shook his head. "Ninety-six. Been in cars with more people."

"Small town," Sam said. He stuck his face out the window and took a deep breath. He was both nervous and excited to be here.

One street divided Lake Eagleton's three blocks of one-story shops. At first glance, the town looked prosperous. The Grocery Bag was obviously brand-new, as was the bank next to it, with its electronic message board offering high CD yields. In the middle of the town, a stately redbrick courthouse sat atop a slight hill. Reflections, a clothing store, seemed inviting, its white clapboard fresh and bright in the evening, an enormous planter by its front door spilling flowers.

Yet despite its best efforts, there was an aging sadness to the town, an end-of-the-day weariness. A number of the other buildings were old and sagging, their corrugated tin roofs half-rusted. His Place, a greeting card store, was leaning dangerously to one side, and Jacob's Gifts was cheerlessly weathered, despite its colorful red, white, and blue sign. A live bait store at the end of town was simply a gray shack with a dirty window.

"Look like a ghost town," Willie said.

Main Street ended at a small harbor, empty, with the exception of a single sailboat bobbing in the water, its mast naked. Lining the harbor was a park. Swings, slides, and metal monkey bars stood empty in the dying light. Sam took in the scene, searching for some sign of life, when he noticed something by the water.

"Hey, stop," he said.

"What? Why? Is this where you supposed to go?" Willie pulled to the curb, across the street from the park.

Sam pointed. "What's that over there?"

Willie leaned toward Sam's window and looked out. "I don't know. Looks like a statue." He sat back up. "Getting hungry," he said.

Sam got out of the car.

"Where you going?"

"Wait here. I'll be right back."

Sam walked across the park and approached the statue. The light was just about gone, and he couldn't see clearly. It wasn't until he got within a few feet of it that he confirmed what he suspected. The statue was Sister North, a large, bronzed Sister North.

She was peacefully gazing down at him, a forgiving smile on her owl-shaped face. Her habit flowed behind her, her arms were outstretched in welcome. Sam tentatively reached out a hand and touched hers. It felt smooth and cool. He closed his eyes and waited to feel something.

"You're not supposed to touch her," a voice said.

Sam jumped back. A gangling man emerged from behind the statue. He was clutching two brown paper bags and wearing a baseball cap with a broad brim. The cap was pulled so low over his eyes, he had to tilt his entire head backward to see Sam.

"You're not supposed to touch her. Louis says," the man said. He studied Sam again, then worked his mouth in an odd way, side to side. In the fading light, he looked to be old, though Sam couldn't be sure.

"I'm sorry," Sam said.

"Here," the man said. "Hold this." He handed him one of the bags. Sam glanced inside and saw that it was full of small, garden tools.

The man knelt on the ground. "Put the bag here."

Sam placed the bag next to the man. "Are you planting something?"

"Impatiens. I always plant them now. They go all the way to October if they're watered right."

The man started to dig with a hand hoe. Sam heard a door slam, and, over his shoulder, he saw Willie leaning against the car.

"This is a big statue," he said.

"It's not that big," the man answered. "It's only eight feet. But it sways in the wind." He pushed it with both his hands, but the statue didn't move. "Last week, we had a big wind, and I saw it moving."

Sam glanced past the statue at the lake, a few feet away. "It's pretty close to the water."

"Got it so the sun catches it when it sets. Looks on fire sometimes. That's when miracles happen. They did that part right at least."

"Where does Sister North live?"

The man kept digging. "Up in the woods."

"Do you know her?"

"She's the only reason I still draw breath." The man stopped digging and started to pull small plastic boxes from the second brown bag. Each box held tiny pink-and-white flowers. Sam watched as the man delicately pinched a flower between two fingertips and dropped it into a hole in the ground at Sister North's feet.

"Do you see her a lot?" Sam asked.

The man smoothed the ground. "Used to see her every day. Now, I got to figure things out by myself. Now, I have to figure things out on my own, I think."

Sam didn't know what the man was talking about and didn't care. It was a beautiful evening, and, for the first time in a long while, he felt good, felt something stirring inside him. A sense of relief, hope.

He put his hands in his pockets and rocked back and forth a little on his feet. A breeze picked up off the lake.

"You here to see her?" the man asked.

Sam stopped rocking. "Yes," he answered quietly. He checked his watch and saw that it was almost eight. "Is there a place we can eat around here?"

The man didn't look up. He dropped another flower in the ground and covered it up. "Big Jack's. Follow the road by the lake. About a half mile or so." He patted down dirt with the hoe and reached into the bag.

"Thanks," Sam said. He watched the man plant one more flower. "Good night."

"Don't listen to anything they tell you in there," the man said, as Sam was turning away.

"What?"

The man stopped digging and stood up with remarkable quickness. He approached Sam, pointing the hoe at him. Close-up, Sam could see his deep-set eyes, dark and wild, and his tight, windburned face, all sharp angles and bones. He wasn't nearly as old as Sam had thought.

"If you could tell Jesus one thing, what would you tell Him?" the man asked. He tapped Sam on the chest with the hoe.

Sam backed up. The man was obviously the town crazy. "I don't know," he said.

"The truth." The man pointed the hoe toward the sky. "You'd tell Him the truth."

With that, the man returned to the statue and slowly knelt.

"Lies," he said. "The lies are starting." He reached into one of the bags and pulled out another flower. "She said they might, and she was right."

Big Jack's Bar and Grill overlooked the lake. It was a low and wide restaurant with large windows, a U-shaped bar, and a cramped dining area overflowing with small and, for the most part, empty tables. A number of mounted, glassy-eyed fish lined the wood-paneled walls. Sam took a deep breath and inhaled stale beer and dank lake water. He liked the place.

"You got a great life," he said to Big Jack. He had been sitting at the bar for close to three hours, steadily drinking beer. He had no idea where Willie was, though he had a sense that he was still around somewhere. He was focusing all his attention on Big Jack, owner and operator, though he was having trouble seeing him very clearly.

"Own your own business on a lake. No one can fire you. How much money do you make a year from this place?" Sam asked. "You know, two years ago I made $245,000. You believe that? You believe that? Now I make a lot less. But I can still pay for my beer. I still got some money for beer. But I don't got much. Not as much as I used to. My wife got the rest. I still got about fifty or sixty grand left. But that's it." He picked up his glass of beer and swallowed the last bits of foam as they slid toward him. "It was all hers anyway. Her father's really. She was rich." He swallowed a belch. "Real rich."

Through the deepening fog, Sam could barely make out Big Jack. From what he could tell, he was an old man with a crew cut.

"You sure you're Big Jack?" he said. "You seem little. I would think that Big Jack was big. Bigger."

"I'm six-four. That's big enough."

"Yeah, that's big. But, I thought you'd be huge. Like the Hulk or something. Hulk-big."

"I'm big enough," Big Jack repeated.

"Yeah, you're pretty big." Sam picked up his empty glass, then put it down. "Hey, do you know Sister North? The nun on TV? She lives here, doesn't she? In town somewhere, right?"

"Yeah, I know her."

"What's she like?"

"Listen, pal. We had this conversation already. About ten times."

"I wanted to see her, but I think it's too late. So I'll see her tomorrow."

Sam could sense that Big Jack had stopped moving and was suddenly standing over him.

"She's nice I bet." Sam closed his eyes, but opened them right back up when he felt himself spinning. "Hey, you want to hear something really weird, something really fucked up? Some guy tried to kill me. You believe that? He was standing right in front of me and shot a gun but missed. He shot Maureen. Then he killed himself right in front of me. Some of his brains flew out and landed on my shoe. It was on the news. I threw those shoes out."

Sam saw a hand reach through the fog and take away his glass. "You've had enough," Big Jack said.

"He was standing right in front of me. A few feet. How could he miss? He was so close."

"Time for you to go."

"I don't want to go anywhere. Want to stay right here." Sam felt himself slipping off the barstool and fought to regain his balance. "Waiting for Sister North."

"She won't be here tonight."

"Where is she? Can you tell me where she is?"

"Time for you to go. I'm going to call for a ride."

"I'm driving him." Willie had somehow appeared. Sam saw him holding up car keys.

Sam leaned forward and pressed his face onto the bar. "I'm not going," he said. "I got to see Sister North now. Call her up on the phone. I know she's got a phone. It's free, so just call her and tell her I need to see her."

"Get him out of here," Big Jack said.

"Let's go." Sam felt Willie tugging from behind. "Come on, Sam. Parked right out in front."

"Leave me alone," Sam said. He pushed Willie's hands away and clutched the top of the bar, hugging it.

"I said get him out of here," Big Jack said.

"Fuck you," Sam said. He closed his eyes and felt the bar spinning again. "Fuck all of you. I'm staying right here. Right here." Somewhere, a part of him was aware that he was yelling.

He felt hands grabbing at him again, trying to lift him, but it was too late. He was already slipping off the barstool, falling onto the floor and into the dark hole that he knew was always there.

Seven

Sam woke up naked from the waist down. He was lying in a bed in a strange room that was empty except for a plain wooden dresser. Everything in the room was white: the walls, the carpet, the bed-spread, the curtains. Sam thought he might be in heaven or an igloo.

He lay in bed and tried to piece together the previous night. He remembered drinking at that bar. He remembered drinking a lot. How he had transitioned from that place to this place he wasn't sure.

He got up and walked around the room, holding on to the walls for balance. His hangover was already in overdrive, and his equilibrium was off. He moved to the dresser, where he found his neatly folded pants, next to a short note completely void of punctuation.

Sam—
took your car you in a bed and breakfast like a hotel but no food
because the cook was fired
didn't take your pants off a guy did you don't got no underwear and
your room is all white and I brought your stuff in in the closet
—Willie Martinez

Sam had to read the note twice, the last time aloud, before he understood it. Then he put his pants on, found his shaving kit in the closet, and headed unsteadily down a hallway to a bathroom, where he showered, while blinking in the sunlight that poured through two frosted windows. He stared at the light and held his hand up into it.

After shaving and brushing his teeth, he returned to his room and pulled on a gray sweatshirt. He perched on the corner of the bed, rubbed his hand over his face, and started to sort things through.

First, an assessment. He was definitely in a fragile state. If he moved too quickly, or thought too deeply, or even attempted to look out of the corners of his eyes, he would break down. He had to take things slow and set attainable goals.

He found his little notebook and pen in his jacket pocket and sat back down on the bed.

He wrote:

?

He had to find out exactly where he was. He needed some point of reference. Knowing this might come in handy in case he wanted to send postcards. He stood up and walked over to the window, pulled the curtain aside, and peered out at a great expanse of water less than fifty yards from his room. A lake. Lake Eagleton.

On the windowsill, he found a brochure: "Monticello Inn by the Lake." There was a black-and-white illustration of Sister North on the bike on the cover and on the inner flap, a short poem:

Silence. Is Golden, unless it is Black.
Then. It is loud.
Contemplate and be.
Happy at the Inn.
The Inn of Peace.

On the back flap was a short list of room rates and checkout times. Over the list someone had scrawled in red pen, *No longer serving breakfast!*

Sam put the brochure down, took one last look around the room, and walked out.

He took a narrow stairway downstairs and found himself in a surprisingly enormous living room with a domed ceiling. Skylights rimmed the dome, letting the sun through in slants. He felt like he was in a cathedral.

The room was sparsely decorated. Two uncomfortable-looking wing chairs and a small television set, with a twisted pair of rabbit ear antennas, were in one corner, and an immense throne of a chair was in another. He moved over to the large chair and sat down, almost disappearing. Its arms were polished wood and its seat and back red leather.

He pushed himself up and went to the window, his footsteps echoing on the hardwood floors, and looked out at the lake again. It was calm, and glassy. He turned and walked into an adjoining dining room, equally large and barren. Other than a narrow oak table, it, too, was mostly empty.

"Hello," he called out. He cleared his throat and tried again, his voice bouncing off the walls and back to him.

He thought the place uncommonly cold and sterile, nothing like the inns or bed-and-breakfasts Carol and he had occasionally stayed at, all of which overcompensated on the warm-and-cozy side and seemed to be built on a foundation of quilts. With its white, bare walls and wood floors, this place seemed more like a condominium someone had yet to move into.

He wandered around the first floor, stopping in an immaculate kitchen with white cabinets. Gleaming pots and pans hung in an orderly fashion over a new stove. He opened the refrigerator, hoping for something to eat, but saw that it was empty.

After scanning the room one more time, he opened the back door and walked out into the afternoon. Shielding his eyes with his hand, he searched the parking lot for his car. As he feared, there was no trace. Resigned to the possibility that Willie had finally gotten around to stealing it, he began to walk down a quiet, wooded road toward what he hoped was the town and food.

He didn't get far. After only a few minutes, he heard a car approaching from behind. Turning, he saw a red trolley bus heading his way. It was a large, double-decker with whitewall tires. On one side a small sign read, TROLLEY. It pulled up next to him and made a clanging sound.

The doors swung open to reveal the driver, a thin man with black, slicked-back hair and a pencil-thin mustache.

"I'm Tony," the man said. "Tony the driver."

Sam nodded.

Tony the driver nodded back. "Going to town?"

Sam looked at the trolley, then at the road ahead. "Yeah," he said.

"All aboard then."

Sam took a seat near the back. Other than an older couple sitting right behind the driver, the trolley was empty.

"Welcome to the Eagleton Trolley," Tony said. He was speaking into a handheld microphone, his voice vibrating from a speaker directly over Sam's head. "How many people on board is new to Lake Eagleton?"

Without hesitating, the older couple raised their hands. Sam peered out the window at the woods, then back at the driver. The man was staring at him through the rearview mirror.

"How many people are new to Lake Eagleton?" he asked again.

Sam slowly raised his hand.

"Welcome then," Tony said. "To the Lake of Many Moods."

"The Lake of Many Moods, that's a strange moniker," the old man said. "Why is it called that?" He cupped his hands to the sides of his mouth when he asked this as if shouting, even though the driver was sitting no more than three feet in front of him.

"It's a moody lake," Tony said.

They drove on the winding road for several minutes in silence.

The old man turned, and said loudly to the woman, "That was a vague answer."

"Lake Eagleton is seven miles round and two miles wide," Tony said. "It's also 237 feet deep. If you approached the town from the hill, you no doubt noticed the amazing roundness of the lake. Its circular shape is a mystery and has been studied for years. According to scientists, a comet or asteroid or something very large and round might have fallen here around two thousand years ago, creating its unusual shape. People sometimes think, because of its shape, it's man-made, like an old rock quarry or something, but it is all natural." He paused. "God's own work."

"Why is it called Lake Eagleton?" the old man asked. He had a loud, barking voice. Sam wondered if he were deaf.

Tony hesitated. "I'll get to that part in a second. It's interesting though."

"I can hardly wait," the old man said. He turned and winked at Sam. He had a thick neck and broad shoulders. His bald head stuck out of his sweater like a thumb. Sam turned back, facing the window.

Tony picked up the microphone. "As I mentioned before in a previous statement, Lake Eagleton was called the Lake of Many Moods by the Native American Indians. Calm one minute, difficult and treacherous the next, it changes quickly, in the blink of an eye. More than fifty people have died in its waters since 1945. That's almost one a year."

"Anyone die this year?" the old man asked.

"Not yet."

"Well, we have that to look forward to."

The trolley made its way uphill, through a short stretch of tree-lined road, and finally out into a clearing. Up ahead, Sam could see the small harbor and soon the town.

"Say, where's this nun live? Sister TV?" the old man asked. "It would seem she would be the star attraction up here." The woman shook her head and said something quietly to him.

"Sister North lives on the other side of the lake. In Lasonia Woods. On top of the hill. That's the second part of the tour. We have to go through town first."

The trolley slowed as it approached the harbor. "This is Eagle's Cove. According to history, Sir Lyell Eagleton, one of the first white men in northwest Wisconsin, first saw the harbor on April 14, 1804, while searching for a tributary to the Mississippi River. At first, he thought he found it, and held a great feast with the Manapacataca tribe, which used to inhabit this area and were serving as his guides. The feast lasted for days, and when it was over, Sir Eagleton set out to sail to the Mississippi, only to discover that he couldn't get out. He sailed around in circles for days. He felt deceived and angry with the Native Americans because he had hosted the elaborate feast, you know, paid for everything, and a battle almost ensued, but legend has it, the chief of the Native American tribe, Chief High Knocker, offered him his only daughter, as a form of apology, before blood was spilled."

"I assume she was attractive," the old man said, "or else it wouldn't have been much of an apology."

Tony was quiet for only a moment, before he continued with his obviously memorized speech. "The daughter was a beautiful woman, who, legend has it, could swim around the entire lake without stopping. Sir Eagleton fell in love with the Native American enchantress and decided to stay in the area and build Fort Eagleton so he would have someplace to live. Unfortunately, it was destroyed in the Great Wind Storm of 1805. He rebuilt it in 1806, but it was destroyed by fire. He rebuilt it again in 1807, but it was destroyed by the Great Ice Storm of 1808."

"What was he making these forts out of?" the old man asked.

Tony glanced back at the man, his face a brief scowl, then

returned to his microphone. "According to history," he said, "Sir Eagleton went back to Scotland in 1810."

"What about the woman? That Native American beauty?"

"She drowned by accident the day before Sir Eagleton left. She was going to go with him. Legend has it, she was fully packed and everything. But she drowned while trying to save her horse, who had wandered into the lake during a storm. Some say she still haunts the lake. You can see her spirit at night sometimes, in the form of a white ball of light that circles the shore, looking for a way out. Only when she meets her true love, can her spirit escape and be free of the circle. Her name is Moanpatec, which means, She Who Swims In Circles."

"Moanpatec," the old man repeated. "Well, we'll make sure to keep an eye out for her." The old woman gently elbowed him.

"What about this strange ball of light?" the old man asked. "Sounds like an old wives' tale."

"It's real," Tony said. He turned to look at them. "I've seen it. People have come up here to study it. They think it has something to do with the Northern Lights, but no one's sure."

"Well, we'll keep our eyes peeled for that, too," the old man said. "Between the Indian woman and the light, we'll stay plenty busy."

The trolley came to a stop. Tony faced them again. "On your left, is the new statue of Sister North. It arrived just a week ago."

"We've already seen it," the old man said. He made no attempt to look at the statue, though the woman stared out the window. "We want to see the real thing now. In the flesh."

"Well, all we have in this spot is the statue. It was commissioned by the town last year and designed by a sculptor from France. The statue is the first part of a Sister North Reception Center that will be built here soon. Or is supposed to be built here soon." Tony stood up. He was very skinny but had a respectable potbelly nonetheless. "We'll take a few minutes here, in case anyone wants to get out and see it again. Then we'll go through town."

No one moved. The old man briefly scratched his elbow.

Tony stared at them and took out a pack of cigarettes from his front shirt pocket, patting it twice on his wrist.

"I'll be right back," he said, and left.

Sam was considering getting off the trolley himself when the old man turned his way and peered at him over sturdy, black glasses.

"Are you here to see this nun?" he asked.

Sam took his time before answering. "I'm just taking the tour," he said. He continued to look out the window, down Main Street.

"Well, we are. Came all the way from Nebraska. She's the primary reason we came."

"May I ask where are you from?" the woman asked Sam. She had a calm, precise voice, and when Sam looked over at her, he could see that she was pretty like a pressed flower.

"Chicago," he said.

"We're from Pleasanton, Nebraska. Have you ever heard of it?" the man asked.

"No."

"No one's ever heard of it. Just once I'd like to live in a town someone has heard of. Have you ever heard of Kearney? Kearney, Nebraska?"

"Yes," Sam said.

"You have, well maybe we should move there then. It's not far from Pleasanton. Where are you staying here?"

Sam saw his reflection in the window. His headache, which had slipped strangely into remission for the last few minutes, was awakening with a roar, and his stomach was growling. He couldn't remember when his last meal had been. "With friends," he said softly.

"Where would that be, may I ask?"

Sam jerked his thumb over his shoulder. "That way."

The man raised his head and peered past Sam as if considering an intricate set of directions. Then he looked directly at Sam, and said, "Our son Todd is missing. He's been missing for almost a year," and turned around.

When Tony returned, he started up the trolley and eased it into town. The streets were fairly well deserted although all the stores and shops were open. When they passed Jacob's Books, Sam noticed a poster-sized picture of Sister North, riding the bicycle—*Go Sister!* He stared at her image as they drove by.

"Next stop, Big Jack's," the driver said.

"We're going on to the nun's house," the old man said.

"We'll be there in about twenty minutes."

Twenty minutes. Face-to-face with the nun. Sam suddenly wasn't ready for her. He needed time to prepare. He rose and walked toward the front, stabilizing himself by gripping the backs of seats as he passed them. When they stopped at the restaurant, he got off.

He didn't think Big Jack would remember him from the night before, but he didn't want to take any chances, so he sat at a table by a large, wide window, as far away from the bar as possible.

"You're the big drunk," Big Jack said as soon as he picked up the menu.

Sam resisted the urge to throw the menu on the floor and run. That would do little to enhance his image locally. Instead, he attempted a smile.

"Sorry about that. I was overserved."

Big Jack leaned forward on the bar and stared at him. He was tall and, despite appearing to be in his seventies, surprisingly muscular. His crew cut was a sharp sheaf of gray bristles and his face, a red fist with a flat nose. He looked like an aging, sunburned boxer.

"Overserved," Big Jack slowly repeated.

"Just a little," Sam said.

Sam felt Big Jack's eyes on him, so he held the menu up in front of his face.

"Are you a priest?" Big Jack asked.

Sam lowered the menu slightly.

"No."

Big Jack nodded, analyzing Sam's response. "We get a lot of priests up here. They come all the time. Most of them are off duty." He fingered his neck. "No collar." He squinted his eyes. "Are you an ex-priest? We get a lot of those up here, too."

"No." Then, to set the record straight, Sam said, "I've never been a priest."

"You look like one."

Sam had no comment for this. Instead, he examined his menu. "I'll have a cheeseburger and fries. And a Coke. I'll have a Coke, too."

Big Jack nodded one last time, before turning and disappearing into the kitchen behind the bar. Sam noticed a slight limp as he walked away.

"Excuse me, Father."

A man with a neatly trimmed black beard had materialized at the table next to him. Sam couldn't believe he hadn't seen him walk in. They were the only two people in the place, and the man was immense. Everyone in the town seemed to be gigantic.

"Excuse me, Father, but I was wondering if I could possibly switch tables with you." The man pointed his finger. "That's my table. I always sit there, in that exact spot."

"I'm not a priest," Sam said.

"Oh, I see." He raised his eyebrows and pointed his finger again. "The table." He silently mouthed the words.

Sam decided the man wasn't kidding. If the place was crowded or Sam had been back in Chicago, he might have ignored him, but since the man was enormous, and the town appeared to be full of insane people, he stood up and gestured toward the table. "All yours," he said.

The man silently mouthed, "thank you," as Sam walked away.

He was on his way out of the restaurant when his hunger got the better of him, so he detoured back toward the men's room, where he splashed water on his face and took several deep breaths. He was feeling light-headed and knew he needed to eat. He took one more gulp of air and returned to the dining area. The giant had switched tables and was still staring at him, his hands cupped over his mouth as if he were praying. Rather than returning to his new table, Sam walked around the bar to the back door, which overlooked the road. Within seconds, the trolley came into view. The elderly couple was nowhere in sight. On the top deck, though, he saw a solitary figure, sitting in the very front, one arm thrown casually over the seat beside him. It was Willie. Too late, Sam opened the door and yelled, just as the trolley wound around a curve and disappeared.

He closed the door. He would find Willie later. He had to eat. He had already decided to sit at the bar, but found his food waiting at the table right next to the strange man's. He quickly sat down and busied himself with his cheeseburger, wishing he had something to read or a cell phone to pretend to talk into. Out of the corner of his eye, he could see that the man was watching him.

"Thank you again for indulging me," he said. "I don't get out much."

Sam nodded, his mouth full. He focused on the bar. Big Jack was leaning over a newspaper. After a few seconds, he looked up, and their eyes locked. Sam quickly looked back down at his plate and seriously considered eating with his eyes closed.

"May I ask how you are feeling today?"

Sam stopped shoveling food and glanced at the gigantic man. He had a terrific, anvil-shaped head, amazingly long and narrow. His flowing black hair fell halfway to his shoulders and his eyes were dark and sad. He was wearing a flowing white muumuu with a red-trimmed collar. Sam assumed he was connected to Sister North in some way. He looked like Jesus on steroids.

"You were in quite a state when they brought you in last night," he said.

Sam swallowed. "What do you mean?"

"To Monticello."

"Oh," Sam said. He took a bite of the burger. "Are you staying there?"

"Yes. I'm the owner. The proprietor." He said this last word deliberately and held his chin high. He had an affected way of speaking that made every word seem more important than it was.

"Oh," Sam said again.

"I helped put you in bed. I undressed you."

Sam stopped chewing.

"I put you in one of my favorite rooms. The white room. It catches the light in the afternoon and has a nice lake breeze. Very cheerful room. And it's near the bathroom."

"Thanks."

"I was planning on painting each one of my rooms a specific color, but I ran out of paint. Right now, I just have the white room and the green room."

Sam nodded.

"The green room is green."

Sam nodded again and swallowed.

"May I ask you another question?" the man asked.

Sam shoved a handful of fries into his mouth, almost biting his hand in the process.

"You're not planning on killing yourself anytime soon, are you?"

Sam coughed a portion of the fries out of his mouth.

"I had someone do that last month in the white room, and it really was unpleasant. A man about your age. He was a priest. We get them up here all the time. More and more of them are suicidal. Are you in any way suicidal?"

"I'm not suicidal," Sam said.

"That's not what I heard."

Sam was picking up the fries off the table and putting them back onto his plate when a woman came into the restaurant holding a grocery bag. She breezed past them without so much as a glance and disappeared into the kitchen, only to emerge a moment later holding some roses. She walked over to the huge man and dropped the roses on his table.

"Don't give me any more roses," she said. She turned and walked away.

The man looked crestfallen. He fingered the flowers. "I am Louis," he said. "Would you mind if I bought you a drink?"

Eight

Her name is Meg Lodge," Louis said. "And I expect she might be gay. That's always the wild card."

They were sitting by the window drinking pitchers of beer and watching the sun set, the roses on the table between them. Since Louis didn't appear to be violent and was buying the drinks, Sam decided to rearrange his busy schedule and drink with him. They had been at it for close to an hour. Louis spoke nonstop, and Sam found himself sliding into a familiar and comfortable state of numbness.

"Meg is the reason I come here. I would never come otherwise. I hate this place. But if I sit in this exact spot, I have a panoramic view of the restaurant, which maximizes my view of her. I can see the bar, some of the kitchen when the door is open, and the entire dining room, in addition to both doors, front and back. It's a perfect location. She can't escape my gaze."

"She looked pretty," Sam said, though he had only seen her for a second.

"She's intelligent, too. Well, she's aloof, something I interpret as a sign of intelligence. I can't imagine an aloof dumb person. Of course, I don't know any aloof people. They tend to be, well, aloof."

"Aloof people are sometimes shy." Sam had been accused of being aloof much of his life.

Louis considered this response. "Yes, I suppose," he said. He pulled on his beard, then examined his fingers. "So," he said, "I assume you're here to see our illustrious nun."

The abruptness of the question jolted Sam. He reached for the pitcher of beer and refilled his glass. "I'm just passing through," he said.

"Of course you are. We're all just passing through. Everyone here is just passing through. And while they're doing that, they stop in to see the nun. There's no other reason to come here."

"It's a nice lake."

Louis leaned forward and placed his great hands on the table in front of him. "No one comes here for the lake. They come to see the nun. And I am prepared to offer you a steep discount until she comes back. Say, fifty percent off if you commit for a month." He tapped his fingers on the table. "That offer will expire soon."

Sam put down his beer. Entirely too much information had been thrown at him. "What?" he asked.

Louis stopped tapping. "I said I am prepared to offer you a significant discount on your room if you commit to four weeks. Normally, your room goes for a hundred thirty dollars a night. I am prepared to offer it to you for sixty-five. If the nun comes back early, you won't be able to find a room within an hour from here. My inn has just eight rooms, and it is the only place in town. You'll be stuck at the Sleep Shack out on the interstate."

"Comes back early? What are you talking about?"

"Sixty-five dollars. It's a very generous offer."

Sam held up his hand in an effort to slow Louis down. "Wait a second. Wait." He took a deep breath. "Where is the nun?" he asked evenly.

"She's not here. Technically, not here."

"What do you mean, technically?"

"Well, she's here in spirit."

"What about the rest of her?"

"That part is gone."

"Where is she?"

Louis carefully stroked his beard near his chin. "A leper colony. Micronesia. Club Med. I have no idea. She's always somewhere. Go sister."

"How long will she be gone?"

"I'm not sure. Not long."

Sam sank back in his chair, stunned at the news. "When did she leave?"

"A few days ago."

"But I just saw her show."

"Reruns."

"But I talked to someone."

"You didn't talk to the nun, did you?"

"No, I didn't." Sam sat forward again, staring blankly across the room. Sister North had been his one anchor over the past few weeks, and now that anchor was gone. He had come a long way to have a cheeseburger at Big Jack's.

Just then the door opened, and a small, twisted man in a motorized wheelchair entered the room. He looked the epitome of pain: mouth open, face yellow and full of effort, head tilted at a sharp angle. He was wearing an ugly orange *Sister North Show* sweatshirt with a white stripe down the middle.

Louis watched the man. "I thought you died," he said matter-of-factly.

The man stopped wheeling, and whispered, "Not yet." He grinned and managed a feeble wave with pencil-thin arms.

"Do you need a room then?"

"I'll think about it." The man smiled again and rolled past them.

"You'll have to pay in advance though," Louis called out after him. He turned back to Sam. "My offer. Are you interested? Sixty-five dollars a night?"

"I have to go," Sam said. He had a sudden need to be alone.

"Go? Where?"

"Back to the hotel."

Louis stood up, pressing heavily down on the table. It was only then that Sam could see the true scope of his size. He must have been over six and a half feet tall. "I just happen to be going that way," Louis said, reaching for the roses.

Sam didn't really want a ride, but he was too tired to walk back to Monticello. When Louis opened the door of his small sports car, he climbed in. It took some time for Louis to wedge himself into the car, and when he did, he looked so cramped and uncomfortable, with his body pressed against the steering wheel, Sam wasn't sure if he would be able to drive.

"Good God," Louis said. "I don't remember this steering wheel being here."

Louis fumbled with the ignition, accidentally turning on the windshield wipers. When he finally did get the car started, he ground the engine for such a long time that the parking lot began to fill with exhaust.

"Do you want me to drive?" Sam asked.

"No. I can do this," Louis said. He shifted gears, and the car lurched forward. "I took a class."

They drove slowly through town. The shops had long ago closed, and the sidewalks and street were deserted. Near the harbor, a scrawny black cat crossed the road, stopped in front of the car, and blinked its green eyes into the headlights. Louis braked sharply when he saw it.

"I used to have a cat," he said.

Sam stared out the window, still trying to digest the news about

Sister North. He wondered how long she would be gone, wondered how long he was willing to wait for her.

"Do you think she'll be back soon?" he asked.

Louis patted Sam's knee and shifted back into drive. "She'll return. She always does. Besides, her presence is everywhere. The trees, the lake, the clouds, Monticello. Her physical presence isn't really necessary. She has a website."

Louis slowed as they took a curve into the woods.

"This town comes alive when she's around," he said. "You can't find parking, and my place is always at capacity. I sometimes rent out the basement. I can get a hundred dollars for a cot down there, and that doesn't even include a pillow. This whole town takes on a wonderful, gold-rush feel to it when the nun is in session. Everyone quietly making money."

"Do you know her?" Sam asked.

"Yes, of course I do."

"What's she like?"

"What is she like, what is she like." Louis tapped the steering wheel. "Well, she's religious," he said. "And she's short. Shorter than you think. She sits on a phone book when she does the show. Only her inner circle knows that. And she has a deceptively large head. The camera masks it, but when you see her in person it really is a thing to behold. There are days when I fear she may topple over from the sheer weight of it. I think it's because of her brain. It must be very large as well. She's very intelligent. Big head, big brain, I always say."

"Where does she live?"

"On top of the hill. Over by Lasonia. In the woods, a few miles from here."

"Can we drive by there?"

"There's nothing to see. It's dark, and she's not home."

"I want to see it."

Without hesitating, Louis swung the steering wheel in a full circle. Sam fell against the door as the car whirled around, tires screeching. They were off the road, then back on it again in seconds, heading in the opposite direction.

"I can't believe I just did that," Louis said. He looked amazed.

"Don't do it again."

As they approached Big Jack's, a pickup truck was pulling out of the parking lot. Louis stopped a good distance away and waited until the truck was out of sight before driving again.

"There's Meg," he said. "Leaving after another hard day of pretending I don't exist."

"Where does she live?"

"Out in the country. On the other side of the lake. Very remote. She's a recluse. God knows what she does for sex. One can only imagine, and, believe me, I have. I'd take you by there, but Wisconsin has recently toughened up its stalking laws."

When they reached the end of town, Louis came to a complete stop and began searching the dashboard for something, fidgeting with various switches. He once again turned the windshield wipers on and off. "I'm looking for the bright lights switch," he said. "I read about them. Oh, here it is." He turned it on the exact moment another car approached from the opposite direction. The car flashed its own brights back at them.

"Touchy," Louis said. "Very nice. You don't see many cars like that up here."

Sam watched as the black BMW passed. "Can you turn around?" he asked.

"I thought you wanted to see the nun's house."

"Quick, turn around and follow that car."

"Follow the car? Why?"

"Because it's mine," Sam said.

They followed Willie through town and onto the road by the lake. When a pickup truck passed them going the other way, Sam could clearly see Willie's head silhouetted in the headlights, looking much like a cardboard cutout. He seemed oblivious to the fact that he was being followed.

"Are you sure that's your car?" Louis asked.

"Yes."

"Did someone steal it?"

"No, I don't think so. I lent it to someone, and I want it back. Hurry up, you're going to lose him. He's turning."

"I'm not going to *lose* him. There's only one road up here."

"He's pulling away. Honk your horn or flash your lights."

"I'm doing the best I can," Louis said. He started fumbling with the headlights.

"Hurry up! Honk!"

Louis began frantically pushing at various points of the steering wheel. "The horn is not functioning." He accelerated, and for a moment they gained on Willie. Then they hit a series of sharp curves that ran through some woods, and Willie disappeared altogether.

"Where did he go?" Sam asked.

Louis hunched toward the steering wheel and squinted into the darkness. "I'm not sure. Oh, there he is, way up there. Now, how did *that* happen?"

Sam stuck his head out the window, and caught a gush of cool wind. Up ahead, far in the distance, he could make out the tiny red dots of his car's taillights. When they rounded yet another curve, Willie had once again disappeared.

"I don't think I can catch him," Louis said. "He's very skilled."

"You should have honked. I told you to honk. He probably doesn't even know we're following him," Sam said. "Shift gears. You're in first still."

"I am?" Louis made a confused attempt to adjust the gearshift, but quickly gave up. "I don't know how to do this."

Sam looked over at Louis, who was now breathing heavily out of his mouth.

"This isn't your car, is it?"

"Not really." Louis said this very softly.

"Whose is it?"

"Big Jack's."

"Big Jack's car."

"He leaves the keys in the ignition."

"Does he let you use it?"

"From time to time," Louis said. Then he said, "This being the first time."

"Does he know you have it now?"

"Well," Louis said. "Let's just say, by now, I imagine he knows *someone* has it. I apologize for this. It's the medication."

"What medication do you take?"

"I don't take any. I think that's the problem."

"What's Big Jack going to say about all of this?"

"I don't think he'll be very supportive. He tends not to be."

"Stop the car," Sam said.

"What?"

"Stop the car and let me out. Just let me out."

"I'll take you home. You can drive. You can honk all the way home."

"Stop the car. Now," Sam said.

Louis pulled over, and Sam got out.

"Are you sure of this?"

"Yeah," Sam said. He slammed the door.

"Here, please take these," Louis said, handing him the roses through the window. "I don't want Jack to see them when I bring the car back. They cost me more than sixty dollars. If you bring them back, I'll discount your room an additional twenty percent. Please." He held the roses out to Sam.

"Which way do I go?" Sam asked.

Louis pointed a finger. "That way. You're about three miles. Are you sure you want to do this? I can drive alongside you if you wish. When you get tired you can jump back in."

"I'll see you tomorrow," Sam said. He took the roses and began walking.

He headed in the direction Louis had indicated, growing more sober with each step. As he walked, he felt himself shrinking, diminishing in the face of the pine trees, which towered over him. He stopped once and looked up at them, huge, silent shadows against the sky, and walked on.

When he reached the harbor, he decided to rest. His body was aching, and his feet were on fire. He found a stone bench near the water, in front of the Sister North statue, and sat with a heavy thud. It was then that he realized he was still holding the roses. He unwrapped the plastic, held them close to his nose, and took a deep breath.

He had taken flowers to his father when he was dying. He hadn't known what else to take. He hadn't thought that his father was that sick and had come home from law school reluctantly, buying the flowers at the bus station on the way to the hospital.

He was shocked when he first saw him. His hair had mostly fallen out, and his face was stretched and tight. Sam had stood by the bed and looked down at him, unbelieving. It was the first time he had seen his father in three years, since his mother's funeral.

"The prodigal," his father had whispered when he opened his eyes. "Every father should have one."

Sam had stayed with him for two days, his father sliding in and out of consciousness. When he was awake, he tried to talk, but the effort proved too much, so instead they had watched TV or listened to music on his father's tape player. They listened to Bob Dylan over and over. *Blood on the Tracks*.

At the end of the second day, his father's eyes had opened sharply, and he looked up at Sam.

"I know I should say something, but I'm afraid I'll say the wrong thing," he said. "There's a lot of pressure on your last words, and I promised myself I wasn't going to say anything heavy. I might screw you up more than I already have. But you know me, Sammy, got to get the last word in, so here goes." He actually laughed when he said that, and tried to sit up. Sam, through his tears, propped him up against the pillows.

When his father tried to speak again, he had started coughing so hard that his head bounced up and down off the pillows. "I was going to say a few things, but I better get to the point," he said after he finally gained control of his voice. "Listen, Sammy, I know I disappointed you, know you wanted a different life. A nice house, new cars. And there's nothing wrong with that. Nothing at all." He started to cough again and reached out for Sam's hand to steady himself. He coughed so long that Sam thought of calling the nurse, but his father abruptly stopped and swallowed. "Be good. Be good, and good things will happen to you. The good are always taken care of." He looked up at Sam and squeezed his hand. "Trust me on this. Trust me on this one thing."

Stranded in the middle of the night in a strange town, Sam saw no reason to believe those words. His father had been a good person, and so had Maureen. And here was Sam, who, by anyone's measure, was lazy and selfish. Despite that, though, despite a life of floating and getting by, a good thing had happened to him. He was alive when he should be dead. As far as he could tell, there was no reason for it, no logic or plan that could explain or justify his continued existence. He did not believe in God, did not believe in fate. But still he was curious. A man with a gun had tried to shoot him and missed, killing instead a very good person and leaving Sam to spend the rest of his life feeling guilty and wondering why.

Sam was mulling the issue over, wishing he had his assessment book or, at the very least, some beer, when he noticed a shape not more than twenty yards to his right moving slowly in the moonlight.

At first he thought it was some type of animal, but he soon realized it was a person, a woman. She was stretching her arms upward, arching them over her head and turning her body to one side. Sam watched as she suddenly bent over and touched the ground with her hands.

After she finished, she turned and started to run, slowly at first, then faster, her arms up high and tight on her body, her stride long and fast. In a moment, she would reach him. Sam suddenly thought his being there was an intrusion, so he slipped off the bench and crouched behind it. When she passed, he recognized her as the woman from the restaurant, the woman who had returned Louis's roses.

He stood up and watched her disappear down the shoreline moving in and out of moonlight and shadows. When she was completely out of view, he picked up the roses and threw them into the water and watched as they floated back toward him, one by one.

Nine

Sam spent most of the next morning lying in bed, debating with himself. Finally, he made the decision to stay in Lake Eagleton for a few more days and wait for Sister North. The night before, he had dreamed of Maureen again, walking in the field. When he woke, he felt drained and hopeless in a way that made driving back to Chicago alone impossible. Besides, he didn't know where his car was.

He drifted in and out of sleep most of the day, finally waking to a muffled bang. He rose to look out the window. Seeing nothing, he walked down to the bathroom, where he took his time shaving and showering, allowing the water to run hot and letting the steam surround him. By the time he finally made it downstairs, it was late afternoon.

He found Louis sitting alone at the kitchen table with his hands folded in front of him. He was wearing another muumuu, this one turquoise with a brown collar. A glistening silver coffeepot on a matching tray rested in front of him.

"Hello," Sam said. "Did you get the car back okay?"

Louis looked up distractedly and smiled. "Car? Yes."

"That's good."

"Please, sit with me," Louis said. "Would you like some coffee?"

"Sure."

Louis poured the coffee and carefully pushed a cup and saucer across the table to Sam.

"I apologize for last night," Louis said.

"That's okay."

Louis fingered the rim of his coffee cup. His hair was damp and his face puffy.

"I get insane when I drink."

"A lot of people do."

"If you have a moment, I would like to ask you a quick question."

"Sure."

"Did you know that vacuums can explode?"

Sam hesitated. "I never really thought about it."

"They can," Louis said. "Mine just did, not more than an hour ago. Now, why do you think it would do something like that?"

"What were you vacuuming?"

"That shouldn't matter, should it?"

"I think it might," Sam said.

"A chipmunk."

Sam nodded. "I don't know too much about vacuums, but I don't think they were made to vacuum animals."

"Well, I know that now, don't I?"

"You probably do," Sam said. He picked up his coffee. "I think I might have heard the explosion. Are you okay?"

Louis smiled and nodded. "I'm fine," he said sadly.

Sam drank his coffee and was disappointed to taste that it was instant. He took another sip. He put the cup down.

Louis sighed. "I used to have women do the work around here. Three Venezuelans. They did everything. Cooked, cleaned, chopped wood. I had to let them go last week."

"Business bad?"

"You might say that." Louis sipped his coffee. "At first, they didn't understand what I was telling them and wouldn't leave. Finally, I was forced to turn the hose on them." He sighed. "They scattered like moths. May I ask you another question?"

"Sure."

"Did you know that when mother died she left me $355,000?"

"I didn't know that."

"And do you know how much I have left now?"

"No."

"Zero." Louis made an 0 with his fingers. "Ze-rooo."

"That's not much," Sam said.

Louis ran his hand through his beard, smoothing it against his face and neck. "Mother worked hard her whole life. Her whole life. She was a tiny woman, but fearless, relentless. My father left when I was born. There was no fun in her life, no room for romance. She looked like Cesar Romero, which would have been fine had she been male. She never dated. She had strenuous jobs. She ran a car wash, was a mechanic, made truck axles. Did you know that when she was ten, she was kicked in the head by a goat in her village in Greece?"

"No," Sam said. "I didn't."

"She was in a coma for a week. An entire week. The doctors said the blow should have killed her, but she lived, and when she regained consciousness, she found the goat, killed it, and dragged it home for her family to eat."

"She sounds like an amazing woman."

"Her whole life she was a fighter. She had hoof marks on her fore-head from the goat, but never used makeup, never tried to cover them up, never wore bangs. Those hoof marks were a badge of honor." Louis made circular motions on his forehead with his fingers. "I can still see them, red and defiant. Sometimes, when she put me to bed, she would take my hand and bring it to her forehead, let me feel the scars, trace their shape. I remember thinking that I was feeling something sacred, holy. I remember thinking they were filled with strength. Never give up, she used to tell me. Never." He sighed. "I wrote a poem about her. I called it, 'Hooves of Honor, Hooves of Hope.' It was rejected by thirty-five different publications."

They both sat in silence for several seconds.

"I bet it was a good poem," Sam said.

"It was a terrible poem."

Sam nodded and slowly pushed his chair away from the table. "Well," he said, standing. "Thanks for the coffee. I'm going into town for a while." He headed for the back door.

"She worked hard for nothing though. Because I've lost everything," Louis said.

Sam turned. "You still have this house," he said.

Louis didn't seem to hear him. He closed his eyes and placed his hands over his heart, one on top of the other. "It's all about to end," he said softly.

The walk into town was longer than he remembered, and by the time he reached Big Jack's, his feet were aching again. He hesitated before entering, worried about what Louis might have said regarding his involvement in the car escapade the night before. He briefly considered leaving, but knew there was no other place to go. He sucked in a breath and continued inside.

He was immediately greeted by a small, bald-eagle-looking man with a hook nose and bright, alert eyes.

"Are you here to eat, son?" the man asked. His voice was friendly but low, and Sam had to lean forward to hear him.

"Yes," Sam said. He searched for Big Jack but didn't see him, or anyone else for that matter: The place was empty.

The man motioned for Sam to follow and led him to Louis's table by the window. "My name is Leo. If you need anything, let me know. Meg will be your server," he said.

Sam had just opened the menu when the woman he had seen the

night before, the running woman, appeared, holding a pitcher of water.

"Hello," he said.

She was pretty. Sharp cheekbones, large, suspicious eyes, black hair pulled back tight in a ponytail. Her skin was tan, lightly weathered, a smattering of freckles on her nose.

"Do you want water?" she asked.

"Yes," Sam said.

"Flip your glass."

Sam immediately turned it over and watched as she filled it to the top.

"You know what you want?"

"Yes," he said again. He fumbled with the menu, suddenly nervous. The woman seemed very put out over having to take his order.

"A beer," he said, "and let's see . . . a cheeseburger. And fries."

The woman looked past him, out the window. "Anything else?"

"No. Oh. Coleslaw. That would be good, too."

The woman turned and headed for the kitchen. Sam studied her long, lanky figure, thin legs and arms. She seemed familiar, in a way he couldn't immediately place.

While he was waiting for his food, he pulled out his assessment book. He was suddenly in the mood to reflect and assess.

He flipped through the notebook, found a blank page, then gazed out the window at the lake. It was calm and undisturbed, simply resting in the bright afternoon sunlight.

He wrote:

Nice day.

He put his pen down and stared at the words, wishing that he were reflective or, at the very least, a bit more descriptive. He picked up the pen and tried again:

Really nice day.

He put the notebook away. He was not a reflective person. He got up and went to the men's room.

On his way back, he discovered a small wall rack overflowing with brochures: "Lake Eagleton, Lake of Many Moods." "The History of the Eagleton Trolley." "Interesting Bike Trails in Northwest Wisconsin." "Sir Lyell Eagleton, Star-crossed Fort Builder." "The Legend of Moanpatec, She Who Swims In Circles." "The Sister Maria North Story." He picked up this last brochure and walked quickly back to his table.

"Thought you left," the waitress said. She was waiting for him, holding his food. She plopped a plate, ketchup, and mustard on the table. When Sam thought to ask about his beer, there was no trace of her.

He studied the brochure while he ate. The cover featured Sister North in her now familiar pose on the bike. Sam stared at her image, the thick glasses, the owl-shaped face. She didn't look especially short, and the size of her head seemed perfectly normal. He opened the brochure and discovered it was actually a reprinted article from a magazine.

God's Straight Shooter
By Kenyon Fox

She offers advice like, "buck up," "get a grip," and "help yourself." She prefers John Grisham to the Bible, has run the Boston Marathon three times, and thinks people should believe in each other as much as they do in God.

She's Sister Maria North, author of the New York Times bestseller, The Living Jesus, and a rising cable television star with heavenly ratings the networks can only pray for. Her show, part-Oprah, part–700 Club . . .

"Here's your beer." The waitress was standing over him, her eyes pinned to the brochure. He put it down.

"Where did you get that?" she asked.

Sam motioned toward the back.

"I thought we threw all those out." She picked up the brochure and dropped it into the front pocket of her apron. "You want anything else?"

"No, I'm fine. Just the check."

She started to write on her bill pad. "She's gone, you know," she said without looking up.

"Who?"

"The nun."

"I heard that. When do you think she's coming back?"

The woman stopped writing and studied him so long and so intensely that he felt his cheeks grow hot. He had underestimated her looks. She wasn't really pretty as much as she was beautiful. He stared back at her.

"I don't know," she finally said.

"Well, I plan on sticking around for a few days," Sam said. "I heard she might come back soon."

She put the bill down on the table and turned away. "If that's what you want," she said.

He was finishing his lunch when Willie walked in. Sam watched as he stood in the doorway, then crossed the room toward his table.

"Where the hell have you been?" Sam asked.

"Where you been?" Willie sat down.

"I've been at the hotel."

"Yeah, I was looking for you."

"You must not have been looking very hard. I was there all day."

Willie shrugged. "You were sleeping late this morning, so I went for a ride. Just got back and didn't see you there."

"How long were you gone?"

"Most of the day. Got lost. Don't know the region. No street signs or people to ask. Never thought I'd get back. Your car is okay though. Nothing wrong with your car. I put gas in it in some town."

Sam glanced out the window, at the parking lot, and saw that his car looked no worse for wear.

"Hey," Willie said. "I'm real hungry. You already eat?"

"I just finished."

"Let me buy you a beer, then. Don't like eating alone."

Sam shook his head, not entirely buying Willie's explanation about where he had been but, at the same time, having no reason to doubt it. He was back, and the car seemed fine, so he decided to let it go. He picked up his beer and took a final swig. "I'll have one more," he said.

Willie waved Leo down. "Need the waitress here," he said.

Leo approached them. "My niece has gone for the evening, so I'll be waiting on you."

Sam glanced toward the door. "Niece?"

"Two beers and a perch basket," Willie said. He had opened and shut the menu in seconds.

"Coming right up."

After Leo disappeared into the kitchen, Willie pulled out a deck of cards from his pocket and handed it to Sam.

"Pick a card, any card," he said.

"What?"

Willie nodded and pointed to the deck. "Pick one."

Sam picked a card, the seven of hearts.

Willie took the deck back, held it up to his forehead, and closed his eyes. He started humming and swaying from side to side.

"What are you doing?" Sam asked.

"Connecting with the ancient spirits. Part of the act." Willie resumed humming and swaying. After a few moments, he slowly waved his free hand over his head.

"You know," Sam said, "I don't have to see the whole act."

Willie stopped humming and placed the card over his heart. "I see that Mr. Sammy has chosen a red card. I can see it with the third eye, the one in my soul. A card with hearts. A card with seven pretty, sweet hearts," he said. He opened his eyes. Sam turned the card over and flipped the seven of hearts back to Willie.

"I'm getting good at this. Scaring myself," Willie said. He scooped up the card and shuffled the deck. "Almost there. Need to start doing this in front of people, real kids. Been doing it in front of a lot of mirrors, but that ain't the same thing. Mirrors don't have money. I need kids."

"I don't think there are a lot of kids in this town."

"Yeah, but old people like magic, too. Town got a lot of old people."

"I never see anyone."

"Yeah, they come out early in the morning. Drive over from all those little motels by the highway, way down that way. Most got problems. Saw two blind people walking around town, holding hands. Got those canes with the red tips. Saw another old lady with a retarded boy, holding hands. The boy sounded like he was barking. Crossed the street when I saw them coming. Weird place."

Leo brought their beers over and placed them on the table.

"Not too busy here, are you?" Willie said. He picked up his beer.

Leo shook his head. "No, we're not. It's quiet now."

"That because the nun ain't here?" Willie asked. He sipped at his beer. "That's what Louis been telling me. The hotel owner. Says she brings in the people."

"That's part of it, yes it is. Part of the reason." Leo looked out the window. "Most of the reason. We depend on her too much now. It didn't used to be that way. People used to come up here to fish and swim. Those folks don't come here anymore, and the religious types, well, if Maria isn't here, they tend to stay away. I heard the motels are close to empty."

Sam drank some of his beer. "Is the waitress your niece?"

"Yes," Leo said. His face lit up.

"Does she work for Sister North?"

Leo paused and searched Sam's face. "Yes," he said. "Yes. She helps out at the station a little. They both work out of the new studio."

"She like Mother Teresa? She perform miracles?" Willie asked.

Leo smiled and folded his arms across his chest. "Some people claim she does. She's special."

"Tony, the guy who drives the bus, said they brought some little girl to see her a few months ago. She was dying, didn't know what was wrong with her, thought she had cancer or something. The nun took one look at her and told them the problem, said it was her liver. No one believed that, but they took her back to the hospital, and it checked out, liver was bad. Now she's fine. Miracle, they calling it."

"That's true. I remember that girl. It was right around Christmas. She was from Indiana. Nine years old," Leo said. "Sister North is medically intuitive."

"What's that mean?" Willie asked.

"She can diagnose illnesses by just looking at people. I've seen her do that many times. She's been touched by God. She has His grace."

"Medically intuitive," Willie said. "She charge money for that?"

Leo chuckled and shook his head. "No."

"That's right. Nuns don't charge."

"How long will she be gone?" Sam asked.

Leo's smile faltered. He glanced out the window again. "Not long," he said. Then he said, "Your food will be right up," and walked away.

Willie shuffled the cards again. "Yeah, this nun is a pretty big deal. I ever meet her, you know what I ask her for?"

"What?"

"A longer torso. You know, get me in proportion."

"That's always important," Sam said.

"Important enough. Hey, let me ask you, how long are you staying up here?" Willie started sorting the cards, throwing them onto the table.

"I'm not sure."

"Why'd you come? You got family here? Or you come to see the nun?"

Sam let Willie's question hang for a while, before answering, "I wanted to maybe say hello to her."

"Say hello to her, huh? After you done saying hello, what are you going to ask her for?"

"You know, she's not Santa Claus," Sam said.

"I know, but what you going to ask her for?"

Sam thought for a second. "World peace," he said.

"Yeah," Willie said. "Always important." He flipped more cards over, his hands steady and sure. "Can't go wrong with world peace. Hey, you hear about that guy who killed himself?"

"What guy?"

"Louis told me. Said that a priest killed himself. In your room. Slit his wrists."

"Oh yeah. I heard that."

Willie shrugged and continued to flip cards over. "I never going to kill myself. Gonna keep living. Find out what happens to me. Lot of people I know, dead, man. Lot of people."

Sam closed his eyes and rubbed the side of his head, his fingers probing for the first signs of a headache he was sure would come.

"Chunk dead. Pera dead. Log dead. Zo dead. Hess dead. Zak dead. Q-Ball dying, maybe dead now. Case and Bone deserve to be dead."

Sam opened his eyes. He thought Willie might be reading from some type of grocery list.

"Prio kind of half-dead."

"How did they die?"

Willie flicked up from the cards and shrugged. "Tragically," he said.

"Excuse me. Do you live here?" Sam was surprised to see the pretty, older woman from the trolley standing beside his table.

Behind her, her large husband with the booming voice lumbered toward them from across the room.

"Are you boys from town?" she asked again. Suddenly, she recognized Sam. "Oh, we saw you on the trolley."

"Hi," Sam said.

"Do you know any other restaurants in the area? Is there someplace else to eat?"

"The food is very bad here," the man said, almost shouting. He was standing next to them now and vigorously scratching his elbow.

"Patrick, keep your voice down. And the food is fine here."

"I'm not blaming anyone. But bad food is bad food. No one's fault. Except the person who cooked it. But I'm sure he tried. Maybe he's disabled. A lot of restaurants hire disabled people now. McDonald's does."

"Patrick, please."

The man nodded slightly. Despite his barrel chest, he had a lean, inquisitive face, with alert, blue eyes behind his glasses. His head was an impressive, bald dome, ringed with a thin crust of white hair that appeared well maintained. "Do you think the cook was the owner, this Big Jack, the one with the limp?" he asked. "Maybe that had something to do with it. Maybe he had to cook sitting down."

The lady smiled nervously. She was doelike, with large, watchful eyes and a delicate, turned-up nose. "It's just that while we're in town we'd like to explore the area. We're staying at Monticello By-the-Lake, and they don't serve dinner."

"Hey, that's where we're staying," Willie said. "Got no food there."

"You couldn't tell that by the size of the owner," the man said. "There's food somewhere in that place I imagine."

"He got a thyroid condition," Willie said. "He told me that."

"Well, it looks like he ate a thyroid or two," the man said.

"He's okay, he's all right. He gave me a room by the lake," Willie said. "Fireplace, too."

"We're in back," the man said. "We can see the garbage Dumpster. Smell the garbage Dumpster."

"It's a fine room, Patrick."

"I'm just stating a fact there, Lila. I'm not complaining. We're by the garbage Dumpster. It's no one's fault. Someone has to stay back there. I should have told the fat owner that we would prefer not to have a room by the garbage Dumpster. I never said that, never made that clear, so it's my fault as much as anyone's. He probably thought we wanted that room."

"I think this is the only restaurant in town," Sam said.

Lila's face fell for a moment. She looked out the window.

"I was hoping for a little variety. But this is very nice. We'll just eat here then. The food is fine, I think." She smiled. "Thank you." With that, she walked over to a table by the bar.

Patrick, however, showed no signs of leaving. "Not much of a town," he said. "This nun better be worth it. Drove twenty hours to see her. Got here three days ago, and they told us she's gone." He glanced over his shoulder in the direction of his wife. "It was Lila's idea. She thought that the nun could help us find our Todd. It's an ill-conceived plan. Not thought through." He sighed and looked at Willie. "You a cardplayer?"

"No. Magician. Do card tricks," Willie said. "Other things, too."

"Magician," Patrick said. "This town has everything. Everything but a nun."

"What happened to your boy?" Sam asked.

"Don't know. He's twenty-nine years old and never came home from work one day. I imagine he's dead by now. No reason to think otherwise. You don't get stuck in traffic for a year. But Lila doesn't want to give up, so we came here. The port of last resort. We've been most everywhere else."

"You call the cops?" Willie asked.

"Them. The FBI. Private investigators. Spent fifty thousand dollars so far. They haven't turned up much, so we decided to start looking ourselves. That's how we ended up here. It was one of the stops." He coughed into his hand. "Not much of a town, though," he said again.

"Maybe he get in an accident?" Willie asked.

The old man absorbed this question, his chest inflating. "I hope so," he said. "I hope so, for his mother's sake."

They were quiet for a few moments. The man cleared his throat and jingled some change in his pocket. Outside, across the lake, the first lights appeared, fireflies in the dark. Sam was going to ask the man to sit down and join them, when Lila returned, her face beaming. "Patrick, I just heard," she said. "Sister North is back. She came back not more than an hour ago."

"What?" Patrick asked. He stopped fiddling with his change. "Where did you hear that piece of news?"

"The bar owner. He just got a phone call from someone who saw her up on the road, walking." They all looked over toward the bar, where Leo was wiping the inside of a glass. He didn't look up.

"He thinks we can see her tomorrow." She bobbed up a little on her heels when she said this, hardly able to contain herself. "Isn't that wonderful?"

"Tomorrow? Well, I suppose that's good," Patrick said. He rubbed his eyes and looked sad. "I suppose that's good," he said quietly.

That night, Sam dreamed of Maureen again. He was in the green field, following her as she walked toward the lake, the children close behind, singing a wordless song. The sky was full of fast-moving clouds, and, as he walked, he saw them part to reveal a vast darkness, deep and cold and unforgiving. The darkness went on forever, and Sam was afraid it might swallow him.

Maureen turned to face him.

"I'm sorry," Sam said, though he knew she couldn't hear him.

"Mr. Gamett? Do you think this whole thing happened because

we did something wrong?" she asked. "That we're being punished for something? For something we did, or because of who we were?" It was the first time Maureen had ever spoken in this dream.

"Mr. Gamett? Do you think this was supposed to happen? Do you think when we were both born, God said this was going to happen to us? That everything we did before was leading up to that day?"

"This shouldn't have happened, Maureen," Sam said. "It was all my fault."

Maureen smiled as the children gathered around her. She put her hands on their heads and stroked their hair. There were three boys and three girls, and Sam was afraid to look at them, afraid to see who they should have been.

Maureen said something he couldn't hear. He knew it was important though, knew it was the reason he was having the dream. He stepped toward her but got no closer.

"What? Maureen, what? Please, what?"

"You can't go back, Mr. Gamett. You can't go back."

Sam stood in the field and felt the darkness descend on him, felt himself falling into it. "Where do I go?" he yelled. "Where do I go?" But Maureen and the children were gone, and he woke with a start, his eyes wide and fearful in the night.

Ten

The next morning, Sam waited in front of Monticello to take the trolley to Sister North's house. It was a cold, wet day, and he could see his breath hanging in the air, small white bursts. He stomped his feet a few times to stay warm and regretted not wearing his jacket.

"Hello, there, yes, hello."

Sam turned toward the booming voice and saw Patrick and Lila making their way to him. They were nicely dressed. Patrick was wearing a blue suit and striped tie, and Lila wore a new-looking maroon raincoat and matching high heels. Both were intent on maneuvering the slight downward slope that led to the road. Lila took mincing steps with her arms held high, as if she were fording a stream, and Patrick walked carefully, balancing himself, his hands out to his sides.

"They should put in some kind of walkway here," Patrick said. "It's tricky. Of course, walking anywhere is tricky at my age."

When they reached the road, they both took time to shake the mud off their shoes.

"Good morning," Lila said, smiling.

Sam nodded and continued to stomp his feet.

"I assume you're on your way to see the nun," Patrick said.

"I thought I'd take a ride that way," Sam said.

"Wish we could drive there," Patrick said. "I would prefer to drive there. But they say it's best to take the bus. She's so deep in the woods. Easy to get lost, they say, but I don't imagine that's true. I imagine we would find her. Not a lot of nuns living in the woods. Of course, I'm not from around here, so maybe there are. Maybe the place is crawling with them."

"Did you sleep well?" Lila asked Sam.

"I slept okay," Sam said. After his dream about Maureen, he hadn't slept at all.

Lila smiled again. "It's so quiet here. I slept through the night, and I haven't done that in a long while. It's so nice up here with the breeze coming off the lake."

"Nothing else to do up here but sleep," Patrick said. "No TV. No food. All you have is the bed."

Sam shuffled his feet again and coughed. He hadn't planned on going up to the nun's with anyone else. In fact, he hadn't really thought the process through at all. He was considering heading back to his room and rethinking things, when the trolley rolled into view, clanging down the hill, its headlights piercing the morning fog. When the doors opened, Tony saluted them with one finger to the forehead.

"Well, here she is," Patrick said. "Let's sit on top. They say it's not going to rain until this afternoon. We can take in the sights."

Sam let Patrick and Lila board first and watched as they climbed the stairs to the upper deck, Lila wobbling slightly in her heels. He decided to sit down below and made his way to the rear, passing two women with scarred, red faces—burn victims, he thought—and a young teenage girl who looked pregnant. He wanted to sit in the very back, but another woman, wearing sunglasses and smoking a cigarette, was sitting there. He sat a few rows ahead of her.

"Good morning," Tony said. "Our next stop will be downtown.

This will be our last stop before Sister North's, so if you have to use the rest rooms, my advice is to use them there."

From above, Sam heard Patrick's voice, "We just got on!" He was quiet for a moment, then said, "I'm sorry, Lila, but just because we're old doesn't mean we're incontinent."

The trolley curved through the woods and approached the harbor. Sam watched as the statue came into view, the last of the morning mist a flimsy shroud. Tony reached for his microphone.

"He's probably going to tell us about that bad fort builder," Patrick said.

Tony immediately put the microphone down and stepped on the gas. A minute later, they were in front of the courthouse in the middle of Main Street.

"Why are we stopping here?" Patrick barked.

Tony reached for the microphone again. "The courthouse is a scheduled stop," he said.

"We've only been moving for a few minutes."

Tony sat motionless, staring straight ahead.

"What's the story behind this courthouse of yours?" Patrick asked. "I noticed it's still standing. Must have been built by a different one of your founding fathers."

With that, the driver stood up and walked off the trolley. Sam watched as he crossed the street and disappeared into a store.

"Some tour guide," a voice said.

Sam turned and saw that the woman with the cigarette had moved up and taken the seat directly behind him.

"I'm Dot Pelgers," she said, her voice low and throaty. She blew a stream of smoke and extended her hand toward Sam. He shook it without saying anything.

"This guy is too tempermental. Loses his temper a lot. He should do yoga. It helps me." She took a long drag on her cigarette. "Do you have a name? I didn't catch it. Your name."

"Sam," he said. "Sam Gamett."

"Where you from Sam? New York? You're dressed like you're from New York."

Sam looked down to see what he was wearing, then back at Dot. She was at least ten years older than he, and her heavy makeup reminded him of how his mother had looked at her wake.

"I'm from Chicago," he said.

Dot smiled knowingly. "I knew it. Big city. Big-city people wear black a lot. I'm from Milwaukee. We don't wear black unless we're going to court. You here to see Sister North?"

"Just taking a ride."

"Just taking a ride," Dot repeated.

Sam nodded, then turned to face the front of the bus, his back to Dot. He wished for a book, or a newspaper, something he could pretend to be reading. He finally took out his wallet and began to examine his driver's license, which, he noted, had to be renewed in less than two years.

"This is like my second home," Dot said. "I come here all the time to see Sister Maria. That's what she likes to be called, but the station makes her use Sister North, so everyone calls her that. For ratings probably. They did research and it said that thirty-five percent of all living nuns are named Maria. So they want her to be Sister North. Make her stand out."

Sam turned halfway in his seat and nodded again.

"You watch her show?" Dot asked.

"I've seen it a few times." Sam put his license back into his wallet.

"Yeah, well, I like it, but it's boring sometimes, I think. I told her that, too. I told her that maybe she should have some guests on once in a while. Celebrity types. Good celebrity types. Not like Madonna, or Bruce Willis. Someone like, oh I don't know, former president Jimmy Carter. He's nice. He builds homes for the poor. I think he does that for a living now."

"He'd be good," Sam said.

"I always liked him. I think he would have been more successful if he had a different name, though. Jimmy's not a president's name. Jimmy Stewart. Jimmy Buffett. Jimmy Cricket, Jimmy Dean Sausage. He should have been James, or at least Jim. I wrote him a letter once when he was president and told him to change his name. I got a postcard back from the White House thanking me for my support. It was signed Jimmy Carter." She exhaled smoke out of her nose "Guess he didn't like my idea."

"Guess not," Sam said. He turned around.

The woman was quiet. Sam stared at a sign at the front of the trolley. *If you like the trip, say it with a tip!—Tony*

"You know, I had cancer four years ago."

Sam turned to face the woman again. "I didn't know that," he said.

"I beat it. Everyone thought I was going to die. I made a deal with God though. I said that if I didn't die, I would go to church every day for the rest of my life, which is a pretty big sacrifice for me." She blew more smoke. "If you knew my life. Down deep, I didn't think I was going to live, though; that's probably why I made that deal. Anyway, He came through on His end. So here I am."

Sam moved uneasily in his seat and nodded a bit.

"I go to church every day now. Plus I come up to see Maria a lot. I'm a Sister North volunteer." She stopped speaking and seemed to be waiting for Sam to ask a question, but he didn't. "I volunteer for things, help her out. Me and a few others, raise money, do charity work. We helped raise money for that new statue. She won't let us help her with her own problems though. People forget she's a person, too, and needs help. Her house is falling apart, for instance, but she won't let us fix it."

"That's too bad," Sam said.

"It's all right. We're going to fix it anyway." Dot coughed into her hand for a while. "I've got time to give. I'm retired. Used to sell cosmetics for Mary Kay. I come up here two, three times a month, even when she's not in town. I got nothing else to do. I'm not married."

Dot stopped talking. Sam looked out the window at the court-house.

"The doctors said it was a miracle my cancer disappeared. They wanted to take both my breasts."

Sam turned slightly again and tried not to look at Dot's breasts.

"And I have very big breasts."

"I'm glad you're better," he managed to say.

Dot blew more smoke out of the side of her mouth. "So am I. Rang up some pretty big charge bills though. I'm still paying them off. You married?"

"What? Yes."

"Where's your wife?"

Sam tried to smile. "At home, in Chicago, where she lives." He turned in his seat.

"I was married, too," he heard Dot say. "Where are you staying, Sam?"

"The inn, the hotel by the lake."

"Monticello? I've always wanted to stay there, but it's expensive. They're always talking about opening new hotels in town, but it always gets voted down. A few people here have a monopoly and don't want to change anything, that's my take on it at least. Is it nice there?"

"It's okay."

"Yeah, well, maybe I'll move in there for a couple of days, check it out." She gave Sam a sly smile. "Who knows, I might run into you there."

Sam was considering getting off the trolley when he saw Tony come out of the store.

"He's the one who probably had to go to the bathroom," Patrick said.

"Ready for your ride, Sam?" Dot said.

The trolley lurched forward and inched slowly down Main Street.

As they approached the bank near the edge of town, Sam saw the man he had seen by the statue that first night pushing a grocery cart, bags piled high. When the trolley passed him, their eyes locked, and Sam saw him smile; then, after they had driven past, he was sure he heard him laugh.

Sister North lived about three miles from town, deep in the woods on a hill on the west side of the lake. The trolley strained as it made its way upward, slowing to a crawl several times and even stopping once in the middle of a sharp turn.

"I don't know why she lives way out here," Dot said. "I keep telling her to move to Milwaukee or Duluth. Buy a condo. Live a little."

"Welcome to Lasonia Woods," the driver said, "a one-thousand-acre forest preserve. The woods are home to more than twenty-six types of birds, eighteen types of trees." He paused here. "And over ten million mosquitoes in July and August."

Dot laughed. "Good one," she said. "And true. So true." She laughed some more, then had a coughing fit.

"Sister Maria North was born and raised in these woods. She lived overseas for a few years, then moved back to the family home after the publication of her book, *The Living Jesus*, which was a *New York Times* best-seller for eighteen weeks."

"Oprah should have picked that book," Dot said. "I sent her an e-mail recommending it. I even sent her a copy. But I never heard back. I think she's Jewish. Or that African religion, that Kwanza thing."

"Up until very recently, *The Sister North Show* was broadcast from the basement of her home but is now broadcast from Norton's College in a new, state-of-the art studio. The show is received in twenty-six states, most recently Delaware."

"Delaware," Dot said. "Interesting. I've never been."

"The woods we are traveling through were at one time owned by the North family, but the good Sister donated them to the state of Wisconsin to be used as a forest preserve, which they are to this day. Hers is the only private home in this area, though there is a campsite and public boat launch by the water."

"A lot of volunteers camp here," Dot said, "but I never do. I need a bed and a bath."

Tony yanked at the wheel, turning the trolley onto a small dirt road lined by pine trees and a low, white stone wall.

"You know where you're going?" Patrick shouted from above. "Lila is afraid you're lost."

"More than fifty-five thousand people made their way to Lake Eagleton last year to meet Sister North. A Christian teacher and healer, she welcomes people from all races and religions, offering advice, comfort, and counsel to all."

"That's true," said Dot. "I've met Jews, Catholics, Muslims, up here. Even met one of those Scientists, you know, from that religion that worships Tom Cruise."

"According to her book, she first heard her calling while walking in these very woods as a teenage girl," Tony continued. "Engaged to be married at that time, she eschewed her fiancé and decided to enter the sisterhood instead at the age of nineteen. She mentions all of this in her book, *The Living Jesus,* which is currently on sale at most Lake Eagleton shops for $24.95. All copies purchased in town are signed by Sister North herself."

Tony put down the microphone and grabbed the steering wheel with both hands. The trolley was bouncing so wildly that Sam had to grab on to the seat in front of him.

"Slow down," Patrick yelled from above.

They finally came to a stop in a clearing in front of a small, two-story, frame house. Even from a distance, Sam could tell it was in need of repair. The white paint was peeling, and the walkway leading up to the front door was cracked and buckling. A handful of dying evergreen bushes, all brown and branches, lined the walkway. The lawn was overgrown and untamed, a series of wild patches of grass, separated by mud. Next to the house was a satellite dish, its face up and pointing toward heaven.

"Is this the place?" Patrick shouted.

"This is the place," Dot said, her voice quiet.

Sam sat motionless in his seat, surveying the house, as the trolley trembled to a stop. The two disfigured women glanced back at him and smiled. Sam smiled back and quickly averted his gaze. The pregnant girl took out a Bible and kissed its cover.

Tony slowly stood up, got off the trolley, and walked toward the house. He paused at the front door, his manner hesitant and uncertain. He smoothed his shiny black hair back with a hand, then knocked.

"She's not here," Dot said. "She always greets us. She's never inside. She's not here, I bet."

Sam's heart pounded, not sure what he felt at that moment, anticipation, fear, hope. He kept his eyes trained on the door, waiting, his hands curled into fists.

After a few more knocks, the door opened, and the driver disappeared inside. Sam turned in his seat for Dot's reaction.

She shrugged. "This is new," she said.

Sam turned and hung his head. When he envisioned this moment, he had pictured it differently, just the nun and himself talking, Sam confessing all.

When he looked up, he saw Tony walk out with Meg, the waitress from the restaurant. They stood for a few seconds on the front steps, talking, Meg's arms folded across the front of her chest. She went back in the house and shut the door while Tony returned to the trolley. A second later, they were moving down the hill.

"What's the problem?" Patrick yelled. "Do you have the wrong address?"

The driver picked up the microphone. "I'm sorry to report that Sister North is not at home. And is not due back for another week or so."

"I was afraid of this, another rumor," Dot said. "I thought it was strange, her coming back so soon."

"Well, that's some piece of news," Patrick said, as the trolley bounced down the road and back toward town, past the pine trees and stone wall and everything else that Sam couldn't see, as his eyes were clenched and already filling with tears.

Eleven

Later that day, Sam went to Big Jack's for lunch. He sat at Louis's table and stared out the window, his chin in his hand. The day had grown cloudier, the lake was gray and the sky brooding. He had ordered a chicken salad sandwich from Leo but left it mostly untouched on his plate.

He was trying to assess how he felt about Sister North's not being there. On the one hand, he was relieved; he didn't necessarily want to relive the shooting again, see the gun, Roger's eyes, Maureen lying faceup, eyes open, her head swimming in brownish red blood.

On the other hand, he was disappointed; he knew he needed to talk with the nun, needed to talk to someone. Things were building, rising. He searched in his back pocket for his red assessment book, pulled it out.

He wrote:

Need to talk!

"You like the Beatles?" It was Meg. She had materialized in front of his table, holding a tray full of ketchup bottles. Her face was drawn and tired, her eyes squinty and red. She looked like she had been sleeping. Or crying.

"Yes," Sam said. "I like the Beatles."

"Me too." She picked up the ketchup bottle from Sam's table, then turned and disappeared back into the kitchen. Sam watched her go, expecting her to return with a CD, or an old album, but she never came back. Instead, Leo emerged, wearing a short-sleeved white shirt, with a bow tie neatly in place. He stood by the bar.

"Do you need anything else, son?" he asked from across the empty restaurant.

Sam shook his head.

"Are you sure?"

"Yes."

"Anything you need, please be sure to let us know. Business is slow, and we want to take care of our steady customers. Where are you from, may I ask?" he asked.

"Chicago."

Leo came closer and placed a hand on his hip. "Chicago. Isn't that something? Nice town. Haven't been there in years. A lot of nice restaurants down there?"

"Yes."

Leo nodded. "A lot of nice restaurants. Isn't that something?"

Sam didn't say anything. He wasn't sure if he had been asked a question.

"Do these Chicago restaurants have entertainment? The nice ones?"

"Yes," Sam said. "Some of them do."

"I was in a restaurant once that had a polar bear in it, a live polar bear. It wore a black top hat. Every half hour it would stand on its hind legs and ring a bell, then someone would throw it some fish. Can you imagine that?"

Sam tried. "Not really," he finally said.

Leo smiled wistfully. "It was something. Brought in the business. We're thinking of adding some entertainment here. My niece wants us to offer it."

"Who?" Sam asked. "The waitress?"

"Yes. She's my niece."

"Is she some kind of runner? I heard she was."

Leo's whole face brightened. "Oh yes. At least she used to be. Set the state record for the mile in high school. Still stands. Broke it by five seconds. Set all sorts of college records. That was a while ago." He gazed at the door. "Almost made the Olympics, too. But she fell at the time trials. She tripped on something. We were never sure what. She doesn't like to talk about it. It was on TV though." Leo pointed at Sam. "On ESPN. They played it over and over again. She kept falling. I finally changed the channel."

"Does she still run?"

"Oh, no. That's all over." He scrutinized Sam. "She's only thirty-six years old. Pretty as they come. Smart, too. Good grades. Always got good grades. She was on TV in Appleton once. On a show called *The Best of the Badger State*. It was a show about outstanding young Wisconsin teens. She read an essay about the environment, and why we need one. It was a while ago." He was about to say more when Meg rushed in from the kitchen. Leo was frightened by her sudden return and jumped when he saw her.

"There's a storm coming," she said. "From the west. A tornado touched down in Princeville. I just heard about it on the radio."

Sam looked out the window at the transformed lake, by then alive and angry, boiling with whitecaps. On the other side of the shore, he saw yellow lightning in a sickly green sky. He stared, stupefied. Only minutes ago, everything had been a solid gray mass.

"Let's close up," Meg said. She started punching the keys of the register, her face tight and focused.

"We still have customers," Leo said.

Meg glanced up at Sam.

"I'm leaving," he said. He finished his beer in two swallows, as if he had somewhere to rush off to, as if he had some home to protect, kids to pick up.

"We shouldn't rush our customers, Megan," Leo said.

"It's okay," Sam said standing. "I better get going." He had his hand on the door when he remembered that the trolley had dropped him off, and he didn't have his car. He paused, felt Meg and Leo watching him, then pushed the door open and walked outside.

"Holy shit," he said.

The rain hit him instantly, a punishing torrent of water that bit and stung. He covered his head with his arms and broke into a confused jog through the parking lot. His plan was to get to town and wait it out in one of the shops. He quickly gave up on the idea though and turned back to the restaurant, fighting his way against the wind.

He ran as fast as he could, but the rain was falling so hard he lost his bearings. The lights of the restaurant were bouncing and disappearing. He feared he was running in circles, the water turning him around. He stopped and crouched, saw more lights, this time right in front of him. A horn. A truck. A door swinging open.

"Get in," Meg yelled.

Sam felt his way around the truck, found the door, and jumped in.

"Where did you park?" Meg asked.

"I didn't drive," Sam said.

Meg swung the truck around in a circle. "I have to get to my house. All the windows are open."

"It's pretty bad out," he said. He closed his eyes, his senses overloaded. He had never been frightened by weather before.

Meg drove onto the road, stopped, and turned the truck around again. Sam slid against the door.

"Where are we going?" The rain was beating so hard he felt breathless.

Meg jerked to a stop. "We're not going to make it. We have to go back into the restaurant."

"I'm not going back out there. I'm staying here." He had to yell this to be heard.

"If that's what you want," Meg said. She pushed the door open and was halfway out when she turned to face him. "Open your fucking door and follow me."

Sam watched her disappear into the rain, then jumped out and into the parking lot. He was running toward what he hoped was Big Jack's, when he felt someone take his hand and drag him in the opposite direction.

"Stay away from the windows," Meg yelled once they were inside.

He followed her behind the bar, where he knelt next to shaking bottles of scotch and bourbon. Meg was silent, her eyes closed, her face impassive. When the lights went out, there was a shattering of glass, and the room began to shake. Sam grabbed hold of the bar and heard a loud rumbling sound like a train approaching, far off but getting closer.

"Hold on," he yelled. The roof and walls trembled. He reached for Meg's arm, but she crawled away.

"Where are you going?"

"I have to find Leo. He's in the kitchen."

He crawled after her, his head down, his eyes half-closed. Glass was scattered everywhere, so he moved slowly around glistening, wet shards. Rain shot through the broken window, spraying him in the back. Fearing that another window might shatter, he pushed himself up and lunged at the kitchen doors, bouncing through them and falling onto the floor.

"Watch yourself, son," Leo said. He was lying under a stainless-steel table a few feet away, holding a Bible to his chest, his bow tie askew. He appeared calm, like he was about to doze off. Meg had curled up next to him and was holding his hand.

"Get under here," she said.

Sam crawled under the table, on the opposite side, and pressed close against Leo.

"This will be over soon," Leo said, taking his hand. Sam closed his eyes.

After the thunder faded, the wind died down, and Sam stopped shaking, Leo said, "Well, that wasn't so bad."

"Yeah," Meg said. She stood up and quickly walked out into the restaurant. Sam stayed with Leo, his heart still pounding. The storm had disoriented him, knocked him silly, and he had no intention of getting up just yet.

"It's over, son," Leo said. He crawled out from underneath the table.

"Maybe it's not over," Sam said. "Maybe we're just in the eye."

"Tornadoes don't have eyes," Leo said.

"Maybe this one has an eye." Sam made no effort to move.

"Tornadoes don't have eyes," Leo repeated. "It blew itself out over the lake before it got here. They all do. The lake protects us." Leo adjusted his bow tie in the reflection of the swinging door's window. "Come on out now."

Sam slowly stood. His pants were wet, and his shirt was sticking to his back. "That was unbelievable."

"We've had worse," Leo said. He pushed open the doors and held them wide for Sam.

The restaurant was a mess, though not nearly as bad as Sam would have expected. Most of the tables and chairs were thrown to the side or upside down, and the floor was littered with silverware and soggy napkins. One of the mounted fish had landed on the cash register, its glassy eyes wide with surprise, and a smaller one was lying delicately on the jukebox. Sam glanced up at the roof, saw that it was still in one piece, and knocked on the bar to make sure it was solid. Other than the shattered window and a cracked Miller High Life mirror, the place was intact.

"Everything okay in here?" Sam asked Meg. She was off in a corner, slowly sweeping up.

"I think we got lucky," Sam said to her.

"Yeah," Meg said quietly. "We won the lottery." Sam thought he saw her roll her eyes but couldn't be sure. Her head was down, and her hair was hanging in her face.

Leo walked up behind him and started working, righting tables and chairs, picking up glasses and lining them up on the bar. They both worked with a casual efficiency, as if cleaning up after a birthday party.

"Do you get a lot of storms like that?" Sam asked.

"We get our share," Leo said. He was cradling one of the dead fish in his arms, holding it like it was a bride he was about to carry across the threshold. "A few years back, I got caught out in the parking lot and was blown all the way up by the road. I flew fifty feet backward. Fifty feet in the air, can you imagine that? I felt like I was riding a roller coaster. I didn't get a scratch. Landed safe and sound."

"Why do you live here then?" Sam blurted.

Leo and Meg both stopped working and stared at him. His question seemed to confuse and startle them at the same time. Meg leaned against her broom and pushed back her hair. Her expression was flat, though her laser brown eyes were locked on him. Behind her, Sam could see the sun breaking through the clouds, pure, clean streaks of light that caught the center of the lake.

"Because," she said, her voice deadpan, "it's exciting."

Leo pointed the snout of the fish at her and laughed.

• • •

Sam stayed at the restaurant for a while, helping move tables and chairs. He even mopped up. After an hour, when the place began to resemble itself, Leo thanked him.

"Megan can give you a ride back," he said.

Sam glanced over at Meg. She was behind the bar, holding her broom, daring him, it seemed, to take up Leo's offer.

"That's all right. I'll walk."

"You sure?" Leo asked.

"Yeah, I don't mind."

As if to prove his point, he exited the restaurant with gusto and strode through the parking lot at a brisk pace, dodging fallen branches and broken tree limbs. About a half mile from the restaurant, he stopped dead in his tracks. There, sitting in the middle of the road, was a rowboat in perfect condition. A few feet up were its oars, lying peacefully next to each other. Sam picked up the oars and slowly walked back to the boat and placed them carefully on one of the seats.

When he reached town, he found it strangely alive. More people than ever were strolling about, inspecting the damage and marveling at the randomness and savagery of the storm. A small crowd had gathered by the end of Main Street, gawking at the bank. Its roof was gone, but its walls were still standing.

"Picked off clean," someone from the crowd said.

Farther up the street, another group of people stared at what was left of the Grocery Bag's garden nursery. It looked like it had been flattened by a huge fist. Remnants of plants and flowers blew throughout the parking lot, scattering in the breeze. Sam saw a handful of yellow tulips on the grocery store's roof lying in a bouquet as if they had been intentionally and delicately placed there.

In front of Reflections, Sam passed a bald man in a wet white monk's robe. He was sitting cross-legged on the sidewalk, talking to the twisted man in the wheelchair.

"I was standing in the middle of the street when the storm came," Sam heard the man in the robe say. "I felt myself being lifted up." He pointed to the sky. "I thought it was my time. I thought I was finally going home."

"To heaven?" the man in the wheelchair asked.

"To Milwaukee," the man said. "That's where I'm from, originally."

Sam crossed the street. In front of the courthouse, two elm trees were lying on their sides, their roots exposed like entrails. The red courthouse door was twisted and hanging off its hinges. An old man in a felt hat stared at it, his hands behind his back.

"I painted this door myself," the man said. He glanced over at Sam. "Painted it red. Took me three days." The man shook his head. "Everything is insignificant in the eyes of the Lord. Everything. Especially doors."

Sam walked on. At the end of town, by the harbor, he found the live bait store leaning to one side as if it were still in the process of falling down. Sam once again crossed the street and gently touched a wall with one finger.

"Judgment came close," someone said. Sam turned and saw the unkempt man from the harbor. He was holding a brown paper grocery bag and grinning, his bony face red. "We get scared, but we won't change," he said. "We never do. We know right from wrong, know punishment is waiting, but we do what we always do."

"That was some storm," Sam said.

"She's gone, you know."

"What? Who's gone?"

"Sister North. He took her back because she doesn't belong here. I saw her fly away."

"She'll be back," Sam said

"No, she won't." The man grinned again and shuffled away.

· · ·

When Sam finally got back to Monticello, Willie was waiting for him in the parking lot. He was wearing a Lake Eagleton, USA, baseball cap on backward and eating the last of an apple.

"Thought you might be dead," he said. He finished the apple and tossed the core aside. "Storm was a killer, but we got off okay. How's the town?"

"Not that bad," Sam said. "It could have been worse."

"Yeah, we didn't get nothing over here. Just some branches down. Hey, Louis says he wants to take us out in his boat. Take a look at the damage around the lake."

Even though Sam had walked close to five miles, the storm and its aftermath had energized him. His adrenaline was pumping. He knew it would be hours before he could sit still, much less sleep.

"Where is he?"

"Down by the dock. Got an old boat. All wood."

Sam squinted past Willie, toward the lake. It had been a long time since he had been on the water. "Let's go," he said.

Louis was waiting for them in the boat, wearing a nautical-looking muumuu with narrow blue-and-white stripes. Up close, Sam could see tiny anchors etched on the sleeves.

"Ahoy," he said.

The boat was a classic wooden Chris-Craft. It sat low in the water and looked like a floating couch. Its red leather seats were wide, and there was plenty of leg room. Sam sat in the passenger seat next to Louis and stretched out as far as he could.

"This is nice," he said. "How old is it?"

Louis started up the boat and pushed off from the deck. "I'm not exactly sure."

Sam thought for a moment. "This is your boat, right?"

"Yes, of course. Mother won it in a poker game."

The engine was a rich, deep gurgle, and the ride smooth. Louis seemed surprisingly at ease behind the wheel, steering with one hand, the other dangling over the side.

"You look like you know what you're doing," Sam said.

"Boats are easier than cars," Louis said. "You really can't drive off the road."

Louis drove slowly, maneuvering around storm debris, mostly branches and floating knots of garbage and seaweed. They headed toward shore, slowing to an occasional crawl to inspect a twisted dock or an uprooted tree. Near town, they saw a sailboat listing badly, its mast almost perpendicular to the water. A few feet away, Willie fished out a basketball and declared it still usable.

"Keep it," Louis said. "There might be a reward."

It was a beautiful late afternoon, the sky clear and blameless, the air humid. Sam soaked it all in, the hum of the boat lulling him into a comfortable trance. He glanced over his shoulder and saw that Willie was sound asleep, his mouth wide-open.

"Nice out here," he said to Louis. "You know, my grandfather used to have a boat. I used to fish as a kid. I used to go with my father. Do you fish?"

Louis straightened up in his seat, peering toward shore. He didn't seem to have heard Sam.

"I used to catch perch and small bass," Sam said. "Sometimes, sunfish. Those flat things."

Louis kept staring at the shore. He looked confused, then worried. Finally, he said, "Oh, my God."

Sam sat up and scanned the shoreline. "What are you looking at?"

"Oh God."

Sam tried to follow Louis's gaze. "What? What are you looking at?"

Louis pointed. "Over there. What do you see?"

Sam cupped a hand to his forehead. "I don't see anything."

Louis turned the boat sharply inland. "Exactly," he said.

Sam continued to stare at the harbor. It wasn't until they were approaching the town dock that he realized what wasn't there.

· · ·

They found Big Jack, Leo, Tony the driver, and the strange man with the bags standing at the former site of the Sister North statue, gawking at a depressed circle of mud and flattened flowers.

"Now, where the hell do you think that thing went to?" Big Jack asked the group.

"It's gone," Tony said.

"I know it's gone. What direction? How far out? Did anyone see anything during the storm?"

"I wasn't paying attention," Louis said. "I was too busy worrying about waking up in Oz."

"The statue has to be in the water, Jack," Leo said. "We would notice if it were in town. The storm blew it into the water."

"I know it's in the water. But I've been up and down the shore for the past two hours, and I've gone fifty feet out, and I can't find the damn thing. How does an eight-foot bronze statue that weighs, what, two thousand pounds, disappear?"

"If we knew that, Jack, we wouldn't be standing here," Leo said.

Jack exhaled slowly. "We paid enough for that damn thing, and we better find it." He glared at Louis. "This was all your idea. You commissioned the thing. Did you insure it?"

Louis ran his hand nervously through his beard. "You can buy statue insurance?"

Big Jack shook his head. "Perfect. Goddammit, everything is just perfect. This is just what this town needs now."

"I say we drag the lake for the nun," Tony said. "She couldn't have gotten far."

"She's gone forever," the strange man said. He was still holding his bag.

"Shut up, Billy!" Big Jack said. "Now, Tony is going to give everyone some chains. When you find it, wrap the chain around her and drag her in. You got those chains?" he asked Tony.

"Yeah, in my truck."

"As soon as you get a chain, everyone get in a boat and look for that thing. It's getting dark. Go about seventy-five feet out, and work your way in. It couldn't have gone any farther. That storm wasn't that big."

"It was pretty big. It was on CNN," Tony said. "They even mentioned the town. But they called it Lake Feebleton. Those assholes can't get anything straight."

"She's dead," the bag man said.

"What?" Willie asked.

"She's dead."

Big Jack whirled around and knocked the bag out of the man's arms. Some clothes, old shirts, and a black tennis shoe scattered on the ground. "I said, shut up, Billy," he said. He stepped close to him. "Shut up."

They drove up and down the shoreline for an hour, trolling for the statue, heading out deeper and deeper. It was almost dark, and Sam thought their efforts would soon be in vain. He hadn't been able to see the bottom of the lake for the last thirty minutes.

"It has to be out deeper," he said. He was driving the Chris-Craft. Louis claimed to have excellent night vision and was leaning over the side, examining the water, the boat tilting in his direction. He had taken the search very seriously, insisting on total silence while he looked.

"Hey, getting late," Willie said from behind them. "We can find the statue tomorrow. Ain't going nowhere. Lake's a circle. Can't get out."

Louis leaned back and shook his head. "It could be anywhere," he said softly. "It could be in Canada by now."

Sam laughed and turned the boat back toward land. "It's not like it can swim. It's here somewhere, under some seaweed or trapped under a tree. Something that heavy couldn't have gone that far."

Louis closed his eyes. "It wasn't as heavy as you think," he said.

"It was made of bronze," Sam said. "It was heavy."

Louis let out a small groan. "It wasn't really made out of bronze. Technically."

"I thought it was," Sam said.

He steered the boat to within fifteen feet of the shore, then turned it around again for what he hoped was one final search. Off to his side, about fifty yards away, he saw the lights of Big Jack's fishing boat bobbing, heading back to shore.

"What was it made of?" Sam asked.

"Some other kind of metal. Titanium something. They make golf clubs out of it. Very lightweight." Louis groaned again. "Only the feet are bronze. The rest is only painted bronze."

"Only the feet are bronze?"

Louis glanced over his shoulder at Willie, who was drifting off to sleep again. "Not many people know that," he said in a low voice. "In fact, no one knows. It's a cheap statue. The man who was originally going to make it, a well-known sculptor from France, wanted an outrageous amount of money, so I hired his third-world equivalent, someone from Thailand. He probably had children make it in a statue sweatshop. It doesn't weigh much at all. Certainly not as much as I do. There was some type of base, or something that we were supposed to attach it to, an anchor, but the instructions were very confusing. Everyone thinks it's all bronze."

"And no one has figured it out?"

"It just arrived. The only way they could tell something was unusual was if they tried to pick it up or push it over. I think Billy Bags suspects, or knows. He's always sniffing around the thing."

"The guy with the bags?"

"Yes. This year's town schizophrenic. In Eagleton, it's an elected position."

"You're not going to fool anyone for long, especially Big Jack."

"I'm aware of that. I was going to get around to telling him, but I could never find the right time. The town entrusted me with the responsibility, and I let them down." He turned to face Sam. "I have no idea why I'm telling you this. I think it's because, in my heart, I still think you're a priest."

"I'm not a priest," Sam said.

"You have a solemn dignity about you, and you look so sad all the time. Most of the priests we get up here are quiet and sad."

"Well, I'm not a priest," Sam said again.

Louis reached out and took hold of Sam's arm. "I wish you were. I have so much to confess."

Sam pulled his arm away. "It's pretty late, why don't we call it a night and look tomorrow, in the light?"

"Please." Louis closed his eyes and put both his hands over his heart. "Drive to the other side. It may just be landing now."

Sam drove fast across the lake, the wind whipping his face, scoops of stars overhead. A ribbon of moonlight sparkled on the water, and he followed it, using it as a path to the opposite shore.

Despite the absurdity of their mission, he was enjoying the evening. He hadn't been on a boat in years and felt reckless and released, like a boy in spring. He held the top of the steering wheel with both hands and considered humming.

"Drive over there," Louis said, pointing at the approaching shore. "Toward that light."

Sam slowed. "Why?"

"I want to check on something."

Sam turned and headed in that direction. The shore quickly came into focus. Soon, he could make out the tree line, then a small dock.

"Get closer, as close as you can," Louis said.

"Who lives there?" Sam asked.

"Someone."

"Who's there?" a voice said. Sam instantly recognized it as Meg's. She was standing on the dock, holding a flashlight.

"Oh God," Louis whispered. He ducked his head. "It's her. I'm not really dressed for this." He turned back toward the dock. "It's us. Me. Louis. And some other people. We just came by to see if you were all right."

Meg didn't say anything. Sam stared at the flashlight and squinted against the light as they floated closer.

"People were killed. By the storm. Over in Princeville. So naturally we were quite concerned. Are you all right?"

Meg was still quiet. They continued to drift toward the dock.

"I wasn't killed," she finally said.

"Well, that's a relief."

"My—" Meg started to say something, then paused. "My dog died," she said quietly.

"What died?" Louis asked.

"My dog died."

"I didn't know you had a dog," Louis said.

They were gently bumping up against some rocks, the boat squeaking. Sam could see her clearly in the moonlight. She was wearing dark shorts and yellow running shoes. Her hair was pulled back in a ponytail, and her face looked tired but, as always, determined.

"I need help burying him," she said. "Throw me the rope."

Louis was flustered. "Yes, yes, yes. Of course. You need help. Willie, throw her a line."

"You mean, like a rope?"

"A rope. Yes. Throw her a rope."

Sam glanced back at Willie who was halfheartedly searching the back of the boat. "I don't see any rope. Oh, here's one."

Willie tossed the line to Meg, who caught it and walked to the far end of the dock.

"You must help her," Louis whispered to Sam. "She's never asked me for anything before. I can't do it. I'll never make it up that hill." He looked back at Willie. "Be her *amigo,* and I will be yours."

"Tired and hungry," Willie said.

"Please," Louis whispered. "I will include breakfast in your stay. "Complimentary, starting tomorrow. I will cook all night." He turned back toward Meg, who was tying the front of the boat down to the dock. "My friends will help," he said again. "I insist."

"What about the statue?" Sam asked.

"Forget the statue. I don't want to find the damn statue."

Meg walked over and looked down at them in the boat. Her jaw was set, and her eyes were focused on Sam. He swallowed hard.

"Bury a dog," he said. He didn't want to do it, but when Meg extended her hand, he took it.

They followed her up a steep hill, Sam trying not to trip in the darkness.

"Watch where you walk," Meg said. "There's a lot of shit on the ground."

"Did you get hit bad over here?" Sam asked. He was trying not to breathe too hard, but he was already sweating.

Meg stopped and pointed her flashlight farther up the hill, revealing a small cabin. It was leaning to one side, its roof gone. What was left looked like it could fall over at any minute.

"Sneeze, and that thing go down," Willie said.

Meg flashed the light directly into Willie's face. "Don't sneeze," she said. She flashed the light past the house and at another broken shape. "That's my barn. Was my barn."

They walked around the teetering cabin toward the smashed barn, all sheets of tangled wood and tin piled high. Sam stumbled over something hard and sharp, bent over, and picked up a weathervane. It was still in one piece, its four arrows pointing in different directions, a rooster in the middle, its mouth half-open. "Here," he said. He extended the weathervane to Meg. "This still looks usable."

Meg took it and immediately threw it off to the side without even a glance. "Albert is over here," she said.

"Your dog?" Sam asked.

"Horse."

Sam paused. "You mean dog."

"I mean horse," Meg said. She stared at him, almost defiantly.

No one said anything. Down by the lake, Louis started up the boat.

"You said dog," Sam said.

"I meant horse."

They were all quiet again. Then Willie said, "That's a pretty big difference."

Meg continued to study Sam, her face expressionless. "Are you going to help?"

"Where is it?" Sam asked.

She swung the flashlight around to the middle of the rubble. "He's in there, under all that shit."

"You sure he's dead?" Willie asked.

"No, he's shy," Meg said. "We need to drag him out and bury him."

"I don't think we can do that," Sam said. "There are only three of us. You might have to call someone to do that."

"I don't want to wait," Meg said. "I don't want him just lying here. I already dug the hole. I know it's deep enough."

Sam wasn't sure he was up to burying a horse. He had never buried anything before. He looked at Willie, who shrugged and spit on the ground, then back at Meg. Her dark eyes seemed about an inch from his face. He knew she had lied to them, but felt sorry for her nonetheless. He couldn't just leave her out here all alone, with her wrecked house, her dead horse, her short shorts, her long legs.

"Is it a big horse?" he heard himself ask.

They worked in silence, lifting and throwing broken boards to the side. Fortunately, everything was light, and they made quick progress, the pile of debris shrinking fast. Sam found the effort invigorating and gained momentum as the night wore on.

"Slow down," Willie said. "Working too fast."

Sam lifted up one last board and gasped. There, lying partially covered under a flimsy, white blanket was Albert. Meg flashed the light on him. His one visible eye was open, and he appeared to be perfectly intact. Sam circled him carefully.

"Are you sure he's dead?" he asked.

Meg knelt over Albert and pulled the blanket aside. "He's dead. He had a heart attack."

"Because of the storm?" Sam asked.

"No. He had it a couple of days ago."

"Before the storm." Sam said, more than asked, this.

"I didn't want to bury him," Meg said quietly. She stroked his mane. "I had him a long time." She put the flashlight down. "Come on," she said. "The only way we can do this is to push him. The hole isn't far. It's right over there. We can push him."

Sam squatted next to her and instantly smelled Albert's dead smell. When he placed his hands on the horse's midsection, he felt short, scratchy hairs.

"One, two, three, go," Willie said.

Sam pushed as hard as he could, but Albert didn't budge.

"Again," Meg said.

They pushed again, Sam grunting aloud this time, but still Albert didn't move.

"Do you have any rope?" Sam asked. "Maybe we can tie him up to a truck and drag him."

"I don't have anything," Meg said, standing up. She was breathing hard.

Sam walked over to the grave, sat down, and looked up at the sky. The yellow moon was by then high and pure white. Meg moved near him and sat a few feet away. Her ponytail had come undone, and some strands of hair fell in her face. Willie remained standing, circling Albert.

Sam looked into the grave and was impressed. It had to be six feet deep and almost as wide. "How long did it take you to dig this?" he asked.

"Two days," she said.

They sat and listened to the wind move branches overhead. Sam glanced at his watch and saw that it was close to midnight. He had no memory of when and where the day had begun and suddenly felt like he might fall over into the grave himself.

"I heard they make Jell-O out of horses' hooves," Willie said. He was squatting by Albert's feet. "Once they die, I mean. Was surprised when I heard that," he said. He shook his head. "Don't taste like horse's feet."

Sam shot Willie a glance and shook his head. Down by the lake, a horn blew, once, then twice, then again.

"That's Louis," Willie said. "Maybe we got to go," he said. "He been down there for a while, waiting. I'm going. Got to get something to eat. You coming?"

Sam studied Meg. She was staring into the grave, her eyes narrowed like she was thinking hard.

"We have those chains in the boat, don't we?" he asked Willie.

"Yeah. For the statue."

Sam stood up and wiped some dirt off himself. "We can do this," he said.

It was almost daylight when they finally finished burying Albert. The dark line of the eastern shore was coming into focus, black turning gray and pockets of fog were making their way across the lake. Sam threw one last shovel of dirt and felt he might keel over.

Getting Albert into the hole had been relatively easy. Right after Willie left, they hooked up his legs to the back of Meg's truck with the chains. He fell neatly into the grave with a dull, soft thump.

"I think that's it," Sam said. He dropped the shovel and sank to the ground.

Meg worked a little while longer, then knelt and patted dirt on the grave, pressing hard. When she finished, she sat down and examined her mud-covered hands.

"Thanks," she said. "I wasn't sure we were going to be able to do that." She rubbed the tops of her hands. "Did you ever bury anyone before?"

"My parents. But I didn't do the digging."

"When did they die?"

"About twenty years ago."

"Did they die at the same time?"

"No. My mom died about three years before my father. She had a heart attack."

Meg thought for a moment. "Dying is weird," she said. "You're here, then gone. You'd think by now we'd have a better understanding of it."

"What do you mean?"

She shrugged. "We've been dying so long, and it's still this mystery. We don't know any more about it than the caveman." She pointed at the grave. "We disappear, and that's it. It's still a big blank. It seems like we should all think about it more. But we don't. No one really thinks about it unless we're already dying." She picked up a clump of dirt and threw it. "My mom died when I was nine. I never knew my father, but I heard he's dead, too."

"Did your uncles raise you?"

"Yeah. They gave me Albert. I haven't told them he's dead yet. They liked him a lot. They took care of him when I was away."

"Do you like horses?"

"No, not really. I just liked Albert. He was around a long time. He and I were friends. I'm going to miss him a lot. Animals are easy to get along with. They don't want much. Albert didn't want anything."

Sam looked over at her, staring blankly at the grave, her face sad and fading. He tried to think of an appropriate comment.

"I had a hamster once," he finally said.

She looked up at him.

"He died, too."

Sam closed his eyes. He couldn't believe he had just said that. He was so exhausted that he feared he was losing control of his thought processes.

"Where are you from?" she asked.

"Chicago."

"Is that where you used to be a priest?"

Sam opened his eyes. "I never was a priest," he said slowly. "Why does everyone think I was a priest? Everyone keeps asking me that. I don't even know any priests."

"Sorry, I heard you used to be one." She looked at her hands and rubbed at the mud again. "We get a lot of priests up here; that's probably why everyone thinks you're one. They come up here alone and kill themselves a lot."

"I am a lawyer."

"Oh," she said. "That's pretty different than a priest."

"Well," Sam said, "I do hear a lot of confessions." He stood up and stretched, then sat right back down. He wondered how far they were from town.

"Have you lived here your whole life?" he asked.

"No. I lived in California for a while. I came back a few years ago."

"Why did you come back?"

Meg picked up another clump of mud and threw it off into the woods. "A lot of reasons." She went back to her hands again and started picking at a finger. "Why are you here?"

"A lot of reasons. Do you know the nun?"

"Everyone up here knows the nun."

"I mean well?"

"Yeah. I've known her a long time. She's smart. I like her a lot."
She picked up a twig.

"Do you work with her?"

"I answer the phones for her sometimes. She used to have a whole
crew working for her." She turned the twig around in her hands. "Are
you here to see her?"

"Yes."

"Everyone is. A few months ago, a guy from Alabama came here
with his dog. He wanted Sister North to bless his dog so he could win
some competition. He drove three days straight. After she blessed
him, he got in his truck and drove home. I can't believe this place,
what it's become. It wasn't like this when I was growing up. It's crazy.
Everyone here is crazy."

"I think I'm crazy, too," Sam said.

"Why? Did you bring a dog with you?"

"No. A man tried to kill me though. He killed my secretary
instead. He shot her right in front of me, then he pressed a gun
against my head. He asked me if I believed in Jesus, and I said yes
even though I don't. He shot himself instead of me." Sam's voice
caught and he put his hand over his mouth. He felt light-headed,
breathless, like he was running uphill. He hadn't expected to say any
of that.

Meg put the twig down. In the gray light and mist, she looked as
though she were disappearing.

"I tried to call Sister North, but I got you instead," Sam said. "I
talked with you on the phone. You kept putting me on hold, so I
came here. I thought she might be able to help me. I don't know how,
but I thought she might."

He stopped talking, suddenly out of words. A strong breeze blew
off the lake, scattering branches and leaves and chasing the fog up
the hill. He closed his eyes again, but felt Meg watching him. He was
embarrassed at what he had just told her, a stranger.

"Coming up here was a good idea," she said. Her voice sounded different, softer. He opened his eyes.

"It was?"

"Yeah." She smiled a little, and, in that instant, he saw her clearly through the mist. "It's been good for me," she said. "I bet it will be good for you, too."

Twelve

For breakfast the next day, Louis left a box of cinnamon Pop-Tarts and a note on the kitchen table. *"Bon appetit!"* the note read.

"Kind of expecting a little something more, maybe eggs and bacon," Willie said as he plugged in the toaster. "Kind of led me to believe that."

After they ate their Pop-Tarts, they drove into town. Even though Sam was exhausted—he hadn't gotten home until after five—he couldn't sleep, so he decided to do some shopping. He needed everything: shirts, socks, toothpaste. As he drove, he added sunglasses to his list. The day was bright and unseasonably warm for early June.

"Hey, Sam, how long you staying up here?" Willie asked, as they passed Big Jack's.

"I don't know," Sam said.

"I think I'm going to stay for a while," Willie said. "Get away from everything."

"What about all those kids in Minnesota? They're dying to see your act."

"They can wait. Need a rest. This place is quiet. Never stayed by no lake before. Yesterday was the first time I ever was in a boat. You know that? Say, you screw that Meg last night or what?"

"What?"

"Figured that's why you stayed there. Know you wanted to. That's why I left. Louis thinks you screwed her, too."

"Well, I'm sorry to disappoint you guys," Sam said. "But I didn't. And I wouldn't tell you if I did."

Willie slumped down a little in his seat and tapped his feet. "Yeah. She's good-looking, but she seems like a bitch. She got those tendencies."

"What do you mean?"

"You know, always looks pissed off. Got those black eyes staring at you. Never smiles."

"Brown eyes," Sam said.

"Yeah, well, reminds me of a cop. Women cops, man, they the worst. Take everything serious."

They wound around the last bend of trees before coming to the harbor. Sam turned off the air conditioner and opened his window halfway. He wanted to smell the lake.

"What you do for a living again?" Willie asked.

"I'm a lawyer. Was a lawyer."

"What do you mean, was? You retired?"

"I think I might be," Sam said.

"You ever do any criminal defense work?"

Sam glanced over at Willie. "Some. Why?"

Willie slouched down lower in his seat. "I don't know," he said.

When they passed the harbor, Sam slowed and opened his window the rest of the way.

"Statue still gone," Willie said. "Weird. Makes you appreciate the Statue of Liberty. Been there forever."

Sam turned down Main Street. Most of the stores were open, and a handful of people were strolling about, mostly elderly couples. Sam saw the burned women again. They were wearing large floppy hats and sunglasses and were walking arm in arm. The twisted man in the wheelchair was following right behind, his head cocked at a painful angle. He was wearing the same orange Sister North sweatshirt, with the white stripe across the middle, and clutching a roll of toilet paper.

"Weird town," Willie said.

Sam parked, got out, and looked around. Other than the two fallen trees on the courthouse lawn, and the roofless bank, there was little trace of the previous day's storm.

"Cleaned this place up pretty fast," Willie said.

Sam agreed. "Yeah, they did." He looked across the street. "I'm going to do a little shopping. I have to buy some clothes."

"That place got clothes," Willie said. He pointed to Reflections, the shop with Sister North's picture in the window. "Been in there before. Mostly God clothes though. Lot of crosses and Bibles. Who'd buy a Bible? Get one free in any motel room."

They crossed the street and peered in the store window. Two mannequins, wearing white T-shirts with *Lake Eagleton, USA!* stitched across their fronts, were on display, standing like sentries on either side of the Sister North picture. When Sam stepped closer, he could see two small black crosses under the T-shirts' front pockets.

"Well, well, well." They both turned just as Dot Pelgers approached them, walking a white poodle. The dog was wearing a red ribbon with a single silver bell tied around its neck. Dot had on sunglasses, tight black stirrup pants, and heels so high that when she stopped, Sam thought that, given the slightest breeze, she would certainly fall over.

"Hello, Sam." She nodded at the store window. "Doing a little window-shopping this morning?"

"Need a few essentials," Sam said.

The poodle jumped off the curb and into the gutter, where it began to sniff a candy bar wrapper. Dot pulled lightly on the leash.

"This is Carson, my dog. Guess who he's named after?"

Willie shrugged. "Johnny Carson."

Dot peeked over the top of her sunglasses, then slid them back up her nose. "You're good," she said, her voice a low purr. "You're *real* good." She opened a small, gold case, took out a cigarette, and tapped it once against the top of the case. "I always liked Johnny Carson," she said. "He was the best. You know what I liked most about him? He left classy. One day he was there, then boom." She snapped her fingers. "The next day, he was gone. You don't see him on *Hollywood Squares* or *Larry King*. Doing commercials. It's like he's dead. That's the way to leave. You act like you're dead." She lit her cigarette with a matching gold lighter, then blew a stream of smoke out of the corner of her mouth.

"He was pretty good," Willie said.

Carson was licking the candy wrapper, his tiny pink tongue darting in and out of his mouth. Dot pulled a little on the leash.

"You going into Reflections?" she asked. She was peering over the top of her sunglasses again.

"Thought I'd take a look around," Sam said.

"Watch your money in there. Big Jack owns the place, so you know it's overpriced. It's all Wal-Mart stuff anyway. They just slap on a cross and mark it up. It's a racket. This whole town is a racket, if you ask me. Big Jack, Louis, Leo, they're all in on it. Rip everyone off. That's why I'm staying at the Sleep Shack out on the highway. No frills, but cheap." She shook her head and took another drag. "Say, I almost forgot. We're all getting together for dinner tonight. Patrick, Lila, and me. Going to Big Jack's. It's Beatles Night there or something. Going to be playing old Beatles songs. They're going to have a disc jockey. You should come." Dot snapped her fingers and shook her head a little. Sam backed away; he didn't want her to fall on him.

"We're busy," Sam said.

"We are?" Willie asked.

"I'm busy," Sam said.

"You sure?" Dot said. "We could use the company. Kill some time together. Have a few drinks. Tell a few lies." She began to snap her fingers again, then wiggle her hips ever so slightly.

"You like to dance, Sam?"

"Not really."

"Too bad. I would have taken you for a real dancer. A good one. How about you?"

"Naw, I am not into it too much," Willie said.

"I am sorry, but you two are just no fun." Dot stopped shaking and dropped her smoke on the sidewalk, grinding it with the toe of her shoe.

"I'll be seeing you, boys," she said. She tightened the leash around her wrist, then yanked on it once to bring Carson to her side. "And don't be such a stranger, Sam." She winked and walked away.

"She hot for you," Willie said after she was gone. "Pretty obvious."

A cool blast of air greeted them as they entered Reflections. The store was narrow, but deceptively large, with rows of clothing racks extending far back. It reminded Sam of the old dime stores he used to frequent when he was a kid, sweet air and sticky floors. Up near the front were shelves of books and magazines. Sam picked up a book, *No Wrinkles on the Soul*, put it back, picked up another one, *Bearing Your Cross Alone*, then put that back, too. He looked for Sister North's book, but couldn't find it.

"Can I help you?" The clerk, a tall and skinny teenager with punk green-and-black hair, looked up from behind the counter.

"Do you have Sister North's book?" Sam asked.

"You mean the one she wrote about Jesus?"

"No, her latest thriller."

"What?"

The clerk looked genuinely confused. "I'm sorry," Sam said. "The Jesus one."

The clerk checked a notebook, then glanced over Sam's shoulder toward the book section. "We're out. Some lady was in here early this morning and bought, like, thirty copies because they were auto-graphed. She's going to sell them on eBay I bet. They always do that if they're autographed."

"Well," Sam said. He tapped the counter once. "Thanks."

He wandered back to the book section and found Willie reading a magazine, *Revelations*. His lips were slightly moving as he read.

"You think the end of the world is coming?" he asked. He didn't look up from the magazine. "Says here it is. Says it's all been foretold. Says all the signs are in place. All we need now is for the Antichrist to reveal himself. Says here he may already be alive, you know, blend-ing in with us, waiting to make his move." He held up the magazine for Sam to see. "Got a list of suspects, people we got to keep our eyes on in case they the ones. People with a lot of influence." Willie held the magazine up close to his eyes. "Who's Dr. Phil?" he asked.

Sam ignored the question and picked up a copy of *Riding for Jesus*, by Jenny Bailey: America's Top Female Rodeo Star. On the cover was a picture of Jesus riding a bucking bronco, one arm extended upward as if he were trying to keep his balance.

"This looks good," Sam said.

"Really?"

Sam looked at Willie. "No," he said quietly. He put the book back and picked out another one: *Reconciling Wealth with Christ, the Wilbur Fuller Story*, then put that back as well.

"Never heard of any of these books," Willie said.

"You a big reader, Willie?" Sam asked.

"I read some, but can't do it too much, because of my condition."

"You mean your torso?"

"No, I think I'm a little dyslexic. Read slow."

They made their way over to the men's casual wear section. Sam carefully inspected a few T-shirts and picked one out with the warn-ing "MESS WITH JESUS, YOU MESS WITH ME!" written on it in bold, defiant letters.

"You going to buy that?" Willie asked.

"Probably not," Sam said softly. He put it back and pulled out a black sweatshirt. Over the breast pocket was a small drawing of Sister North's face etched in gold. It cost forty-five dollars.

"Good store if you the Pope on vacation," Willie said, moving away. "I'm going to the bait store down the street. I'll see you there maybe."

"Maybe," Sam said. The door jingled again when Willie left. Sam put the sweatshirt back and headed toward the front of the store. The clerk was leaning on the counter, engrossed in what Sam assumed was some sort of Christian punk rock magazine.

"Do you have any other clothes here?" he asked.

The clerk straightened up, confused again. "What do you mean?"

"You know, without pictures of crosses and things."

"Oh. No. Sorry. All we have is Jesus and Sister North wear. We don't have like normal stuff here."

Sam nodded and glanced at the clerk's black-and-purple Mötley Crüe T-shirt. "When do you think you'll be getting more of Sister North's books in?"

"I don't know. They're kind of hard to get lately. We've been selling a ton of them mail order. Everyone's stocking up because of the rumor."

"What rumor?"

"That she's real sick."

Sam jumped a little. "Who's sick? Sister North is sick?"

"Yeah. That's what I heard. It's on the Internet. That's why she left town. She's being treated somewhere. In England or someplace. That's what that woman told me this morning. Everyone wants a copy of her signed book in case she dies. Could be worth a lot. We're the only place that has signed copies. She won't sign them anywhere else."

"What's wrong with her?"

"I don't know," the clerk said. He lowered his eyebrows and looked serious. "You know, maybe I shouldn't have told you that. It's just a rumor."

"I won't tell anyone," Sam said.

"Promise?"

"Promise." He left the store.

He strolled down Main Street toward the harbor and stopped and stood in the middle of the circle of mud where the statue had been, scanning the sky, looking for clues. He stood there for a while, before crossing the street and wandering into Tony's Tackle Box, the store the trolley driver owned. The building was slanted at an off-angle because of the storm, and Sam initially felt disoriented in it. Everything—fishing rods, lures, boots, caps, and T-shirts—was scrunched together in a corner as if they had slid there. At the top of the slight incline were the counter and two large tanks that presumably contained live bait somewhere in the murky, green water.

Willie and Tony were leaning over the counter, facing each other, studying a fishing magazine. Neither of them looked up when Sam approached.

"They're garbage fish," Tony said. "And they're mean."

"Lousy sons of bitches," Willie said.

"They eat everything in sight."

Willie shook his head. "Mean mothers. They bite people?"

"Been known to. Yeah."

Willie pursed his lips. "So, these things are like little sharks?"

"They can't eat people. Not entirely. You know what I use when I fish for them? A little piece of a rag dipped in motor oil."

"You shitting me," Willie said. "Motor oil?"

"They love the stuff. Swear to God. They're dumb. Probably the dumbest of all the fish."

Willie took this in. "Dumb fish, huh? What's the smartest fish then?"

Tony squinted. "That's a tough one. I got to say trout. Got to go with trout. They're like miniature dolphins IQ-wise. And dolphins are like people. Dumb people, but still, you know, they have human-style intelligence. They did a study once that said they could drive cars if they had arms."

"That's pretty smart," Willie said. He straightened up when he saw Sam. "Hey, that's my partner, Mr. Sammy," Willie said. "Tony, the driver here, is teaching me the ways of the carp. Mean, dirty fish."

"I've heard they can be pretty tough," Sam said. He walked over to a shelf filled with T-shirts and picked one out. It had a graphic drawing of two fish having sex. One of the fish had a huge, human-style penis. Sam put the shirt down, picked out another one. It had a picture of a small mouse having sex with an elephant from behind. Sam put that one back too. When he glanced over at Tony, he saw that he was grinning at him.

"Dress for success," Tony said.

"Do you have any other clothes?" Sam asked.

"What do you mean?"

"Just plain shirts? Without, you know." Sam pointed to the shelf.

Tony's face had a look of total incomprehension on it. When he pushed away from the counter, Sam could see that his own T-shirt sported two men in a boat, using their penises as fishing rods. "You mean you want a shirt without a picture of a dick on it?"

"Yes," Sam said. "They're more my style."

"I don't got any like that," Tony said. "If you want a shirt like that, you got to go somewhere else."

"Where?"

"Milwaukee. Minneapolis, maybe."

"Wild shirts," Willie said. He leafed through the magazine. "Humorous."

"It's a gag. An adult book store on the interstate was going out of business a few years ago, and I got them cheap," Tony said. "Men buy them, go out fishing, maybe not catch anything, but at least they've got the funny shirt. A little memento to remember the weekend.

They aren't selling too hot anymore though. In the old days, used to sell a lot of them. Before the nun took over. Now the zombies just buy God clothes."

"So there's no other place I can buy clothes at?"

Tony shrugged. "Leo and Jack got some shirts, promotional shirts, at their restaurant. You know, sweatshirts. They always got some promotion going on over there. They got something going on tonight. I was thinking of heading over there."

"A Beatles thing," Sam said.

"Yeah, something like that. Two old mean son of a bitches always got a scam going. Making money hand over fist. They own the whole town. One waiting until the other one dies so he can get it all. They hate each other. I feel sorry for the girl. She's sort of in the middle."

"Who?" Sam asked. "Meg?"

"Yeah. She's so hot. I listen to her show all the time."

"What show?" Sam asked. When he approached the counter, he noticed that the very top of Tony's forehead had faint, black smudges on it. At first, he thought it was dirt, but then realized it was probably traces of hair dye. Tony's hair was jet-black, and he looked to be at least fifty.

"Radio show," Tony said. He reached behind him and turned on the clock radio that was on a shelf. "She's the DJ. Plays oldies. Big Jack owns the station out on the highway, by the college. He's always after her to play Christian rock, but she won't do it. That's her now." He turned up the volume. Sam heard a woman talking about an upcoming charity softball game in another town. He closed his eyes. It was definitely Meg, though she sounded odd, hesitant.

"This ain't live. She tapes the show. I heard this show last week. It's like a rerun. I complain about that to her, but she never listens to me. She's pissed at me because I don't advertise. That's why she doesn't come in here much. She used to when she first came back."

"Where'd she come back from?" Willie asked.

Tony lowered the radio. "California. She was a big-time runner. Almost made the Olympics, but she fell. I used to go see her run at high school track meets over in Princeville. We all did. She was hot back then. She used to ignore us. She's always been a man hater."

Willie looked up from the magazine. "You mean a lesbian?"

Tony considered Willie's comment. "I don't think she's one of those yet. But she's getting there, getting ready to cross over. Personally, I think all women are part-gay, secretly, part-gay. At least the ones I know. They don't know it themselves maybe, but down deep, it's brewing inside of them. That's my theory."

Willie nodded and slowly turned a page in the magazine. "Good theory," he said. "Maybe you should send her some of your shirts. Get her in the mood, get her thinking along those lines."

Tony lightly patted the top of his black hair. "Yeah, well, I'd like to give her more than a shirt."

"What's the story with her uncles?" Sam asked. "How come they hate each other?"

"Oh, Jesus, lots of reasons, lots of reasons," he said. He briefly picked at something inside his ear. "Basically, they kind of fight over her, that's what I think. Big Jack and Leo raised her. Big Jack's an asshole, and Leo's basically all right, most days. So they're different in that regard. Hey, you know Big Jack's got a fake leg, don't you?"

"What you mean?" Willie asked.

"What do you mean, what do I mean? He's got a fake leg. Ain't real. Phony."

"He got a wooden leg?"

"Naw, it ain't wooden. It's something else. Plastic I think. Won't rot. I seen it once. It's water-resistant. He swims with it."

"What happened to his real leg?" Willie asked.

Tony waved a hand. "Got blowed off, or something, destroyed. It happened in World War II. According to Jack, it was all Leo's fault. They were both in the air force. Leo was a navigator. Big Jack was a paratrooper. It was like D day or something, and there was some mix-up and they ended up on the same plane, which wasn't supposed to happen to brothers. Anyway, Leo got things all screwed up and dropped all the paratroopers off in the wrong place. They all landed right in the middle of the wrong place."

"Where did they end up?" Sam asked. Mention of World War II made him nostalgic for the History Channel.

"To hear Big Jack tell it, he landed in Hitler's backyard during the middle of his birthday party. Anyway, Big Jack got captured, so he blames Leo. I don't know the rest of the details. I think some Nazi broke Jack's leg or something. Cut it off. He never wears shorts, but I seen his leg from time to time. It's a real phony all right." Tony stretched. "Anyway, you guys gonna buy anything or what? I'm just talking here."

Willie put down the magazine. "You buying a shirt, Sam?"

"No." The Tackle Box was hot and damp and he needed air. Sam started toward the door, then stopped.

"Hey, have you heard that Sister North is sick?" he asked Tony.

Tony looked surprised, his eyebrows rising. "I didn't hear nothing about that. She's old. Sooner or later, she's going to kick, then this town is going to dry up and blow away, just like that statue. Hey, tell me that whole statue thing isn't weird. I mean, we can't find it? Like it vanished? Come on. Big Jack had me out there again this morning. No trace of the thing. The thing had to weigh a ton. It was all bronze. The whole thing is strange."

"Yeah. This town kind of strange," Willie said. He yawned and turned a page of the magazine. "But I like it all right. Quiet."

"Yeah, well, it ain't that quiet when the nun is around. Like a three-ring circus. You should see the freak cases walking around. Sick, dying, cripples. I blur my eyes when I walk down the street sometimes. I don't want to see too clearly. It affects my appetite. But, you know, they come here for help, I guess, so you got to feel sorry for them." Tony looked at Sam. "The nun is medically intuitive, you know. She can figure certain things out."

"That's what I heard," Sam said.

"She diagnosed my cousin's disease right away," Tony said. "He came all the way from Duluth. Figured it right out by looking at him." He snapped his fingers. "Instantaneously."

"What did he have?" Willie asked. "Cancer?"

"Worse." Tony shook his head. "Herpes."

"Herpes bad, man."

"Yeah, tell me about it. Came as a shock to him. Shocked his girlfriend, too. She was standing right next to him when the nun told him. Ex-girlfriend now."

"Bad way to find that out," Willie said. "Maybe she should have sent him a letter. Keep things private that way. That's the way I would have liked to find something like that out."

Tony yawned. "Yeah, well, the nun don't work that way. Tells it like it is. God's Straight Shooter and everything. She's all right. It's not her fault this place is nuts. Mostly its Jack's and Leo's and Louis's fault. Those three, what a pair."

Without warning, Tony pulled off his T-shirt and put on a new, blue golf shirt with a cross on it. "I'm heading up to her house now, making a run up there. You two coming?"

"Why are you going there?" Sam asked. "She's not home."

"There's some volunteer meeting. They're organizing some kind of cleanup effort for the nun's house. Nun people, the zombies, are coming in to fix her house because of the storm. It's some bullshit thing; I'm sure Big Jack or Leo is behind it to get people to come here. They probably trashed the house themselves; I wouldn't put it past them."

Sam felt himself sag. Lack of sleep was catching up with him, and he needed to take a nap. The prospect of a trolley ride, then work, seemed impossible.

"Meg is organizing the thing," Tony said. "She'll be there."

Sam immediately perked up. He stretched his arms toward the ceiling and bounced a bit on his toes. "Yeah," he said. "Maybe I'll go."

. . .

The trolley picked up Patrick, Lila, and Dot in front of the court-house, but it had to wait for close to an hour for other volunteers at Big Jack's. By the time they got to Lasonia Woods, Sam was dead asleep.

"We have to stop here," Tony said.

Sam jumped awake and looked around. They were on the small road that led to Sister North's house.

"Why don't you take us to the house?" Willie asked. He was sit-ting across the aisle from Sam, behind Patrick and Lila.

"It's too muddy. I don't want to get stuck. You'll have to walk from here. It ain't too far. I'll be back in about two hours."

"Well, we'll get our exercise," Patrick said. He stood up and offered Lila his arm.

"You coming?" Willie asked.

Sam tried to stand, but was too tired. He was going on close to two days with no sleep, and the initial momentum he had felt at the Tackle Box over the prospect of seeing Meg had long since evapo-rated.

"You know, I'll catch up with you guys. Give me a few minutes."

"You okay?" Willie asked. Lila turned and gave him a concerned look.

"Just tired."

Willie shrugged. "See you up there, maybe," he said.

Sam watched as the others disappeared, Lila and Patrick holding hands, Dot, Willie, the burned ladies, and the man with the white robe following them. With their heads bent, they looked like retreat-ing refugees, defeated and lost.

He closed his eyes and listened to the tree branches stir in a soft wind. He was just slipping back into sleep, when Tony yelled, "Hey, what are you doing?"

Sam popped up in his seat, not sure where he was. He cleared his throat. "Nothing," he said. "Resting."

Tony moved back and sat in the seat ahead of him. He lit up a cigarette and shook his head.

"These nun people crack me up, swear to God they do," he said. "Working for free like that." He motioned toward the dirt road, in the direction the group had headed. "This crowd ain't so bad, though. At least there ain't no cripples. Those women, though; Jesus, can they put a bag over their faces? I mean, I feel sorry for them and everything, but that don't mean I got to look at them all day." He took a drag on his cigarette. "Still, they're better than the young zombies who come up here, the teenagers. Those are the real nuts. Go around reading the Bible all the time. Quoting scripture. Smiling like they're drunk. All the broads look like hell. Fat, braces. Zits. The nun is their only hope, that's why they come here. They can't afford plastic surgery. They come up here and pray for new faces."

Sam stood up. "Hey, where you going?" Tony asked.

"To the house."

Tony took another drag, shook his head, and snorted. "The house," he said.

Sam headed up the hill, walking through slants of sunlight that shot through the pine trees, brightening the road in patches. The lake came into view on his left, shining and calm. He paused to catch his breath before walking on.

Eventually, the road met up with the low stone wall that signaled the approach to Sister North's house. Unable to go any farther, he sat down on top of the wall and closed his eyes again, allowing the stillness of the woods to surround him.

He was in a drowsy fog, wondering what he was feeling—contentment, exhaustion—when he heard someone approaching.

"Hey."

He opened his eyes and saw Meg striding up the hill, her eyes fixed on him. She was wearing blue sweatpants and a shapeless gray sweatshirt that covered her like a bag.

"You lost?" she asked as she approached.

"No."

"You coming then?"

He slid off the wall. "I'm on my way."

"Take your time," she said. "We won't start for a while." She passed him without stopping.

He watched her walk in and out of shadows and light, admiring her grace, the synchronicity of her arms and legs. She was out of sight in seconds.

He rested for a few more minutes, then resumed his hike. The road continued to run uphill, though, and after only a few minutes, he was forced to stop and sit down on the stone wall again. He was fantasizing about taxicabs, when he noticed a small sign nailed to a tree a few yards in front of him: CHAPEL IN THE PINES. The sign marked the beginning of a path that led off into the woods. Sam stood up, glanced over his shoulder once, and left the road.

The narrow path was blanketed with soft brown pine needles and rambled uphill, around rocks and exposed tree roots. Gradually, it broadened, and he soon found himself in a small clearing filled with a number of wooden benches carved from logs. At the front of the clearing was a large, six-foot cross made from thick tree branches. Sam gazed at the cross, then sat down on one of the rough benches and tried to lose himself again in the silence and the shade.

If ever there were a time to be reflective, this was it, he thought. He closed his eyes and tried to conjure up something appropriate, about his life, his parents, Maureen, but all he could think of was the movie *Cool Hand Luke*. He had watched it at the Get Down. He remembered the ending, when Paul Newman escaped from the chain gang and hid in an old wooden church. Paul Newman prayed, asking God to talk to him, send him a sign. "All right, old man," he said after some time. He got down on his knees and prayed some more. Finally, he opened one eye, looked up at heaven, and smirked. No sign. No God. When Paul Newman stood back up, he was shot.

Sam opened one eye, did not smirk, but did not pray. Instead, he just looked at the cross and waited.

"Hello, there, yes, hello. I didn't think I'd find you up here."

Sam turned and saw Patrick emerging from the trees, using a stick as a cane. His heart sank. "Hello," he said.

Patrick sat down in front of him with a heavy sigh and wiped his forehead with the back of his hand.

"Nothing to do at the house yet," he said. "The whole effort seems poorly planned. No one's even sure when the meeting is supposed to start. Saw the sign for the chapel on the way up, and I grew curious. It was built by one of her flock. They don't even have a church in this town. Apparently, this is it."

Sam stared at the back of Patrick's neck, which was beet red.

"Yes, sir," Patrick said. "An interesting place, I suppose." He grew quiet. "Yes, sir," he said again.

They sat in silence for a few minutes, Sam growing more and more uncomfortable. He didn't like sitting there in the woods with Patrick. He had wanted to be alone.

"You a regular churchgoer?" Patrick turned to ask this question.

"No."

"Well I am. But I go to please Lila. I admit that. I admit that to you, not to Lila. She's a strong believer. Has faith. I admire that. Always did. I wish I had it. Most of the time when I go to church, my mind wanders. I can't keep it focused on the sermon. I try, but I start thinking about other things. What we're going to have for dinner. What has to get done around the ranch. What football game I'm going to watch that afternoon." He shook his head. "You like football?"

"Yes. I like football."

Patrick sighed again. "I like football, too. My son Todd was a football player. For the University of Nebraska. He was a Cornhusker.

You ever hear of them? You must have if you like football. They're a national power."

"Yeah, I know them," Sam said.

"Of course you do. He walked on, but he stuck with it, and, his senior year, they gave him a scholarship, a full ride. He was a safety, a defensive back. He actually played a little in the Orange Bowl. We used to go to all the games and watch him standing on the sidelines in his uniform. Here." Patrick fumbled for his wallet in his back pocket, slowly withdrew a photograph, and handed it to Sam.

It was a picture of the inside of a football stadium. There was a long line of players standing on the sidelines watching the game, their backs to the camera. The picture was taken over the heads of people and was slightly out of focus.

"Todd is number ninety-eight," Patrick said. He took the photo back and carefully replaced it in his wallet. "We haven't heard from him in almost a year now. One day he didn't come home from work. He lived in Lincoln. He was in the insurance business. He's dead now. I know it. Lila thinks he'll come back. Thinks coming here will help." When he said this he gazed blankly at the ground.

"How do you know he's dead?"

"I just do. Where else would he be? We've looked everywhere. Called the police. The FBI even got involved. We hired a private detective. Best one in Nebraska. Actually, we've hired a few."

"People leave all the time," Sam said. "Then they come back."

Patrick looked up at the cross. "No. He's gone. I'm sure of that. Todd was into a lot of things, his whole life. Things his mother didn't know about. In and out of trouble, his whole life." He didn't say more, left it at that.

Sam rose and put his hands in his pockets, aware of every gesture. Patrick continued to stare at the cross while sitting slumped over on the bench.

"I wasn't a very good father to him. I know that now. I knew it then, too. I always put myself first, wasn't there for him. I was always working on the ranch, or away. I was gone long stretches of time. Six months, eight months. I would come home sometimes, and I wouldn't recognize him. He would change so much, so fast. Grow taller. Stronger. Once I came home and he had a little mustache. He must have been fifteen, sixteen by then. As soon as I saw it, I made him shave it off I was so damn mad."

"Why were you mad?"

"Because he grew up. I was angry at myself, though, not him. I knew it was too late. Knew I had been gone too long. Loving a child isn't enough. You have to be there, too, you have to be there."

"Where were you?" Sam asked.

Patrick sighed and waved the question away. "I was everywhere. It's a long story. I tried to make up for it, tried to get involved, but it was too late. There are certain things you have to do when your children are young; otherwise, the damage is done. You never make up the distance. Never catch up. Do you have kids?"

"No."

"You don't? Well, I don't know if that's good or bad to be honest. Life is easier, I imagine, without them. Not having children minimizes your room for error. It's a never-ending task." He pointed up at the cross. "Are you religious?"

"Not really."

"I used to be. I used to pray when I was young. Said my prayers every night. Every damn night," Patrick said. He turned around again quickly and looked at Sam as if seeing him for the first time.

"What's your name? Here I am talking to you like I know you, and I don't think we've formally met."

"Sam. Sam Gamett."

"Well, I'm Patrick Carlson," he said. He reached out and they shook hands. "Well, I didn't mean to burden you with my problems.

Thank you for listening." He stood up and looked past Sam into the woods. "You ready to head back down that path?"

"Yeah," Sam said. "I'm ready."

"It's a little tricky."

"I know," Sam said. "I know."

Thirteen

It's a long and winding road," Tony said as he poured himself a beer from one of the pitchers on the table. "That's probably my favorite Beatles number. Sums up my life. You know, driving the trolley. Driven that thing a lot of long and winding miles."

"Yeah, a lot of curves in the road up here," Willie said. "Been noticing that."

"Tell me about it. You got to be sober when you drive up here. And not just a little. I mean sober, completely."

They were sitting at a table by the boarded-up window at Big Jack's waiting for the Beatles part of Beatles Night to begin. For the past hour, they had been watching Meg as she methodically set up equipment near the far end of the bar, barricading herself behind speakers, microphones, and turntables. She worked alone, lifting, plugging, and hooking things up, oblivious to the fact that a roomful of people were watching her and waiting for the show.

"Lot of people here," Willie said. "Most people I ever seen since I got here. Too bad none of them came to the nun's house to help out."

The meeting at Sister North's house had been blissfully brief.

Only a handful of people had shown up and Meg, clearly disappointed by the small turnout, dismissed the group with an abrupt wave and a promise to reschedule the next day.

"Yeah, place is packed," Tony said.

Sam finished his beer and scanned the room. Big Jack's was close to packed. The man in the wheelchair was sitting a few tables over in his sweatshirt, sipping a soda from a straw. Another man, shockingly white, held the bottle for him. The two burned ladies were there as well, brightly attired and drinking large frothy cocktails, tiny green umbrellas protruding from their oversize glasses. Another woman, with a horrible scar across her neck, was hovering over the jukebox, shaking her head to a Beach Boys song. Off in the corner, two teenage girls held hands and prayed, their lips moving in silence.

"You remember that bar scene in *Star Wars?*" Tony asked. "Welcome to Big Jack's on Saturday night. All we're missing is a midget. We used to get a lot of them up here. Don't see them much anymore though. Hey, see that guy over there? He may be nut number one." He pointed to the bald man in the flowing white robe whom Sam had seen right after the storm. He was eating a hot dog with one hand, chewing vigorously. When he saw them looking his way, he winked and nodded.

"How you doing tonight, Judas?" Tony yelled to the man.

The man swallowed. "Lazarus," he said, and smiled.

"My mistake," Tony said. Then he said, "You fucking nut," under his breath.

Most of the other people were elderly and healthy-looking, content, it seemed, with watching Meg work. A small and definitely out-of-place group of college kids stood by the bar drinking beer and eating french fries, bopping up and down to the Beach Boys song. Sam watched them bop as they dipped fries in ketchup.

"Where those kids come from?" Willie asked. He had pulled out a deck of cards and was shuffling them.

"There's a college about an hour away," Tony said. He filled Sam's glass, then stood up. "Going to get some more," he said.

One of the college kids, a tall, thin boy wearing a backward baseball cap, walked over to Meg and was soon helping her plug in some wires. Sam considered offering to help, but thought the better of it, afraid she might accept. He knew next to nothing about hooking up sound equipment, or any equipment for that matter. He decided to stick with his one area of expertise: He picked up his beer and quickly drank it.

"Well, well, look who changed their minds."

Sam looked up, just as Dot Pelgers sat down next to him, purposely bumping his shoulder in the process. Sam nodded hello.

"Are you boys ready to boogie?"

Dot wiggled in her seat and looked over at Willie, who was pulling out all the colored cards from the deck and laying them on the table in a straight line.

"Playing a little cards, are we?" Dot asked. She took out her gold cigarette case and flipped it open. "Mind if I smoke?"

"No." Sam picked up his empty glass and searched for Tony.

Dot took a deep drag. "You a cardplayer?" she asked Willie.

"No. Do magic."

Dot narrowed her eyes. "Want me to tell your fortune?" she asked.

Willie stopped sorting. "What, you mean . . . with the cards?"

"Yeah. I can do that. I'm good at it, too."

Willie collected all the cards and pushed them toward Dot.

"All right. Tell me how rich I'm gonna be."

Dot picked up the cards and shuffled them, then placed them in the center of the table. "What's your name again?"

"Willie."

"Okay, Willie, pick three cards from the bottom of the deck."

"The bottom? Okay. The bottom." Willie pulled three cards from the deck.

"Now pick three from the top."

"Take three more," Willie said. "I'll do that."

"Now, put the first three on the table, faceup. Then put the next three facedown on the table, on top of the other cards."

Willie did this slowly, carefully arranging the cards. "Now what?"

"Now we'll see what they say," Dot said. She turned one card over, a seven of clubs. The card beneath it was a nine of spades.

"That first group is your past," Dot said. "You have lived an interesting life, Willie. Exciting. Full of danger."

Willie's eyes widened.

"Yeah. Sometimes a little dangerous."

"You're a risk taker. You take risks."

Willie suddenly looked serious. He puffed up his chest and glanced around the room. "Yeah," he said softly. "Sometimes do that."

"You've moved around a lot."

"Yeah. I'm always somewhere."

"Now flip over the next card. Those two tell you about your character."

Willie paused for a moment, uncertain, it seemed, on whether he wanted Dot to go on. Finally, he said, "Character," and flipped over the next card, the six of hearts. Under it was the six of spades.

"Two sixes," Willie said. "That good?"

"Very interesting. Very unique," Dot said. She studied the cards for a long time and tapped her index finger on the tabletop. "Very unique."

"What?" Willie asked.

"You're one thing," Dot slowly said.

"Yeah?"

"And another."

Willie thought about this, then agreed. "Yeah," he said. "That's me, all right. Complicated."

Over Dot's shoulder, Sam saw Patrick and Lila enter the bar and make their way over to the far side of the room toward a table.

Patrick was wearing his safari hat and a black windbreaker that had U.S. ARMY written in large, gold letters on the back.

"You are a very intelligent person, Willie. Smart. Strong. Reliable."

Willie nodded gravely.

"And brave. You're brave."

"Yeah," Willie said.

"You don't fear many things."

"Naw, I ain't afraid of shit."

"You embrace challenges."

Willie nodded. "Some days I'm like that. Depends what I got going on."

"Now flip over the last card and let's take a look at your future."

Willie turned the card over with his index finger. It was an eight of hearts. Underneath it was an eight of clubs.

"Two-of-a-kind, again," Willie said. He looked scared. "Kind of weird?"

Dot nodded and flicked an ash onto the floor while she studied the two cards. "Two eights. I've never seen this before."

Willie leaned forward and nervously licked his upper lip. "What's that mean? Gonna die?"

Dot was quiet. "I don't think so," she said absentmindedly. She was still focusing on the cards.

Willie looked very nervous. He leaned even closer to Dot. "What do you mean, don't *think* so?"

Dot kept her eyes trained on the cards. "I think it means you're at a crossroad."

"What's that mean, crossroad?"

"It means you will be making some decisions soon, big decisions."

"What do you mean?" Willie asked. Off in the corner, Meg took a seat behind the fortress of speakers and put headphones on. The jukebox was suddenly quiet, and people rearranged their tables and chairs to face the bar.

"It means you might be making some changes soon."

"Kind of changes?"

"I'm not sure," Dot said.

"Something bad going to happen to me?" he asked.

"It's not about bad or good. It's about decisions."

"Decisions." Willie leaned back and exhaled loudly. "Nothing else? That it? All you got?"

Dot looked at the cards a few seconds longer, then quickly scooped them into her hand with one swoop. "That's all I got," she said.

Willie chewed on his upper lip. Then he pushed away from the table and stood up.

"Where are you going?" Sam asked. "The show is starting."

Willie just shrugged and headed for the bar.

"Welcome to Beatles Night," Meg said. "I'm Meg Lodge." She immediately played the song "A Hard Day's Night," without any introduction.

"Good song," Dot said. She began shaking her head and snapping her fingers.

Meg followed "A Hard Day's Night" with "I Want to Hold Your Hand" and "She Loves You." The audience sat politely, listening to the music boom from huge speakers that ringed the room. Meg peered through her bunker over the crowd, her face expressionless. She removed her headphones and fiddled with them.

When she launched into "Paperback Writer," Dot said, "Not much of a show. I expected something more than this." She tapped on the table. "We need to get this place moving." She grabbed hold of Sam's wrist. "Come on, let's dance."

"No," Sam said. He pulled his arm gently but firmly away.

"Come on!" Dot said.

"I don't want to. I really don't."

"If you don't, I'll dance by myself."

"Be my guest," Sam said.

Dot started to rise, then sat again. "I'm not going to dance by myself," she said. "I've only had one drink. Where's your friend, Willie?"

"I don't know."

"Well, I'm not going to dance by myself."

After the last song finished, Tony finally returned, holding a pitcher of beer with one hand and a stack of new plastic cups with the other. He placed the pitcher in the middle of the table before sitting next to Dot. "Evening, Dorothy," he said. He saluted her with one finger.

Dot nodded and smiled, a slightly amused look on her face. "Tony." She reached over and took a plastic cup and poured herself some beer.

"Everyone?" she asked, holding out the pitcher.

Sam and Tony nodded.

"This Meg, I don't know," she said as she poured. "She's not very lively. I think you have to be lively to be a DJ."

"Yeah," Tony said. He took his beer from Dot and sipped some foam off the top. "I think she needs to talk more. She's lacking in that department."

"She's odd," Dot said. "A little . . . what's the word?"

"Aloof," Sam said. He drank some beer and tasted mostly foam. Dot was a terrible beer pourer.

"Here's a good one," Meg said. "It's not really a Beatles song. It's by John Lennon." She flipped a switch and the song "Imagine" filled the room.

"This is a sad song," Dot said. She closed her eyes and rocked her head gently back and forth. "Makes me think."

"About what?" Tony asked.

"About heaven." She opened her eyes and motioned over to Meg and the music. "The line from the song, 'Imagine there's no heaven.' Do you ever think about that?"

Tony shrugged. "Not too often. Usually I'm pretty busy." He finished his beer and poured himself another one.

Dot stared at the boarded-up window. "You know," she said, "I used to work for a big accounting firm. I was an executive assistant. This was before I started selling cosmetics. I worked in an office that didn't have any windows. Anyway, every day, at six o'clock, the lights in the building would go out for one minute. It had something to do with the electricity. The building had to switch over to a different generator at night or something. Every night, everything would go black for exactly sixty seconds, you couldn't see your hand in front of your face it was so dark. You couldn't do anything. All you could do was wait, think. At first I didn't mind it, it was okay sitting there, only a minute. Then it got so I hated it, then finally I got scared of it. I kept thinking, what if the lights never go back on? I mean, what if this is it? Just this darkness. It used to scare me, just sitting there alone in the pitch-black, thinking, waiting for the lights to go back on. It used to scare me a lot."

They were all quiet, the music washing over them. Sam's thoughts went immediately to Maureen. He saw her pretty face, blue eyes closed forever, lost in darkness, searching for light. He closed his own eyes for a moment, and when he opened them he saw Dot stand up and walk over to Patrick and Lila's table. Tony watched her go, a serious, almost melancholy look on his face. Finally, he turned to Sam, and said, "She has a pretty good rack on her, don't you think?"

"I'm going to the bathroom," Sam said.

He stood up, walked toward the bar, and smiled as he passed Meg. She looked at him and leaned into the microphone, and said, "'Help!'"

Sam stopped. "What?" he asked.

An instant later, the song "Help!" blasted through the massive speakers. Sam jumped back a little and kept walking.

Inside the bathroom, he splashed cold water on his face, rubbing his hands over the back of his neck. When he returned to the table, Willie was in Dot's old chair, pouring Tony a beer.

"Place thinning out," Willie said.

Sam took in the half-empty room. Almost all of the older couples had left, but most of the college kids were still present. "This Beatles thing, kind of a bust," Willie said. "No point to it."

"Yeah, not too organized," Tony said. "I was expecting more, a little something else. You know, dance contests, prizes, Beatles impersonators, costumes."

Sam saw Meg staring into nothing as "Hey Jude" played. He poured a fresh beer and headed toward her, working around tables and chairs, concentrating on not spilling his drink on Big Jack's floor.

"Here, looks like you need this," he said.

Momentarily confused, Meg took the beer and drank off half. "This sucks," she said.

"It's all right," Sam said. "You still have some people here."

Meg finished the beer and handed him the empty cup. "I'm going to play some more songs. I may as well. It took so long to set everything up."

Sam returned to the table and started in on another pitcher of beer, listening to Meg work her way through dozens of Beatles songs, songs he remembered singing and dancing to when he was a boy, in high school, in college. He finished the pitcher, then a new one that magically appeared before him. Soon, he was rocking his head back and forth, letting the music flow through him. The Beatles, he thought, were all good guys. All of them. Happy, funny. They were the best. The best. Too bad half of them are dead. He remembered watching them on the *Ed Sullivan Show*, imitating them with a tennis racket. His mother laughed as he danced and sang in front of the TV. Do Paul, Sammy, do Paul, his mother would urge, and he would shake his head and sing, his eyes bright and wide. Do John, Sammy, do John, and he would sing and dance. Do George, do George, and he would continue to play and jump around, trying to look as earnest and as happy as the Beatles seemed. When his mother urged him to do Ringo, though, he would put the tennis racket down. "I don't do Ringo," he would say. "He looks ugly." His mother laughed until she cried. He poured more beer. His mother was always eager to laugh, a fact his father had noted in her eulogy.

Eventually, Meg took a break. It was only then that Sam noticed that Big Jack's was almost empty. Only three or four college kids remained, nursing their beers and talking loudly.

When Meg returned, Sam saw she had changed into shorts and a T-shirt. She moved behind her barricade again, and, without pausing, said, "Thanks for coming, everyone." The college kids clapped and whistled.

"One more, one more," Sam yelled from across the room.

The college kids took up the chant and began yelling, "One more, one more" as well. They sounded as drunk as Sam.

Meg smiled. "What do you want to hear?"

" 'Dear Prudence,' " Sam yelled, a second before the college kids started shouting their requests. Meg rolled her eyes, but put it on.

Sam walked up to her. "Let's dance," he said.

Meg's eyes went wide. "You can't dance to this song."

Sam held his arms out to her. "If you don't dance with me, I'm going to fall down."

Meg stared at him. He wasn't sure if she was smiling or grimacing.

"I've had exactly forty-six beers," he said. "I'm going to fall down right here. And it's going to be your fault for keeping me up all night burying a horse."

She looked at him a little longer, then walked out from behind the equipment and took his hands. They danced slowly, their bodies only inches apart. When Sam tried to lean into her, she pulled away.

"You're really good," he said.

"You're really drunk."

"I'm not drunk. I'm happy. Happy to be dancing with you."

"You'd be happy dancing with Tony right now."

"I'm asking him next," Sam said as he twirled her around.

When they finished, the college kids hooted and hollered, and one of the boys asked Meg to dance.

"In your dreams," she said, unplugging some equipment.

Sam sat on the floor and watched her work. He saw her T-shirt ride up her back when she bent over, and saw the tops of her white panties when she stretched to reach. He was sitting there in a happy daze, just watching her, when he heard a voice.

"What are you staring at?" It was Big Jack. He was standing over him, looking down, smiling.

"Nothing." Sam smiled back. Meg disappeared into the kitchen. "Just taking in the sights." He winked at Big Jack. Big Jack's smile grew.

"You think she's pretty?" Big Jack asked.

"I definitely do. And I've seen a lot of women, trust me."

"You have, have you?

Sam laughed. "You know how many women have wanted me?"

Big Jack folded his arms across his chest. "No, tell me."

Sam laughed and pounded the floor with his hand once. "A lot. That's all I have to say. A lot."

"Is that so?" Big Jack shook his head, then motioned for Sam to stand up. "Hey, buddy, come here a second," he said. "I need a hand in the bathroom. It'll just take a second." He again motioned for Sam to follow him. "Come on. I need you to help me move something."

"Sure," Sam said, getting to his feet. "I'm here to please."

"I bet you are," Big Jack said,

As soon as they got into the bathroom, Big Jack locked the door behind them.

"Someone told me you used to be a priest," he said.

Sam laughed again and held on to the edge of the sink to steady himself. The bathroom was spinning slightly. "I thought I told you, I never was a priest."

"Oh yeah, that's right," Big Jack said. Then he walked close to Sam and punched him in the stomach.

Sam fell to the ground on his knees, struggling to breathe. Big Jack grabbed him under the arms and pulled him up.

"Listen, buddy," he said, his burned red nose inches from Sam's face. "If you so much as look at her again, I'll kill you, you understand? You leave her the hell alone." He jammed a finger into Sam's chest. "She's been through enough in her life."

"Look at who?" Sam asked. He tried to smile though he was having a hard time breathing.

"My niece," Big Jack said.

Sam's head momentarily cleared. "Oh, yeah, that's right, she's your niece. I didn't think about that."

"Well, here's a little reminder, just so you don't forget again," Big Jack said. He reached back, and, this time, he hit Sam in the mouth.

Meg found him lying facedown on the bathroom floor a minute later. She was holding an ice bag.

"Are you all right?" she asked. She helped him roll over and pressed the ice to his mouth.

"I'm fine."

"Jack's an asshole sometimes."

Sam sat up. "You really think so?"

"Come on," she said. She took his hand. "Let's get out of here."

They walked out of the restaurant and down the road for a while to the harbor and sat on the stone bench. Sam kept taking deep breaths, the cool air clearing his head.

"How's your mouth?" Meg asked.

Sam puckered his lips and gently worked his jaw around. "Okay."

"He used to box in the army. He's still pretty tough."

"Yeah. Well, he's just lucky I was drunk."

"Oh yeah, what would you have done if you weren't?"

"Ducked."

"Well, sorry about this. Jack is pretty protective."

Sam moved his jaw around again. It felt fine, though he wondered if it was because he was still drunk. "He's just looking out for his favorite niece," he said.

"Yeah, I guess you're right. I mean, I am only thirty-six."

Sam laughed a little and held the ice bag to his mouth again.

"Pretty shitty night," Meg said.

"It wasn't so bad. The Beatles music was good."

Meg studied her fingertips. "I'm not a very good DJ. It's hard. I just started."

"Why did you become one?"

"Maria, Sister North, told me to try it. She thought it would be good for me."

"Why?"

Meg kept examining her fingers. "I don't know. Make me talk more. I'm not much of a talker."

"Talking can be overrated," Sam said. He dropped the ice bag on the ground and worked his jaw around one last time. His mouth really did feel fine.

"Sister North seems like one clever nun," he said.

"She's smart. She's always thinking about ways to help."

"Has she ever helped you?" Sam asked.

Meg was quiet. "She helps a lot of people," she finally said.

They stared out at the dark lake. The wind had shifted, and the waves had picked up, running hard against the rocks. Sam touched his jaw again, then, without warning, put his arm around Meg and kissed her.

"Well, I can see your mouth still works," she said. She kissed him back, hard, and stood up.

"What are you doing?" Sam asked.

"Going for a run."

Sam was confused. "Run? You're kidding, right? We were in the middle of something."

Meg smiled a little, and her shoulders shook in a silent laugh. "We were at the end."

"It's after midnight. It's too dark to run."

Meg started her stretching routine, bending down and touching her toes. "What difference does that make?"

"You can't see where you're going," Sam said.

"I have X-ray vision." She squinted at him. "I can see through things."

The scene had changed entirely too fast for Sam. He watched her stretch for a few more seconds.

"Well, I'm coming then," he said. "I used to run in high school. I'll run with you."

Meg stopped stretching. She was surprised, the idea of running with someone a foreign concept. "I don't run with other people," she said. "I have to go. I'll see you later."

She took off before he could say anything else, disappearing into the darkness. He stood up and was scanning the lakeshore for her shape, when he heard her call out to him.

"Hey! Sam!"

Her voice seemed to be coming from the right, by a patch of trees swaying in the breeze.

"How long are you staying here?" she yelled.

"Where are you?" He moved closer to the trees and into the wind.

"How long are you staying here?"

He continued to look for her. "I don't know. Why?" He stopped beside the trees and searched the shoreline. Still, he couldn't see her.

"I want to know," she said.

"For a while."

The wind picked up, and he was surrounded in the sudden rush.

He stopped walking and reached out and held on to a tree, feeling helpless and lost in the dark.

"That's good," she said, her voice far away.

He stood there, clinging to the sound of her.

"That's good," he said to himself, his heart skipping a beat.

Fourteen

The next morning, Sam and Willie went to Big Jack's for a volunteer breakfast meeting to discuss the rehabbing of Sister North's house.

"They serving a big country breakfast," Willie said, waking Sam up. "That Meg is organizing it. Heard it on the radio. Flapjacks at Big Jack's. No Pop-Tarts."

"I'm not going," Sam said, lying in bed. The prospect of seeing Big Jack again was not especially appealing. He gingerly touched his jaw. It felt a little sore.

Willie started pulling the bedsheet off Sam. "Come on, man. Meg called here personally. She wanted to make sure we came. Says she needs people. She wanted me to tell you that Big Jack won't be there. Wanted you to know that for some reason."

Sam touched his jaw one last time and slowly got out of bed.

When they reached the restaurant, Leo led them to a round table by the bar where Patrick, Lila, Dot, and Tony were quietly eating. They all nodded simultaneously when they saw Sam and Willie.

"Well, that's two more," Patrick said, as they sat down. "That makes six."

"Hey, don't count me in," Tony said. "I'm here for the food. I got other obligations."

Patrick shook his head. "Five then. Not much of a volunteer group."

"More people will come," Lila said, reaching for her coffee cup. "Meg said she's been calling people."

"Seems to me that the size of her flock being what it is, we'd have hundreds of people here," Patrick said.

"This doesn't surprise me," Dot said. "They don't come unless the nun is here, or they know for sure she's coming."

Tony agreed, "The volunteers aren't what they're cracked up to be," he said. "They hole up in their rooms on the Misery Mile and watch cable all day."

"The Misery Mile? Where's that?" Lila asked.

"That's what we call the highway with all those motels. Like a zoo."

Dot put down her coffee. "That's where I'm staying. And you're right, it's depressing."

"Why aren't there more hotels and restaurants in town here?" Patrick asked. "It seems like there would be more."

Tony smirked. "Zoning don't allow for more building. Unless, of course, Big Jack or Leo is doing the building." He leaned forward, over the table. "Big Jack is county zoning commissioner." He smirked again.

Sam kept his head down and ate quickly, devouring a stack of pancakes in a frenzy. He hadn't realized how hungry he was until he smelled the food. He grabbed a handful of bacon from a serving dish and tossed it onto his plate, afraid that if he didn't set some aside, it would be eaten by Tony or Willie, who were eating even more furiously than he.

"They're very good pancakes," Lila said.

"Is there something wrong with your mouth?" Patrick asked. Sam stopped chewing. Patrick was peering at him, his fork in midair. "You're chewing funny."

"Oh," Sam said. "I had an accident. I fell."

"On your mouth?" Patrick asked.

Sam shrugged and returned to his plate. As he ate, he occasionally caught glimpses of Meg peeking out the small, circular window of the swinging kitchen door, her face expressionless.

"Any word about the nun?" Patrick asked. "Any news about her whereabouts?"

"She's in Angola," Dot said. "That's what I heard."

"Where did you hear that?" Patrick asked.

Dot swallowed. "Friend of mine called me. She goes there a lot."

"Your friend goes to Angola?"

"The nun does."

"Where is Angola?" Willie asked.

"Africa," Patrick said.

"Africa," Tony said. "Yeah, she's big into that place."

"She's there for a conference on limb reattachments," Dot said, "for people who lose limbs in wars."

"Now, I've heard a bit of a different story," Patrick said. He stopped chewing and lowered his voice, although it was nothing even close to a whisper. "I heard this nun is sick. Dying maybe."

Lila was alarmed. "Now where did you hear that?"

"A number of sources. A number of the shopkeepers. I've been hearing it since we got here, truth be told. She's off somewhere convalescing. Or trying to. They're trying to keep it quiet."

"I heard that, too," Sam said.

"News to me," Dot said, "and I usually hear about things like that."

They all fell quiet. Sam sipped some coffee.

"Well," Lila said. "All I have to say is God bless Sister North, wherever she is."

"Here," Meg said. She had quietly appeared next to their table, carrying a platter overflowing with pancakes.

"Do you have any more bacon?" Patrick asked.

"We're all out." She turned and left.

"Not an overly friendly girl," Patrick said.

"Patrick, please."

"I'm not saying that's a bad thing, Lila. I'm sure she has her reasons for being unfriendly and rude and mean-spirited. I'm sure they're perfectly fine reasons. I'm just saying that she's not friendly. It's an observation, I'm not judging. I could just as easily say that she was tall or short or fat."

"She ain't fat," Tony said.

"Naw, she ain't fat," Willie agreed.

"I ran into her at the gas station this morning, and I tried to engage her in conversation, some chitchat," Patrick continued. "Inquired about the weather. I thought that was a pretty important topic, the weather, this being a tourist town after all. She looked at me as if I weren't there. Just pumped her gas and drove away."

"Maybe she didn't hear you," Dot said.

"That's not usually an issue with me," Patrick said. "Anyway, I thought that was rude. Here I am a visitor, putting my hard-earned money back into her own town, in a sense into her own pocket. You'd think she might spare me a few words."

"That's not her way," Lila said. "My goodness, she organized this breakfast, and she's involved in trying to restore Sister North's house. She's busy and probably doesn't have time to make small talk with a stranger."

"Hello isn't small talk," Patrick said.

"She's busy, and in her own way she means well."

Everyone quietly returned to their food. Then Tony asked, "Well, you probably know the real reason she is the way she is, don't you?"

"What's that?" Sam asked sharply.

"She killed a guy." He didn't elaborate.

"Where did you hear that piece of news?" Patrick said.

"Common knowledge. He was her track coach in college. She killed him. In Santa Monica," Tony said.

"My God," Lila said.

"Was it an accident?" Dot asked.

"Yeah," Tony said. "If you call shooting someone in the face three times an accident."

"In the face?" Dot asked.

Tony set his coffee cup on the table and made the sign of a gun with his hand and pressed it against his cheek.

"Face is bad, man," Willie said. "Connected to the brain."

"Where did you hear that?" Sam asked. He was naturally alarmed by this news and instinctively searched the room for Meg. But she was back in the kitchen.

"Like I said, it's common knowledge. Jack helped her out; she beat the rap and came back here. I don't know all the details. It was right after she fell in that race. I think she blamed the coach and shot him. Wrong place, wrong time for that guy, probably. You know, she was upset and reacted in an emotional manner, I think."

At that exact moment, Meg reappeared and slowly began to wipe down the bar with a sponge. Everyone watched her.

"Such an attractive girl," Dot said.

"So hard to believe," Lila said.

"How come you never said anything about this before?" Sam asked. He didn't believe Tony.

"Let's just say a certain relative discourages conversation on that subject and that particular relative happens to be very influential in this town and would probably have my legs decapitated."

They continued to watch Meg wipe the bar. She was scrubbing it, her face growing red with the effort.

"I've always thought something wasn't quite right with her," Dot said.

"Explains a lot of things," Willie said.

"Like what?" Sam asked. He was becoming annoyed by the conversation.

Willie shrugged and reached for the platter of pancakes. "Her ways."

"What do you mean, her ways?" Sam asked.

"Nothing. Her personality."

"She's aloof," Dot said.

"I don't think she's aloof," Sam said. "She's just quiet. There's nothing wrong with being quiet."

"It must have been self-defense," Lila said. "Maybe she was trying to protect herself."

"That's possible," Tony said. "Except he was sleeping." He looked around the table. "Faceup."

"Hey, everyone," Meg said. She had once again appeared next to the table, holding a clipboard and pen.

Everyone started at once. Lila actually popped out of her seat.

"Well, hello there, yes, hello," Patrick said. He reached over for Lila's hand and patted it.

"Thanks for coming. I think more volunteers are on their way, but right now, it's just us."

"I ain't helping," Tony said. He wiped his mouth with his napkin and got to his feet. "I've got some other projects to do today. I told your uncle about them." He put his hands in his pockets and slouched away, avoiding all eye contact with Meg.

"Anyone else leaving?" Meg asked.

No one moved.

"Good," Meg said. "We can get started today."

"What all needs to be done?" Patrick asked.

"Lots of things," Meg said. She passed out sheets of paper to everyone. "I made a list."

Sam took a sheet and scanned it. Six things were listed:

1. New Roof
2. Chimney Repair
3. Floors Sanded
4. Interior Painted
5. New Electrical (replace old fuses with breakers)
6. Replace Front Windows

Sam's heart sank. There was nothing on that list he felt qualified to do. He would embarrass himself, break things, ultimately cause more damage. He would be revealed as useless. He had spent his entire life in apartments and town houses. He had paid people to fix things, paint walls, unclog sinks. He would have to explain that to Meg when he had the chance and try to make her understand.

"There's quite an ambitious list," Patrick said. He was holding the paper up close to his face.

"We have a lot to do," Meg said.

"Now, some of this doesn't seem storm-related," Patrick said. "The painting, for instance."

"I know. She's been putting off a lot of work for a long time. I figured we may as well as do everything now. While we have the help."

"Help?" Patrick said. He glanced around the table and shook his head.

"More people will come," Meg said.

"Who is going to pay for all this?" Patrick asked.

"It's all paid for. The town pays for it. And insurance."

"All paid for." Patrick chewed on his upper lip. "Well," he said. "I imagine I can handle the electrical, if you have the right tools. I can put the windows in, too."

"I would be happy to help with the painting," said Lila.

"Me, too," said Dot. "As long as we do it with the windows open." She waved her hand in front of her nose. "The fumes give me a headache."

"I can do the roof," Willie said.

Sam felt everyone's eyes shift to him. He held the list up high in front of his face.

"What can you do?" Meg asked.

A good question. Sam stared at the paper, searching for a loophole. "I can do anything you want," he heard himself say.

"Good," Meg said. She started writing on her clipboard.

"Say," Patrick said, "do you know anything about your good nun's health? Word is, she's not doing so well."

Meg looked around the table, and her eyes narrowed slightly. "She's fine," she said. She grabbed the sheets of paper and returned to the kitchen without another word.

CHAPTER

Fifteen

Sam was placed in charge of growing Sister North's grass. When Meg first told him this, he was confused.

"How do I do that?" he asked.

"You'll figure it out," she said, handing him a hoe.

Over the years, the huge yard, apparently once lush and well maintained, had fallen into ruin. It had become a jungle of weeds, dying bushes, stunted plants, and scraggly flowers. Her lawn was essentially nonexistent, small, unconnected patches of prairie grass lost in a sea of dark, rocky mud. A nice yard was something Sister North should have, Meg said, something she deserved.

It was a difficult job and better suited, Sam thought, for someone with yard work experience. He was a city boy, whose only real contact with grass had been while playing golf. He had briefly considered lobbying for a desk job, handling the insurance forms for example, but decided instead to throw himself into the project. For more than two weeks, he pulled, dug up, and dragged dead shrubs, bushes, and branches to the front of the house.

He worked alone, the only unskilled laborer among the Sister

North volunteers. Willie worked on the repair of the roof, Patrick on changing the electrical system, and Dot and Lila on painting the inside rooms. Meg had a hand in everything; she jumped on a ladder to inspect a gutter, or shinnied on her stomach to check the crawl space. She came and went unexpectedly, roaring off in her pickup truck to get supplies or meet with insurance people, disappointed that only a small number of volunteers had turned out to help.

"No one else is coming," she said, more than once. "We're going to have to do this ourselves, at least for now."

Occasionally, a stray volunteer reported for duty: a woman from Oshkosh, who walked with a limp because of mild cerebral palsy, showed up for two days and helped inside. An overweight man who ran a youth center in Minneapolis only made it through a single morning before disappearing at lunchtime. Clyde, the man in the wheelchair and Sister North sweatshirt, came by from time to time, but was unable to do much. He spent most of his days reading the Bible aloud under a tree in a halting, high voice that sounded like a child talking in the wind. Once, late in the afternoon, Billy Bags stood on the edge of the woods that bordered the backyard. When Sam asked him for help in dragging a branch to the front, Billy waved him away and left.

Even though it was hard work, Sam didn't mind. The backyard was mostly shaded by drooping weeping willows that formed a cathedral of budding greenery, and he found the cool darkness comforting. He soon began to regard the yard as his private domain, his sanctuary, and he moved about it silently, lost in shadows and thought.

Mostly, he thought about Meg. They had not spent much time together since that night in the harbor, and he wondered if that was by design or accident. She didn't seem to be avoiding him—they often had lunch together on the front porch with the others and shared snatches of conversation throughout the day—but she didn't seem to be going out of her way to see him alone either. When he asked her to have dinner or a drink with him, she claimed she was too busy.

He had concluded that she was a woman who had to be earned. Simply showing up with his hair combed and striking one of his old model poses wasn't going to win her over. He needed a strategy.

He wrote:

Get in shape.

Be helpful.

Appear religious.

He started to jog early in the morning, in front of Monticello. Meg was an athlete and placed a premium on fitness, so he thought getting fit couldn't hurt. In addition to running, he began doing sit-ups, hooking his ankles under his bed and clamping his hands hard behind his head. He did forty one morning, then fifty, then fifty-one. He felt lean and mean and studied himself in the mirror with his shirt off.

He also volunteered for extra projects around the house, hauling garbage, running errands, encouraging others in their efforts. More than once, he offered his suggestions to Meg on paint color or wall-paper. Though he had no idea what he was talking about, he thought she appreciated his initiative and the earnest way in which he conveyed his opinions. He also made it a point to be the first one there in the morning and one of the last to leave in the evening.

Finally, he tried to behave "spiritual" around her. This was a key intangible that could make or break him. Since she was obviously religious—after all, she worked for a nun—he took to carrying a small Bible around. He would read it during lunchtime on the front steps, or at the bar while waiting for his food. He retained nothing, however, the begets, thees, and thous ricocheting off his brain, back to the dense pages. Once, at Sister North's house, when he saw Meg caulking the kitchen window, he made a pathetic show of sitting under a willow tree and trying to read Genesis again. It was a hot afternoon, and he inevitably fell asleep and dreamed he was having sex with her in a variety of exotic positions. When he woke up, she was glaring at him through the window. He stopped carrying the Bible after that and focused on doing more sit-ups. He did fifty-two that very evening, fifty-three the next.

That he was attracted to her was no surprise. She was, he thought, beautiful. Tall and lanky with large, dark, questioning eyes, and an angular face that could appear both serious and, on occasion, amused, he found himself staring at her whenever she was near.

As much as he was attracted to her looks, he was equally attracted to her sense of control, her calmness. She was, as far as he could tell, unflappable. One morning, when the fuse box in the basement was shorting, shooting out hot, white sparks, she reacted without alarm. Pushing Patrick and Sam aside, she identified the source of the problem and, quickly wrapping a rag around her hand, yanked the offending fuses and clipped two small red wires without so much as a word.

"She's cool under fire, I'll give her that much," Patrick said, after she was gone.

Sam admired her steady response to things, the way she always seemed to have an answer, a plan, a schedule. He was convinced she knew things, had life figured out or, at the very least, understood it better than he.

What he liked the most about her, however, was the way people responded to her. Despite her abrupt manner, the volunteers all vied for her approval, her respect. Once, after Willie uncovered the source of a leak in the kitchen ceiling, she briefly squeezed his hand. Afterward, Willie beamed for hours, his day complete. Another time, when she sought out Patrick's opinion on installing triple-track windows, Patrick tried hard not to appear too flattered, then spent hours driving back and forth to Princeville to research options.

But no one was more under her spell than Sam. He had been with many women, but none had made him want to shovel mud or seriously contemplate how a certain wallpaper looked in direct sunlight.

He was as much intrigued by his own response to her as he was with her. She made him want to be a better person and, in the process, she made him feel better.

Despite his growing attraction and his efforts to impress her, she remained elusive, if not aloof. As a result, he feared that the kiss in the harbor was never going to amount to anything more than a kiss, and worried about it daily.

"How the grass coming?" Willie asked him one morning. He was striding toward him while eating a Pop-Tart. Sam hadn't seen much of him over the past few days. Willie spent most of his time either up on the roof, shopping for supplies, or playing cards at night with Tony.

"Okay," Sam said.

Willie surveyed the muddy, desolate ground. "Roof going pretty slow, too. Have to pull off the whole thing. Lot of water damage." He finished his Pop-Tart. "This a big yard. Like a football field."

"It's fifty yards long and thirty yards wide," Sam said. He had measured it earlier in the week, using a tape measure he had found at Monticello.

"How come there's no grass here?"

"I don't know," Sam said. He was digging up a dying evergreen bush by the back door. He had been putting it off because of its size and had made little headway that morning.

"Yeah, well, it'll get there." Willie stuffed his hands into the front pockets of his jeans. "Hey, you going out with Louis tonight? We're looking for the statue again. Said he won't charge me for my room if I help him."

Sam stopped digging and leaned on his shovel. "I might be busy," he said. He had hoped to talk Meg into grabbing dinner with him.

"I'm going. I like driving the boat. Louis let me drive it. He's okay."

Sam nodded. Over the past week, Louis had taken a liking to Willie, letting him move the inn's only TV into his own room late at night and offering him orange juice with his Pop-Tarts free of charge.

Sam suspected it was because recently Willie told Louis he was thinking of growing a beard like Louis's, something Louis found flattering.

"Yeah, he and you are real buds," Sam said. He resumed shoveling, working to get leverage under the bush. He didn't want to dig the
bush up without getting its roots. Meg had been very clear on that.
She didn't want things growing back.

"Hey, Sammy, let me ask you a question. How long are you staying here? Been here more than a month now."

"Why, you want my room?"

"Serious. You got any friends or family back home? People missing you?"

Sam let Willie's question sink in. "No."

"You an orphan or something?"

Sam hesitated again, thinking. "You know, I guess I am." He dug
and pitched some dirt. A bead of sweat fell from his forehead onto
the ground.

"Hey, let me ask you another question here. This one kind of
weird. Been talking to Lila, that Clyde guy in the wheelchair, talking about God and everything, and I was thinking, what do you
think is bad?"

Sam stopped working again and leaned again on the shovel.
"What are you talking about?"

"God, what do you think He thinks is bad? I mean, what would
keep someone out of heaven, piss Him off the most?" Willie looked
serious.

"I don't know. Killing someone, maybe," Sam said. "Killing someone on purpose. Murder, I'd have to go with murder."

That choice seemed to cheer Willie. He pointed his finger at Sam
and smiled. "That's what I was thinking, too. I think everything else
is okay, permissible. He let you slide on everything else probably.
Everything else is small-time."

"Let's hope," Sam said. "Can you give me a hand here? Pull the
branches away so I can get down there."

Willie did as he was told, grabbing the tops of the bushes and bunching them up so Sam had a clear angle at the base of the bush. Within minutes, he had it uprooted, and Willie pulled it out of the ground.

"Thanks," Sam said. It had come out much easier than he had expected.

"Got to tell you something else, Sam. Kind of weird, too. Confidential though."

Sam didn't say anything. He just grabbed the bush and began to drag it to the front of the house.

"You know, when you picked me up at the gas station that time?" Willie asked.

"You jumped in my car, you mean."

"Yeah, well, I was really coming up here. I was heading up here all along."

Sam stopped, his back to Willie. "You mean you were coming to see the nun?"

"Yeah. I was. Kind of weird, huh? That you were coming here, too, to see her too, I mean. You picking me up like that. All the cars, and you the one I get in with. Strange, don't you think? Like it was all planned out."

Sam thought about it, then started dragging again. "A lot of people come to see her and head that way."

"Yeah, but we were about two hundred miles away, though, when I seen you. And I wasn't waiting for a ride either. Made that up. I just got there a minute in front of you. Guy just dropped me off. Saw you in the store there, waiting in line, saw you drop that shit on the floor and just followed you. Had this feeling."

"What do you mean?"

"I don't know. A feeling. Knew right away you was going to see her, too."

"How did you know that?"

Willie shrugged. "Had a feeling."

Sam shrugged, deciding not to read anything into it. "A lot of people come this way."

They reached the road, and Sam dropped the bush into a pile with some others. The trucks would be by the next day for another pickup.

"So," he asked. "You watch the nun?" He had never considered the possibility that Willie was a nun person. He was surprised by the realization, but it all made sense. Him coming here, staying here, him helping out.

"Yeah, a little. I used to watch her a lot while I was at State."

"You mean Statesville, the prison?"

"Yeah, that's the place."

"How long were you there?"

"Judge dropped a nickel on me, but I got out in two."

"What were you in for?"

"This, that."

"First time?"

Willie grimaced and scratched the back of his neck. "You asking a lot of questions, Sammy. I already got a lawyer. Dave Fewkes."

"I know him. He's good. I used to go up against him a lot."

"He's okay. Knows his stuff."

Sam rearranged the bushes, making a pile. The county workers had recently complimented his work, commenting that his neatly stacked brush made their jobs easier, and he didn't want to disappoint them.

"So you came up here to talk to Sister North," he said.

"Yeah. Why not? Used to watch her show. Liked it okay. You know, she talks straight. Don't talk down. Makes everything seem simple. She's always saying life isn't complicated. We make it complicated, you know, we fuck things up. There's right and wrong. That's the way God set everything up. Set it up simple, made the rules pretty clear. You choose wrong, you pay. You choose right, you coast. Made me think. Don't read the Bible or nothing. Tried to when I was inside, but couldn't do it, couldn't follow it. Her show was easier. So I came up here. Nowhere else to go."

"What do you want from her?"

Willie spit on the ground and considered the question. "I don't know. Been thinking about that a lot, though, since I got here. Wasn't really sure until a few days ago. Now I know, I think, now I know."

"What do you want?"

Willie shrugged. "Same thing you want, I bet, same thing everyone wants."

"What's that?"

He glanced over Sam's shoulder into the woods, then looked down at the ground and spat again. "Second chance, I guess," he said. "Second chance."

Sam spent the rest of the morning working alone, removing the last of a dying hydrangea bed that was in the center of the yard. After he had finished, he took a break and stood back to admire his work. Meg had wanted everything removed, a clean start, she said, and Sam thought he was close to achieving this objective. Other than a few bushes and a struggling crab apple tree, the yard was for the most part emptied out.

The next phase involved actually planting the grass, something that caused him great concern. Pulling dead and dying things out of the ground and dragging them around had been a straightforward task that he had quickly mastered, but making things grow, giving life, was another matter entirely.

He went back to work, moving slowly, his mind elsewhere. Gradually, his thoughts coalesced, and he began to assess: He had come to Lake Eagleton in search of answers, and so far he had found none. Still he felt strangely content, the raw edges of his life now a little smoother. While digging, he wondered if perhaps he had been living the wrong life all along, wondered if he was meant to do this, live quietly in a small town, working with his hands. Maybe, he thought, he had been granted a reprieve, maybe from now on, his life would be simpler, but richer. He stopped digging, surveyed the dark, cool yard, and wondered if this was his own second chance.

He worked until lunchtime, then dropped a hose at the base of the crab apple tree. Meg had told him to water it every day; it was its only chance for survival. After he turned the water on, he went around to the front of the house, looking for someone to have lunch with. No one was there, so he drove to Big Jack's himself while listening to Meg on the radio. A snowstorm was rolling in from the west, with somewhere between eight to ten inches being predicted. Sam was startled at the news, looked out at the bright, hot day, then realized it was a tape, months old.

When he was seated at the restaurant, he ordered the Farmer's Platter, a combination breakfast and lunch: bacon and eggs, hash browns, and a grilled ham-and-cheese sandwich. He was sitting at the bar and eating greedily, his head bent low over his plate, when he heard the chair next to him squeak.

"Why, hello there," Patrick said.

"Hey there," Sam said. He took a last bite of his sandwich. "Didn't see you at the house today."

Patrick looked at Sam uncertainly. "What's that now?" He was wearing his tan safari hat and looked tired and dusty, as if he had just walked miles over a desert.

Sam chewed and swallowed. "The house. No one was there this morning."

"Oh. Well, I had to take care of some business on the phone," he said. His voice sounded softer than usual.

The waitress, a young college girl with braces, appeared behind the bar with her pad. She waited impatiently for Patrick's order.

"I'll just have the coffee," Patrick said. He removed his hat and positioned it on the bar.

"I got up early today," Sam said. "I was over at the nun's house, working in the yard. Did a lot of digging. I might go back later and finish. I have to plant the grass seed. I'll have to water a lot though." Patrick had no response to any of this. He stared straight ahead at nothing. "So the grass can grow," Sam added.

"What?"

Sam picked up his cup of coffee. "The yard. I was out at Sister North's all morning."

Patrick finally focused on Sam. The waitress put down his coffee and placed his check next to his cup.

"They found Todd today," Patrick said.

"Who?"

"Todd, my son. At least they think they found him. His body. Outside of Las Vegas. I figured that's where he'd wind up. I told them to look there again." He picked up his cup but put it down without drinking. "I have to fly out there and identify it. I'm leaving in an hour. I haven't told Lila anything yet."

Sam swallowed and looked at the counter.

"I'm not going to tell her anything either. There's no need to tell her until I know. I'm going to tell her that I have to go back to Pleasanton to check on something. A problem with the ranch. She doesn't have to know. She can stay here until I know. She's enjoying it here. She needs a vacation. A rest." He stopped in thought. "She'll probably suspect something though. She probably suspects something already. She's pretty intuitive, and she's been a little depressed lately, which isn't her way." He took a deep breath, his chest expanding. "I would appreciate it if you didn't tell her anything about this. I really shouldn't have told you, but I just found out. They just called."

"I'm sorry," Sam said.

"My son's dead," Patrick said. He shook his head. "My only child. We should have had more. Lila always wanted more, but the delivery almost killed her. She isn't equipped to have children. She's small. She miscarried five times before Todd. Five times. She thought he was a gift when he was born. A gift from the Lord." He stared down at his coffee. The waitress began turning ketchup bottles upside down, lining them up in a row on the bar. Sam could see the ketchup slowly slide downward toward the tops of the bottles.

"Lila's had too much sadness in her life, more than her fair share. Her mother died young, and her father killed himself. Threw himself in a river and drowned. Lila found his body by the shore. She was only twelve. She's always been brave, but I don't know how she'll handle this. A woman can only handle so much."

They were quiet. Patrick pushed away from the counter and slowly rose to his feet. "Do you suppose you have to believe in God for miracles to happen?"

"What?"

"Do you think that good things can still happen to you if you don't believe in God?"

"I hope so," Sam said.

Patrick nodded. "I've considered this issue. Especially since I've been up here. I think about it all the time." He sighed again. "Well, I have to go. Can you keep an eye on Lila? I'll be back in two days, I imagine. It's a long trip to Las Vegas from here. It will take me a while. Another reason I don't want to tell her. She'd want to make the trip with me." He picked up his hat and left a dollar on the check.

Sam wanted to say something, but didn't know what. Finally, he offered, "I'll look after your wife."

"Thank you. I appreciate your help." He was halfway toward the door when he stopped and turned again. "I've been meaning to tell you that you're doing a nice job on the yard there. A nice job, Sam." He put his hat on and left.

When he got back to Monticello, Sam found Dot Pelgers in the living room, holding a powder blue suitcase that perfectly matched her too-tight pantsuit. She was standing by the picture window that overlooked the lake. She didn't hear Sam walk in at first and seemed surprised when she saw him.

"Oh. Sam," she said. She gave him an appraising look, a hint of a smile on her face. "Rolling around in the mud, were we?"

"I was working in the yard at Sister North's house."

She nodded. "A hardworking man." She moved closer to him, toward the center of the room. "I just got back from Appleton. I decided to leave Carson with my sister for a while. She loves him. Neither one of us has any kids. On the drive back I decided to check in here. I was staying at the Sleep Shack, but it's too far out. I thought I'd move closer to the action. Say, how's the food here?"

"There isn't any," Sam said.

"I thought it was a bed-and-breakfast."

"Just a bed," Sam said, immediately regretting it.

Dot walked closer to him, a smirk riding up her face. "That's all I really need," she said. "And sometimes, I don't even need that."

Sam was about to head up to his room, when Lila came through the front door, holding a bouquet of bright, yellow flowers.

"Hello," she said. She looked tired and worried, and her hair was uncharacteristically disheveled.

"Daffodils," Dot said. "Nice."

Lila absently examined the flowers. "Yes. They're blooming everywhere. I picked these by the road. I'm going to put them in water," she said. She smelled them and blinked at Dot. "Then I think I'm going to lie down for a while." She headed for the stairs.

"That's a great idea," Dot said. "You go relax, hon. You go just take it easy."

"Louis around?" Sam asked, after Lila was gone.

"He's here somewhere," Dot said. She pulled out her gold cigarette case, flipped it open, and examined her choices carefully before choosing the perfect cigarette. "He's an odd man. He dresses strangely. Those muumuus. They're too much. He should lose a few pounds, show some self-respect. Try to improve himself. I lost twenty-eight pounds." She patted her stomach. "I'm into self-improvement. Working on my voice now. Might have to have surgery if these throat exercises I'm trying don't work."

"Well," Sam said. He started toward the stairs.

"You know, you really should take off your shoes, you're tracking dirt."

Sam inspected his sneakers and saw they were coated with drying mud. He knelt and untied them.

"All the years I've been coming to this lake, this is the first time I've stayed at this place," Dot said. "Pretty quiet." She wandered around the room, her high heels clicking on the bare, wooden floors. She stopped a few inches from where Sam was kneeling. He could see that the very tips of her heels were plated gold. "I'm staying in room eleven," she said. "What room are you in?"

"I don't know." He was still untying his shoes. "It's the white room. I didn't know the rooms had numbers."

"I think Louis said you were in room ten." She moved a little closer and nudged Sam's hand with her high heel. "We're neighbors."

"I'm going to my room now," Sam said. He stood up, holding one shoe in each hand, and headed for the stairway.

"You know, Sam, you really don't have to be afraid of me," she said. "I don't bite. Much."

"I'll see you," he said.

"Can't wait."

He had fully intended on returning to Sister North's to work on the yard, but ended up falling asleep, his face smothered in the quilt on his bed. When he woke, he felt an unfamiliar pain in his lower back, a dull ache. He stood and carefully stretched, touching the floor with his fingertips, then raised his hands over his head. He had no idea what he was doing, but his back felt immediately better.

He walked over to the window and opened it. It was late afternoon, and the clouds that had hung low all day had rolled out, revealing a lake scrubbed clean of gray. The wind had picked up, and the water was alive with whitecaps. He leaned on the sill, felt the warm wind in his face, and inhaled deeply.

He had lapsed into a stupor when he noticed someone moving about by the dock. At first he couldn't make out who it was through the trees by the shoreline, but he soon realized it was Lila. He watched as she removed a robe and stepped toward the end of the dock.

He looked around for Dot or Louis, but saw no one. Lila seemed transfixed by the water, her small body motionless and bent slightly forward. Suddenly, the wind picked up, the trees by the shore leapt to life, and he lost sight of her entirely.

He searched the empty dock, his concern growing. He opened the window wider and stuck his head out to get a better view. Still, he did not see her.

He pulled back into his room and stood motionless, not certain of what to do. He didn't want to overreact; she was probably just swimming, but Patrick's comment about her being depressed and suspecting something would not leave him. Then he remembered her dazed behavior in the living room and felt his heart speed up.

"Oh, shit," he said.

He rushed out of his room and down the stairs and out of the inn, finally breaking into a run.

"Lila," he yelled. The wind threw his voice back at him as he dashed to the end of the dock. "Lila! Lila!"

"I'm right here," she said.

Sam came to a sudden stop. It sounded as if she were beneath him.

"I'm here, under the dock," Lila said. Her voice was calm, as it always was.

Sam knelt and peered through the space between the planks, trying to follow her voice.

"I'm here," she said again.

"Are you okay?" Sam asked.

"Yes, I'm fine. The water is cold though. Dot warned me that it was too early in the year to swim, but I had to try anyway. I think I'm coming out now."

A few seconds later, she climbed up the ladder and put on her white terry cloth robe.

"Did Patrick call?" she asked. She was vigorously rubbing her hair with the bottom of her robe, her smooth face shining.

"No," Sam said. "I don't think he did."

"Oh, I thought that was why you were calling me. He went home. He had to go for a meeting. He said there was a problem that needed his immediate attention." She laughed, her voice a light chirp. "He's been looking for a reason to go home anyway. He's bored here."

She stopped drying her hair and slipped her hands in the robe's pockets.

"I used to be quite a swimmer in my day," she said. "I know you're not going to believe that, but it's true. We used to go up to Minnesota when we were children. My grandfather owned a cabin on a lake. We used to swim for hours. My poor father had to practically drag us out of the water at dinnertime. We don't take water for granted in Nebraska, I guess. When Patrick comes back, I hope I can talk him into taking a swim. He's not much for water, however, so I'll have to be convincing." She laughed her light laugh again. "Use all my charms."

As Lila talked, Sam noticed a familiar bounce in her voice. The water seemed to have energized her, transforming the old, cheerless woman he had seen a few hours ago into this happy, wet person.

"Do you swim?" Lila asked.

"Me? No," Sam said.

"Oh, you should jump in for a minute. Go on. It feels wonderful. It's cold though."

"I don't have a bathing suit."

"Well, you should buy one when you get the chance. There are certain things you should do while you're still young, and enjoying the water is certainly one of them. I tell my son, Todd, that all the time." She stopped talking and turned her attention to the water.

The sun was slowly lowering itself, touching the tops of the trees across the shore.

"He's missing, you know. Our son is," Lila said. Her words were soft, but the wind left them alone, and they hung in the air.

"I know. Patrick told me."

"I know he's somewhere safe though. I know it. Patrick fears the worst. But a mother knows." She touched her hand to her heart. "I know. I just do. He's safe. In some sort of trouble again, I'm sure, but safe."

Sam nodded and squinted into the sun. He tried not to think of the heartbreak Lila might soon be facing.

"We used to take him to the lake when he was young, too. Todd liked to swim. We would play this game in the water. What's that game? It's like hide-and-go-seek? You close your eyes and try to find the other person."

"Marco Polo," Sam said.

"Yes!" Lila said. "Now I wonder why they call it that? Did you play that game when you were a child?"

"Once in a while," Sam said. "My family used to come up to a lake like this. I'm not sure where it is from here."

Lila crossed her legs at the ankles. "I'm sure you have nice memories of that place."

"I do," he said.

Lila cupped her hand to her forehead and looked out over the water. "You can love a place all you want. With your whole heart," she said. "A place won't let you down. My grandfather used to tell me that. A place isn't like a person. It will always be there."

They were quiet, the wind and the waves surrounding them. Sam, overwhelmed in the face of all that energy, closed his eyes.

"Can I ask you a question? Are you here to see Sister North?"

"Yes," Sam said. "I am. I'm here to see her."

"Why do you want to see her?"

Sam swallowed. "I have to figure some things out," he said.

"Well," Lila said, "I hope you do."

She stood up and put her sandals on.

"Oh, I almost forgot, what did you want?" she asked. "Why were you calling me just now?"

Sam couldn't think of a reason so he told her the truth. "I thought that it was too windy to be swimming by yourself." He gestured toward the lake. "I thought you shouldn't be swimming alone."

Lila squinted at him and smiled. "Why, aren't you a nice fellow," she said.

Sam smiled back. And for a moment, only a moment, he almost believed her.

Later that night, Sam took a long hot shower before going to bed, a pool of muddy water circling around the drain at his feet before disappearing. Afterward, he stood in front of the mirror, not sure he recognized himself. His face was leaner, and more tightly defined, and his black eyes seemed more set back. Despite working in the shade most of the day, he was still tan in a way he had never been before, his skin a rich brown. He flexed his arms and was surprised to see muscles, his biceps small, hard rocks. He winked at himself and went to bed.

He was about to fall asleep when he suddenly remembered the hose running under the crab apple tree at Sister North's house.

His initial thought was to ignore the situation. Someone, he was sure, had discovered the problem and turned it off. He rolled onto his side. When he closed his eyes, he envisioned the backyard as a swamp and Sister North's house half-underwater. Then he saw Meg's face and felt the heat of her eyes.

With a loud sigh, he pushed himself out of bed and threw on shorts and a sweatshirt.

He tiptoed past Louis's room, down the staircase, and out the back door. Only then did he remember that Willie had taken his car to play cards with Tony, something he did from time to time. He considered waking Louis up and asking for a ride, but instead decided just to walk. He thought he could make it in a half hour.

The night was warm and smelled of the lake. He made good time, breaking into a slow jog once he got to Main Street. In minutes, he was through town and deep in the woods.

He slowed and walked up the hill, thinking that a little more than a month ago the prospect of being on a country road late at night would have been inconceivable, if not downright terrifying. He was from Chicago and trained to distrust the dark, but now, alone in the woods, he felt safe, and thought of the darkness as a shield. He walked faster, imagining he was gliding undetected past and through things. When he reached the stone wall, he again broke into a jog.

Once at Sister North's house, he immediately made his way to the back of the house, afraid of what he might see. When he reached the yard, he found the hose rolled up in a coil. He moved over to the tree, knelt, and felt the ground. It was merely damp.

"What are you doing here?" It was Meg. She was standing by the back door. "Did you lose something?"

Sam shot up, startled.

"What are you doing?" she asked again.

"I thought I forgot to turn off the hose."

"I turned it off. You didn't have to come back." She glanced toward the front. "How did you get here? I didn't hear a car."

"I walked."

"You walked? All the way?"

"I ran a little, too." He enjoyed what he thought was the impressed tone in her voice.

"That's stupid," she said. "Where's your car?"

Softly, Sam said, "Willie has it."

"I parked on the other side of the woods. Come on. I'll take you back. Follow me."

They cut across the yard and entered the woods. He had a hard time keeping up, her white T-shirt disappearing, then reappearing in flashes around corners and through tree branches. He stumbled over rocks and roots, walking with his arms out in front of him like a blind man. Eventually, he lost her and was about to call out her name, when he came upon her in the Chapel in the Pines, kneeling at the edge of the clearing, observing something moving by the cross.

"Look," she said, pointing.

"What?"

"Look."

Not more than ten yards away, Sam could make out the shapes of three deer. They were frozen in place, their heads cocked in their direction. He knelt beside Meg and watched them. He wasn't sure if he had ever seen deer before.

"Nice," Sam said.

"I hate deer," she said. "Let's go."

They crossed the clearing, the deer scattering in a silent rush, and were through another small patch of woods and to her truck in minutes. When he finally sat down in front, he was breathing hard.

"Why do you hate deer?" he asked.

"I hit a lot of them." She started up the truck. "I've killed three of them since I've been back."

Sam fished around for his seat belt. "Oh."

They drove down the hill quickly, bouncing over potholes. Meg seemed in a hurry, and was preoccupied. She chewed on her bottom lip.

"I haven't seen much of you lately," he said.

"I've been busy."

"House is shaping up."

"What?"

"The house is shaping up."

"It's okay." She chewed on her lip some more.

"How's your own house doing?" Sam asked.

"Still a mess. I'm staying at Leo's."

"Leo's," Sam repeated. They were quiet. Sam lowered his window a little. "Are you mad at me or something?" he asked.

Meg glanced over at him. "Mad? Why? Should I be?"

"I don't know, it seems like you're avoiding me."

"I'm not avoiding you. I have a lot going on."

They were through the woods and nearing town. They passed the restaurant; its parking lot was empty, and its lights were out.

"Have you talked to Sister North lately?" he asked.

Meg popped up a bit in her seat. "Why?"

"I don't know. I just thought you might have. How's she doing?"

"Fine."

"I keep hearing she's sick."

"She's not sick."

"When is she coming back then?"

"I don't know."

"Does she know people are waiting for her here?"

Meg lowered her window. "People wait for her everywhere."

"I'm starting to think she doesn't exist," Sam said.

Meg slowed as they approached the harbor. Across the lake, a single light was visible, and it flickered like a candle flame in and out of the darkness.

"What were you doing at her house so late?" Sam asked.

"I was going to go running. I wanted to run hills. I haven't run hills in a while."

Sam thought about this. "Hey, I didn't mean to keep you from running. I could have walked back."

"It's all right. I'll run down here, by the lake, after I drop you off."

"I want to run with you," Sam said suddenly. "Stop the truck."

"Forget it."

He put his hand on her arm. "Come on. Stop the truck. I can do this."

"You know what time it is?"

"I'm wide awake."

Meg glanced at his hand on her arm, then pulled over to park by the harbor. "Okay," she said. "If that's what you want."

He had run only about a mile when he felt his chest collapsing.

"Pace yourself," Meg said.

"Does that mean stop?"

"It means you're going too fast too soon."

Sam paced himself for another three steps and came to an abrupt stop, bending over his knees. He was completely out of breath.

"Are you okay? You look pretty bad. Put your hands behind your head and walk around," Meg said. She wasn't even breathing hard.

Sam paced up and down the shoreline.

"Are you going to boot?" she asked.

"What?"

"Boot. Throw up."

"No, I'm not going to *boot*," Sam said. He walked farther away from her, down the shore. He was pretty sure he was going to boot.

Meg followed him. "Here, lean on this." She steered him to a tree. "Close your eyes and breathe slowly."

Sam did as he was told and felt a little better.

"How old are you?" Meg asked.

"How old do you think I am?"

"Seventy-three."

"I'm seventy-eight," he said.

Meg laughed one of her silent laughs, shoulders briefly shaking. Sam opened his eyes.

"You know, you could give me credit for trying to keep up with someone as famous as you," he said.

"I'm not famous."

"Yes, you are." He was breathing slower. "I remember seeing you on television."

"You mean when I was running?"

"On *The Best of the Badger State*. The TV show. Your essay on the environment."

Meg's smile momentarily vanished. She looked confused. "How did you hear about *that*?"

"People still talk about it," Sam said. "It changed my life."

She laughed again silently. "Yeah, right. Get out of here," she said. "You're an asshole."

"Such a way with words. It's a shame you stopped writing."

She shook her head, smiling. The short run had ignited her. She was glowing, humming with energy. He wanted to reach out and hold her, but was still afraid he might boot.

She turned away from him and headed back to the lake, where she stopped by a pile of rocks. It was a calm night, and the lake lay still like a carpet.

"Are you married?" she asked.

"Divorced."

"So am I. Do you ever think about your wife?"

"Not that often." He pushed away from the tree.

"Did you love her?"

"Not really."

"Why did you marry her?"

"She was rich, and I was poor." He walked over to her. "Why did you marry your husband?"

Meg didn't say anything. Instead, she looked up at the sky, and suddenly shouted, "Hey!"

Sam tried to follow her gaze.

She cupped her hands to her mouth and yelled, "Hey!" again.

"What are you doing?"

Meg smiled and shouted again.

"Who are you yelling to?" Sam asked. He was almost breathing normally by then, though his chest still felt tight, and his throat burned.

"No one. Everyone," she said.

She moved closer to the water, her eyes still on the sky. "When I was little, my mom and I used to come here at night. She wanted to talk to God, she said. She was sick, and she was praying that she would get better. I wanted to help her, so before she said her rosary, I would yell to get God's attention. It didn't work. She died anyway."

"Did you move in with Leo and Jack then?"

"Yeah, I was lucky. They were good guys. They still are. Most days."

"What was it like growing up here?"

"It was okay. Before the nun and everything, it was just a small town. Everyone knew everyone. I hated Los Angeles. I hated living there. Every day I was there, I wanted to come home."

"Why didn't you?"

"I was training. That's where my coach was. I wanted to go to the Olympics. That's all I wanted. That's all I thought about. Every day, every second. It was nutty. I was nutty. The second I fell at the trials, the second I fell, I knew."

"Knew what?"

"That I wasn't supposed to be there. That I was supposed to be here."

Sam walked toward her. From behind, she looked like a thin, teenage girl.

"You must be pretty religious," she said. "To come up here." She was still looking at the sky.

"I'm about as unreligious as you can be."

"You're always reading the Bible."

Sam didn't say anything.

She turned and looked at him. He expected her to be smiling, but instead her forehead was furrowed and her eyebrows a knot. "Everyone comes up here for the nun," she said, her voice soft and low, the voice he recognized from his phone calls, the voice that he now knew had led him here. "But she doesn't fix anything. She's not God. She doesn't do miracles. Most of what you hear about her is made up to get people to come here. And some of the people who come here go home disappointed. They expect too much."

"I know all that. I just want to talk to her."

She searched his face. "I hope you're not disappointed," she said.

"Don't worry," he said. "I won't be."

Sixteen

They found one of Sister North's feet two days later. Billy Bags found it not more than fifty yards from the harbor, wedged under some rocks and covered in a net of seaweed. Big Jack and Leo immediately performed a thorough autopsy on it, poking it with screwdrivers, shaking it, holding it up to the light. When they were finished, Big Jack turned and gravely told the assembled crowd at the bar, "It's her foot all right." Then he gave it to Tony to clean and polish.

"Why do I got to clean it?" Tony asked. He was staring at it on the counter of the tilted Tackle Box while chewing his mustache. "Jack's always giving me the shit work. Thinks because I drive the trolley for him, I'm like an indentured servant."

"It's in bad shape," Willie said. "Don't even look much like a foot."

Sam circled the foot and agreed with Willie's assessment. It was in bad shape. Dented and dull, it was severed at the ankle at a sharp, thorny angle. He reached out, ran his hand along the jagged edges, and noticed that the baby toe was crushed and the big toe missing.

"I don't know why we're even keeping this thing," Tony said.

"Big Jack said he was going to try and reattach it to the rest of the statue once we found it," Willie said.

"Hey, I got news for you and Big Jack and everyone else in this stupid town. We ain't ever going to find that thing. It's gone. This lake is 237 feet deep in the center. It's down there somewhere in a damn hole. I told Jack that, but he don't listen. I told him we got to rent radar and pay divers to pull it out. Jack is too cheap to do it. He thinks it's going to swim back on its own. Thinks a miracle or something is going to bring that thing back to us. Not that it matters. Who gives a shit about a statue? All the zombies who come up here want to see the real nun. They can get crosses and statues in any church. They want to see a face, hear a voice. That's what they're paying for."

Willie looked up from a fishing magazine. "Hey, not everyone who comes up here a zombie, you know," he said evenly. "Some people got legitimate business."

Tony looked at Willie, then glanced at Sam and shrugged. "Whatever. I don't mean nothing by that. All I'm saying is that we got our priorities screwed up. We should be spending money to track the real nun down, or recruiting a substitute, not paying for statues and fixing her house. That's all I'm saying."

"Have you heard anything more about her health?" Sam asked. He was poking at the crushed baby toe with a pen.

"No. I saw on the Internet, though, she's still in Africa doing something with the Peace Corps, working with some natives. Saw it on a Sister North chat room yesterday. I go there to find out what's happening. You can meet some interesting women on that thing. You know, desperate, vulnerable."

"Guy at the grocery store told me she riding a bike cross-country to raise money for retarded kids," Willie said. "Said he heard it on the radio. She's in Pennsylvania right now, he thought. Said they base the amount of milk and food they order on whether she's in town or not."

Tony reached behind him for a rag and began wiping Sister

North's ankle. "Yeah. The economy of this town is totally nun-based. Maybe she is in Pennsylvania, I don't know. It's not like I talk to her or anything. Hey, knock that off," he said to Sam. "Trying to clean this thing."

Sam stopped picking at the crushed toe. "Who does talk to her?" he asked. The vagueness and endless contradictions over Sister North's whereabouts were beginning to frustrate him. "Who is her contact here?"

"No one, really."

"How about the people who broadcast the show?"

"Don't know how that works. College kids are like the technicians, and cameramen. The people who beam it up and shit, I think they're from Missouri or something. They never come here."

"So no one is in regular contact with her?" Sam asked.

Tony shrugged. "I guess if it's anyone, it's Meg." He finished wiping off the foot and began applying a polish to it with a different rag. "I think she's the only one the nun is really close to. It's like a mother-daughter thing they got going on. They used to spend a lot of time together in the old days. Would take long walks together. Meg knows what's going on, I think, when it comes to the nun. But she ain't saying much on the subject."

"Why not?" Sam asked.

Tony shrugged again. "Ask her," he said.

Somewhere underneath the counter, a phone rang. Tony reached down and pulled out a black receiver and cradled it against his neck while he polished the foot, buffing hard.

"Jesus. I didn't know nothing about it. This for real? Yeah, okay, all right. I'll run up there," he said. He hung up and polished the foot a little more, then threw the rag down.

"Well, boys, speak of the devil," he said.

"What?" Willie asked.

"The old broad is back. Sister North. Supposedly. She's up at the house now."

Sam's heart jumped. "Are you sure about that?"

"Not sure about nothing when it comes to the nun. Jack thinks it's true, said someone saw her a little while ago. An unofficial Sister North sighting. He wants me to make a run up there. You want to come? Got a group at the restaurant I got to pick up first. Probably others. The zombies come out in full force when the nun comes back."

Willie straightened up and coughed. Sam stared at the bronze foot, catching his distorted reflection near the ankle. His face was stretched thin, and his eyes were dopey and wide.

Tony came out from behind the counter. "You coming or what?"

Sam cleared his throat. "Yeah," he said. "I'm coming."

They picked up people along the way: on Main Street, in front of the harbor, and in the parking lot of the Grocery Bag. One of the burned women sat across from Sam on the lower level, a scarf hiding her face. A young man with a huge, brown mole on his forehead sat behind her, reading the Bible, his lips silently moving. Three middle-aged women wearing identical orange-and-white Sister North sweat-shirts got on in front of Reflections, whispering and giggling as they made their way to the back.

At Big Jack's, they picked up an old man wearing a soft felt hat and holding a gold crucifix, a woman with yellow skin and sunken eyes, and two obese teenage girls stuffed into overalls. As the trolley was pulling away, a black man with a bulging green backpack and a tattered trench coat waved it down and got on, making his way to the upper deck.

Sam sat at the very front, next to Willie, amazed at the sudden whirl of people. He had no idea where they had come from. Had they just miraculously arrived, summoned by instinct or some silent call, or had they been there all along, hiding in the cracks and shadows of the town? He took one last look at the tired but hopeful faces, then slouched forward in his seat. They would be there in twenty minutes, Tony announced. Sam closed his eyes and waited.

· · ·

The trolley stopped about a half mile from Sister North's house again, Tony braking sharply as they approached the stone wall.

"As far as I can go on this hill with this load," he said into the microphone. "Only supposed to carry twenty people, and I got more."

No one questioned him. Instead, everyone filed out and began the trek up the road, a thin line of people moving like shadows. Sam purposefully fell to the back of the pack, letting Willie and the others pass him. He wanted more time to think, to prepare himself.

It was a cold, gray day, and he turned up his jacket collar and put his hands in his pockets. As he walked, he envisioned his meeting with Sister North. She would be sitting in a chair in a small room, her habit spread out behind her like great dark angel wings, her owl face wrinkled and wise. He would bow as he approached her, and possibly kneel.

"Hello, Sister North," he would say.

She would nod and, of course, smile. "And what is it that you want? What brought you here?"

A good question. Here Sam's imagination froze. What exactly *did* he want? The vagueness of his quest was now staring him full in the face. Here it was, finally crunch time, and he still wasn't clear why he was walking up a muddy road in the woods to see a nun.

He quickly began to make a mental assessment.

He thought:

I want to know why I wasn't killed.

No, he wanted more than that, he knew that now.

I want to be forgiven.

I want to know how to change.

I want to be better.

"I want to sit down," a voice said.

Sam turned and saw the black man approaching him from behind, breathing hard, the heavy backpack on his shoulders.

"We're almost there," Sam said.

"I hope so." The man stopped and removed thin wire glasses and ran a handkerchief across his forehead.

Sam waited while the man replaced his glasses, watching as he worked them carefully around his ears. He was tall and distinguished-looking, his short-cropped hair speckled gray and thinning, his posture ramrod-straight. Sam thought he might be a priest or a reverend.

"How much farther?" the man asked. His voice was deep, bottomless.

"It's just over the hill," Sam said.

"Just over the hill," the man repeated. He pushed his backpack up higher on his shoulders and resumed walking. "I tend to think in terms of metaphors lately, looking for meaning in every phrase, every sign. Most of our destinations are just over the hill, just out of view. But we keep walking, regardless, we keep walking, taking it on faith that we are heading in the right direction. There are more metaphors for faith than there are stars in the sky, I am convinced of that. Where are you from?" he asked.

"Chicago."

"Chicago." He considered this for a moment before asking, "Is Sister North very popular in Chicago?"

"I think she has a decent following."

"She is particularly influential in smaller towns. They seem to be her chief areas of support."

"Where are you from?" Sam asked.

"It will be two months tomorrow that I left my home in Iowa City. I walked out my front door on Windsor Court and haven't stopped since."

Sam examined the man. His face was deeply lined, and his tattered trench coat splattered with mud. "You mean you walked the whole way?"

"Yes, I have."

"That's unbelievable. That must be . . ."

"Four hundred and eighty-seven miles."

"That's a long walk."

"You will get no argument with me on that, my friend. I arrived in the area two days ago and spent some time at that motel with all the other pilgrims." He turned and took Sam in. "I don't believe I saw you there."

"I'm staying in town."

"Ah, in town. One of the chosen. What is your name, Mr. In Town?"

"Sam Gamett."

"I'm Daniel Preston Johnson." He extended his hand to shake Sam's as they walked.

"Are you familiar with this process, Mr. Sam Gamett?" Daniel asked. "Meeting with the sister? Have you done this before? Is this routine for you?"

"No."

"Then we are both new to this. I think that's true for most everyone in this particular group. We had a meal this morning, and it became apparent as we talked that most of us are novices."

"How did you hear about Sister North coming back?" Sam asked.

"I heard from someone in our group. Someone in the next room. I'm not sure how she heard. I took it on faith that she had accurate information, took it on faith that Sister North was just over the hill."

They walked farther, passing the small path that led to the Chapel in the Pines. Daniel's stride was long, and Sam struggled to keep up. They soon caught up to the other people: the two fat teenagers, the old man in the hat, the burned lady, the three women in Sister North sweatshirts, everyone falling behind. Willie and a few others were still ahead of them, walking fast, their heads bent down as if walking into a gust of wind.

"Does she still broadcast her television show from the house?" Daniel asked.

"No. They built her a new studio near the college. That's about an hour from here."

Daniel laughed, a clap of thunder. "A new television studio. Incredible. Her word can now reach more people than ever. Her influence grows. Grows. Grows. She is a master at what she does." He readjusted his backpack again. "What exactly is it about her that appeals to you?" He was looking straight ahead when he asked this, squinting at the road.

Sam paused. "I think she's honest."

Daniel laughed again. "Honest! Oh my goodness. Do you believe in this honest nun?"

Sam was becoming a little put off by Daniel and his line of questioning. He answered slowly. "I'd like to meet her," he said.

"Well, I am looking forward to meeting her also. My wife and I tried to meet her when she was in Iowa once, during her book tour, a few years ago, but we missed her. This time, I decided to come to the mountain myself."

"I wonder if she's really here," Sam said. "She's been gone, and there have been a lot of rumors."

"Rumors?" Daniel seized on this word.

"Where she is, when she's coming back, if she's coming back. Her health."

"Rumors," Daniel repeated. "Speculation. She likes to keep people guessing. Likes to keep them waiting for her. It's all part of who she is. Being mysterious is part of her allure. She is so good at so many things."

"Seems like you follow her closely."

"We've watched her for many years. That's why I am so excited finally to come here. It's a meeting that is long overdue." He stopped and wiped his forehead again, gently patting it down with the folded handkerchief. Then he took a deep breath and quickly smiled, his teeth a blur of ivory. "I look forward to meeting her. I look forward to finally telling the blasphemous bitch what I think of her."

· · ·

When they arrived at the house a few minutes later, it was raining lightly, the tops of the pine trees and weeping willows slipping behind a veil of mist. Sister North's house rested silent and dark in the gloom, alone and oblivious to the converging crowd. Daniel drifted away, toward the porch. Sam stood in the middle of the muddy, front yard and watched him as he paused at the door, then disappeared around back.

"No one home," Willie said, walking up to Sam. "Another false alarm, maybe." He coughed and glanced at the house. "A couple of people think she went out for a walk, maybe be right back. I don't know though. Not exactly walking weather. What do you think?"

"It doesn't look too good." Sam looked over his shoulder and watched the others file into the front yard. When word spread that she wasn't home, confusion and concern set in. Some people gathered by the road to confer, while others tentatively sat down on their coats and sweaters. The three women in Sister North sweatshirts fell to their knees and began saying the Lord's Prayer. No one left.

"Yeah, it don't look good," Willie said. He shook his head and disappeared back down the road.

Sam walked over to the house and peered in a window. The living room was dark and, other than a small stepladder, empty. He picked up a shovel lying on the front steps and propped it up against the door, then walked back toward the road and sat down. Out of the corner of his eye, he saw the burned woman making her way over to him, weaving around groups of people. He considered getting up, but decided it was too late to move. A few seconds later, she was sitting next to him.

"I heard she'll be back in a few minutes," she said. She smiled at Sam, but when he tried to smile back, his stomach turned. She had no lips. In their place were thin, white scars. He looked away.

"Chris and I have been waiting for her for over a month now. We're sharing a room in one of those motels by the highway. Chris is there now, taking a nap. I was in town shopping when I heard Sister North was back. Where are you staying, may I ask?" Her voice was light and feathery, and Sam tried to look at her again.

"In town."

"Oh, at Monticello. I've always wanted to stay there, but it's too expensive. Chris and I have to watch every dime. Is it nice there?"

"It's quiet. There isn't any food though."

"We don't eat much." Her scarf fell open partway, revealing ravaged cheeks, waxy red ridges, and blue veins. Sam turned away again.

"My name is Susan," she said.

"I'm Sam."

"Are you an actor?" Susan asked. She wrapped her scarf up, carefully tying the ends under her chin.

"An actor? No." Despite his unease, he had to laugh a little at this. At least she didn't think he was a priest. "No, I'm not."

"Chris and I have been playing this game. We try to guess what everyone does up here. I guessed that you were an out-of-work actor asking Sister North to help your career."

"I'm a lawyer. I guess that has its theatrical elements. I don't practice anymore though. I gave it up."

"Why?"

"I didn't like it. Plus, I wasn't very good at it."

"Well, if it will make you feel any better, I'm in the midst of a career change myself. I used to be a teacher, but I stopped."

"Why?"

"It's difficult to teach when children are afraid to be in the same room with you."

Sam couldn't think of a response, so he rearranged himself on the ground and kept his eyes on the house. A few people began wandering down the road, back toward the trolley. Most of the group, however, stayed and waited, their voices murmurs.

Susan sneezed. "We're all going to catch our death out here." She retied her scarf.

They both watched as the old man in the felt hat walked haltingly up to the house. He stopped at the satellite dish and touched it, running his hand along the inside. Then he slowly sank to his knees and began praying, holding the gold crucifix in both his hands.

"How long are you staying here?" Susan asked.

"Probably a few more minutes."

"No, I mean up here. In the town."

"Oh. I'm not sure. A while. A few more weeks at least."

She fell quiet. Overhead, the pine trees danced in and out of the mist. "I hope I'm not imposing," she said. "But I was wondering if I could ask you a favor."

Sam was quiet.

"Could you give Sister North something? In case she doesn't come back today? It's a letter. I wrote it last night. I think we may be leaving soon. Tomorrow even. It's time to go home, I think." She held out a plain white envelope. Sam stared at it, not sure he wanted to take it, not sure he wanted to be part of this woman's quest.

"I'd mail it, but I like the idea of its being hand-delivered by someone I met up here," she said. "Someone I talked to myself. The letter tells about what happened to Chris and me." She pushed the letter closer to Sam. "Most of the people are leaving soon," she said. "You're the only one staying that I know of."

Sam caught the woman's green eyes, clear and unmarked, and took the letter.

"I'll make sure to give it to her," he said. He carefully folded the envelope and slipped it in his jacket pocket.

"Thank you." Susan smiled again, her hole for a mouth stretching. Sam wondered if such a simple act hurt.

"Are you a big fan of Sister North's?" she asked.

"I've watched her show some."

"Christine and I watched it every day after we got out of the burn unit. We went through everything together. Christine, Sister North, and I. Quite an eclectic little group." She laughed quietly.

Sam swallowed. "What happened?"

Susan waved a hand. "It's a long and very ugly story. The important thing is that we survived. At first I didn't want to, I wanted to die. Who wants to go through life like this? But I got over it. I found a new place in the world. Things are different now, but not necessarily worse."

Sam was amazed at her attitude and was suddenly ashamed to be sitting next to her with his vague problems and needs.

"Why do you want to see the nun?" he asked.

"That is probably the most asked question up here," she said. She laughed again. "That's all we want to know. I sometimes wonder if we're all really trying to one-up each other. Who has the most advanced stage of cancer? Whose husband beat them the worst?" She waved her hand. "Dear God, I think I've become a little jaded over the past few weeks." She picked up a pebble from the road and tossed it. "Well, let's just say I want to meet Sister North because she helped make me believe again."

"In God," Sam said.

"In people," Susan said. "That's what saved me. That's what will save all of us."

"Have you ever talked to her?" Sam asked.

"Yes. On the phone a few times."

"What did she tell you?"

"She talked to me about hope, how hope can heal. She believes the whole world is based on hope. At least that's what I took away from her."

She picked up another pebble but held it this time. Sam noticed how smooth and young-looking her hands were. He wondered how old she was. He couldn't tell with the scarf and the scars.

"Why do you want to see her?" she asked.

Sam swallowed. "Lots of reasons."

"Well, you only get fifteen minutes with her, then she charges double you know."

Sam saw her eyes spark. She reached out and touched his wrist. "I'm kidding," she said.

Sam laughed. He liked this woman, felt relaxed with her. He stretched his legs out in front of him and leaned back on his hands. It was then that he saw Daniel standing on the front porch, holding a small axe.

"Dear brothers and sisters," he said, his voice ringing loud and deep, a preacher's voice. "I think it's important that we have an honest discussion as we wait for our illustrious Sister."

"Oh God," Susan said. "I was afraid of this."

Daniel paused and scanned the crowd, smiling. "Now, I spent some time with you the last few days. Not enough I know, not as much as I would have liked, but some. We shared our meals, our stories, our pain. And while you may not regard me as a friend, I regard you all as friends."

Everyone fell quiet.

Daniel smiled again. "And as your friend, I have to ask all of you a simple question. An honest question. An important question." He once again took in the crowd. "How much longer are we going to deceive ourselves with this lie?"

No one spoke or moved. The crowd was mesmerized by his voice and stared at him, watching his every move. Daniel took a single step down from the top of the porch and shook his head. Sam kept his eye on the axe.

"The truth is one of the things we all claim to seek, yet it is always the last thing we accept," Daniel said.

He took another step down.

"In our hearts we know what we are doing is wrong. Being here is wrong. Waiting for Sister Celebrity is wrong." He stopped. "Sister North is wrong," he said quietly.

He took the final step to the ground. "Yet still we wait." He shook his head again. "But we are waiting for the wrong person. This is not a woman of God we are sitting in the rain to see. In our hearts we know that. In our hearts, we know that a woman of God does not appear in *People* magazine, or on the television, or on the radio, or on the *Oprah Winfrey Show*."

One of the women in the sweatshirts struggled to her feet. "Sit down. Be quiet!"

Daniel looked amused. "I will not be quiet," he said. "I have been quiet too long. We have all been quiet too long. We have all put up with this lie, tolerated it, encouraged it."

"Sit down right now. Sit down and shut your mouth!" another one of the women yelled.

Daniel fixed his gaze on her, his face glistening with sweat. He inhaled deeply and marched back up the porch steps.

"We've all come here for different reasons," he said, turning. "I've heard your stories. I've cried over them. I've prayed over them."

He stopped again and hung his head, and let his words and the rain fall over them. Down by the lake, thunder rumbled, muffled and low, a beast stirring.

Daniel continued. "We all have pain," he said. "It is part of living. And we all have hope, it is part of being human." He pointed at the two obese girls sitting by the satellite dish. "You two have come because of your gluttony. You hope she will help turn your bloated bodies into something else." He smiled. "But only God Himself can change you, not a television personality."

He walked down off the porch again and pointed at the old man in the hat. "You came because your wife has suffered a stroke and is lying in a hospital, comatose, her brain wasting away. Her doctors want to discontinue their efforts, but you won't give up hope, so you've come here. But your hope is misguided, it falls on fallow soil."

He wandered into the crowd and pointed, this time at Susan.

"And you have come here for a release from your shame. You were burned by your own mother as you lay sleeping with your lesbian lover. You were in the throes of passion when the flames engulfed you. And you've come all this way, hoping the good sister will quiet the fire that burns you still. But Sister North cannot heal your scars, cannot take away your sins. She is not your confessor or confidante or even your friend. She is a creature of our times. She exists because we let her exist."

Susan took Sam's hand and squeezed it. "I thought you were a holy man," she called out, her voice calm but loud.

"I consider myself a holy man. I also consider myself a humble man in the face of God. Sister North is neither holy nor humble." He was now shouting. "She is not worthy of our respect or our prayers or our hopes. She is a lie, a terrible, terrible lie."

He abruptly strode back to the porch and bounded up the stairs, holding the axe high. "I am here to end this lie."

With that, he smashed the small axe into the front door. A gasp rose up from the crowd. He pulled the axe out and hit the door again and again until it cracked at the center. He then began hacking at the front of the house. A window shattered, wood splintered and flew.

"Stop him," Susan yelled. She scrambled to her feet. "Stop him!" She raced through the crowd, one hand on the back of her head, holding her scarf. Sam followed her, running as best he could around clusters of people. Up ahead, he saw Daniel bring the axe down on another window, heard more glass break, people shriek. The three women in the sweatshirts quickly descended on the porch, their faces desperate, frantic. Within seconds Daniel was surrounded.

"It is not my intent to hurt anyone," he said. He was breathing hard. "But I will not be deterred."

Susan stood at the bottom of the steps, her scarf slipping down her neck. Sam was right behind her, breathing hard. "This isn't the right way, Daniel," she said. "Please drop the axe."

Daniel's eyes searched the small knot of people closing in on him. "I call on you all to help me. Help me do God's work."

"This isn't God's work," Susan said. Her voice was soft and disarming. She took one step and extended her hand.

Daniel pulled the axe back farther. "I will not be deterred." His voice cracked. He looked wild, frightened.

Susan took another step closer. "Please, Daniel."

"She killed my wife. She killed her with false hope," Daniel said. "She was dying, but the nun made her believe things. She believed she was going to survive, she believed she was getting better. She believed in hope. The nun is a liar. She is a goddamn liar!"

"Daniel, please. We talked about this. This isn't the way. It never is."

"This *is* the way," he yelled. With that, he swung the axe downward, missing Susan's head by inches. Sam bolted up the steps and grabbed her hand, yanking her off the porch. Daniel lunged after them, falling forward, knocking them to the ground, where they landed in a tangle. Sam felt Daniel's hot breath against his cheek, then pushed out from under him and crawled up the stairs to reach the shovel by the door. He turned and saw Daniel lying facedown on top of Susan.

Sam stood. "Get off her!" he yelled. "Get off her!" He jumped off the porch and stood over them, the shovel held high.

"Get off her!"

"It's all right, Sam," Susan said, from beneath Daniel. Her voice was quiet and unafraid. "Everything's all right now." The axe was lying harmlessly next to them. Daniel started to cry, his chest heaving with deep mournful sobs.

"I'm sorry," he said, his face pressed against Susan's shoulder. "Dear God, I am sorry."

Susan's arms encircled him.

"It's all right," she said again.

Dazed and breathless, Sam scanned the terrified and shocked faces staring up at him, then the blank house.

"Goddammit!" he yelled. He heaved the shovel at the broken front door and sank to the ground, into the mud and the rain that was falling harder than ever.

Seventeen

The next morning, after the state police had come to take Daniel away and after Susan and her partner, Chris, had left for home in Boston, Sam decided to walk into town for some oatmeal. He thought a nourishing breakfast and some exercise might do him good after the tumultuous events of the previous day. He had decided to make every effort not to let what happened propel him into a downward spiral. A healthy start was just what he needed to keep moving forward.

When he reached the restaurant, he was greeted by Big Jack and quickly led to a table by the window. The man with the brown mole was already sitting there, eating his breakfast. Confused, he looked up at them, a piece of toast in midair.

Big Jack grabbed the toast out of his hand. "Get up," he said, "and move over there." He pointed to another table by the bar. Terrified, the man scurried away.

"Why did you do that?" Sam asked.

"He was just finishing," Big Jack said. He started clearing the table. "Besides, it's a nice morning, and I thought you might like a nice view. Got the window fixed and everything."

Sam glanced at the man with the mole, who was bent over his Bible, and sat down.

"Heard what you did yesterday," Big Jack said, holding his chin high.

"I didn't do anything."

"Took a lot of guts to help that woman. A hell of a lot of guts. You probably saved her life." He was looking at Sam closely, reconsidering him. "You did a good thing."

Sam was going to protest again—he really didn't think he had done anything—but instead picked up his menu. "I'll have the oatmeal."

Big Jack pointed at him. "On the house," he said.

"With raisins."

"I'm going to have to charge you for those." Big Jack headed for the kitchen.

Sam settled back in his chair and watched a sailboat glide through the water, slightly tilting as it rode the waves. Small, cotton ball clouds drifted over the lake. Big Jack was right, it was a nice morning. He wanted to feel happy, fall into the warm, bright day, but he felt his resolve giving way. He was angry and tired.

He dug out his assessment book.

He wrote:

This town is nuts.

"Well, hello there, yes, hello." Patrick, wearing his safari hat and wraparound sunglasses, was standing over his table. Big Jack held his chair for him.

"General," Big Jack said.

"Thank you, Jack," Patrick said. He removed his hat and glasses. "And you don't have to call me 'General.' I prefer if you don't."

"Yes, sir," Big Jack said. He handed Patrick a menu and left.

Sam waited until Big Jack was back in the kitchen before asking, "Did he just call you 'General'?"

Patrick was seriously studying the menu, frowning. "Yes, I believe he did."

Sam picked up his own menu, his black mood briefly lifting. "Why did he call you that?"

"What? Oh, because I am one. Was one, I should say."

"In the army?"

Patrick kept looking at the menu. "Yes. That's where you'll find most of your generals."

"Do you know Big Jack? Were you in the army together?"

"I don't know him," Patrick said. "I imagine he knows me though. A lot of old men know me."

"What war did you fight in?"

Patrick's eyes appeared over the top of his menu. He leaned forward and squinted. "What?"

"What war were you in?"

"What war? Oh, well, pretty much all of them. World War Two, Korea, Vietnam. You name it. One of the great things about America is that we're always trying to kill someone. Keeps a man young."

Sam tried to place Patrick on the History Channel. He was about to ask him what battles he had fought in when he remembered that he had just returned from his trip in search of his son.

Patrick closed his menu. "Where did all these people come from? Is the nun finally back?"

Sam glanced around the restaurant. It was almost full, mostly with people he recognized from the day before: the two big girls, the man with the hat, the three women in sweatshirts.

"No. There was a rumor she was, but she's not. I think most of these people will be leaving soon."

"Where did the rumor come from?"

"I don't remember."

"Well, I heard the same rumor." He pointed at the kitchen.

"From Jack. That's twice he's told me she was in town, and twice he's been wrong. I'm beginning to think the nun is one big rumor herself."

Sam put his menu on the table. "So," he said. "How was your trip?"

"Oh, fine, fine," Patrick said. "I ended up stopping over in Nebraska for a while on the way back. Took an extra day to meet with my bankers after all." He was reading the specials card, which was clipped to the back of the menu.

"When did you get back?"

"An hour ago. I flew to Duluth and drove up. Lila wasn't at the hotel though."

"How was your flight?"

"Oh, good, good, fine, fine. Flew first-class. Always a treat."

Sam sighed. "Did you find your son?"

Patrick looked confused. "What? Oh, no, no. That's right, I forgot about that, our discussion. No, no, it was another dead man. Someone else's son." He finally put the menu down. "I think I'll just have coffee and a roll after all. I ate something at the airport." He slid the menu toward the middle of the table and smiled. Sam thought he might ask something about Daniel, but instead he said, "Can you keep a secret?"

"A secret?"

Patrick's smile stretched ear to ear. "I watched a pornographic movie in Las Vegas," he said. He drummed the table with his fingers when he said this, and winked. "Yes, sir, I did."

Sam had difficulty processing this information. "Oh," he said.

"Have you ever seen one of those? I tell you, you get your money's worth. Watched it in the hotel room after I got back from the morgue. I've never really watched one of those before. I must admit, it held my attention. Doesn't leave much to the imagination. *Horny Housewives*, it was called. Have you ever heard of it? Nothing wrong with those movies, I imagine, once in a while." He looked around the restaurant, then back at Sam, still smiling. "I was hoping old Lila would have been at the hotel with me. I have to admit, that movie gave me a little spark. I thought about her the whole way home."

"Those movies can be very inspiring," Sam said.

"You have that right," Patrick said. "*Horny Housewives.*" He took a deep breath and exhaled loudly. "You married?"

"No. I used to be."

"What happened? Your wife die?"

"I'm divorced."

"Divorced? Well, you must watch your fair share of pornography then. You must have a lot of free time on your hands."

Sam leaned over the table. He had no desire to discuss porno movies with Patrick in a crowded restaurant, especially in the mood he was in. He just wanted to be alone. "I don't want to talk about those movies right now," he said softly.

"What's that?" Patrick asked. "Speak up."

"I don't want to talk about those movies," Sam said.

"You mean pornographic movies?" Patrick shouted, as if hailing a cab in New York.

"Yes."

"Are you prudish? I didn't take you to be prudish."

Sam glanced around the room. An elderly woman sitting two tables away was looking at them.

"I'm not *prudish*. I don't want to talk about them, that's all."

"You know, I have to admit, one of the actors, the man in *Horny Housewives*, looked a lot like you. Dark, curly hair. Slender. About your build. He played the role of a plumber in the film. Could have been your brother. You don't have a brother, do you? Or brothers? Didn't have many lines, but he stayed plenty busy."

Sam hunched his shoulders and tried to make himself smaller. In addition to his rising irritation, he was becoming embarrassed.

"You know something," Patrick continued. "Throughout the movie, I kept wondering where the word *horny* comes from."

"Can you lower your voice, please?"

"What does it mean, *horny*? You should know, being divorced and all. I imagine it means pent-up. You must be in a constant state of it. A frenzy."

"I don't know what it means." Sam rubbed his forehead. Out of nowhere, a headache had erupted. He hunched as low as he could.

"Something wrong with your back?" Patrick asked. "You're sitting funny. You throw it out?"

"Can we talk about something else?"

"You don't want to talk about your back?"

"I don't want to talk about those movies."

"You mean the pornographic movies?"

"Yes." Sam leaned back. "Those."

"Oh, that's fine. That's fine with me. Probably not daytime conversation anyway." Patrick reached for his water glass. "You know, that comment about you looking like the actor in *Horny Housewives*, Vince, his name was, I didn't mean anything by it. It was just an observation. You were the spitting image. Throughout the entire movie I kept thinking it might be you. Of course, I've never seen you with your clothes off."

"No," Sam said, "you haven't."

"But the resemblance was striking."

"Maybe it was my evil twin."

Patrick's eyes grew wide. "You have a twin?"

Sam sighed, and for a moment wished for Daniel's axe. "I don't have a twin," he said.

Patrick drank more water. "You know, those movies must appeal to sexually frustrated people. I'm not sexually frustrated, never have been. Did you know that Lila and I have sex every night we're together?"

Sam closed his eyes and massaged his temple. "Lila never mentioned that," he said.

"Well, we have, every night for forty years, except for religious holidays. Christmas, Easter, Good Friday, or when I'm in a war. Other than those days, we never missed it. Part of our routine. We brush our teeth, wash our faces, then get busy. I've talked to other people about their sex lives, and I'm starting to think we're unique."

"You're definitely unique," Sam said.

"I was calculating how many times we've fornicated. According to my calculations . . ."

"Can we change the subject?"

"Why?"

"I don't want to talk about your sex life right now. I'm not in the mood."

"What do you want to talk about then?"

"Nothing. I had a pretty bad day yesterday."

"You did? Because of rain? Oh, you mean about the nut with the axe. The lunatic. Heard something about that when I was at the hotel. I can see that putting a crimp in your day. That and the rain."

"It was a bad day."

They were quiet. Sam searched for Jack and his oatmeal. Patrick repositioned his hat on the table.

"When you were married, how often did you have sex?" Patrick asked.

"I said I wanted to change the subject."

Patrick looked genuinely confused. "Well, we did. We're talking about your sex life now. Not mine."

Sam felt the back of his neck grow hot. "I don't want to talk about anything right now."

Patrick's eyes narrowed. "The axe thing really bothering you, huh? Getting you down? Well, I can see how that could happen.

Especially if you're new to violence. Sometimes talking about it can help. We used to talk about things after battle. You want to talk about what happened?"

"No."

"You don't?"

"No."

"You don't want to talk. Well, if you don't mind me saying so, that's your problem. You never want to talk. You're too damn quiet. Everyone says so. You come up here, you should make an effort to fit in more, mix a little. You keep to yourself too much. Always in the backyard by yourself. We're all in this together. You're not the only one with problems."

Sam didn't say anything.

"See?" Patrick said. "Right there. Quiet. See, we know that's your problem."

Sam snapped. "You don't know me, so just shut up," he said.

Patrick's eyes grew wide. "Settle down now, just settle down. We're all your friends. We're just trying to help you."

"You're not my goddamn friends," Sam said. "This whole town is nuts. Everyone up here is nuts. This whole thing is pathetic. Everyone up here is pathetic."

"You're up here," Patrick said.

Sam pushed back his chair and walked over to the bar. He had just sat down when Big Jack burst through the kitchen doors with his oatmeal.

"Why did you move?" Big Jack asked. He seemed reluctant to give Sam his oatmeal now that he was sitting at the bar. "You had the best seat in the house."

"I like it better over here."

"But you were sitting over there."

"I'm sitting here now."

"But that's the best seat."

"I changed seats," Sam yelled. "I got up, walked over here, and sat down. It's not that complicated."

Big Jack looked over at Patrick, then back at Sam. He put the oatmeal on the bar. "I didn't have any raisins," he said, and left.

Sam ate slowly, his anger rising. He was sick of this town, sick of all these people, sick of waiting for a silly nun. The more he thought about it, the more ridiculous everything seemed. For the first time since he had arrived in Lake Eagleton, he seriously considered leaving. He could be back in Chicago before nightfall.

"Excuse me."

Sam turned and saw the man with the mole standing next to him, his eyes focused on the floor. Up close, his mole looked like a spreading coffee stain dripping down his forehead. He opened up his Bible and began to read in a hushed voice.

" 'Greater love has no one than this, that he lay his life down for his friends.' "

He closed the Bible but stayed focused on the floor. "Susan is my friend," he said. "Thank you for what you did." He reached out and touched Sam's shoulder and shuffled away.

Sam stared into his half-empty bowl of oatmeal, his anger and despair leaking away. He sat for a while, letting the sounds of the clanking dishes, the chatter of voices, and music from a radio all console him, calm him. He glanced around the restaurant at the lost people and wondered about all the pain in the world, wondered how and why everyone kept going. Is it because we have no choice, or do we really believe things are going to get better? Does some abstract hope keep the world spinning or, as Susan said, is it a belief in others that will save us?

He was fishing for his assessment book when Big Jack walked up to him.

"You want some coffee?" he asked.

Sam, still deep in thought, looked at him. "What?"

Big Jack held up a pot. "Coffee. Ever hear of it?"

"Coffee. Yeah, good. Coffee, but bring it over there." Sam pushed himself off his stool and headed back to Patrick's table.

A few days later, Meg showed him the right way to plant the grass seed. He thought there would be some scientific way of doing it, a process that involved the reading of manuals and the studying of intricate diagrams, but Meg just took a handful of seed from a wheelbarrow and threw it onto the upturned mud, then covered it up again, using the hoe. When she was finished, she turned and faced him.

"You have to water a lot," she said.

"How do I do that?" Sam asked.

For an answer, Meg left and returned a few seconds later with two sprinklers.

"The hoses are in front," she said. "They're a little short, so you'll have to move them around to get the whole yard." She took a step closer to him, her eyes serious, and her mouth, as always, drawn tight. "It's important that you water," she said. "If you don't water, the grass won't grow." She gave the instructions slowly, as if talking to a young child or, possibly, a highly intelligent dog.

Sam examined the seedless ground. "Okay," he said. Then he pumped his arms back and forth slightly like he was running. "Maybe we can jog a little tonight," he said. He raised his eyebrows in hopeful anticipation. "I think I can go a little longer now. I've been practicing."

Meg stared at him. "You don't practice run. You just run," she said.

Sam stopped pumping his arms. "Oh."

"Anyway, I can't. Not tonight." She mumbled this, distracted, and headed to the house. When she got to the door, she glanced back at him. "Sorry," she said, with a weak smile, then went inside.

Sam watched her go, disappointed. There was no trace of the other night's run together, the light gone. He turned and reluctantly addressed the yard.

It was a very big job, he thought, and he wasn't sure he was up for it. He was worried that somehow he would do something wrong, and the grass wouldn't grow, or worse yet, he would somehow manage to ruin the soil, rendering it useless for future generations. He had no idea of what he was doing.

"What's up?"

It was Willie. Sam was happy to see him. Maybe he could help.

"Hey, Willie. What's going on?"

Willie worked a toothpick from one side of his mouth over to the other and studied the ground.

"Nothing. Waiting for a delivery. Tiles for the roof. Gotta get going on the second half. Figured might as well do the whole roof. Meg say the insurance will pay for it."

Sam dug a little with the hoe, loosening up the earth, then went over to the wheelbarrow, took a handful of grass seed, carefully crouched over the ground, and gently tossed it, almost placing it in the mud. He felt Willie watching him and waited for his comment or instruction. Willie said nothing.

Sam stood up, his eyes still on the little pile of mud now filled with grass seed. Willie stared at the seed, too, then back up at Sam.

"Ain't going to grow right away," Willie said. "Ain't like a magic beanstalk."

"Do you think I put too much seed there?"

"I don't know. Spread it out a little."

"Spread it out? What do you mean? You mean, spread it out?"

"I don't know. Use that thing. That shovel thing."

Sam looked at his hoe. "You mean, this?"

"Yeah, that shovel thing. Spread it out."

Sam moved some seed around with the hoe. "How's that?"

Willie shrugged. "I don't know."

"I have to cover it back up with mud now." Sam waited for Willie to say something, to grab the hoe, push him away, and say, "Here, let me do it." Instead, he let out a small burp.

"Getting sick of Pop-Tarts, man," he said.

Sam covered the seed with dirt, then took a step back and studied the small plot of earth, which measured about one foot in total space.

"Pretty shady in here," Willie said. "Hope it grows. You using the right kind of seed?"

"Are there different kinds?"

"I don't know. Yeah, I think so. I think there's seed for shady areas."

"Shady seed?" Sam was suddenly suspicious. He looked at the seed in the wheelbarrow accusingly.

"Yeah, something like that." Willie took the toothpick out of his mouth and threw it. "Hey, you hear Leo asked me to do a magic act at the restaurant? I said I'd consider it. Don't think it's my crowd, though, but I'll try." He coughed into his hand and stomped his feet a little. "Cold, man. Louis let me move into that big room with the fireplace last night. No extra charge. Room right next to his."

"Really?" Sam grabbed some seed and inspected it, then threw it on the ground. "You mean the one with that big bed with the canopy?"

"Yeah. The blue room."

"That room's not blue."

"Yeah, well, he's thinking it might be if he ever gets more paint."

Sam reached for more seed. "You must have gotten on his good side."

"I help him out around the house. Do things. Empty garbage. Don't do much. He ain't really been charging me anyway. He's all right. He lets me practice my act in front of him, gave me a few tips, you know, about how to act, attitude-wise. He says, I got to be more of a performer, act more mysterious. Aloof, like you."

"What does that mean?"

"Aloof? I don't know. That's what he said." Willie sniffled and put his hands in his front pockets and rocked back and forth on his heels. "He's trying to think of a stage name for me."

"A stage name," Sam said. He squatted and, using his index finger, carefully began to separate the seeds from each other.

"Yeah," Willie continued. "He's okay. Lets me drive his boat. Watch his TV. He pretty worried about business, though, says the town is dying. He's trying to come up with new ways to get people to come up here. He wants to get away from just promoting the nun. You hear what his new advertising slogan gonna be?"

Sam stood up but kept his eyes on the seed. "No."

"Lake Eagleton: Come for the nun, stay for the fun. Going to take out ads in some papers."

"That's brilliant."

"Yeah. That's a good word."

Sam resumed working, throwing seeds, then covering them up. Willie made no effort to help. He just stood with his hands in his pockets, occasionally coughing.

"Working pretty hard here, Sammy," he said after a while. "Tony, he thinks you doing all this to win Meg over. Says this has nothing to do with the nun. Says all the motivation coming from a desire to get in the woman's pants. Those are his words. I ain't saying this, just telling you."

Sam stopped working. "Tony's got a big mouth," he said.

"Yeah, that's what I'm thinking. Meg's okay. Something going on with her though. Saw her crying yesterday."

This news caught Sam totally off guard. "Crying? When?"

"Real early. I was looking for the tool kit, I wanted to put on some new doorknobs, and I walked in on her in the nun's house. She was sitting at a desk, crying. Upstairs. She was crying soft, you know, she wasn't like weeping or anything, sobbing. But she was crying okay. Had her hands over her face and everything."

"Did you ask her why she was crying?"

"Naw, that's private property, people crying. She saw me, though, but we didn't say anything. I just left. Hey, don't tell her I told you about this. Like I said, it was private. I shouldn't have been up there maybe. Kind of like her house, almost."

Sam went back to work, but the image of Meg crying stayed with him. He wondered if she was sick.

"You got the hots for her, don't you?" Willie asked.

"I like her," Sam said.

"Yeah, I can see why. She's a good-looking woman, but she's not my type." He stamped his feet and coughed. "Want my advice, Mr. Sammy? About women?"

"What?"

"Never go after a sad girl. They sad for a reason."

"What's the reason?"

"Only they know that," Willie said. He stamped his feet some more and drifted away.

Sam dug and planted most of the afternoon, fighting a fear that he was doing things wrong. He was concerned that he might be using too much grass seed in one area and not enough in another. He was also worried that he was covering the seed with too much soil in certain spots. He knew he was managing to complicate what was an extremely simple process, but he couldn't help himself. He wondered if there were some kind of pamphlet he could read, a book possibly— *Chicken Soup for the Lawn.* The more he worked, the more concerned he grew.

He stopped around five o'clock. He was hungry and very thirsty. A small pain had once again surfaced in his lower back from all the bending, and he needed to get off his feet. He dropped the hoe on the ground and tentatively approached Sister North's house, silent in the afternoon shadows. He walked around to the front, saw no one, then circled around to the back again and went inside.

In the kitchen, he stood at the sink and drank a glass of water. It tasted like iron, but it was cold, so he drank another. He then searched for an apple or a banana, or maybe some bread. He was hungry and needed something fast.

In a walk-in pantry, he found a few cans of soup. Sister North's soup. He tried to imagine her eating it, blowing on it, shopping for it, waiting in line at the checkout counter at the Grocery Bag. He wondered if she clipped coupons. He was having a hard time accepting the fact that she was a real human being, that she existed at all.

He selected a can, baked bean, his favorite, and searched for an opener, checking inside drawers and cupboards, all of which were empty. He finally found one inside the pantry, opened the can, and poured the soup into a small pot that was already on the stove. Then he stirred it twice with a spoon, and turned the back burner on low.

While the soup was heating, he decided to tour the house. He had been inside a few times but only briefly to use the bathroom or to voice an unsolicited opinion on wallpaper to Meg. Now would be the perfect time to take a complete tour.

The kitchen was small and modern, with white cabinets and a new refrigerator Meg had ordered. A small, sleek microwave was built into the wall. An empty bookcase was off in the corner.

He walked carefully into the living room, around buckets and ladders, and noticed the front door had been replaced. Meg had hung it herself, as well as installed two new windows, the day after Daniel's attack. He glanced around the rest of the room, and saw it was entirely covered with a blue painting tarp. He peeked under one corner of it, saw brushes and paint cans, then let the tarp float down to the floor and headed up the narrow staircase.

Upstairs, he found a bathroom and two small rooms on opposite ends of a short hallway. He entered one of the rooms. Except for an old, chipped wooden desk and an aluminum folding chair, it was empty: The walls were also bare, no pictures, or photos. He glanced out the window overlooking the front yard, saw that it was deserted, then walked back to the desk and opened a drawer. As he now expected, there was nothing in it. He closed it and opened another, then another. In the bottom drawer he found a yellow legal pad. On the top sheet, someone had written, *Dear Maria*. On the very next sheet an address was written in very large, very neat print:

230 Printemps
Lyon, France
Attention: Wilbur Fuller

He stared at the address for a while then at the name, Wilbur Fuller. It was familiar, but he could not place it. He put the pad back in the drawer, and went over to the closet. Nothing but two wire hangers. He heard them clang together when he closed the door.

Next he wandered across the hall into the bedroom. Except for a small bed stripped bare, it was also empty. No trace of anyone having lived in the house.

He sat on the edge of the bed and tried to think things through. Up until now, he had chosen to ignore signs, chosen to keep his suspicions submerged and out of reach, but he could no longer deny the fact that things were a little strange. He admitted to himself that when it came to Sister North, something was definitely off. It should be obvious to anyone who chose to think. The confusing reports on her whereabouts, the rumors about her health, the town's obsessive reliance on her. Billy Bags's strange comments about her.

Sam lay back on the bed, his head spinning. A thin white curtain danced in the open window. He felt the cool breeze of the approaching evening on the side of his face and smelled the lake and pine trees. He wanted to sort through things, assess, but he felt his eyes close.

He immediately fell into a shallow sleep, just below the waterline of consciousness, heard and saw things. He saw the lake from high above, the nun's house, the yard, Meg's face, the poster of Sister North on the bike. He saw them all individually, like pieces of a puzzle. He then heard a great voice cutting through his vision, loud words that shook him, scared him. *God*, he thought. *God is talking to me.* He opened his eyes and saw Patrick hovering over the bed, eating soup from a bowl.

"Hope you don't mind," Patrick said.

Sam sat up with a start. "What?"

Patrick extended the bowl slightly forward. "The soup. I assume you're the chef." He spooned some into his mouth and swallowed. "I was hungry, and it was coming to a boil."

Sam ran a hand over his face and swung his legs over to the floor.

"Are you staying here?" Patrick asked. "I didn't know the nun had rooms for let."

"I was just resting."

Patrick swallowed. "Resting," he repeated. "Well, I didn't mean to disturb your rest. You can keep resting." He ate more soup, slurping a little.

Sam sat on the edge of the bed, still a little bit dazed. He sat for a while, until his head cleared, then asked, "Do you think it's strange that the house is so empty?"

"It's not completely empty. There's soup." Patrick spooned up some and shrugged. "They packed everything up when work began. I imagine that would be standard operating procedure for a job of this size."

"Everything? I mean, there's not even a picture?"

"What's your point?" Patrick asked. He seemed more interested in the soup than Sam's question.

"I don't know," Sam said. "I just think there should be a few things left over. Some sign that someone was living here. Or is coming back."

Patrick thought about this, his mouth full of soup. Then he swallowed. "To be honest, I've considered that issue. Actually, I've considered a number of issues concerning the nun. Can't seem to get a straight answer when it comes to her. Everyone has a different story. The man at the grocery store says one thing, Jack and Leo say another. The fat man, Louis, is especially vague. He doesn't even answer me when I ask anymore." He scraped the bottom of the bowl with his spoon, shook his head once, then left the room.

Sam followed Patrick downstairs. When he reached the kitchen, he found Willie at the table, eating the last of the soup.

"Hey, Sam," Willie said.

"That was my soup," Sam said. "I made it myself. Is there any left?"

Willie stopped eating and looked at Patrick.

"I doubt it," Patrick finally said, his face thoughtful and even sad. He patted Sam on the shoulder. "We spilled some." He pointed to a small puddle of soup on the floor by the door. "Over there. What we didn't spill, we ate."

"Yeah, it's good," Willie said. "Hit the spot. Baked bean."

Sam shook his head and walked over to the pantry and picked out another can, green split pea. He opened it, then poured the soup into the pot and turned the stove back on.

"Think the nun has anything to drink in here?" Willie asked.

"There's water," Sam said, motioning to the sink.

"Any beer?" Willie asked.

"There's some soda back here," Patrick said. He went inside the pantry. "Root beer."

"Bring it out," Willie said. "Better than water."

Patrick emerged from the pantry holding three cans of root

beer and a box of Ritz crackers. "I found some of these in a drawer," he said. He put everything in the middle of the table and sat down.

Willie reached for a root beer and opened the can. Sam turned off the soup and began eating it right out of the pot while leaning against the stove. It was hot, and he burned the tip of his tongue.

"Kind of surprised the nun likes root beer," Willie said. He softly belched.

Patrick opened his can. "I agree, root beer isn't something I would expect her to drink."

Sam snorted into his soup. "What do you expect her to drink? Holy water?" He was cranky over there not being any baked bean soup left.

"I don't know," Willie said again. He pulled a few crackers out of the box. "Sometimes I forget that the nun is a regular person. Eats regular food. Brushes her teeth."

"She's a person, like the rest of us," said Patrick.

"But she's different," Willie said. He finished the crackers and brushed crumbs off his hands before reaching for more.

"I disagree. We're all the same. We all have the same basic needs and desires."

"She's close to God. Closer than we are."

Patrick thought about this. "That's debatable," he said. "She's more committed to God maybe, but there's no guarantee He likes her more than the rest of us."

"You don't think God likes the nun more than you and me?"

"I like to think He doesn't play favorites," Patrick said.

"He got favorites, and the nun is one of them," Willie said. He took a sip of root beer and looked around the kitchen. "Wonder where she is. Been gone a long time."

Everyone was quiet. Sam walked over to the back door, still holding the pot of soup. The light was fading, and the yard looked dull and lifeless. He ate his soup and watched some sparrows flit around the crab apple tree, which still hadn't blossomed. He decided to pull it out. It was probably dead.

"So you think God likes you just as much as the nun?" Willie asked. He was still focusing on the issue.

"Well, maybe not me in particular," Patrick said. "But I'm probably not the best example. I would venture to say that He likes Lila, though, as much as the nun."

Willie mulled this over. "Lila versus the nun. Yeah, that's pretty close," he said.

Patrick reached for the box of crackers. "People are human," he said. "We have a tendency to judge them on their reputation and image, rather than who they are. I remember once seeing Patton jump away from a wasp that was buzzing nearby. Here he was, one of the most decorated men in the army, and he was afraid of an insect." He ripped open a sleeve of crackers and popped one into his mouth, whole. "People are human," he said again.

"Patton? You in the army?" Willie asked.

"Yes, I was."

"You in a war?"

"Yes, I've been in a few."

"You were in World War Two, right?" Sam asked.

"Yes, sir, the Deuce. I was there. I was only nineteen, but I was there."

"What was the worst part of the war?" Willie asked.

"The worst part?" Patrick chewed thoughtfully on another cracker. "Well, the food was pretty bad. Actually, I can't say any part of it was enjoyable. I missed Nebraska. I would have to say D day, though, was the worst. When we hit the beach. That was bad. That was as close to hell as I'd like to get."

Sam was suddenly very interested. He had watched dozens of shows on D day on the History Channel. It had always amazed him what took place there and he often wondered if he were capable of such bravery. "You were at D day?"

"Yes, I was. At a little place called Omaha Beach."

Sam was impressed. "Wow," he said. "What was that like?"

"I don't remember anything about it. I passed out as soon as I hit the water, I was so scared. Someone dragged me to the beach. I was out the whole battle. When I woke up it was over. Forty-nine boys in my unit were killed, and, for all practical purposes, I slept through the whole thing."

They were all quiet. Willie finally said, "You must be a pretty sound sleeper."

"I've been accused of worse things," Patrick said. He stood up and headed for the bathroom down the hall, only to return a second later, looking concerned.

"Excuse me, gentlemen," he said. "We have a developing situation here. Our foreman is back."

"Who?" Willie asked.

Patrick jerked his thumb over his shoulder toward the front of the house. "Miss Congeniality, if you forgive my sarcasm."

Sam stopped chewing. "Meg?"

"Yes. Her. She's pulling up in front." He focused on Sam. "I assume you had clearance to throw this little dinner party."

Sam swallowed and took in the mess: dirty bowls, spoons, cracker crumbs, root beer cans. Sister North's kitchen. Sister North's food.

"I didn't really. I mean, I just opened a can of soup. You guys opened the others."

"You opened all the soup here," Willie said. "Thought you had the okay."

Patrick nodded in agreement. "You were sleeping in her bed, making her soup. Your actions led me to believe that you had permission to throw this hootenanny. That was a wrong assumption on my part, and I'm sorry I made it." He glanced over his shoulder at the front door. "If Lila hears about this, I'll catch some hell. That was private property we consumed, private soup."

"Meg is not going to like this," Sam said.

"You mean, she didn't say it was okay to eat the nun's food?" Willie asked. He looked over the table. "Pretty messy in here, too. Soup on the floor even. Should have cleaned that up."

"Sam," Patrick barked. "Get outside and detain her. We'll clean up in here. Everyone, keep low." After saying this, he immediately fell to the floor on his hands and knees and began reaching up to the table for the bowls and spoons. "Move around like this. Stay away from the windows."

Sam felt a rising sense of panic. As soon as Meg looked at him, he would break down and give up the jig. He would ask for immunity, testify against everyone at the trial. He paused at the door.

Patrick gave him a hard stare and waved violently. "Put a move on now, mister! Double time. Move *now!*"

With a burst, Sam rushed outside and literally ran into Meg, who was standing by the door. She stumbled backward a few feet.

"Hey!" she yelled. "Watch it!"

"Sorry. Are you okay?"

She didn't say anything. Instead, she gave him one of her looks before turning to scan the yard.

"You didn't finish planting yet, did you?" she asked

Sam groaned a little. "Not really."

"It's getting pretty late." She walked away from the back door, her hands on her hips. "Have you at least watered what you've planted?"

"I was just about to. But I had to do something else."

"What?"

Sam thought about this. "I had to go to the bathroom," he said.

"How long were you going to the bathroom?"

Sam decided it would be best to be vague here. "A long time," he said. Meg raised one eyebrow and headed for the back door.

"Where are you going?" Sam asked.

"I want to take the paint inside."

"Wait." He tried to get in front of her, but it was too late, she was already opening the door. He held his breath and followed her inside, expecting to see the kitchen a mess. Instead, he found Patrick sitting in the dark at the table, waiting, it seemed, to be interrogated. He was alone, and the place was spotless.

"What are you doing?" Meg asked.

"Well, hello there, yes, hello there," Patrick said.

Meg eyed the kitchen "What are you doing?" she asked again.

"Well, I'm just sitting here."

"Why?" Meg asked.

"I sprained my ankle. Sprained it coming up the front steps."

Meg walked over to the wall and flicked on the light switch. "So you're just sitting here in the dark?"

"Yes, I am. My options were limited."

Meg looked at him, then over at Sam, who cleared his throat.

"I'll be right back," she said.

When she left, Patrick covertly gave the thumbs-up sign to Sam, but kept his eyes trained on the table. "Willie's upstairs," he whispered.

"Okay," Meg said when she got back in the room. "Let's go. Can you walk?"

"Yes. But slowly."

"Grab a shoulder," she said to Sam.

Sam initially assumed the sprained ankle was a ruse, but the way Patrick was limping, and holding on to him, made him wonder. It was entirely possible that during operation cleanup he had twisted it. When they got to Meg's truck, he gave a very convincing wince when he sat down.

"Bless it, it hurts some," he said.

"You'll have to get that checked," Meg said.

"I will make that a priority," Patrick said.

"Here," Sam said. "Stretch your leg all the way out."

"Where are you going to sit then?" Meg asked. She got in behind the wheel.

"Out in the back."

"It's full of junk," Meg said.

Sam glanced in the back and saw it was jammed with buckets, tools, and plastic garbage bags.

"It's okay," he said, closing Patrick's door. "He needs room. Just drive carefully. I don't want to fall out."

Meg's face softened. "I'll drive careful," she said, and started up the truck.

Later that night, Sam waited by the harbor for Meg. It was cold, and he was wearing a new Sister North sweatshirt. There had been a big sale at Reflections on Sister North wear, and he had reluctantly bought a number of things out of sheer necessity.

"Are you waiting for her?"

Sam turned and saw Billy walking toward him, pushing a shopping cart brimming with bags. His baseball cap was up high on his forehead, revealing his skinny, narrow face.

Sam waved a greeting. "Billy," he said.

"You waiting for her, aren't you?"

"Who?"

Billy smiled, his tight face relaxing. "Meg Lodge."

"I thought I'd surprise her."

Billy peered out over the lake. It was breezy, and the water was choppy. On the opposite shore, a few lights flickered in the growing dark. "She's pretty," he said in a slow, flat voice. "About as pretty a woman as I have ever seen."

"Have you seen a lot of pretty women, Billy?"

His smile disappeared. "I was married to one. She left me though. Living with me was too hard."

"I'm sorry."

"Not your fault. I'm not sure whose it is, but it's not yours."

"How long have you been up here?" Sam asked.

"About three years. I'm from Monroe, Louisiana."

Sam was surprised. "Louisiana? You don't sound like you're from the South."

"I lost my accent in medical school in Baltimore. They surgically removed it. They won't let you have a Southern accent at Johns Hopkins."

"You were a doctor? I mean, you're a doctor?"

"You were right the first time. Used to be a surgeon. Went back home and married a beauty queen. Miss Louisiana 1992. I had it all. Big home. Five bedrooms, a pool. Have to have a pool in Monroe. We were going to have a lot of kids. Tammy wanted a lot of kids." He extended his hand. "My name is Billy Parkson."

Sam studied the hand before slowly reaching out to grasp it. He was having a hard time connecting this calm, rational man to the person he was accustomed to seeing.

"You a runner?" Billy asked.

"Not really. I used to run a little bit in high school."

Billy smiled again, and under the unshaven gray beard and dirty hair, Sam glimpsed a man, a normal life, saw the five bedrooms and pretty Tammy lounging by the pool. "If you're going to try and keep up with her, you better be fast." He made a motion with his head and stared past Sam toward the water. Meg was running their way, her shape silhouetted against the lake.

"One of the reasons I stay up here is I get to look at her face every day," Billy said.

"Hey, Billy, do you mind if I ask you a question?"

"I know what you're going to ask. I've never been with her, though I tried."

Sam glanced back in Meg's direction. "No, not about Meg. I want to ask you about the nun. Do you know her?"

"I know her."

"So she really exists? She's real?"

"As real as you and me."

Sam felt relieved. "Is she sick then? I keep hearing these stories."

"No. She's not sick," he said slowly, distracted by Meg. "If I were a different type of man, I wouldn't just let you run off with her. I'd try one more time," he said. "But she's all yours. I gave her my best shot. I think she's prejudiced against schizophrenics."

Meg stopped a few yards from them and nodded hello. "Hey, Billy," she said. She was breathing hard.

"Meg," he said. He smiled and tipped his cap before walking away from them, pushing the cart.

"How are you feeling, Billy?" Meg asked.

"I'm fine," he said over his shoulder.

"Are you keeping with the program?"

"I'm trying to," he said. "You know that, Meg, I'm trying, just like you told me. I'm trying to be good."

Meg watched him for a full minute, her hands on her hips.

"What program?" Sam finally asked.

"His pills," she said. Her eyes were still on Billy.

Sam watched Billy cross the street and disappear into the woods. "How far have you run?" he asked.

"I don't know." She was still looking in Billy's direction. "About six miles."

"Six miles? Already?"

She turned, and Sam saw that her face was red and raw from the wind. "I felt like running tonight."

Sam jogged in place a little, bringing his knees up high in an exaggerated fashion. "Feel like running a little more?"

She shook her head and started to run. But she waved her hand for him to follow.

They ran down Main Street next to each other, their shoulders occasionally bumping. When they passed the courthouse, Sam saw that the door had been replaced and the two fallen trees had finally been cleared from the lawn. Once they were at the end of town, they doubled back and ran down the other side of the street, toward the lake and the harbor. Sam knew she was setting a very easy pace and felt he could keep up. He had been running quite a bit on his own in the morning and had developed what he hoped was a respectable amount of stamina.

"Do you ever think you'll compete again?" he asked.

"No," she said. "I'm too old. I was about fifteen pounds lighter back then. I'm fat now."

"You're not fat," Sam said.

They turned at the harbor and headed up the shore in the direction they had run the time before. Despite the cold night, Sam felt loose and warm. He ran a little faster, scooting ahead of Meg. He heard her laugh behind him.

"Want to race?" he said.

"No," she said. She ran slower, so he slowed, too, falling in beside her.

They ran for a while. Sam considered asking her about her crying, or at least probing the issue, but decided against it. Instead, he asked, "Why do you run so much? There are easier ways to get around, you know."

"It makes me feel better."

They were close to the water now, moving over a small, flat path that separated the trees and the lake. The waves slapped against the shore, occasionally spraying them. Sam licked water off his upper lip and tried to ignore the first stirrings of a stitch in his side.

"Makes you feel better," Sam said. "When does that part happen?"

"If you stick with it, it will happen. Running burns the bad out of me. Makes me feel new."

"You have bad in you?"

"I have a lot of bad in me," Meg said. She ran a little faster. "What were you and Billy talking about?"

"Nothing. He seemed pretty normal tonight. What's his story?"

"He's been around for a while. He used to be a doctor. He's in pretty bad shape now. I feel sorry for him. He's schizophrenic."

"Where does he live?"

"He has a little cabin, up by the bluffs. He does okay. We keep an eye on him. When he takes his pills, he's fine. Almost fine."

The path narrowed, and they had to run in single file, Meg in front. Sam stared at her long, bare legs, more out of admiration than desire. He was amazed at how fluid she was. She looked as though she were gliding.

By the time the path broadened, he was struggling. The stitch was now a sharp pain, and his lungs felt on fire. He tried to keep up but soon fell behind.

Meg slowed to a jog. After a few minutes though, even this proved too much for Sam, and he stopped, put his hands behind his head, and started walking.

"Sorry, you go on ahead," he gasped. He paced back and forth on the shoreline.

Meg stopped. "Why are you doing this?" she asked.

"What? Why am I running with you?"

"This whole thing." She stepped in front of him. "Why are you doing this?"

Sam tried to slow his breathing. "What are you talking about?"

"You know what I'm talking about. What do you want?"

Sam stopped pacing. "What do you mean?"

"You know what I mean. Where do you think this is all leading?"

"I don't know. I don't plan things out. I just want to run with you, be with you."

Meg was quiet, her eyes on him.

"I wasn't sure what I wanted when I came up here, but now I do," he said. He took a deep breath. "Now I know."

She shook her head. "This is the wrong time for something like this."

"Why?"

"It just is."

"When would be a good time then? Tomorrow? Next week? I can wait. I'm not going anywhere. Time is the one thing I have."

She concentrated on him again, her eyes moving back and forth like she was reading. He thought she was leaning toward him, but, instead, she turned and started to jog down the path.

"Come on," she said.

"I don't think I can."

"Yes, you can," she said. "Come on. We'll take it slow."

Eighteen

Over the next few weeks, Sam fell into a rhythm. He would awaken early and half jog, half walk over to Sister North's house to work on the yard, then catch a ride back to the restaurant in the afternoon for a late lunch. Evenings were occasionally spent watching TV with Louis and Willie on the small, black-and-white set, or swimming off the dock with Lila.

Quite often he would run with Meg, meeting up with her at the harbor, where they would stretch for fifteen minutes, swinging and straining their arms and legs. They always ran three miles, Sam's limit, keeping to the narrow path that hugged the lakeshore. Meg effortlessly chatted throughout their runs, talking about the day, the radio station, or the progress on the house. Sam seldom said anything; it took all of his strength just to keep up. But he kept up.

After they finished, Meg would make a quick exit, jumping into her truck and driving back to the restaurant, or Leo's house, where she was staying, or to the station to tape a show. Sam always held out hope that she would take him up on his offer to stay and watch the sun set, or drive into Princeville for a movie, but she never did. After a while he stopped minding and took to watching the sun set by himself, sitting on a rock on the shore, amazed by the changing colors.

He slept soundly at night, his body exhausted but satisfied, his dreams now a patchwork of vivid images: the lake, the yard, the woods. Sometimes he dreamed of nothing but a clear sky, achingly blue and empty. In the morning he would lie in bed with the window open to the breeze, thinking, assessing, wondering if he had a right to be happy.

His guilt found him at odd times, throwing him off-balance. Once, at the restaurant, when Meg was bringing him his lunch, she became Maureen for an instant, alive and smiling. Another time, he saw a new Sister North volunteer with white hair who looked so much like Roger that Sam had to leave the yard and walk down to the Chapel in the Pines to calm himself.

He pushed these moments aside, though, and accepted each day as it came, choosing not to look too far ahead. He ate, he slept, he worked, he ran. This is enough, he thought. His sporadic entries in his assessment book now included simple, but complete, sentences: *I feel content and satisfied*, and *I am sleeping much better*. One evening, while sitting on the dock, he tried to describe the way the tops of the trees looked as the sun caught them, how they seemed to be glowing, tinged with fire, but quickly gave up the effort, embarrassed.

He should have added *I am exhausted* to the assessment book, for he worked hard every day, clearing brush, planting grass and now flowers. The yard was his obsession, a reflection of him, and he threw himself into the effort in a way he had never done before.

Unfortunately, the yard wasn't responding. Despite its being July, the grass refused to grow, a fact that was beginning to cause him great anxiety. The rest of the house was progressing at a good pace. Willie was nearly done with the roof and chimney, Patrick was almost finished with the electrical work, and Dot and Lila were well into the painting and decorating. Only the yard remained unfinished, or, more accurately, a mess.

His growing sense of concern was fueled by the news that a major event celebrating the completion of the house had been scheduled for August. People from around the country were planning to attend the unveiling of the resurrected house. Word was that Sister North would be there as well. Leo had received a letter from her and posted it on the bulletin board at the restaurant next to the jukebox. It was just a few lines, reporting she was safe and well and traveling with a friend in France. It also said she would be home soon. Sam read the letter over several times, noting the large, neat handwriting.

Even though he had his doubts about her return, he had to assume the party would take place, and this added to his sense of urgency in regard to the lawn. He worked harder.

"What are you supposed to be growing?" Dorn, the punk clerk from Reflections, asked one morning. He was standing on the back porch eating an apple, having been recruited by Meg to help with the installation of a new septic tank that was supposed to arrive any minute.

"Grass," Sam said.

Dorn had no comment. Instead, he took one final bite of the apple before throwing the core high up into the air. It landed in the middle of the yard with a thick thump, and stuck out of the mud, terribly white against the hopeless darkness.

"Don't do that," Sam asked.

"It's biodegradable," Dorn said.

Sam gave him a look.

"Sorry," Dorn said. He walked gingerly across the yard and carefully picked up the core, pinching its stem between two fingers.

"Got it," he said. He held it up for Sam to see before placing it in his pocket.

"Why do you think nothing is growing?" Sam asked. He didn't think Dorn would have a clue, and he was right.

"Don't know," Dorn said. He tiptoed back to Sam.

"I've done everything. I've seeded, watered, everything. This is embarrassing."

"Yeah, I bet." Dorn took the apple core out of his pocket and began to pick some mud off it. Then he took a tiny bite out of it with his front teeth. "Maybe you should grow something else."

"Like what?"

"I don't know, tobacco maybe." He put the core carefully back in his pocket and sniffled.

"Tobacco," Sam repeated. He flicked away the first beads of perspiration from the back of his neck. Despite the early hour, it was already hot. While getting dressed that morning, he heard Meg predict the first ninety-degree day of the year on her radio show.

"Hey, are you going out with Meg?" Dorn asked.

"Why do you ask?"

He shrugged. "She's my cousin."

"She is?"

"Yeah."

Sam looked at Dorn a bit differently. His hair was greener than usual this morning, and his skin, in sharp contrast to his black Metallica T-shirt, a white sheet. "I don't see much resemblance," he said.

"She's like my third cousin or something, so we don't have a lot of the same, you know, DNA."

"That explains it," Sam said. "Did you grow up with her?"

"Yeah."

"What was she like?"

"A lot of fun. She's a lot older, so I don't remember much. But she was funny. She used to watch me and a friend of mine a lot, you know, baby-sit. She always made us laugh. She would make us sing and dance, put on these little shows for her. She's different now."

"How? What do you mean?"

"She's pretty serious all the time. She came back that way, from California. But she's still pretty cool. We both like music. I keep telling her to play different stuff though. Music that's happening now.

She's been so busy lately. Hasn't had time to broadcast live much. I like it when she does her shows live. I call in all the time. Did you ever hear me?"

"No," Sam said.

"I disguise my voice sometimes, so it sounds like different people are calling in. No one ever calls. I do it to help Meg out. You've probably heard me but just didn't know it."

"Probably."

Dorn cupped his hands over his mouth. "Hey, I'd like to hear 'Stairway to Heaven,'" he said in a low, rough voice. He smiled. "Recognize that one? I use that one a lot. It's my old dude voice."

"It's good."

"Want to hear my young dude voice?"

Sam stared out over the yard. "No," he said.

Dorn nodded. "Last year, I did live reports from Summerfest in Milwaukee. I called them in. Like a roving reporter. A rock and roll correspondent. I used my real voice for that. I almost interviewed the BoDeans. Ever hear of the BoDeans? They're from Wisconsin, I think. But when I got close to them, a security guard tackled me."

"He tackled you?"

"Yeah, well, I didn't have any pants on." Dorn offered no immediate explanation. Sam looked at him.

"I was really wasted, and I forgot to put them on," he finally said. "Don't tell Meg that though. She's antidrug."

"I won't."

"She gets pissed pretty easy. She's real pissed that not many people showed up to help with the house."

"Do you really think Sister North is coming back this time?"

"Yeah. She's due. She's never been gone this long, so she's due."

"Do you know her?"

"Yeah. She and I talk about stuff sometimes."

"Like what?"

Dorn shrugged. "Stuff. Everyday stuff. Music. She likes rock and roll. Just oldies though. She's the one who told Meg to play that instead of Christian rock. She wants me to go to college. She told me to move away and live somewhere else. She told me not to stay here."

"She did? Why?"

"I don't know. I don't think she likes it here anymore."

"Why?"

"I don't know. She doesn't like new stuff. The statue, the trolley, the new studio, the new bank, and all the stores, all that stuff. That's why she's gone so much. I think we're, like, chasing her away."

Sam scrutinized Dorn, his perceptive comments catching him off guard. He was about to ask him other things, when he heard the truck with the septic tank struggling up the road out in front, hissing and sputtering.

Dorn reached into his pocket and took the core and threw it deep into the woods, where it fell out of sight. "Time to go to work," he said.

Later that evening, Sam returned to his room and tried to review a rough design of a promotional brochure Louis was developing about Lake Eagleton: *Come for the Nun, Stay for the Fun!* The cover of the brochure was ridiculous: a picture of an older woman, who looked suspiciously like Sister North minus the habit, water-skiing, an insane smile on her face. In the background, billowing clouds loomed over her shoulder. When Sam turned the brochure at a particular angle, as Louis had suggested, the clouds joined together to form the profile of Jesus Christ wearing sunglasses.

He put the brochure down, lay back in his bed, and rubbed his eyes. Louis had been frantic the past few days, complaining about business and money. One night, earlier in the week, he had knocked on Sam's door and drunkenly began asking questions about bankruptcy.

"When you declare bankruptcy," he had asked, "exactly whom do you declare this to? Is it like telling people you're gay?"

Rather than declare bankruptcy, he began selling Pop-Tarts and fruit to his guests in the morning. Willie had suggested this, and Louis, after running his hand through his beard several times, agreed, declaring Willie "brilliant." The day before, he had bought an immense watermelon and had been selling it for a dollar a slice, cutting it with great fanfare at the kitchen table with a large butcher knife.

Thoughts of food made Sam's stomach rumble. He had worked so late in the yard, he had forgotten to eat. He rolled out of bed and headed downstairs, where he found Willie and Louis in the living room, watching TV. Louis was sitting in the big chair, knitting what looked to be some kind of red shawl. He seemed to be fairly well along in the process, the shawl already falling from his lap to the ground.

"What are you doing?" Sam asked.

"Reading," Louis said. He didn't look up from his lap, where his thick fingers were quickly moving.

"I didn't know you knew how to do that."

"I'm full of surprises," Louis said.

Willie was sitting in one of the two high-backed chairs, leaning forward toward the TV. "Where's the other chair?" Sam asked.

"Broken," Louis said. "I sat on it by accident."

"Are you going to get a new one?"

"Yes. I'm knitting one as we speak."

Willie looked at Sam and put a finger to his lips. "He tense," he whispered.

Sam went into the kitchen, took a peach out of a wooden bowl, and ate it while standing over the sink. He dropped fifty cents into a jar marked FRUIT, wandered back to the living room, and sat cross-legged on the floor. *Ripley's Believe It or Not* was on. A man from South America was about to legally marry an eight-inch doll he believed was inhabited by the spirit of his late girlfriend, who had been killed by a snake. The man wept as he walked down the church aisle in his black tuxedo. The camera zoomed in on the little doll in her tiny, white wedding dress. She looked innocent and fragile, her mouth and eyes wide-open.

"Believe it or not," Willie said. "Believe it or not."

"What are we watching here?" It was Patrick, standing by the staircase, eating some grapes and wearing a red baseball cap with LAKE EAGLETON, USA! stitched across the front.

"Some dude just married a doll. Thinks it's got his dead girlfriend's spirit. Doll only eight inches."

"Only eight inches? Well, that's not much of a doll to marry." Patrick squinted at the TV, swallowing some melon. "Say, did the girlfriend in question get killed by a snake?"

"Yeah," Willie said.

Patrick nodded. "Then I've seen this episode." He walked farther into the room and looked around. "Still a little light in the chair department, I see."

Louis ignored him and kept knitting. Patrick moved closer to Louis and the big chair, finally standing directly over him.

"Well, I guess I'll just stand here," he said.

Louis knitted faster, his hands a blur.

"With my bad ankle."

With that, Louis put down his ball of yarn and needle and heaved himself out of the big chair, pushing so hard that it moved backward several inches. Patrick turned, winked at Sam, and plunked himself into the chair.

Louis straightened his muumuu and glanced around the room. "What are you smiling at?" he asked Sam.

"Nothing," Sam said. He looked at the TV.

With a grunt, Louis turned and headed into the kitchen, dragging the half-finished shawl behind him.

"You took his favorite chair," Willie said.

"I am a paying customer," Patrick said. He licked his fingertips clean, then ran his hands over the big chair's thick, mahogany arms. "I feel entitled."

"He kind of depressed."

"I believe that may be a permanent condition."

Willie glanced down the hallway where Louis had disappeared. "Business is bad," he whispered. "Plus, his poem got turned down by a magazine. About his dead cat. Blue Bell. Kind of a famous cat. Was in a lot of magazines. Won a lot of awards. Had like blue paws," Willie said. "Light blue."

"Blue paws?" Patrick asked.

"Believe it or not," Willie said.

"I never heard of such a cat. I don't fancy cats myself. They are too feminine a creature."

"You like dogs?"

"No, I can't say that I do. I don't really like animals as pets. I own a cattle ranch. I raise animals to kill."

"How many cattle you got?" Willie asked.

"We have about ten thousand head, including calves."

"A lot of cows, man. You got a lot of land there?"

"I guess so. They tell me I'm the biggest private landowner in the state of Nebraska. I hire people to run the show now though. I am just the benevolent owner at this stage of the game. I just sign the checks. I cash my share, too."

"Yeah, place sound like Bonanza. I like to be on a ranch, ride a horse. You got any Mexican people out there?"

"We might. I don't know every one of our hands personally." Patrick pointed at the TV. "What are we watching now?"

"I don't know," Willie said. "*Ripley* over. Nothing now."

"Well, put on the A&E channel. *Biography* should be on. It's nine o'clock."

Willie changed the channels with the remote, eventually finding *Biography*. The life of Liberace was being featured.

"Who's he?" Willie asked.

"Liberace. A very famous homosexual pianist. He never said he was homosexual, never admitted it though it was obvious." Patrick gestured with his head toward the kitchen. "Like our friend here," he said.

Willie took in Patrick's comment, glanced toward the kitchen, then back at Patrick.

"What you talking about, Patrick?" he asked.

"Our large friend."

Willie's eyes shrunk into slits. "You mean, you think Louis a fag?"

"Well, he wears a dress, knits, and pines for a cat. From my vantage point, those are the classic earmarks of homosexuality."

"But he got the hots for Meg."

"She has a certain masculine element to her, if you ask my opinion."

Sam got to his feet. He couldn't bear to see the look on Willie's face. Shock, suspicion, confusion. Sam, too, had recently suspected Louis was gay, or at least had a crush on Willie. "I'm going to bed," he said.

Patrick stood as well. "That sounds like a good idea. We've been driving around all day, looking at property, and I'm a little beat. Meg was showing us around."

"I heard you might be buying something here," Sam said.

Patrick shook his head and sighed. "Yes, I believe we may. Lila's smitten with the place. Wants a summer home here on the Lake of Many Moods. Thinks it's sacred ground." He sighed again. "Well, she's younger than I am, so if this is where she wants to end up after I'm gone, that's her prerogative. I would rather she stay in Pleasanton, but I imagine this place is nice enough." He started for the stairs. "Good night, gentlemen."

Sam followed him upstairs, walking slowly down the hall. He was wonderfully exhausted. After months of dreading sleep, he craved and even looked forward to it, the Maureen dream now more the exception than the rule.

The light was already off in his room, so he quickly got into bed, too tired to brush his teeth or even to take off his running shorts or T-shirt. He was falling asleep when he felt his foot graze something. Another foot. He opened his eyes, then slowly reached over in the darkness and felt, first a head, then a face, then, finally, very large, female breasts.

"What a coincidence," Dot said. "Running into you here."

Sam bolted upright. "I'm sorry. I'm in the wrong room."

He tried to get out of the bed, but Dot yanked his arm back and in one quick motion managed to get on top of him. "No, you're not," she said, once she was safely sitting on his chest. "I'm in the right room."

"Can you get off me, please?"

Dot hovered over him and looked into his eyes, her white, powdery face a grinning ghost. She was wearing a loose-fitting nightgown that was slipping off her shoulders. "I like the view from up here," she said.

"I'm having trouble breathing. You're on my chest. Please. This is not good."

"How do you know? We haven't tried anything."

"We're not going to." Sam tried to push her off but she was surprisingly strong and kept him pinned down, her legs straddling his chest.

"If you move, I'm going to scream," she said. "That would upset a lot of people."

Sam stopped pushing.

"Listen, pal," she said in her husky voice. "I'm not looking to raise a family here. All I want is a little roll in the hay. Could you be a team player on this? It'll be over in a few minutes. It doesn't hurt or anything."

"I don't think I can help you. Maybe Willie can. He's just down the hall. He talks about you a lot."

Dot laughed. "Nice try." She sat back a bit. "You don't have any problems down there, do you?"

"No."

"Are you gay?"

"No."

"And you're not married, I heard that, even though you told me you were. So what's the problem then? It's not like I'm asking you to change a tire."

"I just don't want to do it."

She leaned back even farther and crossed her arms over her chest. "Don't want to do it with me, you mean. Everyone wants to do it." She nodded a little, thinking. "I know what's going on here. You're in love with Meg Lodge. That's what's going on. I was afraid of this. I made my move too late. Should have acted sooner before Miss Hard Body came running." She shook her head. "I want to tell you something, buddy. In my prime, it wouldn't have been close. Wouldn't have been close. I had my pick of men. My pick."

"I'm sure you did."

She shrugged. "I knew it was a long shot. But at my age, you take risks. Go for it. That's what Sister North is always telling me."

"Sister North tells you to go for it?"

"Yeah. Don't act so surprised. She's a woman. You should hear some of our conversations. Make Dr. Ruth blush. She was engaged for two years before she turned into a nun. Was engaged to some guy who used to live here. The stories she told about herself and her boyfriend. He ended up owning a big electrical supply store. I think she missed the boat on that one. They're everywhere. They used to do it like rabbits when they were kids."

"I don't think I want to hear this."

"You know, it's been six years since I had sex," Dot said. "And fifteen years since I made love."

Sam didn't say anything. Dot was just now coming into focus in the dark. He could see her shape in her long, slinky nightgown. He had to admit, for an older woman, she had a nice figure.

"Reconsidering my offer, Sam?" she asked.

He cleared his throat. "I think you better leave," he said.

"Not just yet."

Sam sank back in the bed. It was then that he heard someone walking down the hall. A moment later, there was a knock at his door.

"Sam?" It was Louis.

"Oh," Sam whispered. "Shit."

"Sam? Are you awake?"

Sam and Dot were quiet.

"I know you're in there. And I know you're not sleeping. You just went upstairs. I have a problem in the kitchen. The microwave, there's smoke coming out of it." He knocked again. "Please. It's acting violently."

"Unplug it," Sam said.

"I did that. But I'm concerned about the smoke. It seems to be *billowing*."

"What did you put in the microwave?"

"That shouldn't matter, should it?"

Sam sighed. "It might."

"A toaster."

Sam started to ask why, then decided not to bother. He tried to rearrange himself under Dot.

"I wanted to heat up some toast," Louis said.

Dot sat up straight and cupped her hands around her mouth. "Hey, Louis, go ask Willie," she half shouted. "We're busy in here."

There was a muffled gasp followed by deep silence, then finally a sharp burp. "My apologies," Louis said, and walked away.

"Thanks," Sam said. "That's going to be all over America tomorrow."

Dot shrugged. "Hey, the next best thing to having sex is people thinking you're having sex."

"Can you leave now?"

"What's your hurry? Relax. You're always so uptight. I just want to get to know you a little. You're a mystery. Always by yourself in the backyard digging, reading the Bible. Everyone wonders about you."

"Dot, listen, I think you're an attractive woman. So don't take this wrong, but I don't think we're right for each other." He made an effort to sit up, pushing on his elbows. Dot pressed down harder on his abdomen.

"I think you're wrong there, buddy. I think we're a lot alike. We've been through the same thing. From what I've heard at least."

Sam groaned and sank back.

Dot finally slid off him and rolled over on her side, her back to him. Sam, relieved of her weight, took several deep breaths.

"You know," she said. "When they told me that my cancer disappeared, I didn't believe them. I went to three different doctors. Finally, I went to Mayo, and after they told me it was gone, I went out and drank a half a bottle of vodka. I found an all-night liquor store in Rochester and drank it in the parking lot. I almost killed myself. They had to rush me back to the hospital. I almost died of alcohol poisoning. Almost drank myself to death. Can you believe that?"

Sam sat up and looked at her back.

"I couldn't understand what happened, how it just went away like that. No one could. I felt happy, of course, grateful, I still do, but I feel guilty, too, like I got away with something." She was quiet for a moment. "It's hard, I tell you," her voice now low. "Real hard. I want to make a difference, pay God back, but I'm not sure I know how. I don't know if I'm doing enough, or doing the right thing, or doing it for the right reason. Am I being good to help people, or am I doing it so I don't get cancer again? I tell you, I get dizzy thinking about it. I just do. I thought maybe you'd understand, from what I heard."

They were both quiet. Then Dot's shoulders started to shake a little and she began crying, short sobs. Sam hesitated, then slowly reached out and put his hand on her back.

"Hey," he said. "I think you're doing a great job."

She rolled over and looked at him. Her makeup was running, her eyes melting into thin black streaks. "You think so?" she asked.

"Yes. Absolutely."

"Well, I'm trying, you know." She sniffled. "I go to that little Chapel in the Pines every day and pray. I pray for everyone, everything. I even said a prayer for you. I'm helping out as much as I can at the house. I gave $1,000 to the Jerry Lewis telethon last year. A thousand dollars. I called it in, I charged it on VISA. But I don't know if I'm doing enough." She stopped and shook her head and sniffled some more. "I tell you, Sam, being a survivor is a hassle sometimes," she said. "A real big hassle."

"I know," Sam said.

"Do you feel guilty? About that girl who was killed, the one you worked with? I heard about that."

Sam's body tightened and sagged at the same time. "Yes, I do. She shouldn't have been working there. She was always afraid. I knew it was dangerous, but I didn't care. I just didn't care."

"Is that the reason you want to talk to Maria? Sister North?"

"One of the reasons."

"What else do you want to talk to her about? Or is that none of my business?"

Sam considered this question. "I'm tired of being me," he said. "I'm sick of it. I want to know how to change. I want to know if it's really possible." He shook his head. Spoken aloud, his quest sounded absurd. "Pretty stupid, huh?"

"What?"

"Come all this way to ask something like that?"

Dot smiled. "Nothing stupid about that." She reached out and squeezed his hand. "Changing can be pretty hard, though. Trust me. Not many people can do it, I bet." She sniffled a few more times and rolled over, her back to him again. "Do you mind if I stay here for just a little? Just for a few minutes. Is that okay? I don't want to be by myself."

Sam saw her shoulders shaking again. He reached over and patted her back, then lay down and put his arm around her.

"You can stay," he said. "You can stay as long as you want."

Nineteen

The next day was Willie's big show at Big Jack's. Sam got to the restaurant early and took a seat at the bar next to Willie, who was wearing a too-tight, long-sleeved white shirt and a black bow tie. He was obviously nervous as he studied a small, elevated stage in the middle of the room.

"What kind of house you think we gonna get here tonight?" he asked.

Sam scanned the room and was surprised to see that it was almost full. Clyde, the man in the wheelchair, was sitting directly in front of the stage, his head jerking and bobbing as he tried to read the Bible he always carried. A ghostly, pale woman wearing an ill-fitting wig was sitting next to him, her hands neatly folded in her lap, a silver crucifix lying flat against her pressed black blouse. The cheerless man with the mole walked quickly past the bar on his way to a table by the window. Up front, a white-haired priest with a hearing aid dozed, his arms dangling loosely at his sides. About three dozen others, in crisp, summer clothes, sat patiently, waiting for the show to begin.

"It's a good crowd," Sam said.

"Yeah. More people than I thought." Willie pulled a deck of cards from his green duffel bag and tried to shuffle them, but fumbled, cards spraying onto the bar.

"Shit," he said. He reorganized the cards. "Tense, man. Louis say I got to channel my nervousness into positive energy and envision my success. He been practicing with me. Coaching me. He was gonna lend me a cape he got. He used to wear it. Too big though. I was tripping over it."

"Is he coming tonight?"

"Naw, he ain't coming. Says he be too nervous. Let me ask you something here. You think he a fag?"

"I don't know."

"Yeah, I don't either. Could be though. But he got it for Meg. Used to talk about her all the time."

"You can like men and women," Sam said.

"Yeah, I know people like that."

"He's lonely," Sam said. "I think he just wants people to like him. And you're pretty nice to him."

"Yeah, well, I ain't that nice to him. I like women." Willie fooled with the cards again. "But he's okay. Offered me a job, helping to run the place with him. He needs help."

"Are you going to do it?"

"I don't think so. I may be going soon."

"Well, hello there." Patrick and Lila approached them, holding hands. Patrick was wearing a white linen sport coat and a pink polo shirt, and Lila was dressed in a collarless light blue dress and a strand of pearls that draped nicely across her chest. Sam was continually impressed with their elegant clothes.

"Isn't this exciting?" Lila said. She reached out and squeezed Willie's wrist. "We're all cheering for you."

"Yeah, thanks," Willie said. He reached for Sam's water and took a couple of gulps. "Excited myself. First time tough, I guess."

"First time?" Sam asked.

Willie shrugged. "Yeah. Never really done this before, you know, in front of a crowd before. Practiced it a lot. In front of Louis mostly."

"It can be a terrifying experience getting in front of a crowd. Especially if you don't know what you're doing," Patrick said. He looked at Sam. "I used to sing a little, you know."

Sam hesitated. He had a sense of where this might be leading. "I didn't know that," he said.

"Yes, I did. I picked it up in the military."

"Thought you were a general," Willie said.

"I was an officer and a singer. It doesn't say anywhere you can't be both. When they promoted me I stopped singing in public. Nixon put the word out for me to knock it off after he saw me perform while he was touring Pendleton. I sang 'Shenandoah.' My tour de force. He was a hypocrite. He shook my hand after my act, said he enjoyed it. Then he told the brass that I was a general, and if I did it again, he'd ship me to Laos. I've been a Democrat ever since." He scanned the room and nodded at Dot, who was sitting down near the front. "I had quite an aptitude for it though, singing, so much so that I've been thinking about picking it up again."

He waited for someone to say something, but no one did.

"Yes, I have," he finally said. "I know I can still do it."

"I'm sure you can, dear," Lila said. She patted him once on the chest and smiled nervously at Sam. "I'm sure you can."

"Don't patronize me, Lila," Patrick said. "I'm liable to jump up onstage and sing a little tonight."

Lila took Patrick's hands and held them. "This is Willie's night," she said. She appeared worried, her eyebrows knotting. She obviously had reason to be afraid.

"He can sing, I don't got no problem with that," Willie said.

"You see that, Lila? He doesn't care. Music and magic. The complete entertainment package."

"Please, dear, remember the last time?" She patted the top of his hands.

"One bad experience does not discourage me, Lila. That was an aberration."

"And that time in Paris?"

Patrick was quiet. "That was a while ago," he said. "Those people were French, and they were rude."

Lila turned to Sam. "We were in Paris. In a bistro. Patrick was arrested."

"Rude people, the French. And I wasn't arrested, as a point of clarification. I was escorted off the property. They released me immediately back at the station. They even gave me a ride back to the hotel. They were very apologetic. Hell, I helped save their damn country."

Sam laughed, then pretended to cough when Patrick glared at him.

Lila took Patrick's hand again. "You're right, they were rude, dear. Now, let's go sit down and enjoy the show. We'll talk about your singing later."

Patrick puffed out his chest and gave Sam one last look. He hooked his arm in Lila's and turned toward the tables.

Willie reached for Sam's water glass. "Kind of a strange dude," he said. "Never figured him for a singer. Picture him killing people more than I can picture him singing." He drank off most of the water, then put the glass down and rubbed his hands together. "You know something? I'm getting real nervous. Lot of my tricks ain't ready for prime time. Plus, my act is geared more toward kids."

"This won't be a tough crowd," Sam said. "They're mostly old folks, and they're not going to be able to see most of your tricks anyway so just explain them out loud, explain what you're doing. That might work. Talk loudly though."

Willie began packing the cards into the box. A young couple, probably still teenagers, walked past them, searching for a table. The man had long sideburns and was wearing a T-shirt that said PRAISE HIM! The girl, moonfaced, with long disheveled, yellow hair, followed close behind.

Willie finished packing up the box. "Hey, let me ask you something else here. You ever have weird dreams? You know when you sleep?"

"Yes."

"I never used to, but now I do. Pretty soon after I got up here, I started getting them. What do you think that means?"

"What are they about?"

"Last night I had a dream I was talking to the nun. We were sitting here. Right here, talking. She was sitting right where you are now. Except she was drinking a beer. I remember that I thought that strange. A Corona. And she had on big sunglasses, mirrored ones, so I couldn't see her. Just saw my own face."

"What were you talking about?"

Willie shrugged. "I don't know. I told her shit, you know. Things I don't tell anyone. Like confession used to be. Like when I went to church when I was a kid. Told her a lot of shit."

"What she tell you?"

"She told me everything be all right, mostly what she said. But then she told me to watch my back."

"Sister North told you to watch your back?"

Willie nodded. "Yeah. I mean, she said it in more of a, like, holy way, like a religious way. But that's what she meant. Be careful. Then I woke up. Weird dream. Been thinking about it a lot, though. Stayed with me all day."

"I have a lot of them, too," Sam said.

"What are yours about?"

"Nothing lately. I used to dream about this woman I knew, she was killed. Now, though, I dream about this place."

Willie looked around the bar. "You mean Big Jack's?"

"No. The lake. The sky. The clouds."

Willie considered Sam's dream. "No offense, Sammy, but it sounds pretty boring. Good thing you already asleep when you're having it."

"I like it. It's peaceful."

"You know Tony; he says everyone has weird dreams up here. Everyone talks about them. He gets them, too. He sets an alarm clock by his bed for two hours after he go to sleep so it will wake him up in case he's having a bad dream. Then he resets it for another two hours and goes back to bed again. Sleeps with a light on, too. Kind of feel sorry for him. Waking up all the time, lights on. Kind of"—Willie stopped to think—"what's the word?"

"Pathetic?"

"Yeah, he kind of that way, Tony. Pathetic. You know what I told him?"

"What?"

"Told him he needs a woman, someone to wake him up when he's having a bad dream. Everyone needs someone like that. Someone to wake them up when they having a bad dream."

Sam finished his water and searched for Meg.

"Thinking about that shit more lately, thinking maybe it's time I get a woman. Had a few, but not in a while. Married once," Willie said. "Thinking if I don't, I'm going to end up like Tony, sleeping with the lights on."

"Maybe you guys can move in together," Sam said. "Take turns watching each other sleep. Wake each other up."

Willie grinned. "Hey, I'm trying to have a conversation here. Being serious. You know, having a heart-to-heart. About to face a firing squad. Getting my last words in before I go down. Making my confession to you."

"You got a lot to confess?"

Willie drooped forward on the bar and began picking at the box of cards. "Who doesn't?" He picked at the box some more. "Hey, something else I got to mention to you. Been meaning to bring it up, you being a lawyer and everything."

"What?"

Willie shrugged. "Well, say I got this friend who did some shit and was out on bail but decided to jump and leave the state. What kind of trouble he get in?"

"I'd have to know more about what he did."

Willie was quiet. "Well, I think he stole some cars. That's what I was led to believe. This was his third time he was being sent down, and he didn't want to go. Wasn't hurting nobody, just stole cars for parts. Insurance pays everything, no one gets hurt. He was a hard-working guy, but got tripped up. So now he's in deep shit or something?"

"Maybe."

"What would you recommend he do, what would you counsel him?"

"Turn himself in probably. But I would have to know more."

"Yeah, well. That's all I know, you know, all I know."

"I hope he does the right thing," Sam said. "Stuff like that can catch up with you." He stood up and patted Willie on the back. "I've got to go to the bathroom."

"Yeah."

Sam had to work his way through the growing crowd, past and around a number of small, extra tables that Leo and Jack had set up to accommodate the audience. There was a line in the bathroom, and he had to wait for close to five minutes. When he finally returned to the bar, he found Tony sitting where Willie had been.

"Showtime," Tony said. He rubbed his hands together and picked up his glass of beer. "I'm nervous for Willie. Hope the kid can pull it off. This crowd could get ugly real fast."

"He'll be all right. Most of this crowd is pretty old."

"Don't matter. They'll turn. Trust me. He don't produce, they'll eat him alive." Tony rubbed his hands again. "Where's your girlfriend?"

"Meg?"

"No. Louis. Yeah, Meg. Wondered what she was going to wear tonight. Thought maybe she might get dressed up. I never seen her in a skirt before. I'd like to see her in a short skirt and something cut low. Black. Classy, but sexy." Tony lowered his head and picked up his beer. He took a very slow but loud sip. "I like my ladies that way. Classy, but sexy," he said. "Oh, here she comes. Shit, she's got jeans on."

"Hey," Meg said. She was wearing her hair up in a tight bun, and Sam could clearly see she was nervous. Her eyebrows were scrunched up, and her face looked unusually small and pinched.

"Where's Willie?" she asked.

They searched the bar, but there was no trace of him.

"I don't know," Sam said.

"Maybe he split," Tony said. "Couldn't handle the pressure. Maybe he took off. I seen it happen. Performers can't take the heat. They crack up, turn to drugs, get caught with a hooker." He shook his head. "It happens."

"I'll go look for him," Sam said, standing.

He found Willie sitting on the bench on Big Jack's dock, holding a small shoe box with holes punched in the top and smoking a cigarette.

"When did you start smoking?" Sam asked.

"Five minutes ago."

"What's in the box?"

Willie blew smoke, and threw the cigarette in the lake. "Mouse. Part of my act. Found a mouse in Louis's basement. He gave it to me."

Sam stared at the lake. The sand bluffs to the east were slipping into shadow. They appeared ominous, mysterious as they disappeared. "You got a roomful of people waiting for you inside."

"That's why I'm outside."

"You're going to disappoint a lot of people, you know."

Willie stood but didn't move. "Don't think I can do this."

"Come on," Sam said. "You can do it."

"Ladies and gentlemen, it is my pleasure to introduce Martinez the Magician," Sam said.

"And who are you?" Patrick called out. He and Lila were sitting right in front of the stage.

"His assistant," Sam said. He bowed as the room clapped.

Sam turned to Willie. "Tell me what you want me to do," he whispered.

"Hand me the bag," Willie said.

He started to shuffle a deck of cards and suddenly fumbled, dropping a few cards in the process. Sam quickly knelt and picked them up while Willie offered a sheepish apology.

"Weird," he said. "Never did that before."

When he shuffled again, he dropped a few more cards and abruptly froze, staring at them like they were bloody body parts. His face was blank and uncomprehending, and the room was silent.

Patrick turned to Lila. "Is this part of his act?"

Sam once again collected the cards. When he handed them to Willie he whispered, "You might want to try something else."

Willie put the cards into his pocket and pulled out a short string and scissors from his bag. He held the string up for everyone to see, then cut it carefully into three, small pieces.

"Got three pieces here," he mumbled.

"He's got three pieces here," Sam repeated loudly.

Willie looked at him, then put the pieces on the table, covering them with a red napkin.

"Gonna sprinkle some magic dust on them now," he said, swallowing his words. He reached into a green felt bag and dropped a pinch of white powder onto the napkin.

"Magic dust," Sam said.

Willie looked at him again. "I just said that," he whispered.

"I said it louder," Sam said.

Willie nodded. "Oh. Okay."

He reached into his bag for a thin black wand and waved it over the napkin like a conducting maestro. With his left hand he quickly pulled the napkin away to reveal the piece of string, once again whole and intact. When he held the string up for the room to see, everyone enthusiastically clapped.

Willie stood stoically on the stage, his hands in his pockets, his chin on his chest. When the applause died down, he reached behind his ear and pulled out a quarter and threw it up in the air and caught it. He then opened his hands so the audience could see that the quarter had disappeared. A second later, he leaned over the stage and pulled the coin from behind Clyde's ear. Clyde made a high-pitched squealing sound, and everyone clapped again.

Buoyed by this success, Willie immediately repeated the trick, pulling a quarter from the ear of the ghostly white woman sitting next to Clyde. The woman nodded and smiled demurely as Willie held the quarter over her head. Once again, the crowd applauded, this time more vigorously.

"You're on a roll now," Sam said. He backed up to the side of the stage.

His confidence surging, Willie quickly launched into more ambitious tricks. First, he made an entire pitcher of water disappear, covering it with the red napkin and snapping it away with a flourish to reveal it gone. While the crowd was still marveling at this feat, he deftly pulled a handful of daisies with short-cut stems from his sleeve and presented them to Lila with a bow of his head.

A series of quick, simple card tricks followed, each one pleasing, if not amazing, the crowd. Sam surveyed the room, saw the rapt, eager faces, amused and entertained, and felt happy for Willie, happy for everyone.

For his final trick, Willie made a gray mouse vanish from inside a small, gold cage, then reappear under a napkin. The crowd oohed and aahed, clearly and justifiably impressed at this feat.

"Now how did that happen?" Patrick yelled.

Sam clapped loudly, proud. While Willie's act was short, it was smooth, and, despite the shaky beginning, flawless. The tricks with the water and mouse had especially surprised him. He had never seen Willie practicing those and wondered how long he had been keeping the mouse.

Willie began packing up his things, but the crowd kept applauding. Patrick and Lila stood up. Soon the entire room was standing and clapping. Willie bowed a few more times, strutting back and forth in front of the stage, his chest puffed out, his grin wide. Finally, when the applause showed no signs of abating, he stopped and pumped two fists in the air.

"You people fucking rock!" he yelled. He pumped his fists one more time and jumped off the stage.

The people in the front row stopped clapping, their mouths open. The old priest pressed his hearing aid against his ear and looked confused. "What did he say?" he asked.

"He wants to know if we want to see an encore!" Patrick said. He stood and turned toward the room. "Who wants to see an encore?" he yelled.

Everyone started applauding again. The teenage boy with the sideburns stood up and whistled.

"And who here wants to hear me sing?" Patrick yelled, smiling. He pumped his fist in the air.

The clapping died down; the teenage boy with the sideburns stopped whistling.

"Patrick! Please!" Lila said. She grabbed his hand and pulled him to his seat.

Willie bounded onto the stage, and the clapping immediately resumed. He held his hands out for quiet. "Hey, appreciate your support," he said. "Means a lot. Bad news is, I don't have any more tricks. You want to see some of my old tricks again?"

"May as well," Patrick yelled. "Do the whole thing. No music lovers here."

Willie considered this. "You want me to do my act again? The whole thing?"

The crowd clapped its response, and Willie, beaming, reached into his bag.

"Well, you saved the day," Meg said, after Willie had finished his second show. She was standing next to Sam, who was back at the bar. She was holding a beer and looking at him strangely, her eyes half-closed, her lips half-parted. It was a look he used to get years ago from other women in other bars. He wondered how many beers she had drunk.

Sam nodded toward the stage. "Better sign Willie to a contract fast," he said. "Or else he'll charge you double next time." A group of people, led by the man with the brown mole, were gathering around Willie, watching him perform some of the card tricks for a third time. The man with the mole seemed particularly interested and was loudly asking Willie questions.

Meg took a long drink of her beer. "This is the first time any kind of promotion ever worked here," she said. "Everything else bombs."

"It's magic," Sam said.

Meg was quiet and picked at the label on her bottle. "Hey, do you want one?" She held up the bottle.

"No. I'm good."

She gazed at him. "I bet you are," she said. She finished her beer, her heavy eyes still on him.

"You want to run later?" he asked.

"No," she said. "I feel like doing something else. Why don't you meet me in the park when I'm done here."

"What do you feel like doing?" Sam asked.

"I don't know." She smiled. "Probably the same thing you feel like doing." Before he could say anything else, she disappeared into the kitchen.

Sam sat at the bar for more than an hour, drinking water and eating cashews from a red plastic bowl that Leo kept by the register, waiting for the place to empty out so Meg could leave. Willie's act seemed to have some type of cathartic, unifying effect on everyone, and most of the crowd remained, standing in small clusters, chatting and drinking coffee. Finally, around ten o'clock, convinced he was going to be there all night, he ordered a grilled chicken sandwich and a Coke from Dorn, who was bartending. From time to time, he caught a glimpse of Meg through the kitchen door window, holding a tray, or scrubbing a pot in the sink. He tried to wave her over, but she never saw him.

He was considering going into the kitchen and offering to help when he felt someone tap him on the shoulder.

"Can I talk to you?"

He turned and saw Billy, unshaven and looking more gaunt than usual. He was wearing his cap down low and smelled of stale food and old gym clothes.

"Sure." Sam patted the empty seat next to him. "Have a seat."

Billy didn't move. Instead, he looked at the floor.

"Outside," he said.

Sam glanced around the bar, then took one last bite of his sandwich. "Hold on," he said, swallowing.

He followed Billy through the parking lot. It was a marvelously clear summer night. The air smelled sweet, like washed fruit, the sky crowded with stars. When they reached the road, Sam asked where they were going.

"To the harbor," Billy said.

When Sam asked, "Can't we talk here?" Billy was quiet.

They walked quickly down the road, Billy's face up toward the night sky.

"Keep your eyes peeled," he said. "You might see some interesting things."

Sam walked faster. All he really wanted to see was Meg.

When they reached the harbor, Billy turned to face him. "I found Sister North today," he said.

Sam was confused. "What do you mean? Where is she?"

"Under the water. She's all the way on the other side, a mile away at least. Thing must have been like a rocket. She's about twenty feet out, by the bluffs, stuck in a sandbar. She's almost out of the water. I could touch the top of her head from my boat."

Sam nodded. "The statue," he said.

"It must have been stuck in that sandbar, but it got loose. It's been pretty windy the last few days. Probably loosened things up. They stopped looking for it. They think it's in the center, out deep, but I found it. They will, too, soon enough, I guess, if it stays on that sandbar. I could have dragged her out myself if I had some chains. She's real loose. She'll pop right up."

"Did you tell Jack yet?"

"No." Billy looked past Sam, out over the water. It was a calm night, and the lake was still. "Look over there," he said.

"What?"

"There. Look there. I thought we might see it tonight."

Sam turned his head and saw a flickering circle of white light, bouncing from one side of the shore to the other.

"What's that?" he asked.

"Moanpatec's spirit," Billy said, smiling.

"What?"

"The Indian princess. She's circling the lake now."

Sam watched the light, then walked closer to the lake, looking for its source.

"Where is it coming from?"

"Heaven," Billy said.

Sam continued to stare, amazed. He peered up at the star-filled sky, then back down at the shore. Although it was small, he could see it clearly: a circle of light, darting randomly over the water and the shoreline. "Where do you think it's coming from?"

"I don't know. But it's trying to get out. It's looking for a way out of the circle. Just like the rest of us. We're all looking for a way out of something."

Sam watched the light for a few seconds, straining his eyes at what he thought had to be an optical illusion. "What did you want to tell me, Billy?"

"I wanted to tell you about the lie. Because I know you're going to figure it out."

"Figure what out?"

"Sister North is dead."

Billy's words fell like a brick to the ground. Sam was silent.

"Jack told me, but I've been suspicious. I know you suspect, too. You're smarter than most people who come here. That's why they're worried about you. They don't want lawyers from Chicago driving BMWs up here. They want old ladies with stage-four cancer from West Virginia. People with inoperable melanomas, people going blind. Alcoholics." He stopped. "And schizophrenics from Monroe, Louisiana. That's where they make their money. Desperate people who only see what's put in front of them."

Sam was still quiet.

"They don't want anyone to know. They want to keep the lie going as long as they can so the town doesn't go under. They just built that bank and the grocery store. That TV studio out by the col-lege. They want to keep it going until at least that big party. They're in deep, and they need every dime."

"Who's trying to keep it quiet?"

"Everyone."

"Who? Jack, Leo, Louis? Meg?"

"Meg," Billy said. "Especially Meg. She owns this town. Or she will soon enough. She's a hard woman. She'll do anything to keep you from finding this out." He smiled again. "Even make you fall in love with her."

Sam followed the light across the lake. It was on the far shore now, by Sister North's house, bouncing crazily. "How long has she been dead?"

Billy bent over to pick up a small rock and threw it into the water. "About two months. She died in France. Lung cancer. Other people are going to figure it out soon. You can't keep it quiet forever. You sus-pected, didn't you? I could tell by looking at you."

"Yeah, I did."

Billy wandered to the edge of the water. "This is a pretty place. I enjoyed my stay here, but it's time to go. No point in staying any longer."

"Where are you going?"

"Home to Monroe. I think I'm ready to try again. I never thought I would be, but I think there comes a point when you have to. I'm going to live with my brother Nicky for a while. Get things right."

"When are you going?"

"I'm leaving right now," he said. "I've got a car. I can drive. I'm not as crazy as everyone thinks. I can drive."

He turned and headed across the park, toward the street where a white, compact car was parked at the curb.

"Hey," Sam called out. "Are you going to tell anyone about this?"

Billy didn't stop walking, but over his shoulder he yelled, "I just did."

• • •

Sam sat on the bench in the park, watching the swings sway in the breeze, thinking, assessing. While he had never fully articulated his suspicions, he had known something was up almost from the start. He had chosen to look the other way for an obvious reason, the same one everyone else had—he wanted to believe. He was surprised by how unaffected he felt over the news of Sister North's death. He thought this was because from the moment he had arrived, he had replaced Sister North with Meg. He knew now that as soon as he had seen her, she had become his reason for staying, not the nun.

And she had lied to him.

He walked to the lake and searched for the light. It was gone. The shores were dark and still, waiting.

"Hey."

He turned and saw Meg approaching. She had changed out of her jeans and was wearing a long, sleeveless sundress. Her hair was down, and her feet were bare. When she got close, Sam could see that she was holding flowers in her hands.

"Did you see the light? It's weird," she said. She stood next to him. "It only comes out once or twice a year. No one knows what it is. They think it has something to do with the Northern Lights. Everyone was watching it from the dock when I left, like it was part of Willie's act."

Sam kept his eyes on her.

"He gave me his daisies," she said. She held them out to him. "They're real. I thought they were fake."

Sam took the daisies and dropped them to the ground.

"Hey! What did you do that for?" She knelt and scooped them up. "What's the matter, you don't like magic flowers?"

"I don't like being lied to."

Meg kept smiling. "Who's lying to you?"

"You are."

"What do you mean?" Her voice went flat. "What are you talking about?"

"Sister North is dead, isn't she?"

Her smile vanished, and it was only then that Sam knew for sure. "Who told you that?"

"Billy."

"Billy doesn't know what he's talking about. He's crazy. Where is he? Did you just see him?"

"He went home. To Louisiana."

Meg dropped her arms to her sides, deflated. One of the daisies slipped out of her hands and fell to the ground.

"This whole setup is a lie," Sam said. "Anyone who spent half a minute thinking about it knows this is a scam, and you and your uncles are making money off it. Keeping the nun alive as long as you can. Lying to sick, old people. Dot. Willie. Lila. And you're right in the middle of it, aren't you?"

"You don't know what you're talking about."

Sam felt his face flush hot. "Why didn't you tell me the truth? How could you see me every day, talk to me, run with me, work with me, and not tell me? How can you look at me every day knowing why I was here and not say anything?" He grabbed one of her wrists and shook it. "How could you do that?"

"Get your hands off me!" She yanked free. "Don't you ever do that again. *Ever.*" She spit those words and looked wild.

Sam backed away, frightened by her sudden transformation. "I'm sorry," he said. "I'm sorry."

Meg's chest pumped furiously, her eyes locked on him. "What did you think was going on between us? We run a few times together, we . . . we fix a house together. So what? Do you know how many people I've met up here? Do you know how many crazy, desperate, nutty people come through here every month, every week, every day? Do you know how many people's stories I've heard? People who want to be my best friend, who pour their hearts out to me, who I never see again? I just met you. I don't know you. You could be anyone."

"I'm not anyone," Sam said.

She shook her head. "You know, this isn't all about you. It's bigger, a lot bigger." She started to say something else, but decided against it. Instead, she turned and walked away, flinging the daisies into the darkness.

Twenty

Sam stayed away from Sister North's house for the next two days and seldom left his room. In the evenings, he avoided everyone, choosing to read in bed or to stare out the window at the lake, imagining it was a river that flowed far away from this strange place. Once, Louis knocked on his door late at night, a wineglass in hand, and asked him if he was all right. Sam told him he was sick. Louis gave him a long, soulful look before leaving. The next morning Sam found an entire watermelon by his door with a note, *No charge!*

He made quite a few entries in his assessment book during this period, short sentences full of anger and betrayal.

Meg lied to me.

Everyone in this town lied to me.

I was an idiot. And:

I am going to end this whole thing.

He had every intention of doing just that, although he knew it would be more difficult than he had originally thought. He had no real proof, no dead body. He only had the words of a schizophrenic and the look on the face of a woman he thought he might be falling in love with. He feared his claims would be dismissed as simply another rumor.

He considered calling a television station or a newspaper and offering his theory, encouraging them to get on the trail. It wouldn't take long for a reporter to uncover the truth. He also considered walking into Big Jack's on a crowded night and making an announcement, to get other people to think and ask questions. The town was slowly filling up, and the restaurant was busier than ever.

Ultimately, however, he decided to do nothing. He was confident that the truth would soon reveal itself. It would be impossible to keep the secret for much longer. He also held out hope that Meg would come forth and end the charade. If she could do that, she would redeem herself, at least in his eyes.

On the evening of the second day, he put on his running shorts and went down to the kitchen. Louis and Dot were sitting at the table, eating red grapes from the wooden bowl and reading old issues of *Cat Fancy* magazine. Louis eyed him apprehensively, but Dot kept her head down in the magazine.

"So which one was Blue Bell?" she asked.

Louis glanced at the open pages and pointed. "That one, that one, and that one." He flipped a page. "And that one. She was in this magazine more times than any other cat."

"She was like a celebrity then, like Meg Ryan," Dot said.

"Yes. Exactly. She was the Meg Ryan of cats. She was everywhere."

Dot held the magazine up to her eyes and squinted. "I can see her blue paws. Amazing." She brought the magazine even closer to her face. "Is that an emerald on her collar? The green jewel?"

"Yes. It was mother's. She gave it to me a few weeks before she died."

"What happened to Blue Bell again?" Dot asked.

Louis closed his eyes. "She fell out of the boat, into the water. I was holding her and lost my balance, and she just slipped out and went under. I never found her body. I searched for days."

Dot took Louis's hand and squeezed it. "That must have been terrible."

"Can I take the boat out?" Sam asked.

Louis opened his eyes, confused.

"Are you going to look for the cat?" Dot asked.

"I just want to take it out," Sam said.

"Where are you going to take it?" Louis asked.

"For a ride," Sam said. "Is it on the lift?"

"Yes." Louis still looked nervous. He glanced over his shoulder at the lake, then ran his hand over his mouth. "The keys are in there."

"Thanks," Sam said.

He walked down to the dock and got into the boat, searching immediately for the chains. The ones he had used to bury Albert the horse were still there. He backed off the lift, the boat's motor gurgling to life, then quickly turned and headed toward the sand bluffs.

It was another mild evening, the lake mirror smooth. Once he reached deep water, he slipped the throttle all the way down and felt the engine respond and jump. Soon he was cutting through the water, warm air clearing his mind. He glanced up and saw small swirls of clouds, then the etchings of a crescent moon. Any other time, he would have been content simply to move over the water, but tonight he felt barren, and saw nothing but shadows.

When he reached the other side of the lake, the trunks of the pine trees were already dark and disappearing. He slowed as he approached the shore, cutting the engine to trolling speed.

The sand bluffs were high and steep and clung to the last remaining light. He inched closer to them, then straightened the boat out and ran parallel to the land. For more than a half hour, he drove back and forth in front of the bluffs, heading out deeper with every pass, his eyes trained on the water. He was about to give up when he saw something solid and black lurking just below the surface. He cut the engine and let the boat drift sideways. When he floated close to the shape, he looked over the side of the boat and into the eyes of Sister North.

Despite the darkness, he could see her clearly. Her peaceful face was gazing upward, her smile rippling with the movement of the water. He reached down and felt her cold, hard head.

He knew that what he was doing was foolish, even dangerous— he couldn't swim—but, if Billy was right, he felt he could do this.

He quickly dropped anchor and jumped into the water, tightly clutching the chain from the back of the boat. Billy was right, the statue was on a sandbar, and if he stretched out, he could touch bottom.

He walked on his toes through the water until he reached the statue, then straddled it with his legs, wrapping the chain tightly around its neck two times. After yanking on it to make sure it was secure, he heaved himself back into the boat. When he started it up and gave it gas, the big boat jerked and strained forward. After just a few minutes, the statue oozed out of the sand, floating free on its back.

Though it was now completely dark, Sam kept the lights off and drove slowly. When he was reasonably sure he was in the center of the lake, he cut the engine and drifted in silence, astonished at the distance the statue had covered in the air. He was still at least two miles from the harbor. He looked up at the sky and tried to imagine the statue flying through it, hurtling upward, streaking toward heaven in a blind rush, the clouds parting to greet her. He next saw the descent, saw her falling, tumbling head over heels, her face calm and accepting, at peace.

He sat there with the statue under the sweeping night sky, feeling helpless. Then he made his way to the back of the boat, where he saw the silhouette of Sister North darkening the surface of the water.

He hesitated before doing what he had come to do, wondering if criminals also balked before pulling the gun or sticking in the knife. The moment passed, however, and he reached down and unlatched the chain from the boat. Then, he peered over the edge and watched the shadow of Sister North disappear for what he presumed was forever.

· · ·

Later that night, while lying in bed, he tried to describe his experience in his assessment book, but all he could write was, *"Alone."*

He was staring at the word when Louis knocked on his door. Sam debated whether or not to answer it before reluctantly dragging himself out of bed.

"I thought you might enjoy this," Louis said. He extended a bottle of wine to Sam. "Absolutely no charge. Completely. It's a Pinot. Light. Perfect before bed."

Sam pushed the bottle away. "No thanks."

Louis raised his chin and appraised him with sober eyes. "As you can imagine, we're all very worried about you."

I bet you're worried about me. "How's business?" Sam asked.

"Oh. I can't complain."

"Everyone coming to the big party later this month. To meet the nun."

"Yes."

"I've been meaning to ask you, how is Sister North doing, Louis? Have you talked to her lately?"

Louis examined the floor and pulled on his beard, yanking hard. "No, not really. I've been busy. I've been working on a poem. It's about you."

Sam had nothing to say to this.

"It's called 'Solitary Man.'" Louis fished into his muumuu and pulled out a sheet of paper. But before he could read, Sam closed the door in his face.

About a half hour later, there was another knocking. He initially ignored it, but it kept up. Finally, his temper rising, he jumped out of bed and yanked the door open, prepared to tell Louis off.

"Hey," Meg said.

"Oh. Hi."

"Can I talk to you?"

Sam opened the door wider.

She entered the room and walked directly to the open window. The wind had picked up, and the white drapes fluttered crazily like moth wings. She stood with her back to him.

"What do you want?" Sam asked. He closed the door and stood by it.

"You know, my uncles raised me. They were my mother and my father," she said. Her voice moved slow, each word precise. "They drove me to school every day, picked me up. They packed my lunches. They came to every track meet, no matter how far it was. They saw me run, they paid for my travel. They even hired a personal coach. They didn't have much money back then, and what they had, they gave to me."

"Why are you telling me this?"

"Because I want you to know that they're not bad people. They don't want to hurt anyone. They didn't want any of this to happen. They made some dumb decisions when it came to the town and the nun. They got carried away. Everyone did."

"They should tell the truth."

She turned to face him. Her eyes were red-rimmed, but her face was impassive, unyielding. "You know, everyone who comes up here is broken, Sam. They all need help. Believing in the nun a little longer isn't hurting anyone. It gives people hope."

"And while they're being hopeful, they can spend their money."

"This town gives people somewhere to go. It gives people a chance to meet each other. That's how the nun made a difference. She brought them together. There's nothing wrong with them finding each other, helping each other."

"You can tell yourself that," Sam said.

"I'm telling you this because I know you'll understand. You're always helping people."

Sam was taken aback by this. "What are you talking about?"

Meg looked straight at him. "You help everyone. Everyone wants to be around you. You make everyone feel better. Patrick, Willie, Lila, Dot." She stopped there. "Me."

Sam swallowed. He had never been accused of being helpful before. He cleared his throat and worked hard to maintain his anger.

"You should have told me about this. At least told me."

Meg folded her arms across her chest. "I'm going to tell everyone the truth at the party. Everyone's going to know then," she said.

"So everyone gets one last payday."

"So everyone gets to believe a little longer," she said. "I'm sorry about this. I didn't mean to trick anyone. That's not what I want to do. I know you think that, but it's not true. I don't care about money."

"Why are we fixing the house then?"

"You don't have to if you don't want to."

"Yeah, but Lila and Patrick. They're working hard on it. Everyone is now."

"They're enjoying it. You know that. It gives them something to do. It takes their minds off their problems."

"It's a waste of time. She's dead."

Meg paused here and tucked the ends of her hair behind her ears. "Making something beautiful, fixing something, isn't a waste of time." She stopped and looked off to the side, at a blank wall. When she spoke again, her voice was just above a whisper. "You know, I just found this out a little while ago. When we started the house, I didn't know. I knew something like this might happen, but when she left she didn't tell me anything. I didn't even get a chance to say good-bye. I want the house to be our good-bye."

She took a step back and waited for him to say something.

"So," she said. "What are you going to do?"

"What do you want me to do?"

"If you can just keep this quiet until the party. I'll tell everyone then."

The drapes fluttered again, billowed up behind her, then fell limp. Sam took a deep breath.

"Okay. All right."

"Good," she said. Without another word, she walked past him and left the room.

That night, when Sam finally fell asleep, he dreamed he was falling through a dark space filled with voices. He sensed good intent, but could not hear words. When he landed, he was in the familiar field, watching a woman dressed in white, walking away from him, small children following. He ran to catch up with them, thinking it was Maureen, but when she turned to face him, he saw it was Meg.

He woke with a jolt and lay in one position for hours, listening to his breath and watching the night fade through the open window. He stayed in bed as the morning arrived, looking at the fog move across the lake, the image of Meg clinging to him. Finally, he got up, dressed, and slipped out the back door. He walked up the gravel driveway at a good pace, his rhythm smooth and easy. When he reached the road, he started to run.

The fog drifted inland, swirling around, surrounding him. As he moved in and out of clouds, he felt like he was disappearing, so he briefly hugged his chest with his arms to get a palpable sense of himself. When the fog clears, he thought, I will know where I am.

He picked up his speed, the ground revealing itself through patches of mist. He turned off the road and up the hill. Though he could not see it, he knew the stone wall was to his right and the lake to his left. He worked the hill hard, pumping his arms at his sides. Sweat dampened his forehead, and his breath felt hot and dry. When he came to the top of the hill, he stopped to get his bearings, then took the path to the right, following it as it gently sloped downward. Within minutes, he was at Sister North's house. He found his hoe leaning against a tree by the front door. There was one last section of the yard that he wanted to plant, and if he hurried, he could have it finished by noon.

When he reached the back, he stopped dead in his tracks. The yard was different. Through the mist, he scanned it from corner to corner, then took a few steps forward and knelt. A thin green blanket was poking through the mud. He stood and walked around the sides of the yard, his heart racing. It was growing by the woods, in the center where the tree trunk had been, by the house. It was sparse in most areas, but almost dense in others. He stood in the shadow of the house and clutched the hoe in disbelief. His grass was growing. He glanced over his shoulder, then around the yard again. He wanted to show this to someone. Patrick, Willie, Meg. His mother. "Look," he wanted to say, "look at what I did." The grass, it was everywhere.

Twenty-one

With the party fast approaching, Lake Eagleton sprung ferociously to life. The stores along Main Street began offering new merchandise, filling their windows with Sister North pictures, books, and clothing. Seemingly overnight, the town had swelled. Old and sickly people now crowded the sidewalks, window-shopping, or merely strolling about, their faces peaceful but expectant. The lines at Big Jack's stretched into the parking lot, with dozens waiting patiently for a table while leaning on walkers and canes.

A week before the party, a dusty yellow school bus filled with nuns rolled into town. They were all elderly and stooped, and waddled like ancient penguins, their habits lifeless wings, their expressions blank.

The next day, a group of former priests showed up in a parade of minivans. Two of the priests were married and had small children. One was dying of prostate cancer. Another was peddling a self-published book of religious poetry.

Business boomed. Leo and Jack opened a frozen yogurt stand in the park, featuring twelve flavors as well as old-fashioned lemonade.

Tony packed up all his obscene T-shirts and tripled the number of daily trolley runs to Sister North's house, his tip box overflowing.

Reflections sold out of Sister North wear.

Monticello was at capacity. Louis raised his rates.

The number of volunteers working on the house also increased. Nine or ten new people showed up to help each morning: an Asian couple from New York; a pregnant woman from Illinois; two pretty, twenty-year-old girls with pierced noses from Lily, Kentucky. A chunky, former stripper from Dallas. In a rush, the last bit of paint on Sister North's house was applied, the new shingles placed on the roof, the wiring completed, and the floors sanded and refinished. A new, cedar shed with a red-shingled roof that matched the house was quickly erected in the far end of the yard, compliments of Fiber, a hymn-singing carpenter from Chicago. With some leftover wood, Fiber also built a small deck that extended off the back door.

The lawn, however, remained Sam's private domain. When a young man with a Grizzly Adams beard from upstate New York asked if he could help fertilize, explaining that he was a landscaper, Sam said no thanks, he had it covered.

Every morning, he would wake up at five-thirty and run the three miles to Sister North's house, where he would turn on the sprinklers and watch as the water covered the yard in smooth, steady waves. Later, when he turned them off, he would stand on the new deck and gaze at the glistening lawn, silent and soaked. Occasionally, he would pick up a leaf or pull out the odd weed. For the most part, though, the lawn was done, and the surge of pride he felt every time he looked at it sometimes embarrassed him.

He kept mostly to himself. His conversations with Meg were brief, and he avoided the eyes of the others. He hated to see the hope reflected in them as they waited for the return of the nun. When talk turned to her arrival, Sam would drift to a corner of the yard or go up to his room.

He sensed a growing tension among what he now considered the ringleaders of the conspiracy. Big Jack and Leo seemed irritable and stressed, snapping at customers and eyeing Sam suspiciously when he came in to eat. Louis finally broke down and wept one evening while watching a Purina Cat Chow commercial on TV, pawing the air with a fat hand and drunkenly mouthing "meow" as tears streamed down his face. Later that same night, he knocked on Sam's door and asked him if he would hear his confession. Sam lay perfectly still in his bed until he walked away.

He found solace in his work and kept busy. In addition to watering the grass three times a day, he assisted with the long-overdue removal of the old satellite dish from the front yard. Under Meg's supervision, he and a number of volunteers dismantled it and hauled it away.

"Hello, there," Patrick said one morning, as Sam was planting some pink begonias by the front porch. He had bought them on sale at the Grocery Bag.

Sam straightened up. Patrick was wearing a black cowboy hat and blue jeans, and was still limping. He appeared lopsided as he hobbled across the yard.

"How's your knee?" Sam asked.

"A little stiff. Say, you've done a nice job," he said as he neared.

Sam wiped his hands on the back of his pants. Even though he had received this compliment many times over the past few weeks, he never tired of hearing it.

"Thanks. It's coming along. I need more flowers though. More color."

"Color." Patrick smiled. "Where are you from again?"

"Chicago."

"That's right. Well, you have a green thumb for a city boy. I might need some work done on our new place over by the bluffs. We bought some land there, you know."

"That's what I heard."

"A ranch home on three acres of pristine lakefront property, according to the Realtor. Realtors like the word *pristine*. They use it a lot. They must think it appeals to our pioneer spirit. The house needs a little bit of work. Lila will enjoy it."

"So will you," Sam said.

"Oh, I don't think I'll have much time to enjoy it. I'm not long for this world."

"What do you mean? Is there something wrong with you?"

"Yes. I'm afraid there is."

"What?"

"I'm almost eighty years old."

Sam paused. "But there's nothing else?"

"That's enough. Old age is a disease, just like any other. Except there is no known cure, and treatment options are limited. I don't expect to be around much longer. You know your history?"

"Not that well."

"Abraham Lincoln foresaw his own death. A few days before he was shot, he dreamed he was walking through a roomful of crying people, then he looked into a casket and saw himself lying there. It's been documented. I had the same dream recently."

"You did?"

"Yes, I did. I dreamed I was walking through a roomful of crying people and looked down into a casket."

"And you saw yourself?"

Patrick shook his head. "No. Actually, I saw Lincoln. Damnedest dream I ever had." He took his cowboy hat off and examined the inside. "Yes, sir, when you're my age, you think about death a lot. That and fiber."

Sam knelt back down and tried to continue his work.

Patrick was in the mood to talk though. He coughed once into his hand. "Heard from our posse yesterday," he said. "Our band of highly compensated private detectives looking for Todd. They said they may have a lead on his whereabouts. They seemed serious this time, said they're closing in. I don't believe it though. Not after all this time."

"Where did they say they saw him?"

"Mexico. They were light on the details. Probably another false lead though."

"Why do you think he disappeared?"

"He owed people. I'm sure of that. Owed them big. I bailed him out more than once. We're talking big money here, too. Last time it was more than one hundred thousand dollars."

Sam stopped digging. He couldn't help himself. "You have that kind of money?" he asked.

"For my son I do." He shook his head. "I wasn't much of a father to him. I had him late, too late really, and was too stuck in my ways to pay much attention to him. After I retired from the military, I took a military consultant job, so I was always in Washington, or off in some foreign country teaching foreigners how to kill. Missed most of his birthdays. Lila taught him how to bike. She even taught him how to kick a damn football. I'd have liked another shot at raising a child. I would do better, I think, the second time around. That's the problem with having one child; you only get the single chance to get it right." He coughed again and looked away.

"Looks like they may be getting close," Sam said.

"I haven't even told Lila about this latest news. Hope can be cruel. I don't want her to get her hopes up." He was quiet for a while and studied his hat. Overhead, a mourning dove cooed, and a last pocket of mist disappeared from the middle of the yard.

"Yes, sir," Patrick said, "not much to do around here anymore. Everything's about done now. The women are down to working on window treatments. Window treatments. By God, I've been hearing that term from Lila for forty years. Just yesterday I realized she means curtains." He put his hat back on. "Say, I couldn't interest you in a breakfast over at the restaurant, could I? My treat."

"No. I want to finish this. Thanks though."

Patrick squinted at Sam. "You're really into this whole thing, aren't you? Throwing everything you got into it. I know Lila's impressed with you. Speaks highly of you. Thinks you're a fine young man. Her words. I've been impressed, too, though up close, to be honest, you don't look all that young."

"Thank you."

"Well, I can tell you can handle the truth. That's why I'd like to confide in you, talk about something."

Sam dug a small hole with a hand hoe and dropped a begonia into it.

"This isn't about porno movies, is it?"

"No. It's in regards to our famous nun friend."

Sam stopped working. "Who?"

"Our mysterious nun friend. I think there's trouble in River City. Suspect that at least."

Sam stood up. "What do you mean?"

"Things aren't right when it comes to the nun. I know you suspect, too. Your comments about her house being so empty the other day. I know you share my suspicions."

Sam nodded but said nothing.

"Something's seriously wrong there," Patrick said. "The whole thing is wrong. No one seems to know too much about her, where she is, her health. I've been hearing some things and doing some deducing, and you know what I think? People are obscuring the truth. I think she's never coming back. I think her health is worse than everyone lets on. In fact, I think she's dying. I hope I'm wrong for Lila's sake and everyone else up here who believes. I hope I'm wrong."

Sam knelt again and went back to work. His heart was racing, but he resisted the urge to tell Patrick what he knew.

"What do you think?" Patrick asked.

Sam shrugged and kept working.

"You must think something."

"I don't know what to think. It's strange."

"Strange." Patrick squinted at Sam again and nodded. "Well, taking a different track, assuming I *am* wrong, and that is a possibility, and the nun does come back for this big shindig, how do you think the process works?"

"What process?"

"Meeting her. Do we all rush up to her and tell her our problems? Do we need an appointment? Is there a system in place? It all seems vague, and I don't like vague things. I don't even like the word."

"We'll see, I guess," Sam said.

"That's a pretty vague answer." Patrick marched past Sam and onto the front porch and stood directly behind him. "If you get your chance, what are going to say to her?" he asked.

"I'm not sure," Sam said. He didn't look up at Patrick.

"Not sure. Not sure," Patrick repeated. "Well, the way I figure it, most people want two things, forgiveness or hope. I've concluded this. When it comes to religion, I mean. I imagine most of us can be divided into those two camps of need. That's all religion boils down to. What camp are you in?"

"I'm not sure," Sam said again. He stopped digging and looked up at Patrick, saw his tired, sad face, his wrinkles more like creases. "Maybe both."

Patrick stared across the front yard, far off. "Well," he said softly, "that makes two of us, then. That makes two."

Later that day, after he had finished in the yard, Sam returned to Monticello and took a dip in the lake. This had become a ritual for him, and he looked forward to it. Occasionally, he would find Lila on the dock finishing her swim, and they would end up talking about their day until the light was gone, Lila always smiling and inquisitive about the inner workings of grass growing. From time to time, she would ask about his life, his parents, his job, questions Sam didn't mind answering, so earnest was her interest.

This evening, there was no sign of Lila, so he eased himself into the water and floated on his back, watching the sky fade and feeling the strain of the day leave his body.

When he was young, his mother had encouraged him to swim, not float in an inner tube or on a raft. "Girls like swimmers," she used to say, "not floaters." Sam hated swimming; his skinny body could never adjust to the cold water, nor, it seemed, did he have any natural ability to stay afloat for long. Anytime they went to a pool or a lake, he would sit on a raft or plastic orange ring or, at the most, float on his back, ignoring his mother's pleas to do the Australian crawl or the breaststroke. Sometimes she would stand on the edge of the pool and demonstrate what stroke she wanted him to do, turning her head from one side to the next, moving her arms in a rhythmic motion. Sam would just float away from her whenever she did this and pretend she was someone else's mother.

Once, when he was about ten, they went to the beach, and his mother wouldn't let him have the orange ring, insisting he swim. Sam refused, and stood in the water, waist deep, his hands on his hips. He stayed there for close to an hour, neither he nor his mother relenting. Finally, she called him to shore and took his hand and led him to the car. When they got home, she made him take a bath. After he was in the tub, she handed him the orange ring and left without a word.

Floating in the lake, facing the sky, Sam felt deep pangs of guilt. His mother had asked very little of him over the years. Push himself a little, learn to swim, speak his mind. He had failed her in most regards. He was not the person she wanted him to become. This realization stung him so much that he stopped floating, turned over onto his stomach, and tried to swim. He gave up after a few strokes, however, his body sinking fast. He tried again, then again, flailing away.

"Keep trying," a voice said.

His mother. He stopped and pulled himself onto a slimy rock. When he blinked water away, he saw Lila on the dock in her flowered bathing suit and matching cap, hands on her hips, smiling.

"You can do it, come on now."

"I can't," Sam said. "I've never been able to swim."

Lila laughed. "Oh, of course you can. That's like saying you can't walk. Here, I'll help you." Before Sam could say anything, she dropped her towel on the bench and dived cleanly into the water, with barely a splash. She emerged a few feet from him, her eyes wide and wet.

"Come on, now, you're almost there," she said.

"No. I can't."

"You're bringing your head too high out of the water. Keep it level to the water and turn it a little bit to the side. Just a little. I'll hold you."

"No. Please." Sam didn't move off the rock.

"Come on." Lila moved closer. "I know you can do this."

"Jesus," Sam muttered.

"I heard that, and praying won't help. Come here." Lila moved closer. "Lie flat on your stomach."

"I'm too heavy."

"Not in the water."

Sam finally relented and extended himself, lying facedown in the water. He felt Lila's hands on his stomach.

"Kick, Sam. Kick."

Sam kicked.

"Now move your head to one side, just a bit. Just a bit."

Sam did as he was told, keeping his eyes shut. Then he felt her let go of him.

He immediately sank and came up to the surface sputtering.

"Well," Lila said. "I think that's a start. You just need to practice. Do you want to try again?"

"Not right now. This could take years."

"Are you sure?"

"I'm sure."

They both stood in the water, facing each other. Water dripped down the sides of his body. Overhead, the first stars appeared against a blue sky, tinged black at the corners. Lila smiled and looked up at them.

"Something inside of me opens up in a place like this," she said. "I feel a part of me opening up."

"It's a nice lake," Sam said.

"Yes, it is," she said. "I feel God's presence here. I feel Him close to me."

Sam didn't say anything. The evening was cooling off. He lowered himself into the water, until his chin was just above the surface.

"Do you believe in God, Sam?"

"No," he said. "I don't think I do."

"Yes, you do," Lila said. "You just don't know it. Everyone does. Otherwise, we couldn't keep going. Down deep everyone believes. Sometimes we can't express our faith. We all have hope that tomorrow will be better. And hope is God."

Sam wiggled around in the water to stay warm. Across the lake, he saw a boat moving slowly against the opposite shoreline, a white arc of waves following in its wake.

"I know Patrick doesn't think he has faith either. But he does. He just doesn't know it. He's been through so much, and seen so much in his life. Too many wars, too many dead boys. Throughout everything, despite what he's seen and done, he's tried to stay good though. And that's what's important. All else can and will be forgiven. All that matters is that you try." Lila crouched down, too, wiggling her legs and arms. "You don't think you're a good person, do you, Sam?"

"A man tried to kill me. He killed someone else instead. A girl. A girl who didn't deserve to die."

"I know. I've heard that," Lila said. "I'm so sorry. I've been praying for you."

"I shouldn't even be here. I shouldn't be swimming. I shouldn't be talking to you right now." He pointed toward the sky. "I shouldn't be looking at the stars. I don't know why I'm still here."

"You were saved for a reason."

"I don't know if that's true, Lila. I don't think there was any reason for me to be saved. I'm not good, I'm not a good person. And I'm not going to do any good or great thing to explain or justify why I'm still here."

Lila tilted her head at an appraising angle, her smile thin and small and sad. "You don't know what's in store for you, Sam," she said. "None of us do. That's one of God's gifts." She studied him a little longer, then jumped up and dived lightly into the water.

Twenty-two

He wrote:

I think things are coming to a head. I may stay here for a long time, or I may leave tomorrow. I don't know. I don't know what is in store for me.

The day before the party, Louis shaved his beard but kept his mustache.

"It's the first step toward purging myself," he said. He was sitting at the kitchen table, slowly arranging a bowl of fruit, placing apples on top of bananas and ringing them with peaches. "What do you think?" he asked Sam.

Sam was speechless. Louis definitely looked purged.

"Be honest," Louis said.

Sam circled Louis like he was a car he was considering purchasing. His new face was white and pink, and while puffy, not nearly as big as he would have thought. The beard had added considerable size to his appearance, and shaving it had a slimming effect.

"Patrick was very honest this morning," Louis said. "He said I looked like Saddam Hussein."

Sam nodded, as he assessed. In addition to looking thinner, Louis also looked younger: He had a baby face. His eyes, once narrow slits, now were open and wide and earnest. His nose and mouth, no longer hidden, looked innocent and naive. His long hair was also cut short.

"I think it looks pretty good," Sam said.

Louis was surprised. He ran his hand over his smooth face. "Really? So did Willie."

Sam gave him one more lookover, then made for the door. He had overslept and needed to get to the Grocery Bag to pick up some potted geraniums the store was donating for the party.

"I want you to know something," Louis said. He fingered the bowl of fruit.

"What?"

"I sold my boat this morning."

Sam paused by the door. "You did? Why?"

"I wanted to pay the town back the money I stole."

Sam turned to face him. "What?"

"The statue. I lied. I told the town that the statue cost twenty thousand dollars when it really cost less than half that. I kept the difference. That's why I bought the cheap statue. To make money. To profit. I lied, and I stole, so I could make money." He raised his chin and looked at Sam.

"Oh," Sam said.

"I know you're not a priest," Louis said. "But I may need your help. If some lawsuit results from this, I was hoping you would represent me. Willie told me you're an attorney."

"I don't practice anymore."

"Please. I need your help. The day of reckoning is upon us."

On his way to town, Sam flipped on the radio and heard Meg talking about the party, urging people to get there early so they could enjoy the food and music. Thomas J. Murphy, a well-known Christian folk singer from Cleveland, would be making a special appearance, and Willie Martinez would be performing his special brand of magic as well.

"The official ceremony celebrating the completion of the house will be at noon," she said. Then she played "The Eve of Destruction."

Sam had to wait almost an hour at the Grocery Bag for the geraniums. The store was swamped, and Ralph, the owner, a short, bald man with hair shooting out of his nostrils, was too busy to go find them in the recently rebuilt nursery.

"Never been so crazy," he said after he finally broke free and was loading the pots into Sam's trunk. "Word is the nun is on her way. She landed in Duluth and is driving in."

"Where did you hear that?"

"That's just the word."

On his way over to the house, Sam listened to Meg read the news and weather in her radio voice, which was low and hesitant and completely unconnected to the woman he knew. He closed his eyes for a second as he drove and tried to picture her face, see her mouth move, as she discussed the new county budget, her words broken by awkward pauses.

He had been cordial but cool with her since that night in his room, deliberately keeping his distance, refusing her offers to go running or to have lunch. More than once, he considered her position, lying to him to help her uncles. He had a difficult time reconciling it, but missed her nonetheless, their runs, their talks. He was willing to give her another chance if she came clean at the party tomorrow.

If she didn't, he was prepared to end the charade, possibly enlisting the support of Patrick in some way. Then he would leave and head back to Chicago. To do what, he didn't know. He couldn't imagine staying here though; there would be no reason.

He turned off the radio and drove the last mile to Sister North's house in silence. When he got there, he unloaded the pots from the car and arranged them. There were six geraniums, a combination of

red and pink, and soon the deck was alive with color. He took a step
back to admire them.

"Very pretty." It was Clyde. He had silently rolled up behind
him on the lawn. Sam's first reaction was to check for tire marks
on the grass. It was still very young and vulnerable. He knew the
party tomorrow would be rough on it, and he wanted to save it
from any unnecessary stress if he could. He considered asking him
to move, but when Clyde started jerking and twitching, he kept
quiet.

"Very nice," Clyde said again in his thin voice, a reed in the wind.

"Yeah," Sam said. "Looks good."

"Sister North likes flowers," he said. His head jerked to the side,
then his body began to shake. "Have you . . ." He struggled for air.
"Have you ever met her?" he asked.

"No."

Clyde smiled and pried his twisted arms apart from each other so
he could briefly clap. "She's something else," he said. He barked out a
strange laugh before pressing a button on the wheelchair's arm and
slowly rolling away.

Sam spent the rest of the day busily preparing for the big day,
completing a number of chores: watering, pulling an ominous
patch of weeds by the fringe of the yard, organizing the shed, sweeping and hosing down the deck. He then helped the Grizzly Adams
man from New York load dozens of old roof shingles into a garbage
Dumpster.

When he got back to Monticello, it was already evening, going
on nighttime. He ran into Lila in the driveway, taking her bathing
suit off the clothesline that Patrick had hung between two small trees
the day before. She smiled when she saw him and motioned for him
to hurry along.

"You're just in time," she said. "We're going swimming. Night
swimming. We're celebrating the finishing of the house. Even
Patrick's going in the water, and he hasn't swum in years. Dorn's

down there already. So is Dot and some others. We're going skinny-dipping with our bathing suits on. It's the Christian way," she said, laughing.

"I'm kind of tired," Sam said.

"Meg is down there," she said. "She came over with Dorn."

He paused. "Well," he said. He looked toward the lake and heard laughing and splashing. "Maybe for just a little while," he said.

The dock was overflowing with plastic folding chairs and beach towels. More than a dozen people crowded around, drinking lemonade from red plastic cups and eating watermelon wedges and grapes that Lila had brought down.

Only a handful of people actually went in the water. Grizzly Adams swam vigorously back and forth in front of the dock, his strokes strong and smooth. Dot waded out waist deep and stood there, her arms held uncomfortably high against her sides, her cigarette glowing red in the dark. Three older women, all wearing tight-fitting orange life vests, clustered by the dock ladder, discussing the party and debating whether Sister North was really going to show.

After making a grand display of lowering himself into the water, Patrick spent most of the evening floating on an oversize raft, his body rigid and straight. Whenever he would drift inland, someone would gently push him back out.

Sam sat at the edge of the dock, next to Lila, and dangled his feet inches above the water. He tried not to stare at Meg, but found himself watching her as she raced Dorn out deep and back. Once, when she came in shallow, he could see her clearly. Her hair was plastered against the sides of her head, and her Santa Monica Track Club T-shirt clung to her. He gave her a small wave, but she didn't respond. Instead, she stared at him and lowered herself in the water until just her head was bobbing on the surface. Then she slowly floated away on her back.

Surprisingly, Lila did not swim, choosing instead to sit next to Sam and sip her lemonade.

"It's so nice out," she said.

"Yep," Sam said. He leaned back and took in the night. The air was balmy, the sky raked with stars. The calm water vibrated with, once again, voices and laughter.

"I wish Louis would join us," Lila said. "He's been so out of sorts lately. I tried to persuade him, but he didn't feel like it."

"He's pretty moody," Sam said.

"He's lonely. A houseful of people, and he's lonely. He misses his mother. He misses his little cat, too, I think. It's a shame. I hope he'll come out of it. He just needs a start in the right direction, a little push. Something good has to happen to him."

"I think Willie and he are playing cards."

"Oh, they are?" She glanced over her shoulder, up at the house. "Well, that's nice. Willie looks out for him. He's a special person. I'm going to miss him."

"Where's he going?"

"He told me he's leaving in a few days."

Sam was surprised to hear this. Willie hadn't mentioned any specific plans about leaving. "Really?"

"Yes. He's said he's going to move on after he meets Sister North tomorrow. I think he just recently decided."

Sam stared out at the lake. Even though it was close to ten o'clock, there were still traces of pink light in the western sky. He watched the color fade, then watched as Meg pulled herself onto a raft. She had a hard time staying afloat, though, because Dorn was shaking and pulling on it, trying to flip her over. Twice she fell back into the water. Eventually, she righted herself and escaped, paddling out deep.

"Are you all set for tomorrow?" Lila asked.

"Yes. All set for the big day."

"I can't wait to meet her."

Sam turned and saw Lila smiling in profile. "Do you really believe she's going to be there tomorrow?"

"Oh yes. She'll be there."

Sam sat in silence, recalling what Meg had said about everyone who came to Lake Eagleton being broken. Despite the revelation about Sister North, the past few months had been good for him. He now felt steady, felt that the broken pieces of his own life had somehow formed together to create a raw and new whole. Still, he knew he wasn't entirely fixed, knew that parts of him were shattered maybe beyond repair. He wondered about the other people on the dock with him, wondered how they were broken, wondered how and if they would be able to fix themselves once they learned the truth about Sister North.

"Well, I think it's getting late," Lila said. "I want to get a good night's rest. Meg said she'd introduce me to Sister North as soon as she arrived, and I want to look my best."

Sam's body stiffened at this news. "She said that?"

"Yes. She promised Dot and me some time alone with her. That's very nice of her."

She placed her hand on Sam's shoulder and pushed herself up. "Patrick," she called. "Time to go, dear."

Sam stood up and glanced around. Dot and the other volunteers had gotten out of the water and were already drifting up to the inn, towels draped over their shoulders. A minute later, Dorn pulled himself up on the dock, his thin white body glowing in the dark, a bony ghost.

"I'm beat," he said as he passed.

Patrick got out of the water only after Lila threatened to leave without him. Sam had to help him up the ladder, grabbing hold of his arm and pulling hard. He was still limping a bit when he walked.

"Very enjoyable," he said. He stooped so Lila could dry him with a towel, though he wasn't wet. His body hadn't touched water. "Glad you talked me into it, Lila. Felt I was floating down the Black River back home." Lila patted his back one more time with the towel, then stretched and kissed him once on the cheek.

"Good night, Sam," Patrick said.

"Oh, I should clean up," Lila said. She picked up an empty pitcher and appraised the dock. It was littered with cups.

"I'll get the rest," Sam said.

"Why thank you." She smiled, hooked her arm into Patrick's, and walked away. "I think Meg is still out there," she said over her shoulder. "You might want to keep an eye on her, Sam."

"I will."

He sat back down and watched Meg float on the raft. She was about twenty feet away, aimlessly drifting. It had started to cloud up, and he couldn't see anything but the outline of her legs, bent at the knees. He watched her for a few minutes longer, then called out.

"You awake?" He stood.

"Yeah."

"Are you coming in now?"

"Yeah. I'm coming."

She paddled her way back in. When she got close, she slipped off the raft and handed it to Sam, then quickly climbed up the ladder, trailing water.

"Everyone gone?" She shook her hair, and water sprayed. Sam stepped back.

"Sorry," she said. "I forgot a towel."

"Did you tell Lila that you would introduce her to the nun tomorrow?"

Her eyes caught fire. She stopped shaking and looked at him. "Can we not get into this right now? I'm sick of talking about this party. I'm sick of everyone asking me about the nun. I'm sick of everything. This whole thing is driving me nuts."

She grabbed the bottom of her T-shirt and squeezed water out of it. Then she started to pick up the plastic cups, crumpling each of them in a tightened fist.

She made her way around the dock, cleaning up, ignoring him. Suddenly she said, "Can you give me a ride to her house? I came here with Dorn." Her voice was a mumble.

Sam didn't say anything. She looked up at him. Her eyes were still blazing. "Can I have a ride? I need to go there."

Sam shook his head, but he said okay.

They didn't speak on the drive over. Meg kept her head down most of the way, apparently transfixed by her fingernails. As they passed through town, Sam turned on the radio and heard her signing off.

"One more song and that's it for tonight," she said in her flat, radio voice. The song was Prince's "1999." Meg reached over and turned it off, then went back to her fingernails.

When they got to the house, Sam kept the motor running. "Should I wait for you?" he asked. He assumed she was picking something up.

"No. I'm staying here. I've been sleeping here the last few days."

"So you live here now?"

She looked up from her fingers. "I've been staying here off and on since the storm. I don't want to stay with Leo and Jack anymore. They've been driving me crazy."

Sam lowered his window and cleared his throat.

"Can you come in and help me move a table up from the basement?" she asked.

"Do we have to do that now?"

"It won't take long. Then you can go."

Sam turned the car off.

The house smelled of freshly cut flowers and Lemon Pledge. The living room was picturesque: The walls were freshly painted a rich cream, the sanded wooden floors, stripped of age, now gleamed. A small black couch and Queen Anne chairs with brightly striped upholstery circled a Persian rug. Over the couch, hanging in the center of the wall, was a small wooden cross.

Sam glanced upstairs and saw that the hallway looked equally reborn: Lila and Dot had chosen colorful wallpaper with red flowers and tiny blue birds against a white background. The stairs had also been redone, and they also shone.

"Where's the table?" he asked.

"Downstairs."

He followed her to the basement and found a coffee table with a glass top waiting for them at the foot of the stairs. They each took an end and slowly made their way back up, taking special care not to nick or scrape anything as they approached the doorway. They maneuvered the table into the living room and placed it on the rug.

"That it?" Sam asked.

Meg pushed the table once to center it, then disappeared into the kitchen. She came back a second later holding a towel and a can of Coke, which she silently offered him.

He took the Coke. Even though he was angry with her for what she had told Lila, he didn't want to leave. He sat on the couch and opened the can.

Meg put the towel on the floor and sat on it. "Thanks," she said.

"It wasn't heavy. You could have moved it yourself."

"I mean for everything. For keeping quiet, you know, about everything."

Sam took a sip of his Coke and watched her.

"You know, you're the first guy I've really spent any time with since my divorce," she said. She was looking at the floor. Some water from her hair dripped down the side of her face like a tear, and she wiped it away.

"There aren't many guys up here like you. Mostly they're old or they're dying. Or they're like Billy. I'm not used to guys like you. I'm not good with them. Normal guys like you. Almost normal, I mean."

Sam relaxed, felt his anger fading. He fought a smile. "Almost."

"I have a hard time being around guys since Carlos."

"Was he your husband?"

"Yeah. He was my coach, too. He used to hit me. He hit me all the time," she said, her voice flat again. She kept staring at the floor. "He said I was worthless. For years, he made me believe that I would be nothing without him and running. I believed him because I was young and dumb."

"What did he do to you?"

"After I fell in the race, he pushed me down some stairs and started kicking me. He said I embarrassed him. He kicked me in the head and the stomach. A few days later, while he was sleeping, I tried to shoot him. I had this gun I bought at a pawnshop. I bought it for just twenty-five dollars. I couldn't believe how cheap it was. I shot him in the foot with it." She looked up at Sam. "You know, you can't just kill someone. I thought I could, but I couldn't."

She stopped talking. Outside, wind chimes tinkled, a faraway sound.

"When I first came back here," she said, "I didn't leave my house. I just holed up inside. I never went anywhere, never talked to anyone. Finally, Leo and Jack got the nun to come over. But I didn't let her in. She came every day for a month. Sometimes she brought cookies, sometimes she brought apples. She used to leave them for me on the front steps. One day, I finally let her in. I let her in, and we talked."

"What did you talk about?"

"Everything. God. Life."

"Do you believe in God?" Sam asked.

"Yeah. I do. Do you?"

"I don't think so."

"You either do or you don't."

"I guess I don't then."

"I do," she said again. "There's got to be something out there keeping us all together. You have to believe in something."

Sam drank his Coke. Meg looked at her fingernails again. "One time, Sister North came over to hide from a TV station. They were making a documentary on miracles, and she didn't want to be interviewed. She stayed with me for a few days until they left."

"Why didn't she want to talk to them?"

"She didn't want to talk about miracles. She told me there were no big secrets to life. 'There's just every day,' she said. 'And every day you have to try.'" Meg said all this in her soft voice, the flatness gone.

Sam stared at her. A breeze blew through the window behind him, and he felt it on the back of his neck. He closed his eyes, and when he opened them again, she was standing over him.

"You going to keep trying, Sam?" she asked.

"Yeah," he said. "It's hard sometimes, though."

"I know," she said.

Sam put the Coke down, stood up, and put his arms around her. She felt cold and wet.

"Hey, can you stay here tonight?" she asked. "I don't want to be alone. I'm tired of being alone. I'm always alone, and it sucks."

Sam nodded.

"Come on," she said.

He followed her up the stairs. When they reached Sister North's room, she turned on the lamp on the nightstand. The room was bare except for a single bed made up with a simple white sheet and pillow.

"I bet talking about Carlos didn't really put you in the mood. I guess I'm not good with guys," she said. She pulled off her T-shirt and stepped out of her shorts.

Sam looked at her long, tan body. "You're better than you think," he said.

She lay on the bed with the light still on, her body half in shadows, her arms at her sides. She looked so awkward and so unsure of herself that Sam just stood there, staring.

"Well," she said.

Sam sat on the edge of the bed and tried to turn off the light.

"You better leave it on," she said. "I haven't done this in a while, and I need to see what I'm doing."

Sam laughed and leaned down to kiss her mouth, then her neck. She tasted salty and warm. "It will come back to you," he said. He made his way down to her breasts, then lower, her body a wave, rising and falling with his touch. He glanced up and saw that her eyes were half-open, watching him as he kissed her. She pulled him up toward her.

"Pace yourself," she said.

Sam paused, breathing hard. He had been thinking about this for so long that he feared he might rush things. "That may be easier said than done."

She laughed. "Never mind," she whispered.

When they finished, they lay in each other's arms, pressed close. He felt her breath in his ears and her skin, warm against his.

"You're right," she said. "It does come back to you."

Sam lay on his back, staring at the ceiling. He felt content and secure in a way he had not thought possible. For once, everything made sense, everything was in place. He closed his eyes. This might be what it was like to be happy. He felt himself smiling. This might be what it was like to be in love.

She pushed herself up on an elbow, and inspected him, her head cocked, her face flushed but serious. "She said it was time to do this. She said you sounded like a good person."

"What are you talking about? Who said that?"

"Sister North."

"You talked to Sister North about me?" Sam was now confused. "When did you do that?"

"This morning," she said. She reached over and clicked off the lamp, and in the darkness Sam heard her laugh.

"Can you keep a secret?" she whispered.

Twenty-three

Big Jack had wanted to sell commemorative red, white, and blue "Come for the Nun, Stay for the Fun" T-shirts at the party for $18.95, but Meg wouldn't let him. She also wouldn't let him move the small frozen yogurt stand from the park to Sister North's backyard. She insisted that absolutely nothing be sold, and that everyone who came be treated as a guest of the town, not a customer. It's going to be a quiet event, she said.

Despite her best efforts, however, a carnival atmosphere prevailed at the party, an expectant electricity humming through the crowd. Hundreds of people stood in small circles, clutching cups of coffee and Bibles and talking about Sister North. The word was she was coming and, in fact, would soon be there.

By the time Sam arrived, the celebration was already in full swing. After an hour of sleep, he had awakened before dawn in Sister North's bed and, seeing no sign of Meg, driven alone to Monticello, where he promptly fell back asleep. It was close to noon when he finally returned, shaved and showered and ready for whatever came next.

"Why, hello there," Patrick said. He approached Sam on the deck. He was wearing his safari hat and sunglasses and holding a large green apple. "The big day is finally here. Word is the nun is coming. I imagine the clouds will part soon, and she will descend along with a heavenly host. Gabriel is probably tuning his horn as we speak." He took a bite of the apple and squinted at the crowd. "Unfortunately, your grass is going to pay the price for this blessed fiesta."

Sam scanned the yard. "Yeah, I know," he said. He was resigned to the fact that his young lawn would be damaged, if not outright destroyed, and that there wasn't a single thing he could do about it. At that very moment, at least, it still looked good. He wondered if anyone would notice or comment.

Sam turned back toward Patrick. "How's Lila?" he asked. "Is she all set?"

Patrick chewed thoughtfully. "She's all set," he said. "Looking forward to it. She's going to want to see the nun now I think more than ever." He looked up at Sam. "They found Todd."

Sam didn't think he heard Patrick correctly. "What did you say?"

Patrick glanced over his shoulder, then took off his sunglasses and looked at Sam with tired eyes. "They found him. He's alive and living in a jail in Mexico City. He's been there for six months."

"Are they sure this time?"

Patrick nodded. "I talked with him myself. It's him all right. Too ashamed to call for help, he said. Started crying on the phone. I guess that's progress. He's never been ashamed before. Never cried before either."

"What's he in for?"

"Running drugs. Heroin. Needed the money, he said, to pay off his losses." Patrick puffed out his chest. "It's a mess. He's going to be there a long time."

Sam was quiet, his eyes on Patrick. His shoulders were stooped forward in an unfamiliar way, and his face looked sunken. Sam wanted to say something, but wasn't sure what. He reached out and briefly touched Patrick's shoulder. "Well, he's alive," he said.

"I'm not so sure that's a good thing," Patrick said. He squinted out over the yard. "Lila cried all night."

Something caught in Sam's throat, and he swallowed hard. He couldn't bear the thought of Lila in pain. "This must be breaking her heart," he said.

Patrick turned to face Sam. "Breaking her heart? She's *happy*, dammit. She cried because she was *happy*. Says her prayers have been answered. Her faith rewarded. Her son is alive, that's all she cares about. Talked to him for an hour. Here I want to go down and kill the man myself for what he did, and she's sobbing for joy. All will be forgiven, she said. All will be forgiven." He shook his head again, then rubbed his eyes. "That's one thing about believers. The glass is always half full. Always. I wish I had her perspective on things, her outlook. I think life would be easier. In fact, I know it would be. But I'm not built that way. I'm just not."

"Are you going to go down and see him?"

"If I can help it, no. He can stay down there forever as far as I'm concerned. He can stay down there and rot." He sighed and fiddled with the band of his hat. "Lila, of course, has already made plane reservations. All set to go."

"I was wondering when you were going to get here." They both looked up to see Dot approaching from across the yard. She was wearing a long black dress, cut low and backless, better suited for the Academy Awards than a backyard picnic. She held out a tray of delicate-looking pastries topped with swirls of frosting. Sam shook his head, then quickly changed his mind and reached for two.

"Quite a circus," Dot said. "Where were they all when we needed the help, that's all I have to say. There must be five hundred people here. We could have had the house done in an hour. The place does look nice, though."

Sam and Patrick nodded in agreement. The yard did look nice.

A dozen or so tables, with simple but colorful floral centerpieces, were set up at the edge of the yard, balloons attached to the backs of each chair. A bar offering soft drinks and lemonade was positioned in each of the yard's corners. In the middle of the yard, a long, skirted table was filled with pastries, fruit, coffee, and pitchers of juice.

There was also entertainment. Willie had set up shop near the back of the yard and was performing his act to the delight of several older women, who applauded his every move. Nearby, Thomas J. Murphy, blind singer-songwriter from Cleveland, strummed a combination of Christian and folk songs, his blank eyes wide and earnest. Grizzly Adams sat on the ground in front of him and harmonized, his voice deep and on key.

The old nuns stood in the middle of the yard by the long table, their habits forming a tight black circle that no one tried to enter. Occasionally, one of them would check her watch and glance anxiously toward the house. The tallest of the group wore tiny, round sunglasses and quietly talked into a cell phone.

There were several handicapped people in wheelchairs, a woman who was apparently so horribly disfigured that she wore a thin, black ski mask, a group of antiabortion activists passing out T-shirts featuring photos of smiling fetuses, and Lazarus in his flowing white robes, just back from the dead.

Larson, a stilt walker who billed himself as the World's Tallest Christian, made his way over to them. When he got to the deck, he reached down and took a pastry from Dot's tray.

"Don't mind if I do," he said. He winked and stilted away.

Leo and Jack were there, of course, standing in the back by the woods with Tony, their arms crossed, their expressions grim. When Larson approached them, Jack said something to him. A second later, Larson quickly strode off, his face red and his eyes wide with fear.

Sam was anxious over what was about to happen. He, too, looked

at his watch, then excused himself to go check on the shed. He
wanted to make sure it was locked, though he couldn't imagine why.

He wound his way around groups of people and past the nun circle. When he reached the shed, he found two old ladies, one obese
and the other with a jagged red scar that cut across her face, sitting
directly in front of the door. He had to ask them to move.

"We will certainly do just that," the woman with the scar said.
She helped the obese woman to her feet.

Sam unlocked the door with a small, silver key he always carried.
His rakes, hoes, shovels, and brooms were as he had left them, lined
up in an orderly fashion, waiting for use. He had a sudden urge to grab
a rake or hoe. He wanted to begin the repair of the yard as soon as he
could. He was nervous and wanted to do something . . . anything.

"Everything okay in there?" the woman with the scar asked.

"Yes." Sam closed the door.

The woman was short and stumpy, but had clear eyes and a
friendly smile. She touched the scar and traced it across her cheeks.
"My husband did this to me," she said. "But I tricked him and lived."

Sam walked back to the deck, weaving around blankets, chairs,
and tables. When he got there, Dot was gone, and Patrick was finishing his apple. He was about to say something to Sam, when his jaw
dropped open and bits of chewed apple fell out.

"What's wrong?" Sam asked.

"Well, I guess the clouds just parted."

He was staring off to the side of the yard. Sam followed his gaze
and felt his own mouth fall open. He heard a chorus of delighted
voices, a combination of laughter, shrieks, and screams. Last night
Meg had told him this would happen, but he was still amazed.

Sister North was back.

She was wearing a long, blue jean skirt with red sneakers and a simple, white button-down blouse. Her short gray hair lay flat on her

normal-sized head. Her black glasses, though, were huge and thick and fit loosely around her face. Sam marveled at her size; she was so tiny and doll-like that he feared she would be crushed by the emotional crowd surging toward her.

Sister North seemed unconcerned, though, as she walked quickly to the center of the yard. Lazarus fell briefly to his knees, and screamed, "Rapture," then took out a digital camera from beneath his robe and began snapping away. Larson got off his stilts. Willie put away his cards.

Sister North stopped in front of the circle of nuns, removed her glasses, and wiped her nose. Her eyes were large and watery, and her inquisitive owl face showed the first hint of jowls.

"Sisters," she said.

As a group, the nuns nodded. The tall one with the round sunglasses stood as rigid as a tree.

"It's so very nice to see everyone again," Sister North said. Her voice was plain, and direct, blowing over the yard like a breeze. "The house and yard look beautiful. Thank you. All of you. You didn't have to do this. In fact, I told you not to, but you did anyway. So thank you, thank you, thank you. I'd especially like to thank Megan Lodge. Where is she? She picked me up at the airport and drove me all the way here, and now I've lost her. Oh, there she is." She searched the yard and found Meg off to one side, standing behind an old man in a wheelchair, who was wearing a suit and tie. Meg waved, embarrassed, her face tight. There was scattered applause.

"It's a shame I won't be here to enjoy all this," Sister North said. "I'm moving back to France. I've become fond of French food." She smiled when she said this, but no one laughed. Instead, there was a confused murmuring.

Sister North continued, "I have two other announcements," she said. "The first one is this . . . I'm not dead. I understand some of you had been led to believe I was."

There was laughter and applause.

"The second one is the reason I came back here. I wanted to tell everyone this good news in person. I've known some of you for years, and I didn't want you to read about it or hear about it. I wanted to tell as many of my friends as I could, face-to-face. Some of you know this already." She stopped and put her glasses back on and looked out over the crowd. "I've gotten married."

There was a collective gasp, then total silence.

"That means you're not a nun anymore," Dot said. She was standing near Sister North, still holding her pastry tray.

"That's right, Dot, I'm not," Sister North said. "I was married to God for forty-five years. I thought I'd finally give Wilbur Fuller a chance. He's been very patient."

As if on cue, Meg pushed the man in the wheelchair over to Sister North and stood behind them both. Wilbur was old, but he still had a mop of thick silver hair and cheerful red cheeks. He waved to the crowd.

Sister North placed her hand on his shoulder. "I think some of you know Wilbur. He was born and raised here. We were engaged once, a long time ago."

Wilbur smiled and waved again. The crowd was silent, gaping in disbelief. The nuns were expressionless.

"How can you do that?" the woman with the scar asked. She was standing next to Dot, her camera at her side.

"Because I'm in love," Sister North said simply.

"So you're leaving God?" the woman asked.

"I think God will be all right, don't you?"

"So you're going to leave us all alone?" It was Clyde, jerking up in his chair. He held his twisted hands out as if he were reaching for something.

Sister North gestured to the crowd. "You're hardly alone, Clyde." She smiled, sensing everyone's confusion and shock.

"But we need you to, to tell us things," Clyde stammered.

"I never told you anything you didn't already know," she said. "Be hopeful. Help each other. Try to be good. That's all I ever said. I pray for the same things you do. My questions are the same as yours. I know nothing more than any of you." She smiled again. "I just had a television show, so you thought I did."

"But you heal people," Clyde said.

"I've never healed anyone. Much of what I supposedly did was made up." She gazed briefly across the yard toward Big Jack and Leo.

The crowd fell quiet. A red balloon that had been tied to the back of a folding chair came loose and floated away, breaking free of the trees and soaring into a pocket of blue sky.

No one moved. Finally, the tall nun with the sunglasses stepped forward and faced Sister North and Wilbur.

"Hello, Maggie," Sister North said. "I hoped you'd be here."

The tall old nun stood straight and tall. "I have a question for you, Maria," she said in a voice every bit as loud and clear as Sister North's.

The yard was still. "I assumed you would," Sister North said. "What is it?"

The tall nun pointed at Wilbur. "Does he have any brothers?" All the nuns started to laugh and continued until several wiped their eyes. Maggie marched over and planted a kiss on Sister North's cheek. "Congratulations, Sister," she said. "We'll miss you."

"Thank you," Sister North said, as the other nuns, then everyone else, slowly fell into line to congratulate her. "Thank you," she kept saying over the whispers and sighs.

After Sister North's announcement, Lazarus died, lying in front of the long table in the center of the yard and closing his eyes. Several people tried to coax him back to life, but he refused. "This time it's for real," he said.

Lila was concerned and sat by him, until Sister North told her to leave him alone.

"He'll snap out of it," she said. She leaned over and handed him a chocolate éclair with sprinkles on it.

"Thank you," Lazarus said.

Sam didn't have much time to worry about Lazarus. He was too busy working behind the large grill that Jack had set up in front of the house, cooking hot dogs, hamburgers, and chicken breasts under the hot sun. The shock over Sister North's announcement didn't seem to have any immediate impact on the crowd's appetite. Other than Lazarus and a few older women who wandered around in a quiet daze, almost everyone lined up for lunch. Soon Sam and Willie couldn't keep up, and Meg was forced to enlist Tony's help with the grilling.

"Why bother cooking?" Tony mumbled as he flipped a hamburger over. "As long as it's free, they don't care if it's raw."

Throughout the afternoon, Sam caught glimpses of Sister North and Wilbur Fuller moving through the subdued crowd, Sister North's loud laugh breaking the stunned tension. He hoped that Lila would have a chance to spend some time with her alone. He never thought about seeking her out himself. He was so busy.

When there was finally a break in the line, Tony asked, "So, what do you think of the news?" He was sweating profusely, traces of hair dye leaking from his sideburns.

"Pretty unbelievable," Sam said.

"Yeah. Caught me off guard. I thought she was dead. That's what Jack was telling everyone. He told me the real story last night at the bar though. He got good and drunk and told me. Said it didn't matter no more."

"Why was he telling people she was dead?" Willie asked through the smoke.

"He was trying to start a rush on things, trying to unload all the merchandise before everyone found out she wasn't a nun no more. Being dead ain't gonna hurt sales. Makes shit more valuable, makes them collector's items. If she quits being a nun, though, all bets are off. Maybe people get pissed off, think she's a phony. Maybe no one buys any books, or T-shirts, or posters anymore. Maybe they want their money back. He was nervous."

"Jack tell you all this?" Sam asked.

"Yeah. He was drunk."

"So the nun came back to put an end to all these, like, rumors," Willie asked.

"I think she's sick of this town making money off of her," Tony said. "I think she came back to put Jack and Leo out of business."

"Meg know all this all the time?" Willie asked.

"I don't know," Tony said.

"She knew," Sam said. "She told me last night."

"Yeah, I figured she knew," Tony said. "The nun and her were tight."

"They still are," Sam said.

Sam stayed behind the grill until late afternoon, then organized the cleanup effort, packing up tables and chairs and throwing out garbage. There were so many people helping that it only took an hour or so to finish the job, and by early evening, everything was pretty much back to normal.

His grass, of course, was another story. It looked different, almost sad. It was matted down in some areas, and gouged or dug up in others. From a perch on the deck, he hardened his heart and surveyed the damage. He quickly identified three areas of particular distress, large circles people had placed blankets on. He would focus on those areas the next day, he thought, and begin immediate resuscitation efforts.

"It will grow back, Sam." He turned and saw Sister North standing behind him. He swallowed. He thought she was in the house with the other nuns.

"Meg said you were a real help the past few weeks. And she doesn't offer compliments easily, though we're working on that."

Sam looked down at her owl face, large black eyes, wide and unblinking, a small hook for a nose. "Thank you," he said.

"You're from Chicago, right?"

"Yes."

"What do you think of my town?"

"I like it."

She smiled. "It's changed, but its heart is still pure. I'm going to pray that it gets back to the way it used to be." She rubbed her eyes, then pulled out the familiar pair of glasses from a pocket and put them on.

"Oh, here," Sam said. He dug into his own pocket and presented Sister North with a folded envelope. Susan's letter. "This is for you," he said. "From someone I met. A friend."

Sister North took the envelope without comment. She remained focused on Sam.

"Why did you come up here?" she asked. Her eyes were watery behind the glasses. She blinked.

Sam jumped at her question. He had imagined this conversation dozens of times, but now that it was finally happening, he felt unprepared.

"Something happened to me," he slowly said.

"Oh, that's right. Megan told me. You were almost killed. A friend of yours was killed instead, is that right?"

"Yes. I think she used to watch your show. She was killed right next to me. The, the man—" He stopped and cleared his throat. "The man was really trying to kill me, but he killed her instead. He shot from close-up."

"And you want to know why you weren't killed?"

Sam nodded. "Yes."

Sister North took his hand. It was small and cool like a stone. He felt her fingers intertwine with his, felt his hand grow warm. "I'll tell you the reason you're still alive, Sam. The man who tried to kill you, he was a lousy shot."

Sam's head jerked at this explanation. He thought she was kidding, but her serious face told him she was not.

"Don't look for meaning. We spend too much time doing that. It's not important why you were saved, just that you were. Look forward, not back." She squeezed his hand once. "I have to go now. I'm leaving tomorrow, and I have other people to see."

She headed toward the house, her blue jean skirt trailing behind her. When she got to the door, she turned and faced him again.

"You came up here for something else, didn't you?"

"Yes, I did."

"And you found it, didn't you?"

"Yes."

"Love will take you to strange places." She winked. "Take care of my town, Sam," she said, and just like that she was gone.

Twenty-four

Three days after Sister North left, it started to rain—a light drizzle, then a downpour that gained force and power as the days passed. Thick gray clouds hung low in the sky, inching down every morning until the lake and even Main Street began disappearing in a fog.

People left reluctantly, first in small groups of two and three, then, as the weather worsened, in droves. The nuns were among the last to leave, posing for a photo in front of Sister North's house before boarding the yellow school bus. Dot packed up and went home to Milwaukee, saying she'd come back in the fall for a visit, and Patrick and Lila had left for Mexico to see Todd. A week after the party, the town was a deserted, lonely pond.

Still the rain came.

Big Jack's took in water, and the harbor flooded, the lake overrunning half of the park. The domed roof of Monticello began to leak, leaving the floor dangerously slippery in spots. The storms intensified at night, with heart-pounding thunder and twisted whips of light-

330 · *J i m K o k o r i s*

ning. Sam had trouble sleeping; the wind was so strong there were times he feared the roof might blow off. Convinced the Apocalypse was upon them, Louis began reading the Bible.

"Did you know that when Jesus Christ comes again, all the Goody Two-shoes will get airlifted up to heaven and be saved?" Louis asked one afternoon. He had the Bible open on his lap and was trying to reposition a pink bucket under a leak with his foot as he sat in the big chair. "Do you think weight has anything to do with who gets chosen? What happens if I'm left behind simply because I'm too heavy to lift to heaven?"

Sam ignored him. He sat on the floor next to the bucket and continued to read the letter Louis had written to Jack and Leo, explaining why he was reimbursing the town $12,000.

"Well," Louis said. He closed the Bible. "What do you think?" He gently moved the bucket over with his foot and watched as water splashed into it.

"It's a little dramatic," Sam said.

"Dramatic? In what way?"

"The poem."

"It's a haiku. I thought it more businesslike than a poem. It explains my motives."

"Just cut a check plus interest. They'll drop it. I told you, I already talked with Jack. He's going to forget the whole thing."

"So he says."

"He will. He doesn't care anymore."

Louis stroked his chin where his beard used to hang. "I imagine you would know. You and he being almost family now."

Sam folded up the letter and handed it back to Louis. "They expect the money by the end of the week."

"All of it? I was hoping to pay in small, monthly increments."

"They want all of it."

Louis took the letter. "That damn statue. If it comes back, I can legally sell it, then, is that correct? I own it now."

Sam stood up. "No, the town still owns it. But it's not coming back," he said.

"Hey, Louis, got something for you here." Willie walked into the room holding a black kitten.

"What's that?" Louis asked.

"A cat," Willie said. "Thought maybe you'd want one. Bought it from a farmer. He had a lot of them. Only cost five dollars." He put the kitten on the floor, and it stood there staring at Louis with unblinking eyes, its tongue flicking in and out of its mouth.

"A cat," Louis said softly. He put his hand up to his mouth and looked incredibly sad.

"Hope you like black," Willie said. "They had a butterscotch one, too."

Louis looked at the cat, then back up at Willie. "You're leaving today, aren't you?" he asked.

Willie shuffled his feet and looked at the ground.

Louis looked over at Sam. "He's leaving now, isn't he?"

Sam cleared his throat.

"Gotta go, Louis," Willie said.

"Why? I told you, you can stay as long as you want. Why do you need to leave?"

"Just time to go."

Louis shook his head. "Everyone leaves," he said.

"I'm not leaving," Sam said.

This was apparently little consolation to Louis. He closed his eyes and took a deep breath. Tiny splashes filled the bucket. Willie nudged the kitten with his foot, hoping to push it closer to Louis. It didn't move though.

Louis pushed himself out of the big chair, walked over, and picked the kitten up. It looked tiny in his huge arms.

"She's beautiful," he said. He reached down and hugged Willie. "No one has ever really given me anything before. Thank you, *mi amigo*."

Willie pushed away from Louis. He looked a little embarrassed. "Yeah, okay." He smoothed his hair back. "Take care of the cat. It's still little."

Louis gazed at Willie, his eyes reddening. "I will think of you always when I look at her," he said.

"Yeah, well, you know, you can think about other things, too," Willie said. He looked at Sam. "Ready to go?"

"Do you want some fruit for the trip?" Louis asked.

"Naw, we're good," Willie said.

Louis was quiet. He continued to look meaningfully at Willie. Finally, he said, "I have some peaches. Fresh peaches." He turned and headed toward the kitchen, pressing the kitten carefully to his heart.

Meg was waiting at the top of the driveway as they were pulling out. She was wearing a green rain poncho and a black Sister North base-ball cap pulled down over her forehead. Sam stopped the car and lowered his window.

"What are you doing out here?" he asked. "In case you didn't notice, it's raining."

"I came to say good-bye." She walked over to the passenger side of the car.

"What's she want?" Willie asked. He nervously wet his lips.

"She wants to say good-bye," Sam said.

"To who?"

"To you. You're the one leaving."

Willie drew a deep breath and started to open the door. "These good-byes, killing me."

As soon as he got out of the car, Meg said, "Bye, Willie," and gave him a brief, awkward hug and a new pack of playing cards. Then she walked back over toward Sam's side and leaned into the window. "How's Louis taking the news?" she asked.

"He's probably writing a sad poem."

"Did he like the kitten?"

"I think so."

"I'll go check on him," she said. She didn't move though. Instead, she searched Sam's face. Rain dripped off the bill of her cap onto Sam's lap.

"You're getting me all wet," Sam said.

Meg glanced over at Willie, then back at Sam. The rain drummed on the roof of the car. "Are you coming back?" she asked, her voice strong and direct. "Tell me now if you're not."

It took a few seconds for her question to register. When it did, Sam almost laughed.

"Do you want me to?"

Meg looked him hard in the eye. "Yeah," she said, no hint of shyness.

"Well, if that's what you want," he said. Then he kissed her once and drove off.

An hour out of town, the rain finally stopped and Sam turned off the windshield wipers. An hour after that, the sun came out, streaming through the clouds in thin shafts The road sparkled.

"Ain't seen that in a while," Willie said. He had been quiet so far, nervously fingering the drawstrings of his duffel bag.

"I hope it clears up," Sam said. "I don't think I can take much more rain. I don't think the town can. I've never seen rain like that."

"Louis thinks it's some kind of punishment. The town is getting punished for lying about the nun."

"A lot of other towns are getting wet, too," Sam said.

"Yeah, that's true."

Sam lowered his window a crack and tried to find something on the radio. He finally settled for a Milwaukee Brewers game. They were losing to the White Sox. He turned it up and drove faster. He wanted to get to Duluth and drop Willie off before dark. He didn't like the idea of driving on back roads at night.

"You sure you want to do this?" Sam asked.

"Yeah."

"Where are you going?"

"Bus stop."

"I know, but after that?"

"Know when I get there."

They drove awhile in silence, Willie trying to sleep. Sam reached into the backseat, grabbed a peach out of the bag Louis had given them, and took a bite.

"Hey, Sammy, let me ask you a question here," Willie said. He was slouched down and still had his eyes closed. "You think you're a good person?"

"Not particularly."

"You good with grass," Willie said. "Make it grow. The nun appreciated that. Scored some points there. Grew her yard. Start. It's a start."

Sam laughed but didn't say anything.

"So, you feeling better?" Willie asked.

"What? Yeah, I feel fine."

"No, I mean since you came up to the lake. Feeling better about everything, I mean."

"Oh, yeah, I'm better."

"You seem better. Look better, act better. Everyone says that. I remember that first night in the bar. Drank yourself blind, man. Everyone thought you came up there to kill yourself. Louis was worried you were going to mess up his room."

"I'm better now," Sam said.

"So you got things all figured out now?"

Sam laughed a little. "Yeah, I'm all set."

"Yeah, what you got figured out?"

Sam thought about this for a few seconds but didn't say anything.

"Come on, Sammy. Give me one thing to go on. How come you're better? What secret you got?"

Sam laughed again. "I have no secrets."

"Come on. What have you figured out?" Willie asked again. "Know that's why you went up there. To figure things out."

Sam cleared his throat, trying to put his thoughts into words. "Well," he said, "I think I've figured out that you have to work at being good. I think maybe you have to try."

Willie considered this. "Being good tough."

"Yeah, but it's worth it. Because if you're good, good things will happen to you." He turned and winked at Willie. "The good are always taken care of, Mr. Willie."

"You believe that?"

"Yes, I think I do."

"What? The nun tell you that?"

"Nope." Sam finished his peach and threw the pit out the window. "My dad did." He shook his head. "My father."

Willie sank back in his seat. "Yeah, the nun kind of said the same thing. Said if I did the right thing, everything be okay in the long run."

"Did you talk with her?"

"Yeah. Told her about my predicament, my situation, about jumping bail."

"What did she say?"

"You know, have hope. Then she told me do the crime, do the time. Told me to turn myself in. Gave me a letter."

"A letter? What kind of letter?"

"A letter to give to the judge, saying I jumped to come up and work on her house. She told me to give it to the newspapers, too, if I get hit hard. Said the press will eat it up, make everyone go light on me. She smart."

Sam thought about his own brief conversation with Sister North and was momentarily jealous. "You must have really made an impression on her."

"Yeah, well, I think Meg was behind it all. Meg put in a good word. She's all right, Meg. Took care of the original workers, me, Lila, Dot, we all got good time with the nun."

"I didn't get much time with her."

"Yeah, well, you got Meg. Better than the nun if you ask me. Looks better in shorts. Hey, did she tell you about the nun getting married ahead of time?"

"She told me the night before. I didn't know otherwise."

"Been meaning to ask you that. Figured she would have told you ahead of time."

"The nun told her not to tell anyone. She keeps a pretty good secret."

"Yeah, she's not too big on talking. But she's all right. She's okay."

They drove a little longer in silence, the sun slipping low, then finally gone. The White Sox beat the Brewers. Sam turned off the radio and flicked on his lights. They were about a half hour from Duluth.

"What are you going to do?" Sam asked.

"I don't know. First I said I was going to keep going, just make sure to stay out of trouble, but been thinking about it. Sooner or later I'll get tripped up. Making a bad situation worse by running. Figure I get extra time for running maybe, three years total. Nun said it would go fast. Said she'd pray for me. I don't know. Maybe I should turn around and go back to Chicago right now. Start getting things right." He was quiet, thinking. "Nun told me to do that. What do you think I should do?"

Sam wasn't surprised by Willie's question. Louis had told him that he had asked him for advice on this as well.

"Maybe this is your second chance," he said.

Willie shook his head. "Yeah, I thought about that. Then I thought maybe it's my last chance." He took a deep breath and sank back in his seat, his hands in his pockets. "How far Chicago from here?" he asked.

· · ·

They bought a map at a gas station and traced a route to Chicago, one that approached the city from the west. They drove through the night, making good time, rolling over hilly countryside on roads that dipped through small, clean towns with sturdy names and no stoplights.

In a town named Marshall, they ate at a diner that served their food in a small toy train that ran the length of the counter, and in a town named Columbus, they stopped at a truck stop and bought CDs. The Rolling Stones, The Who, The Beatles. Santana. Occasionally, they would discuss the legalities of Willie's case. More than once Sam offered to represent him. But Willie refused.

"I got a lawyer," he said. "Don't want to get you involved in my shit anyway. Kind of want to keep you and everyone else I met up there in a different place, don't want to be dragging you down into my place." He patted his shirt pocket with Sister North's letter. "Besides, I got my get-out-of-jail card, too. Maybe it will work."

"Can't hurt," Sam said.

They hit traffic outside of Milwaukee, then again two hours later, as they finally approached Chicago. Sam swallowed hard when he saw the familiar skyline, and felt overwhelmed by the size and scope of everything. It was an overcast afternoon, and the dark buildings looked overbearing and harsh against the gray background. He tried to remember what it was like living there, walking the streets, waiting for buses and cabs and trains, hearing the sounds, breathing the air. He tried to conjure up some sense of attachment or sentiment, but felt nothing. Chicago wasn't home, he realized, it was just someplace he had lived. He drove faster.

He dropped Willie off at Twenty-sixth and California, a dirty gray mausoleum of a courthouse on the city's West Side. Willie said he would call his lawyer from there and turn himself in.

"I'll go park," Sam said. "And meet you inside."

"I don't want you to come in," Willie said. "I can get arrested by myself. Got a lot of experience doing that. Don't need no help."

"Are you sure?"

Willie pulled the drawstrings of his duffel bag. "I'm a big boy, Sammy," he said.

"How are we going to hear from you?"

"I'll be in touch. Got lots of time. Tell everyone I'll maybe be back someday."

He got out, closed the door, and leaned through the open window. "You're all right doing this for me. Driving all this way. This whole thing been all right. Meeting you in a gas station. Staying up there. Working on a house for no pay. Louis and everyone. You know when we first got up there and I took off with your car, left you sleeping in the hotel that morning? I was planning on stealing it, was on my way. But I didn't. I turned around and came back. Glad I did. Glad I came back. Been all right, the whole thing. Wished I could have stayed more. You going to stay up there for good? Forever?"

"I might. We'll see what happens."

"Sounds okay to me," Willie said. "Place is like home." He extended his hand for Sam to shake. When they finished, he leaned down and picked up the bag and slung it over his shoulders. "Hey, Sam, got one last question for you. Been thinking about this. You think it too late to change, too late to be good?"

Sam thought about this, saw the question hanging between them, saw Sister North's house at dusk, the yard alive with flowers and grass, the lake disappearing in the night, Meg standing at the end of Louis's driveway, waiting in the rain, waiting for him. He smiled. "I hope not," he said.

Willie looked at him, thinking. "Yeah," he said. "That's a good answer." Then he nodded once and walked away.

READING GROUP GUIDE

1. What do you think Sam was looking for when he went in search of Sister North?

2. Sam changed for the better over the course of the book. What changed him the most? His love for Meg? His friendships with the other characters? Or his own desire to change? Do you think people can really change?

3. One of the messages of the book is that people should try to solve their own problems through love and friendship rather than look for abstract answers. Do you think this message is in any way antireligious?

4. Do you think Sam will stay in Lake Eagleton forever?

5. Do you think Sister North's answer to Sam's question is fair, or did he deserve more elaboration on why he wasn't killed?

6. What do you think Lila means when she says that not knowing what's in store for us is one of "God's gifts"?

7. Sam claims he does not believe in God. Do you think that by the end of the book his views might have changed?

8. What do you think the overall message of this book is? Explain.

9. Other than his good looks, what did Meg see in Sam? What finally changed her mind about him?

For more reading group suggestions visit
www.stmartins.com

St. Martin's Griffin